Parallax

Andrew Dunkley

Contact the author: alliseeismud@gmail.com

Published by: Andrew Dunkley
Title: Parallax
ISBN: 9780648322916
Science Fiction

For Judy

Chapter 1

Superintendent John Stokes pulled up at the crash site, his brand new 1962 XL Falcon Police vehicle, scraping the curb as he pulled up and took in the scene. He swore under his breath.

Sweat beads leaked from his forehead, and he felt a cold sensation under his arms as the fresh stains on his shirt squashed against his chest when he took his hands off the wheel. It was an unseasonably hot October day.

He looked through the windscreen; about fifty yards ahead he saw the reason for being called out. A car had left the road, and his keen eye and years of experience told him it had done so quite suddenly. It was almost wrapped around a telegraph pole with pieces of it spread all over the road and verges like it had exploded.

The burly cop pulled on the latch of the Falcon's door, which creaked when he gave it a push and the gravel crunched under his heavily laden boot as he heaved himself upright.

Superintendent Stokes ambled to the scene, mopping his brow as he squinted at the vehicle in question. He didn't like the heat or humidity and struggled on, his immense frame the result of years of dedication to pastries and four sugars in a minimum of seven cups of tea a day.

Stokes immediately noticed the faces of his fellow officers and emergency workers who displayed what he could only identify as dismay.

No-one spoke as he moved forward, his head moving left and right as he checked each expression.

He spotted Geoff Riley, the local Ambulance Chief who appeared to want to speak but was obviously incapable for reasons John couldn't grasp. They'd been friends for twenty years and seen many an accident, so why was this one different? Geoff wasn't one to get caught up in the emotion of it all, but here he was, totally mute.

Stokes turned his attention back to the wreck, his footsteps amplified by the stunned silence around him.

He noticed that the car was indeed unusual and not because it was almost split down the middle. The paintwork was a deep fire engine red which practically glowed. He'd never seen such a pristine shine before, not even on his new beast.

He stepped on a broken piece of the vehicle which crumpled under his heel and he paused. Lifting his foot, he saw a shiny red fragment and bent to pick it up. He was surprised by how light and flexible it was. It couldn't be metal; it wasn't at all heavy and yet it had strength about it that he couldn't comprehend.

Looking up again he noticed an odd bump on the rear of the vehicle's roof, like a tiny shark fin. What was it?

The badge at the centre of the vehicle's trunk was unfamiliar, what appeared to be a slanted letter L in a circle and the word Lexus on the left of the tailgate. The number plate had a letter and number combination that also confused him. The only thing he recognised was the State, New South Wales. It was a local car at least.

He touched the metal of the vehicle's body; it felt incredibly smooth.

No-one moved as he took in the scene.

Stokes paused and then spotted the trickle of a lime green liquid coming from under the car. He had no idea what it was and decided not to step in it.

As he moved around the vehicle, he realised the back window had a strange stack of parallel lines on it; they were light brown in colour. An odd place to put pinstripes he thought. Upon touching the glass, he realised they were embedded within it. How?

A series of stick figures were pasted to the glass too, a man with a set of golf clubs, a woman with a tennis racquet, a little girl with a doll and a dog; very odd indeed.

He made his way to the driver's window and looked inside. The controls were beyond comprehension; sleek, clean, shiny and very detailed...more like the cockpit of a jet plane he thought.

He then looked down at where the driver would have been seated and gasped. Superintendent Stokes had seen many a fractured body over the years, but he was nonplussed by what was before him here; there was no body; not in the seat, not anywhere. Could it have been flung out? No, there was no way it could have come out because the seat belts were still connected to a buckle. He'd heard of seat belts and there'd been much debate about making them compulsory but hardly anyone had them installed, let alone used them.

There was no chance that a driver could have survived this wreck and yet, the car was empty with no signs of trauma.

Looking again he noticed something crumpled on the floor, down near the pedals. Instead of the pulverised cadaver of the driver there was only a suit jacket. He leaned in and picked it up, pushing aside some weird, deflated balloon on the steering wheel.

Stokes noticed the clothing was almost as shiny as the car. It appeared to be very expensive, but he didn't know why he thought so. The fabric was very thin and light, with a sheen that made his uniform look even drabber. He looked back into the crumpled cabin and noticed a strange device, which looked like a tiny TV. He reached in to grab it but as he touched the front its screen suddenly lit up and he flinched. Looking again he saw the words, "No Signal".

He shook his head, trying to make sense of it all. What kind of car was this? Was it a military experiment?

He rifled through the suit pockets and found a wallet. It was black leather but again, very unusual with an ornately embossed pattern, perfect stitching and gold metal cornering.

He opened it and saw a multitude of strange cards and a photo of a woman with a girl and a dog. He immediately looked back to the stick figures on the rear window then to the photo again. Both females were very thin and quite pretty, but he was somewhat confused by their clothing, very short dresses and tight, colourful fabrics. Their hair too looked different, short cut like a boy.

He then noticed the cash and took it out of the sleeve; it had no creases and was also brightly coloured. It looked like toy money and felt like cellophane. He tried to count it but realised it was in dollars, immediately thinking it was foreign currency; however, the tiny writing indicated it was Australian, but he'd never seen anything like it before.

Stokes then saw a card with the photograph of a man's face on it and whipped it out of the slot, the words Drivers Licence were clearly visible at the top of the piece of plastic.

He read the driver's name; Jason Warwick Milne and the address, Sydney Casino, Level 14 Penthouse, Robinson's Point.

He'd never heard of the place.

Then Stokes saw the man's date of birth. It didn't click at first and he found himself straining to comprehend the numbers, but then...

Superintendent Stokes looked up at his colleagues, his eyes wider than everyone else's as the colour drained from his face. He held up the licence, realising he was suddenly quite nervous and showed the plastic card to Geoff Riley.

Riley peered at the words for a moment trying hard to absorb the data and finally looked back at Superintendent Stokes, shaking his head.

It read 18 October 1962; it was today's date?!

Chapter 2

Christopher Parish: 52 years old, married with a son and a gambling habit.

It didn't start out that way of course. He, like many, only played for fun and if he won, well that was a bonus, but over time the urge to win took over and not long after that the dire need to win was overwhelming. It stopped being fun and became an obsession that began to dominate his life. With that, he began to lose...a lot.

That thought was running through his head as he threw the last one-hundred-dollar poker chip into the pot. There was around $5000 on the table, and three players were still in the game, "I call," announced Chris.

The be-speckled nerd like figure of Damien Lovegrove stared him down, looking for his tell and Chris tied hard not to smile. He wondered if Lovegrove's glasses were wired with sensors to detect changes in body temperature or to magnify his twitches or any kind of involuntary movement. Lovegrove equals the bet.

Johnny Driscoe, a brash young fellow with a devil may care attitude loses more than most, but his dangerous style sees him win big occasionally. He worried Chris the most. Johnny smirked under the bill of his skater boy cap and flicked a chip on the pile, "I'll see you!"

Thank God, Chris thought. He was down to zero and really needed to score this jackpot. He laid down his cards; two Aces, two Kings and a Seven. Damien winced as he spied the cards and a twinge of relief flickered in Chris's stomach ever so briefly, but it evaporated quickly as Johnny started to beam, "Sorry old man, you should stick to betting on horses," and he threw down a full house, Queens over threes.

"Bugger!" Chris said under his breath.

Johnny scraped up his winnings as Chris rose from the table, "Well played Johnny," he said begrudgingly.

"Hey, where you going old timer? I'm on a roll!"

Indeed, he was, but Chris had no more to give, "Sorry Johnny, I'm wiped. Next week perhaps."

"Whatever!"

Damien shrugged and stuck to his seat, as did the other players.

Before Chris took a step a new player swooped on his chair. There was no shortage of people willing to risk their hard-earned cash at a high stakes table these days.

Chris left without another word, walked through the foyer of the Casino with its terrible red carpet and hideous array of statues and gargoyles and made his way to the car park. He climbed into his seat and started the engine,

"Shit! Is that the time?" he blurted to no-one.

It was 11.40pm on a Tuesday night. He'd have a lot of explaining to do if he didn't get to work on time. The fact was he'd have some explaining to do in about half an hour if his wife woke up.

He did a quick calculation and thought he could snatch about six hours sleep before the alarm went off.

He eased his decrepit, 1996 Holden Commodore out of the car park, cruised to the exit and accelerated onto the motorway without hesitation, leaving a huge blue cloud of burnt oil in his wake.

With little traffic to inhibit his progress, he was soon making his way across town and headed home.

He started to feel weary as the drone of the tyres turned on their hypnotic tune and he flicked on the radio to stay alert. He was startled to total consciousness almost immediately,

"Erk, Judy's been in the car," he said in disgust as the strains of some new wave rap crap poured out of the speakers.

Flicking through the pre-sets he found his station and his favourite talk segment which immediately piqued his interest. He screwed up the volume control to better hear what was being discussed.

Despite a layman's understanding of astronomy, Chris always found Fred Wilson a fascinating fellow on the occasions he'd heard him talking about the Cosmos. He was an astronomer with the Australia Observatory and a regular on the Late show.

It dawned on Chris that he'd heard this late-night radio show all too often, which made him feel guilty.

Doctor Wilson was explaining something about solar activity,

"As you know we've been studying the Sun for many years. The SOHO probe is sending back telemetry all the time, and you would think that we've seen everything but that's simply not the case!"

The announcer, David Sanders was clearly very keen on the subject,

"Has anything new shown up recently?"

"Oh yes!" Fred said excitedly, "Only last week the Solar and Heliospheric Observatory detected something we've not yet been able to define. I know that sounds sinister but we're only just piecing it together. I suppose the easiest way to explain it would be to call it a distortion of some kind."

David asked the obvious follow up question,

"What do you mean by distortion? Could it have been a problem with the SOHO camera?"

"We thought the same thing and the answer is no, the camera was fine. The probe seems to have detected something beyond the limit of our normal visible scope, so we weren't initially able to get a picture of the event."

David again, "Please tell me you got something!"

"Well SOHO does have infrared capability and we looked at that. We still can't believe what we saw."

"Don't leave us hanging Fred," prompted David.

"It was a spike!"

"A what?" David asked in surprise.

"A wafer-thin spike of light, no thicker than a needle we suspect. We think it was pure white light, and it was ejected from the Sun rather than being emitted. And here's the thing, we estimate that it was travelling faster than light speed and had an estimated length of seventy-five million kilometres!"

"You're kidding me, what does it mean?"

"That's the sixty-four-thousand-dollar question. The Sun is enormously powerful and, as I said before, there's so much we simply don't know. This could have been going on since the beginning of time, and we've just never seen it. Then again, it might have been a one off."

David pressed him further, "You mentioned it was faster than light, I didn't think that was possible...is it?"

"Well yes and no. That is to say we, human beings, haven't come close to reaching the speed of light, not on Earth and not in Space. Within the confines of our own Universe, light speed is as fast as anything can potentially travel. The only thing we know of that can travel faster than light is Space itself. Based on this discovery, we're wrong about that."

"Please tell us you have a theory," encouraged David.

"Theory is all we have for now. We then test those hypothesise and hope we can come up with a feasible conclusion. Some think it was a glitch in our equipment while others believe it's a change in the Sun's gravitational field allowing a minuscule amount of pure energy to escape...but I have a different idea..."

"And that is?" asked David.

"Well, I think the Sun collided with a very small black hole, or vice versa."

David paused, obviously shocked by this possibility,

"Wait a minute! Aren't black holes' huge voids in space sucking up everything?"

"Sort of BUT we've created miniature black holes on Earth using the Large Hadron Collider, so we know they're not all huge, planet eating monsters. It stands to reason that a tiny black hole could exist in Space and could crash into a star. That may have caused a faster than light spike to escape the gravitational pull of the Sun itself."

"But how? The Sun can't even escape its own gravity. We see that with coronal mass ejections. They just fold back on themselves," David suggested strongly.

"You're partly right, however, we see light hitting Earth every day so that's not the issue. I think I can explain, in theory, what might cause the spike to escape at faster than light speed though. We know that black holes' warp time as you get near them, so if a small black hole collided with a star, then it stands to reason that time, and space could be disrupted on a minute scale and that a faster than light ejection might then occur!"

Sanders paused briefly, not sure where to take the conversation next,

"So, if it was a black hole, this might just have been a one-off incident, right?"

"Yes, maybe, but then who knows how many black holes are out there. Perhaps there's a cluster of them moving about. We don't know; however, it's certainly got astronomers scratching their heads."

"I'm not surprised. One final question...what if a faster than light spike was to happen again and strike Earth?"

"There's really no way of knowing what might happen there either. It may simply pass through the planet, bounce off the atmosphere...or?"

Fred Wilson paused and there was dead air for a few seconds before David Sanders jumped in again,

"Or what Fred?"

Chris was suddenly ripped away from the discussion by the blast of a horn. He hadn't noticed the traffic light turned green and he'd pissed the guy off in the car behind. He accelerated away from the intersection as the driver of the late model sports sedan sliced past, giving Chris the finger in the process.

Dickhead Chris thought to himself as the driver screamed away in a flash of red.

After he calmed down, which Chris often struggled to do, he realised he missed the end of the interview and was suitably annoyed.

He arrived home a few minutes later and edged the car into the garage, quietly slipping through the back door of the house. A fistful of envelopes, all torn open, littered the kitchen table. Even in the darkness, ambient light revealed the words "Final Notice". Chris was pretty sure the rest were of a similar ilk.

He shook his head realising that, once again they would have another fortnight of baked beans on toast for breakfast and dinner.

When he turned into the hallway and moved towards the bedroom, he noticed light leaking from under the door,

Oh crap, he thought. Judy was awake. He skulked into the room and saw her sitting on the toilet in the ensuite bathroom,

"Hi baby, I'm home," he said, sounding anything but innocent.

She just looked at him for a moment before she asked the obvious question,

"How much did you lose this time?"

His face ripened with embarrassment. He was hoping to put this discussion off until at least tomorrow afternoon,

"I dunno, a thousand maybe?" He knew what was about to happen...

"Jesus Chris, it's always the same with you? Did you see that pile of bills? How are we supposed to cover all that? We're broke and behind on the house payments, behind on the school fees, behind on the rates and the insurance. We'll be sold up," she screamed, and she wasn't finished yet, "I'm working my tail off, but my shitty retail job won't cut it. I can't keep propping us up. I got an ear full today because I'm wearing clothes that are out of stock. I'm supposed to wear the new stuff, but I can't afford it!"

Judy burst into tears. The financial pressure they were under had just about reached critical mass.

"I'm sorry baby. I'll get some help, I will!"

Judy looked at her husband of twenty-seven years as tear drops washed remnants of eyeliner down her cheeks,

"What kind of help? You have a problem that's already way out of control. Will a meeting at Gamblers Anonymous get all those bills paid next week? We owe thousands Chris!"

"And the car service is overdue," he added stupidly.

"Stuff the bloody car!" yelled Judy! "I'm fed up with us scrimping for every cent. We just can't seem to get ahead and it's your fault. Drinking, card nights, poker machines, races! You sit in front of that TV with you iPad betting on, who knows what and when I try to pay for the groceries, it gets rejected!"

It was true, they were doing it tough. Both worked full time and earned meagre salaries at best. Judy was a shop assistant where minimum wage was less than the dole and Chris was in a dead-end job pushing paper around for a mortgage broker. In short, they had huge debts and no sign of climbing out of the abyss. And yes, it was all Chris's doing.

Judy made her way back to bed as Chris tried to give her a hug,

"We'll be ok babe, I promise," but she just pushed him away and curled up under the sheets, ignoring him. They'd had this conversation so many times. She was fed up.

Chris didn't believe a word of what he'd said either. In real terms they were destitute.

He wondered how they'd managed to spiral into such a terrible situation. When they met, both had cash in the bank and were very financially savvy, but over time they just didn't seem to get ahead. All Chris's aspirations turned to nothing, and Judy had their first child at the same time as Chris lost his first job. That's how the savings evaporated and the only work he could get after the bank let him go as the result of a merger was as a casual labourer. It was blue collar work, and he hated it, so he chopped and changed jobs over the next several years until he got back into banking. The industry had changed so much over the years it wasn't the career he used to know. His age didn't help either and he was constantly passed over by younger employees.

Judy was forced to go back to work straight after the baby was born when all she wanted to do was be a mum. All up life was a pile of despair and now their relationship was teetering.

Chris crawled into bed next to his wife and somehow managed to fall asleep.

The following morning, things hadn't improved. Chris slept in, missing the alarm. He rushed a shower and got dressed, finding Judy in the kitchen making breakfast,

"You're going to be late again!" She was obviously still angry.

"I know."

Just then their son, Caleb surfaced from his bedroom. He was almost twenty-six, an Arts Student in University and matriculating in video games with a double degree in skipping class. He was what many people referred to as a professional student and had already racked up five years studying, for want of a better word.

"What's for breakfast?"

Chris looked him over, "Eggs on toast! And hello to you too!"

"What"?

"Nothing. Have you done your assignments?"

"Haven't got any."

Chris looked at him and squinted to indicate his doubts.

"I don't! Geez, get off my case!"

"Ok, keep your pants on. It's hard to know what's what with you and all the bills we get from your school," Chris paused and checked the mail pile again, "Nope, nothing today! We get to eat this week!"

Caleb growled at him, "Give it up Dad..."

"Yeah righto."

Caleb just shrugged and took his food back to the bedroom.

Judy and Chris ate silently. There was really nothing more to say. They were in a state of depression, and she hated him right now. Chris kissed her cheek, but she turned her head away, brushing him off, so he left for work.

Driving into the city he heard yet more news about the odd "Sun spikes" as they were being called now.

"NASA reports that the Sun spiked four times overnight our time with at least one of the mystery ejections passing close to Earth. Infrared photographs of the phenomenon are being analysed by astronomers around the World but, despite several theories, the cause and makeup of the spikes is unknown."

It was the talk of almost every radio station Chris switched to, except for the FM rock stations. Can't let news get in the way of the music! The world could get wiped out by one of these things but anyone under the age of twenty-five wouldn't have a clue why.

He eased into the company car park and made the short walk to his office. Rob Dillon, who had the cubicle next to his, stuck his head around the corner,

"Did you watch the game last night?" asked Rob.

"Nah, who won? No wait, let me guess. Sydney by 20!"

"Spot on Chris...you are bloody good mate!"

"Yeah, only when I don't put money down," Chris replied.

Rob and Chris often talked sport and quizzed each other on horse racing, a passion they both shared. Chris could name the winner of every Melbourne Cup as well as the second and third place getters off the top of his head going back to the sixties, but that hardly helped him pick winners.

"So, what do you reckon about those Sun things," Rob asked.

"Dunno. Perhaps they're here to extinguish our personal debts or to kill off bank executives."

"Yeah right, that would be good!"

Just then the boss walked in, Bill Jarvis. He was an arsehole at the best of times and didn't take kindly to office chat. He looked at Rob with laser beam eyes. Rob jumped a mile and practically landed back in his chair as Jarvis wheeled around,

"Parish! My office!"

Chris looked up, stupidly pointing at himself. Jarvis didn't respond and continued marching across the room. Chris leaped to his feet and started after his boss. Rob shrugged his shoulders signifying that he didn't know what it was about. Chris wasn't sure either but given some of the issues in his personal life he suspected a glaring error was about to bring a huge hammer down.

Chris Parish followed his boss though the Manager's door and waited as Jarvis settled into his plush leather chair. He was sure it was worth more than the Commodore.

"Don't sit down Parish, I'll make this quick. You've been off your game lately and I don't like it. You used to be the best broker here, now you're the worst!" He never minced words, "What was that pile of crap you passed off as work yesterday. Spelling errors, messy formatting and in one case three extra zeros on the loan agreement. We're not here to give money away you know?"

"Sorry sir!" he whimpered.

"I haven't finished," Jarvis yelled. He hated being interrupted, "The market's very slow right now and we're not getting the work we used to. People just aren't buying homes or businesses at the moment. These are tough times, so we have to be even better, or our clients will go elsewhere. We've already had to renegotiate contacts to keep business, so the bottom line doesn't erode but we're still falling behind."

Chris wasn't sure where this was going and just stood there with a dumb look on his face.

"Well, what's going on?" Jarvis demanded.

"I'm sorry sir, I..."

"You already apologised! I want to know whether or not you're worth keeping!" Another pause; "Well?!"

"Um, yes sir, of course sir..."

Chris was a jabbering idiot. His job was on the line, and he couldn't find the words to defend himself. He had flashbacks of school, the bullying and the laughter. Jarvis was just like them, bashing him with words.

"Jesus Parish, speak up!"

Adrenalin started swirling around, settling in the pit of Chris's stomach and a layer of sweat started beading all over. There were hot flushes as his anxiety grew.

"PARISH," Jarvis screamed, "I want an explanation. Your shoddy work has become a concern. Don't you want to keep your job? Wake up man...WHAT IS YOUR PROBLEM?!

Chris snapped.

"YOU ARE...YOU'RE MY PROBLEM YOU PRICK!"

And now he couldn't stop. Years of abuse and fear burst out like he'd hit a fire hydrant,

"We work our arses off here and for what? Abuse? Sarcasm? Bullying? Well, you're an arsehole and a shitty boss. You control this place through fear and criticism. I mean, you just can't see what a bitch you really are! You somehow think that treating us like shit is going to make us more productive. Well, that's crap! No-one can be productive under an authoritarian regime! You're a fucking dickhead!"

Just then Chris noticed that the whole office was quiet. His words were no doubt penetrating the thin walls. He suddenly lost his train of thought. Jarvis leered at him, his face pulsating red rage,

"You fucking little turd! No-one speaks to me like that. Get the fuck out and take all your shit with you, you're through!"

Chris, realising his mistake tried to salvage the situation, "Wait, sir, I'm sorry..."

"I know you are, very sorry and you'll no doubt have plenty of time to think about it because there are no jobs out there for a fifty something loser like you. Now get the fuck out of my office!"

Chris looked down at the floor feeling humiliated. He so wanted to take back everything he'd just said but it was too late. He really blew it and it cost him his job.

There was no turning this around. Chris's temper had done its evil yet again and he trembled as the adrenaline worked its way through his body.

He skulked out of Jarvis's office, everyone looking at him but saying nothing. He quickly cleared his desk of personal belongings, which didn't amount to much. He looked at Rob as he sat, mouth gaping open in shock.

"Seeya mate" he said but Rob was still speechless as he pushed through the exit door and walked to the car.

All kinds of things were swirling through his brain, what would Judy say now? How will I explain this? They had enough trouble to deal with and now he was unemployed. He kicked himself all the way home freaking out at how she might react. It would have been easier if she was at work, which would give him all day to settle down and consider a rational response, but it was her day off. Before he knew it, he was in the driveway, still seething. He noticed the curtains flutter as Judy investigated the mystery vehicle out front. She was at the car door before he could blink,

"Please tell me it's a public holiday or rostered day off you forgot about?"

He didn't know what to say but she'd already guessed something was amiss, so he just had to tell the truth,

"I got the sack babe. I lost my job!"

"What? Why? What did you do?"

"I don't really know. I was being hassled and just lost it. Jarvis is an arsehole!"

"Yeah, but he's an employed arsehole. God, what are we going to do? We owe so much money and haven't got it. How much severance did you get?"

"I don't know. I expect they'll post a cheque!"

"WOW! You must really have pissed him off. Did he literally kick you out?"

"Pretty much!"

"You idiot!" and she started towards the front door with Chris hard on her heels.

"Where are you going?"

"I'm calling Michelle to see if I can get more hours. I'll need the money!"

"I'll get a job. I'll start looking today."

"Good, get started and don't you dare come back until you have one. You really stuffed everything up this time and I really didn't think you could make it worse. I've had it. Get the hell away. I can't talk to you right now," and she slammed the door in his face.

Chris left and spent all day job-searching, reading the want ads online and going door to door. Nothing!

Even the car yards were going through tough times and weren't hiring, and that was pretty much his last shot.

He took Judy at her word and decided to lay low for the night, she was a fairly easy person to understand, what she said she always meant so Chris booked into a cheap motel by the motorway. It was dingy and dirty, but the TV worked and there was a bottle shop close by; very handy.

After a greasy take away meal he sank a few beers when the late-night news came on.

The lead story was all about the Sun spikes, "The phenomenon has escalated with multiple spikes erupting from the Sun today, baffling scientists," the Newsreader said.

"Eyewitness reports have suggested that some of these spikes have now broken through the Earth's atmosphere and may have struck the planet's surface in places. What affect that might have is unknown. We'll keep you up to date as we get more information."

How odd, Chris thought. What could it be? He was thankful that there was something distracting him from his plight, but the deep fog of sadness quickly enveloped him again. He swigged down another guzzle of beer, still watching the TV, "In other news, Police are searching for a Sydney man who vanished earlier today. No trace of the man or his car, a red late model Lexus, have been found. Underworld figure Jason Milne was last seen driving away from his office around 3pm but he never made it home. Anyone with information is asked to contact Police."

Chris wondered if Mr Milne had met with foul play through his infamous connections, it'd serve him right, Chris thought.

At some stage Chris fell asleep, not waking until the next morning, still in the motel lounge chair. He showered; put on the same clothes he'd been wearing from the previous day and checked out of the motel, using up his last thirty bucks.

He found an ATM just outside the motel and tried to draw some cash, but the bank account was skint, about eight dollars which he couldn't access.

Logically Chris should have hit the trail again to find a job, but his mind was elsewhere and the pawn broker's shop across the road was hard to ignore. He hesitated but then, like a moth to a flame he was at the counter, "What can I do for you mate?" asked the man behind the counter. He was a big fellow, heavy set and around three days the other side of his most recent shave. Coffee stains on his shirt finished off the look, not that Chris could judge in his current state.

"How much for the watch?" Chris had a fairly new, gold watch that cost about $500, something he picked up after a rare win at the casino.

The man examined the piece and did his best to put on his analytical face, "Lots of these around, not much demand for them these days," Chris rolled his eyes, "I'll give you twenty bucks!"

"You're joking," Chris blurted in disbelief, "That's a 500-dollar watch; you could easily get $400 for it today, give me $250."

The man laughed; "Fifty."

"Oh great, we're haggling now, One hundred and seventy-five."

"Seventy-five," was the comeback.

"How about one hundred?" suggested Chris. The man paused and looked at the watch again, "Please mate, I really need the money."

"They always do," he said dismissively, "OK, one hundred."

"Thanks," said Chris only slightly satisfied.

He filled out the title declaration and then handed it over, taking the cash.

He got in his car, which was almost out of fuel and looked for a petrol station but somehow found himself in the casino car park instead and within a few minutes was at a table.

The place operated twenty-four hours a day, so getting a game at 8am wasn't a problem.

The cash was exchanged for a couple of chips; cards were dealt, and the game was on.

All that was going through his mind was how pathetic he was; how stupid this was. But that thought evaporated as he picked up the first pot and suddenly doubled his money. For the next few hands his wealth increased, five hundred dollars, then a thousand. Chris was winning!

Players came and went but as the hours progressed, Chris was building a nice pile of chips. Around lunchtime he was swimming in them and had no idea of their value. He played on into the afternoon, winning more and more. He looked at his wrist to check the time, but realising it wasn't there he paused. He could have kept going but something snapped in his mind and common sense finally got through. He called it quits, absorbing the applause of a small crowd that had gathered to vicariously share in his good fortune.

He took his winnings to the cashier, and she peeled off a pile of one-hundred-dollar bills and change, Chris had won almost fifty thousand dollars.

Holy shit he thought to himself. This'll pay the bills and some. "You beauty!!" He just couldn't believe his luck and how suddenly things had changed, all for the sake of losing his job and that watch.

As he turned to leave, he literally ran into a man in a suit, "Congratulations Sir."

"Thanks," Chris said, wondering what his game was.

"Simon Jenkins, casino manager," the man said offering a hand. Chris shook but felt apprehensive.

"You're not going to accuse me of cheating, are you?"

"On the contrary, as a sign of our goodwill, we'd like to offer you a suite for the night, completely free," he explained.

"What's the catch?"

"No catch, you'll have a luxury room at your disposal with our compliments, if you want it."

Just then one of the prettiest girls Chris had ever seen sidled up to Jenkins. She had short blonde hair, well-manicured fingernails with red polish, was around nineteen or twenty and perfectly formed, in every way.

Chris was dumbfounded, "Well, um. I..."

"It's completely up to you sir, but Holly here is discrete and will look after your every need. No charge of course and you can drink or eat as much as you like, and she might even throw in a massage." Jenkins winked.

Chris knew he had to leave and make good with Judy, but this was great! Surely one more night won't matter. He could take the money home in the morning. He wouldn't go back to the tables, which is certainly what this bloke wanted, "Yeah, alright. I accept."

"Excellent. Holly?" The girl beamed a smile and fluttered her eyelashes, flashing her big blue eyes at Chris and took his hand, "See you later Sir," said Jenkins with a wry grin breaking through his professional facade.

"Yeah, sure," Chris replied with a hint of sarcasm as he was led away. Holly didn't say anything until they reached the lift doors,

"You know that you can do a lot with that kind of money."

"What do you mean?"

"Well, I do more than a great massage," she prompted, biting her bottom lip provocatively.

"Yeah, I'll bet you can." Chris was certainly tempted. All this luck and attention was unexpected, and his guard was down.

They entered the lift as Holly looked him up and down, her ample breasts nearly bursting from the low-cut dress. She noticed him sneaking a look and smiled knowingly.

A few seconds later the doors of the lift opened on an upper floor and Holly escorted Chris to a room, a penthouse suite no less. The gold number, 14 was on the door. She slid the security key in and out of the slot and the door latch clicked, "Here it is," and she push open the door.

"Holy shit!!!" he screamed, and Holly laughed,

"I wish I had a dollar for every time someone said that," she quipped.

The room was enormous with chandeliers, shag carpet, gold framed mirrors, silk bedding, all the bells and whistles...even the bath was gold. He was in his own version of heaven!

He ran from room to room, and then admired the amazing view over the Sydney skyline, "Wow!"

After the initial excitement began to settle Holly spoke again, "How about you put all that cash in the safe and I run you a hot bath?"

Oh crap, Chris thought, how do I deal with Holly? He was worried she might disrobe there and then and try to take a bath with him.

"Um, I'm married!"

"Ok? Why don't we start with that massage then? Whatever happens after that, well that's your choice, right?"

"Yeah, I guess so," Chris said reluctantly.

He put the money in the small wall safe and set himself a security code while Holly drew the bath, "I'll be right out here when you're done," she called out detecting his reluctance. She didn't want to mess up a golden opportunity and was biding her time. She reclined on the super king bed instead.

"Yeah, OK, no worries," Chris replied as he closed the bathroom door and locked it behind him.

"Oh man, fifty grand!! Woohoo," he screamed, and he heard Holly giggle.

He practically tore off his filthy clothes and stepped into the bath, it was very hot and so very lovely. He sat there with a huge grin on his now whiskery face and soaked up the warmth, closing his eyes and almost falling asleep. He hadn't felt so relaxed in a long time as years of financial pressure washed away. Judy would be so happy, and he made a pact with himself to never gamble again.

In his relaxed state his mind opened and memories of better times leaked through the grey.

He remembered how he and Judy met, the day she stepped onto his train, and he offered her his seat. She was 19 and was coming home from the beach. Her blonde hair, blue eyes and brown tan, very eye-catching. She was a poster girl for Bondi Beach, he thought at the time. No wonder he was attracted to Holly.

Chris recalled how he struck up a conversation and by the time they reached her stop, he had her number and a few days later they went on their first date.

They clicked immediately and continued to see each other over the next few months. He fell in love with her quickly and thought she felt the same.

One night in April of 1986, Chris took Judy to dinner at the most expensive restaurant he could afford. After the main meal he got down on one knee and popped the question. She burst into tears and hugged him and simply said yes, over and over again. The other patrons applauded, and Judy blushed.

He felt a tear leak from his face as he recalled those happy moments, but reality soon erased the thought as he came back to the here and now. Oh, how their lives had come apart, if only he'd made better choices and stopped to think about some of his critical decisions. Maybe things would be so very different.

Now, with some cash to tide them over, he would make things right again.

After ten minutes, his head now clear, he decided to get up, thank Holly for her hospitality, slip her a decent tip and send her on her way. He'd then call Judy and get her over here to celebrate.

Chris was about to climb out of the golden tub when something hit him very hard! Intense pain filled his head, like a bullet has been fired between his eyes.

Dazed, he fell back into the bath and was suddenly submerged. He tried to get up but felt an incredible heaviness over his entire body, the pain intensifying.

At first, he thought someone was holding him down and he gasped for air, water gurgling down his throat.

What's happening, he wondered, straining to see out through the bathwater. He couldn't see much but there was no-one there, he was sure of that. He couldn't understand why he wasn't able to get up, and panic began to take hold.

He then realised that the bathroom was glowing, with little sparks dancing around his eyes, like when your head spins. He squinted through the water as the light intensified. He then thought he saw the room melting into a void, as if he was being dragged away from it at high speed. A fraction of a second later he was enveloped in darkness as the panic manifested itself into sheer terror but before he could react, he was suddenly in the water again, still struggling to take a breath. As he gasped, he was sure the liquid was salty with an odd metallic tang.

He instantly felt an incredible pressure on his skull and a different kind of pain took over from the searing headache which had quickly abated. All around he made heard muffled voices breaking through the darkness.

It now felt like he was in a vice and his head was being crushed, the pain again intense.

He couldn't breathe but as the minutes went by, he realised he wasn't drowning. He tried to reach out but whatever constrained him had him wrapped up tight, like a vacuum pack and he was totally immobilised.

Suddenly the darkness broke away and a bright, white light blinded him,

"I can see the head!" someone shouted.

What? Chris wondered, whose head, who is that? Hands were upon him now pulling and twisting him too easily, big hands that now wrapped around his shoulders and under his arms. The feeling was very strange, and he heard the voice again, "Push!"

Chris started to formulate a scenario in his mind that made sense. He must have been stuck fast under rubble or something, had there been an Earthquake or a terrorist attack? That must be it, some kind of disaster and he'd been buried but that didn't explain how quickly he was found and rescued. None of this made sense.

All of a sudden, he was released from whatever was holding him and swept up by someone and quickly half wrapped in a blanket? He felt instantly cold and was trembling now.

A woman was weeping, and another was reassuring her, "It's all over now, you did well."

There was the sound of a snip, and he felt a tug on his stomach and was quickly bundled up and placed in someone's arms, what the hell is happening? He literally felt small amongst these strangers and his eyes were useless after the trauma he'd been through. He could barely make out any shapes, only seeing shades of light and dark.

A tube was immediately shoved in his nostrils and throat, sucking out remnant liquid. He winced at the discomfort and tried to call out but could only manage a squeak. Something felt dreadfully wrong.

Chris tried once more to open his eyes but found it nearly impossible, only catching glimpses of blurry faces, and flashes of bright light again. He felt exhausted as he was bundled up and cradled into another person's arms. Were these people giants, nothing made sense and his mind swam with confusion.

All of a sudden, he felt calmness take over as a voice, somehow familiar, whispered to him, "Hello little man. Welcome to the world."

He strained again to open his eyes and caught the blurry vision of the young woman cradling him as a man's voice spoke again, "Congratulations Mrs Parish, it's a boy!"

Chris felt a shockwave of realisation pulse through his body, Mum?

Chapter 3

Chris was deeply confused, Where the Hell am I? What's happening, he wondered.

As much as he tried, he simply couldn't focus his eyes on anything, his arms and legs were wrapped up tight but somehow, he knew they weren't going to help even if he could get out of, whatever it was that constrained him.

A woman came close and spoke, "Mrs Parish, it's probably a good time to see if he'll take a feed, if you feel up to it."

"Yes, of course. What do I do?"

There was that familiar voice again, Mrs Parish? Surely this isn't my mother, I must be hallucinating, Chris thought.

He considered that the most likely explanation was that he had actually drowned in the bath and was going through that flashback phenomenon that people talk about, where you live your life over again in the blink of an eye, but if that was the case, why was it not flashing. It was running at normal speed.

He tried to call out, hoping someone would rip him away from whatever this was, "Bgggggggghhhrrrrr," was all that came out.

"Oh, isn't that sweet?" someone said as a warm, soft something suddenly pushed at his mouth.

"Here you are little one. Go on, take it," said the motherly woman.

Take what, Chris wondered. What is that?

"That's right Mrs Parish, gently. He'll know what to do."

The thing tickled at his lips and Chris's reflexes caused him to recoil.

"Oh dear, he isn't interested," the woman suggested, "Am I doing something wrong?"

"Not at all Mrs Parish, sometimes they need a bit of encouragement to take the breast," replied the woman.

The what?!

Chris shuddered, what is all this? It must be some kind of elaborate joke.

He tried to scream out again, "Bgggh," but before he could let out half a syllable something plunged into his mouth,

"There you are little one."

Little one? I'm 5 foot 11!

Chris was mortified. What if this was his mother? It didn't make any sense. And was she doing what it sounded like they were talking about doing. Was his mother's breast actually in his mouth right now?

Chris gagged at the thought and tried to pull away. He had no real control of his body and his efforts to repulse the object were useless.

"He's not taking it!" said the lady cradling him.

"Patience Mrs Parish, give him time."

Time? Time for what?!

Chris began to freak out, and tensed up letting out an almighty scream, "Waaaaaaggggggghhhhhhhhhh!"

The shock of the sound only exacerbated the situation.

What the Hell was that noise?

It was the cry of a newborn. He recognised it from witnessing Caleb's birth.

This can't be real.

"Try again Mrs Parish. You can't give up; he has to take it. Instinct will kick in."

"Alright Nurse. I'll try again."

Nurse? No way, this can't be what it seems.

A minute ago, he was relaxing in a nice hot bath with fifty thousand dollars in his pocket and now.

The breast's nipple teased at his lips again. He tried to fight but he simply couldn't avoid it.

Suddenly a warm, wetness drenched his mouth. Without another thought he succumbed to a hormonal response and latched onto the nipple and began sucking.

"He's got it! Ow, not so rough little one," said his would-be mother.

The warm, sweet collagen suddenly turned on some primal need in him. He quickly relaxed and took in the sustenance with no further resistance.

For now, he would simply accept whatever this weirdness was and hope that he might soon come out of it.

Perhaps it was a coma, or he was dying and just reliving his birth in his final moments? Maybe he was unconscious in some rubble and having a nightmare. Whatever was happening, it felt real enough but he was too tired to fight any more.

He felt an incredible calm sweep over him and there was something else. A small, loving kiss on the forehead followed by the stroke of a hand over his head and down his back. He recalled that was something his mother always did, for all the time he'd know her, right up to when she died in that terrible accident in 1973.

My God! Is it really her?

He absorbed the rich nectar for a few minutes more before releasing the nipple and drifting off to sleep.

A few hours later a deep hunger roused Chris from his much-needed slumber.

As he woke, he heard more voices but couldn't catch any of the conversation. It took a few more moments for him to gain his wits again and he remembered the awful nightmare he just had where he felt like he'd been born again and was suckling from his long dead mother. He shivered at the thought.

He tried to piece together the cloudy thoughts that were swirling around in his head, the casino, cash, cards, Holly, the bath and then he remembered being caught up in some catastrophic event.

He opened his eyes expecting to find himself in a hospital bed or an ambulance,

"Oh Robert, he's awake. Come and say hello to your son!"

What? Not again.

Chris was thrust back into the nightmare and decided he mustn't have actually woken and was still dreaming this weird dream.

"What do you think Rob? Isn't he adorable?"

"Yeah, he's a little ripper alright. G'day mate!"

Dad? What the Hell?

Chris recognised his father's voice. He'd only spoken to him a day or two back and it wasn't a good conversation.

Robert Parish was an alcoholic and a gambler who'd taught Chris everything he knew about losing cash fast. Like father like son.

In the years after his mother's death, Robert went down a self-destructive path and Chris recalled the regular visits from the welfare workers and the long periods when his father was absent and how he lived with his mother's parents.

"Have a cuddle, Rob."

"Geez Sandy, I don't know. He's so small. I might break him!"

Sandy? That's Mums name.

"Go on Rob, he won't bite. That's the way."

Chris felt himself being lifted and turned and finally cradled in a stronger pair of arms. He could smell the district odour of tobacco smoke on the clothing that now caressed his face and recognised it instantly.

"What'll we call him love? I know we talked about it but..."

"Well," said Sandy, "Why don't we name him after your father?"

Robert's parents had died a long time ago, before Chris was born. He never really knew what happened, no-one ever talked about it.

"Jesus, Tyrone? No way...that's terrible," and they both laughed, "how about we name him after your dad?"

"Really Robert, you would do that?"

"Sure, why not?"

Chris listened to the conversation absorbing every word in total shock. Surely, they weren't about to say his name. That would be the final straw.

"If you're sure then? I know Dad will be thrilled but are you certain?"

"Yeah, well I realise we were never the best of friends, I know he probably thought you could do better, but I respect him and he never did anything to get between us," suggested Robert.

This was certainly news to Chris, and he started wondering if this was more than just a dream. He was still having trouble with his vision and wrote it off as some other element of the trauma he was almost certainly experiencing as a result of the earthquake or whatever had happened at the casino.

"Well, if you're certain then we have ourselves a name," suggested Sandy.

"Yeah, we do at that," said Robert as his breath puffed down on Chris's face, "Hi Christopher, I'm pleased to meet you," said Robert as he kissed Chris's forehead.

Holy shit! Dad, Mum...what is this place?

He couldn't quite believe what he was hearing and the absolute realness he felt was impossible to ignore now.

He was soon suckling again, taking in the sustenance that every baby craves. If only he could focus and see what was really going on.

As he fed, he kept listening and caught fragments of a life he'd only heard about in passing when he was a child, before his mother's death and his father's spiral into a personal oblivion.

They talked about having more children, buying a house and simple things about jobs and money. Chris was losing focus as the sweet nectar started to work its magic on him again and he slipped into another welcome slumber.

Waking again he thought he was ready for anything this time but deep down hoped that the whole experience had simply been an alcohol fuelled hallucination after his big win, but he knew that wasn't the case.

This time though, he felt no arms cradling him and no voices. He was somewhere else.

Chris strained to hear something and caught muffled voices but little more. He tried again to look around but realised he was shrouded in darkness. Was it night or had he finally become conscious and was still entombed in the rubble of the casino?

He couldn't make sense of anything and decided to call out for help, "Waaaaaagggggghhhhhhh!"

My God, that was a baby's cry!

He tried again and repeated the squawk.

A light suddenly came on, causing him to wince and he soon felt himself being lifted and wondered if he'd finally been rescued. He was only carried a short distance,

"Mrs Parish? Mrs Parish, Chris is hungry. Time to feed him again," said his carrier.

"Yes, of course," came the familiar voice of his mother in reply.

"I'll give him a change while you get ready."

"Thank you, nurse," said Sandy.

Chris felt the blankets unwind from around him and the thrill of being released from this claustrophobic environment. He stretched out and kicked his legs but realised it was mostly involuntary. The nurse removed his nappy easily despite his attempts to move.

"Hmmm that's strange," said the nurse.

"What is it?"

"He's dry. He should have emptied his bladder and bowel by now."

"Is that a problem?" asked Sandy.

"No, but we'll keep an eye on it."

Just then Chris felt an incredible urge and couldn't stop himself, spraying the nurse in a cascade of urine.

"Oh dear. Well, he's ok as it turns out," she screamed.

Sandy couldn't help but laugh.

Chris was feeding every few hours and slowly accepting that this situation might be real after all.

Every time he woke it was the same, nappy changes, feeding, burping and sleeping.

About a day later his mother had visitors and Chris wasn't ready for the shock.

"Here he is Mum and Dad," said Sandy, "Your Grandson Chris!" She looked at her father as he absorbed the news and he beamed with pride, "It was Robert's idea Dad."

" Well, I never, what a gorgeous boy he is," said Sandy's mother, "I'm so proud of you Sandra! Look Christopher, you have a Grandson."

Christopher Clements looked at the boy, "Well fancy that!"

Chris recognised the phrase. It was Grandpa's go to line whenever he was surprised. Chris loved his grandparents so much; they were the rocks that kept his life together in the years after Sandy's death and Robert going off the deep end.

They were instrumental in so many aspects of his development and tried their best to set him on the right path but every time Robert came back into the picture, Chris seemed to fall to his influence, learning bad habits and skills that weren't going to equip him well for his life.

Chris was gobsmacked, Grandma and Grandpa here right now. He tried to look upon their faces, but his vision was so blurry.

"Have a cuddle with him Mum," urged Sandy.

"Oh no I couldn't," she replied.

"Of course you can Edith, you've been so very excited from the first moment you knew he was on the way," Christopher announced.

"You're right Clem." Edith always called her husband by his nickname, "Give him here," and she swept Chris up and cradled him in her ample arms.

Chris could smell camphor, something that was all too common at Grandma's house.

Edith wept a little which got Sandy started too,

"God strike me, you'll drench the boy," said Clem and everyone laughed.

Chris was overwhelmed by the situation. He felt so much love in that moment, and a pang of bliss rippled through his tummy.

Robert stayed well back during the exchange, knowing how Sandy's father felt about him, but Clem demonstrated the kind of man he was. He turned and reached out to Robert, giving him a congratulatory handshake and nodding his approval, "Well done and thank you!"

Robert smiled and nodded his acknowledgement, "I suppose we'll all have to call you Clem from now on?"

"Fine with me," replied Clem.

Christopher (Clem) and Edith Clements were wonderful people, Chris knew that. They only ever did right by him. He remembered the stories that Grandpa told him about the war and

Grandma's terrible driving whenever she took him anywhere. He had so much respect for them and loved spending time at their little house when Robert was away.

In 1983 his grandfather died, finally succumbing to his smoking habit which had been a daily ritual for over sixty years. He lost his grandmother a few years later, just after announcing his engagement to Judy. They'd lived wonderful, happy lives and were both proud of their legacy. Regrettably they never got to see Chris's wedding or to meet his son, which was something he'd always struggled with even though it was out of his control.

Chris now realised that he hadn't been in a disaster, hadn't been hallucinating and this was no elaborate joke. This was real...he was a newborn child with his parents, and they were young and just starting their lives. How? Why?

He was still in a state of shock and his mind was spinning. On top of that he was exhausted. Finally, he submitted to this strange reality and decided to face, whatever this was, later, much later.

Chris was soon asleep once again.

After a month Chris's vision improved greatly and he could make out objects a short distance away.

He could also recognise faces and was initially shocked at how young his parents looked.

Chris also had plenty of time to think about what might have happened and recalled the Sun spikes and that radio interview with Fred Wilson from the Australia Observatory.

He formulated a theory. He must have been struck by one of those spikes and sucked back to the moment of his birth through some kind of time distortion event.

That's probably what Fred Wilson had said the night he was driving home when he was interrupted by the arsehole in the red Lexus and missed the end of the interview. Time travel! That must have been it.

Well, here he was, living proof that it actually happened. There could be no other explanation, could there?

Other things went through Chris's mind too. He was equipped with an incredible amount of knowledge, a lifetime's' worth to be sure. He came back with a lifetime of experience at his disposal.

He realised quickly that he had an incredible opportunity. He had dates for major events, even times in some cases and started working out ways of using the information into the future, which was essentially his past, his present and his future again. It was mind numbing to contemplate.

Right now, all he had were his thoughts because, as an infant, he was just a blob of flesh and couldn't do anything but think, so think he did. It consumed every waking moment in these early weeks.

One thought dominated, how could he get things right this time, help his family, make good lives for them all, and meet Judy again? The idea made him nervous. He had to be careful not to manipulate events too much in case it set him or someone else on a path that would cause significant change. What did they call it? A time paradox. He had to make sure he met Judy just like before and have her fall in love with him all over again. The timing of it all was critical.

He struggled with something else too. What should he do about some of the major events that would happen? How could he do anything? Who would ever believe him? Assassinations, disasters, financial collapses, terror attacks, wars; he knew about them all, when and how they would occur.

He was making assumptions though. Who was to say for sure that this life path would unfold as it had before? He had a long time to wait and see.

For now, he had to live with the frustration of being a small person in a big world and all the complications and frustrations that entailed for a fully conscious adult mind. He decided to teach himself to walk and talk and practiced every night when his parents were asleep. He made progress very quickly and gained control of his body in ways he didn't think possible and in a very short space of time.

One thing he did find intriguing was the dynamic between his parents. No child ever gets to witness the relationship of their parents so early in their life and Chris was in a unique position to do just that.

He realised just how much they loved each other and that they were indeed starting to create a wonderful life together.

Their happiness was evident and while they had occasional arguments; overall this was a happy home.

Robert had a good job, working for a department store and Sandy was a stay-at-home Mum. Chris liked her friends, probably because they doted over him. She was the first in her circle to have a child and the women were all very clucky. Plenty of tickles and cuddles and the one thing he couldn't control often caught him out at change time. That aside, Sandy didn't understand why he was always dry. Chris's first achievement was to gain control of his bladder.

They all lived in a small flat in suburban Sydney but were very keen to buy their own place soon.

The grandparents, Christopher (Clem) and Edith visited often, and Grandpa played with Chris every time they came over. Chris very much enjoyed these visits, particularly when his grandfather put him to bed and told his stories until he fell asleep.

Unlike his mother's choice of story books which bored him terribly, Grandpa told him war stories from his time on the Western Front. He didn't hold back either; he let it all out like he was getting it off his chest. It was as if he'd never had anyone to talk to in all these years after the war and Chris was perfect because he didn't understand; at least that's what his grandfather thought.

The stories revealed a man that Chris didn't recognise. The close quarter combat, the near-death experiences, the loss of friends and the conditions they faced. While Chris knew about World War 1 and that his grandfather had been a part of those terrible years, it was only now that he got a firsthand account of what it was really like. His admiration for his grandfather only grew as a result.

As the months went by Chris's sight improved to normal and his bodily control developed very quickly. After six months, he'd taught himself to walk and talk but only when no-one was looking. He didn't want to draw any extra attention to himself.

One day Clem and Edith came over and were sitting in the lounge room chatting with Chris's parents. They were discussing the News of United States President, John F Kennedy's speech about going to the Moon, which was all over the newspapers.

"I don't think it's possible," said Clem, "How on Earth will they do it?"

"Rockets, "replied Robert.

Clem laughed, "Like the one that crashed a few months ago? I doubt it."

"Maybe, but they'll learn. They'll figure it out," added Robert.

Chris was a keen listener and so wanted to tell them what he knew. Until now nothing much was familiar in the world, but this was! He remembered Neil Armstrong stepping on the Lunar surface in 1969, seven years from now. He knew what was going to happen. He'd seen it on television!

"Even if they do figure out how to get there, who is going to be dumb enough to go?" added his grandfather.

Just then Clem looked over at his grandson and realised he was intently focussed on the adults and their conversation,

"What is it, Chris? You have an opinion?" asked his grandfather. Everyone laughed.

"He certainly seems very interested in what's being said doesn't he," suggested Edith.

His parents thought so too and Chris, realising he was drawing too much attention to himself pretended to be interested in the stupid mobile hanging from the ceiling.

The adults quickly returned to their conversation and the various topics of the time, many of which Chris wasn't aware of.

That was close, he thought, and he scolded himself for being so obvious knowing he'd only get away with it a few times before they took it seriously.

Soon enough his grandparents said their goodbyes and gave Chris a smothering array of hugs and kisses, which he very much enjoyed before they went on their way.

One of the difficult issues for Chris was nighttime. Having complete awareness made for significant periods of boredom and night was worst. He would just lie there in the dark reluctant to cry out and wake his parents, despite the hunger.

In time it started to take a toll and his little body lacked nourishment which his mother noticed.

"Robert? I think there's something wrong with Chris, " Sandy suggested.

"What is it?"

"I don't know, but he's not been waking for night feeds and I think it's too soon for him to sleep through, isn't it?" Sandy wasn't really sure and neither was Robert.

"I couldn't tell you. Maybe he should see the doctor," he added.

"Yes, that's a good idea."

So off to the doctor they went, and Chris was stripped down naked so the doctor could take a look.

Dr William Chamberlain examined Chris, "I see he isn't circumcised yet; didn't they ask about it at the hospital?"

"No," replied Sandy.

"No matter, I can do it here if you like."

"OK sure, if you think it's necessary," replied Sandy, the uncertainty defined in her voice.

"Oh, its normal procedure these days; it'll only take a few minutes.

Chris was mortified. He hadn't given it a thought, but he remembered the "original" version of himself had indeed been circumcised at some stage, probably under these circumstances. Knowing that many years from now it would be frowned upon, he wanted to tell them not to do it, but he was powerless.

"Right, let's take a look at him then."

The doctor pinched and prodded, making Chris feel more uncomfortable. He took some measurements and checked some charts he had in a draw, "Well I think he a little undernourished, is he feeding well," asked the doctor.

"Yes, he is, well during the day at least. First thing in the morning I can't get him off!" Chris felt himself blush, "But at night, he sleeps through. I'm practically bursting out of my, well you know what I mean," Sandy concluded feeling somewhat embarrassed.

"Sleeping through? At this young age? That's a little odd. Has this only just started?"

"Well, no, he's been sleeping all night for a while," Sandy added.

"Really? That's extraordinary and it would certainly explain his condition."

"Is it a big problem doctor?" Sandy asked anxiously.

"Oh no, not at this stage. If he starts getting all the sustenance he needs from now on, he'll soon catch up on weight. No major problem at all. Is he on solids yet?"

"I have tested a few things on him, and he seems to want more. Should I?"

"Certainly! If he's keen on solid food, then by all means but nothing that requires chewing just yet. Soft foods mainly. And don't worry about him sleeping through. It sounds like a blessing. Every child is different and he appears to be quite settled and getting down to the business of a normal sleep pattern faster than most," explained Dr Chamberlain although he was still quite surprised.

"Thank you doctor. Other than feeding at night, he's a very good boy. I never hear a peep out of him to be honest." Sandy said.

"What do you mean?"

"Just like I said, he's very quiet all the time," Sandy explained.

"Doesn't cry?

"Never!"

"Is that right," asked the doctor who had his interest peaked by the comment, "What else have you noticed?"

Chris started to worry. He might be able to keep him Mum and Dad in the dark about his ability, but a doctor was a different prospect. He might just try to investigate this strange child.

"Well for a start he pays a great deal of attention to conversation and he watches TV intently, like he understands exactly what's happening. He never wets or soils himself; he never cries and if he wants to be fed, he simply shows me," explained Sandy.

"Shows you? How?"

"Well, he just holds out his arms, like he wants something. I figured out, eventually, that it was food he was asking for."

Dr Chamberlain looked at Chris and focussed intently on his eyes. Chris was worried his face would give something away and tried not to react. He wondered what a normal baby might do; hoping he could deflect the unwelcome attention but only managed a guilty squirm.

"You say you never have to change him. He's wet of a morning though?" asked Dr Chamberlain.

"Um, no? He's usually dry and I simply take him to the loo, and he does his business before breakfast. I just give him a wipe or a wash and he's done."

The doctor was getting more and more interested, "What about during the day, surely he soils the nappy."

"Well, no. He tells me he needs to go."

By now the doctor was thinking it was a joke, "You're having me on, aren't you?"

"No! Really, he tells me. Chris will make a noise which I learned was his way of saying it was time."

"What noise?!"

Chris was really worried now.

"It's like a coo; that's the best way of describing it, A sound really."

"What do you mean?" The doctor was more than intrigued and looked at Sandy as intently as he had Chris.

"It's so embarrassing, um like a peeoo sound," Sandy explained, "Peeoo, peeoo."

"They sound like words to me, "The doctor was deep in thought now, "surely not!"

"Surely not what?" Sandy asked.

"It seems to me that he's already developing language skills, beyond the gooing and garring you would expect at this age. Does he dribble?"

"What? That's an odd question, isn't it?" asked Sandy.

"Not really, babies are pretty grubby creatures, the pee, poo, drool and mucus; not the most pleasant of creatures to be frank," he explained

"Oh. Well, I don't have anything like that. We never gave it a second thought really. This is the first child of his generation in the family, not even my friends have kids, so we don't really have any comparisons to make. We thought it was basically normal."

"Well Mrs Parish, if everything you say is true then he's gained bladder and bowel control and has learned to communicate on a cognitive level, which means he actually does understand what's going on around him; but it's impossible at his age, at the levels you're describing anyway." Doctor Chamberlain was completely engrossed now, "Is there anything else?"

"Just one thing I suppose, "Sandy suggested.

"And what's that, "asked the doctor expectantly.

"He talks at night, in his sleep!"

"What!?"

What!? Chris thought, feeling shocked.

"Yes, it's true. I've heard him chattering to himself. He's dead to the world but he's definitely saying something."

"What's does he say?"

"Most of it doesn't make much sense but I've heard him say a woman's name a few times."

Oh no!

"What name?"

Please no, don't say it.

"Judy; he uses the name Judy sometimes," explained Sandy.

"Oh Jesus!"

Chris had no idea. He'd been very careful when practising speech at night and was just as careful in developing a way of getting through to his parents without raising alarms that might make them think he was "too different", but he realised that he simply couldn't control what happened when he was asleep. Now he was thinking that soiling and wetting himself would have been a small price to pay for anonymity, but it was too late now.

"Extraordinary," said Dr Chamberlain, "Who's Judy?"

"I have no Earthly idea. We don't know anyone by that name, not even remotely. What do you think Doctor? Is there something wrong with him?"

The doctor paused and looked at Chris again making him more uneasy, "No, not at all. Quite the opposite in fact. He's demonstrating free thinking, self-control and communication skills. He's absorbing data faster than, well, anyone I've ever come across. He's a savant!"

"A what?"

A what?

"An extraordinarily intelligent person with a superior mental capacity. I mean, I'd have to run more tests to be sure, but that seems to be the only explanation. He's been born with a highly advanced level of intellectual capability. Has this sort of thing come up in the family before?"

"No, not that I'm aware, we're all just normal I suppose," Sandy was in shock, but Chris was relieved. This might keep the doctor off his case now that he had a theory to settle his need to know.

"I'd like you to bring him back for more tests, some cognitive ability stuff if you don't mind. What do you say?"

"Yes, of course."

Oh crap!

"Great, I'm really excited. See my girl on your way out. Now how about that circumcision?"

Chris was mortified and found the process brutal and terribly painful, and he wailed like a newborn.

It took a few days for him to feel normal again and much longer for the wound to heal. In time though he'd forgot about it, he hoped.

He continued to practice his speech and walking at night while his parents slept and he worked on his dexterity. He was constantly frustrated by his chubby little legs, arms and fingers and the ongoing changes his body went through. He realised that taking on much more sustenance created puppy fat which turned him into a little Buddha! He decided to work it off over time and stealthily ease off on the goodies.

To pass the time he used the streetlight through his window to read anything he could find; magazines mainly, which his mother loved and the daily newspaper. He had to be careful not to rustle the pages so he wouldn't wake his parents, and he really loved reading the sports stories, and was surprised by how much he actually remembered about the various sports of the era. It started to give him more ideas.

The next visit to the doctor's office was due and Chris was very apprehensive about it.

When they arrived, Dr Chamberlain was waiting and they got in on time, which was unheard of,

"Hello Mrs Parish."

"Good morning doctor."

"And hello Chris," Dr Chamberlain smiled but Chris chose not to react, "A little shy I see. How has he been?"

"Really good. Nothing to report. He's not wearing nappies now and he's trying to talk!" Sandy said proudly.

"Great. How's his crawling going?"

"Oh, he doesn't do that!"

"Really? Interesting," said the doctor.

Chris cursed himself. He knew that might come back to bite him but there was no way he was going to crawl around on the floor no matter how clean it was. Now he was under more suspicion.

"What else has he started, or not started doing? I suppose he's using a knife and fork?" Dr Chamberlain laughed.

"Oh yes, has that well under control," came Sandy's reply.

Mum? What are you doing?

"You're joking!?"

"Yes, I am, I just wanted to see what you would do."

Both laughed at the joke. Chris was relieved.

"Would you say he's coordinated?" asked Dr Chamberlain.

"I think so. The other day he was sitting on the kitchen floor playing and I dropped a grape right in front of him. Without hesitation he reached out and caught it as it was about to roll past him"

"Fascinating."

"And we were at his grandparent's place yesterday when Grandpa tossed him a stuffed toy and he caught it!"

"Really? That's amazing!"

Chris was freaking out. This guy would want to know what made him tick and would go to great lengths to find out. His mother was unwittingly tearing away his secret life.

"How old is he now?" the doctor asked.

"About eight months."

"I see. Well at this age he should be crawling in some form, rolling over and maybe pulling himself up on objects and standing with support. Anything like that?"

Sandy looked at him, "He's walking doctor. Fairly well too. He doesn't know it, but I've seen him do it when he thinks I'm not watching."

What?

"What? He's walking independently, unassisted?"

Oh shit!

"Sometimes. I was awake one night and went to check on him and saw he'd climbed out of his cot and was walking around the room. I wanted to pick him up and put him back to bed but it was so cute how he was focussed on a newspaper that was on the floor! I just watched him until he put himself back to bed."

The doctor was nonplussed, "And you didn't think that was unusual?"

"Well yes," said Sandy, "but you said he was a savant. I read up on it and given what you told me, I didn't think it was that strange."

Phew, good save Mum.

The doctor didn't have anything to say to that but wanted to investigate the newspaper situation, "So, when he was looking at the paper was he playing with it?"

"No, he looked like he was pretending to read it!"

"What do you mean?"

"I mean he focussed on an article and then he'd turn the page and look like he was reading another article," she explained.

"Extraordinary. Is he copying his father?"

"That's what I think."

"OK, do you think he'll do it for us now?" asked Dr Chamberlain who was getting very excited.

"I don't know."

Chris didn't know how to deal with this but then a thought flashed in his mind. He suddenly remembered his former childhood and watching cartoons on TV. He remembered one in particular where a workman on a construction site found a frog in a box. When he let it out it did a song and dance routine. The man then tried to show his friends, but the frog just sat there and, despite his attempts to make the frog dance, it did nothing, but a croak and the man became a laughingstock.

Dr Chamberlain scurried out of his office and came back sporting a newspaper and placed it in front of Chris. Chris looked at the paper, looked at the doctor and smiled.

Ribbit

Chapter 4

Chris's first Christmas was odd; family members he never knew, family friends he'd never met and presents too numerous to count. He was surprised by how much joy he felt and was swept up in the thrill of the season.

In January 1963, he was christened. He had no idea how devoted his parents were to their faith. They didn't go to Church every Sunday, but they certainly were strong in their beliefs and wanted Chris to be brought up with some kind of connection to the Church.

At the ceremony, the priest took Chris in his arms, held him over the font and poured holy water on his forehead while speaking the holy words. Chris winced as the cold water trickled into his eyes. He let out a little squeak, which made the congregation laugh. Little did they know he almost said "shit!"

By the time Chris was nearing one-year-old, he'd managed to perfect just about everything he'd been practising in his room every night and he was making inroads in plain sight too.

He was eating regular food unaided, walking and running like a tiny athlete; he had total control of his bodily functions and did so without his parents learning the truth. They simply accepted that he was well above average and Chris was careful not to get too clever in front of visitors.

On the downside, he suffered bouts of sadness, verging on depression. Having a fully conscious adult mind would seem to be a huge advantage for a toddler but there was no way of using it. He didn't have anyone to talk to and people, quite naturally, thought he was a baby and treated him as such. He dared not risk doing anything that might draw unwanted attention so, he suffered in silence, fighting off the demons as best he could.

Even more traumatic was having to bathe with his mother and father on occasion. He knew he was more than capable of doing most everything, but he rarely had a moment to himself during the light of day. He loved them dearly but there was no escape.

And then there was his parent's voracious appetite for sex. He tried to block it out but sometimes he was in the room with them and got the full Monty on several occasions. Oh, how they loved to screw. Traumatic doesn't begin to describe how it felt to him!

He was thrilled that they were happy, and he was learning so much about their early time together. The emotional connection between them was so very real and he never gained any such perspective from the photos he looked at in his first stint at this life...but why did they have to bonk every single day?

Yes, it was hard being a kid in these circumstances. The endless monotony and lack of access to basic adult stimulation was driving him crazy. He had to work more stealthily to watch TV news and be ever sneakier about getting the papers after learning that his mother had sprung him reading at night and the walking around the room and spilling the beans to their doctor.

Still, his amphibious attitude with Dr Chamberlain had paid off with the visits becoming fewer over time and finally fizzling out. It was likely the doctor thought his mother was just embellishing Chris's abilities and he was just a stock standard child after all.

The most difficult thing was not being able to partake in any form of conversation. He would hear things and know what was going on or what was going to happen and simply have to keep his mouth shut. To reveal himself now would be a big mistake and he couldn't risk it.

He knew that some babies started talking at around this age, but he wasn't ready for that yet and decided to be a late bloomer, despite the frustration. It didn't stop Sandy from trying to persuade him to say something simple like, "Mummy" or "Daddy."

Ribbit

His first birthday was a crazy day with lots of people and presents. The toys were all designed for, well, a one-year-old and he knew he'd have to pretend to play with them when people were watching. Acting like an excited toddler was a challenge but he seemed to pull it off judging by the joyous responses. Unlike Christmas, he was full on faking his joy this time. For some reason a birthday was a time of reflection, and he remembered what he left behind when he was sucked back to this place and time.

Deep in thought, as he formulated a plan for the future, Chris didn't immediately notice his grandfather's gaze.

When Chris broke out of his mesmerised state he looked up. Clem was watching him closely, very closely as it turned out and this wasn't the first time. There had been several other occasions when Clem had taken a more than cursory glance and Chris wondered if his ruse was failing. Perhaps he was just being paranoid.

To keep himself sane Chris invented little games, like throwing a toy so it skidded behind the couch and was lost for a while or trying to throw a ball so it would have just enough velocity to land on a tabletop without bouncing. It wasn't all that stimulating, but it helped to keep him focussed for a while.

He also recognised some toys as dangerous, like the aeroplane that was coated in lead-based paint. Those laws hadn't been sorted out yet, so he was careful to avoid chewing things that would otherwise go into any other toddler's mouth. Chewing was a necessary evil if he wanted to look "normal".

Pretending to be a baby when your mind is over 50 years of age was indeed exhausting.

It was the next day; while he was sitting in the kitchen pretending to play that he overheard something that excited him,

"I think it's time I took Chris out to meet other children," suggested Sandy, "There's a group of women who meet at the library every week. I could take him there."

"Great idea!" said Robert, "He'll love it."

Chris was excited by the idea for a completely different reason, books! He'd be able to pretend to play and sneak in a few pages here and there. The other kids wouldn't have a clue, and the Mums would be too busy gossiping to notice. This was going to be awesome!

Libraries were never normally Chris's favourite places. He'd always avoided them in the past, or was it the future? He thought they were stuffy and full of geeks and smart arses but now he had a very good reason to want to visit one.

Sandy picked him up off the passenger's seat and carried him across the busy road. He smiled to himself as he watched the 1950s and 60's vehicles; many looking shiny and new. He still couldn't quite come to grips with this strange rebooting of his life.

Sandy clambered up the steps, "Gee you're getting heavy Chris. Are you sneaking out for midnight snacks?"

Chris blushed.

The library was quite large and carpeted throughout. There were rows and rows of bookshelves, all jam packed and quite tidy. Between the shelves, open spaces made way for tables and chairs where people sat in silence absorbing whatever took their fancy or studying.

Blerk, study!

In an open corner at the back of the building was a kid's space where Chris saw several Mums and their babies. Sandy took Chris straight over to the group and introduced herself.

After the greetings one of the ladies made a quick announcement, "Hello everyone and welcome. I'm Ruth and this is my son Jason. This isn't a formal gathering, so chat amongst yourselves and let the children play. That's about it; have fun!"

Perfect, Chris thought. The women will be distracted, and he'll be able to sneak off and stimulate his mind for a while.

A few seconds later he was plonked down with the other kids, their grubby faces and runny noses almost causing him to gag. He decided to sit a while and observe until the ladies were well and truly occupied. He looked at the nearest row of bookshelves, the geography section. Not his favourite subject but really, he didn't care. It was something to do.

A kid started crawling towards him and Chris's instinct to get up and dodge the collision was almost impossible to reign in. He managed to fake a little roll and get out of the way, which the mothers all thought was very cute, judging by the giggling that followed.

The snot faced brat kept on coming and Chris again evaded him with another commando roll, "Oh Chris, don't be so rude," suggested Sandy.

Rack off kid!

"Leave him alone Ben," said the child's mother.

Yeah Ben, the zoo's over there!

The lady grabbed Ben and dropped him well away from Chris much to his delight.

Just then latecomers joined the group, a woman with a little girl on her hip. Chris couldn't see their faces as they introduced themselves to the others,

"Hello, sorry we're late," said the Mum.

"That's quite alright, you haven't missed a thing. I'm Ruth."

"I'm Tracy, Tracy Burrell," announced the lady.

Chris was only half paying attention, so the name didn't click at first.

"Nice to meet you Tracey, and who's this little darling?" asked Ruth.

"Why this is Judy, my daughter!"

What!

"Well, hi Judy, "cooed Ruth, "Why don't you put her down with the others and she can play?"

So, Tracy placed Judy on the carpet right next to Chris. He just sat there totally gobsmacked.

Holy shit! Judy?

He stared at her face, not quite believing what was happening. He was looking at his wife!

"Well, somebody's got eyes for your daughter," announced Ruth.

"Oh my, yes indeed. And who might you be young man?" Tracy asked.

But before Chris had a chance to blow his cover, Sandy chimed in, "Oh this is my son, Chris."

"Nice to meet you Chris, this is Judy," echoed Ruth but Chris didn't need an introduction.

Yeah, I know. We've met.

Chris realised he was attracting way too much attention with his wide-eyed gaze transfixed on Judy's face, but he couldn't help it. He never knew they'd actually met this early in life. Of course, he never retained these memories last time around; he was a baby, with a baby brain. There was no way either of them could ever have recalled such a gathering when they met as young adults so many years later but here, she was.

Chris wanted to talk to her; wanted to say hello. He wanted to hug her! His mind was racing and the emotions were almost overwhelming. He felt incredible frustration and just sat, gazing at her with laser beams. It took all of ten seconds for Judy to start wailing, "Waaaaaagggggghhhhhhhhhh," and tears burst from her pretty blue eyes.

"Oh Chris, you've scared her," suggested Sandy, "I'm terribly sorry. I don't know what's gotten into him."

"That's quite alright. He didn't do anything," Tracy said, "She has a bit of a soft heart."

Chris always liked Judy's Mum. She was always nice to him, even when things went sour in their lives.

Tracy swooped Judy up in her arms and calmed her quickly; breaking the spell she had over Chris.

Oh shit! I'm sorry.

Chris quickly gathered himself and tried to act like a baby again. The women laughed and quipped over the strange encounter until one of them said, "Maybe they're soul mates."

"Or they met in a former life!" said another.

More laughter but Chris knew they were right on the money.

Judy was placed with another child and Chris sat tight until the ladies finished joking around. He watched her closely and Judy kept an eye on him, her instincts making her wary.

Wow, that's the way to start a relationship, Chris. You dickhead!

He gave her time to calm down and watched the women as they got themselves absorbed in conversation, only taking irregular glances at their children. When the chance came, Chris crawled towards his wife. He was careful this time, avoiding eye contact so as not to set off the alarm again; eventually taking a strategic position nearby.

Lots of soft toys littered the carpet and Chris picked up a fluffy pink elephant and offered it to Judy. She looked at it for a moment, hesitated then smiled, revealing two brand new teeth. She looked at Chris and took the toy, shoving it in her mouth.

OK, that's better but you know that meal isn't free right!? Oh, that's just creepy.

Chris watched her chew on the plush toy and tried to act normally, whatever that was, but he couldn't stop himself from gazing at her. She played and crawled and chewed and filled her nappy, which wasn't a memory he really ever wanted but hey, he loved her deeply even if she couldn't control her bowels.

She grew used to him and started smiling and crawling after him whenever he moved. They were like glue from then on and the Mums again chatted and whispered at how cute they were.

By now Chris didn't care what they thought. He was in rapturous joy and felt the love he had for Judy burning deeper than he could have imagined.

After an hour or so group time was over. People gathered up their belongings and their children, "Same time next week ladies. I hope to see you all here!" announced Ruth.

Chris was disappointed at the announcement but at least he had something to look forward to until...

"Oh, I'm sorry. We can't make it I'm afraid, "Tracy announced, "My husband has a job interview and we may be moving."

That's right. They lived in Melbourne until Judy was about seventeen.

Chris suddenly realised that Judy was going away. He was tormented by a new thought; she would be out of his life for another two decades, if he was going to replicate their chance meeting in 1983.

He looked up at Judy, just as she was being carried away, barely paying him a scrap of attention. Chris was suddenly overwhelmed by grief.

A few days later Chris was shuffled off to stay with his Grandparents while Sandy and Rob had a weekend away. No doubt copious amounts of bonking would ensue, and Chris squirmed uncomfortably at the thought.

How is it I don't have a dozen brothers and sisters?

After saying goodbye and pretending to cry as they walked away, Chris settled on the lounge room floor with a few toys while his grandparents pottered around. They ate lunch and Chris had a fake nap during the afternoon.

That evening, after tea, Clem and Edith settled down to watch the news on television. Chris sat on the floor and pretended to play when the bulletin began.

The lead story immediately caught Chris's attention. He stared at the black and white images and the flecks of snowy static caused by the rabbit ears that sat on top of the set,

"It's now been revealed that fifteen thousand US Military Advisors are in South Vietnam in an effort to quell tensions between the South Vietnamese Government and the Communist North..."

Chris knew what this meant. He remembered watching the News as a child when the entire nightmare of Vietnam unfolded. He didn't recall the very beginning because he was so young, but now his consciousness was very much able to absorb what was happening. He also knew where this was headed, the political mistakes, the turmoil, the escalating casualty count and ultimately the defeat. He sat, glued to the screen absorbing every word, knowing that these advisors were steering the United States and ultimately Australia to war. He involuntarily shook his head in response to the futility of it all.

When the newsreader moved on to the next story Chris broke his gaze from the screen and looked towards his Grandparents. His Grandfather was, once again, eyeing him very closely. There was an awkward pause as they stared at each other for a moment,

"So, Chris, do you think this means war for Australia?" asked his grandfather.

Chris didn't know what to do. Was this a rhetorical question or did Clem have him pegged?

"Leave him alone Clem," Edith said, "He's just a baby, how could he possibly know what that's all about?"

"He knows more than he's letting on Edith. This boy is very bright. I've been watching him and he pays attention to things that no child should be aware of," Clem explained.

"What a load of rot. It's a coincidence."

"So, how do you explain him walking at such a young age and reading the newspaper. Sandy saw it!"

"Just a baby at play and the walking, well he's just a bit more advanced than most. Even the doctor Sandy took him to see decided there was nothing to it. Just let it be Clem, "Edith insisted.

"Maybe you're right but I can't help feeling there's more to it. When I tell him stories to put him to sleep, I can see there's genuine concentration there. He doesn't smile or lose focus; he listens to every word! It's not natural."

"Oh Clem, now you're being silly," to which Clem said nothing, but he kept his eyes transfixed on his Grandson.

I've got to fix this and fast.

Chris ripped his eyes away from Clem and latched onto a rattle, smashing it into the carpet a few times and making raspberry sounds. When he glanced back at Clem the man was still looking at him as if he was reading Chris's thoughts.

Chris smiled and threw the rattle, which bounced off the coffee table and landed next to the fireplace. Clem lurched out of his rocking chair and retrieved the toy returning it to Chris. He knelt down and started to hand the rattle over which Chris instinctively reached for, but as he was about to grasp the thing Clem dropped it. Without a thought Chris's reflexes clicked in and he sprung forward and took the catch with ease.

Chris rolled over and sat back up, realising that he'd once again let his guard down.

Idiot!

"Did you see that, Edith?"

"Yes, I did!"

" And?"

"I don't know; I've never seen anything like it!"

"Me either but I'm going to find out what's going on. We've got him all weekend," Clem suggested.

"What are you going to do?"

"Nothing that'll harm the boy, Edith. Just a few little tests, to see what he can do!"

Uh oh!

"Now Chris, let's see how you go with this," said Clem and he dangled a pocket watch in front of the boy.

"Are you trying to hypnotise him?" suggested Edith.

"Of course not, just watch."

Chris wasn't sure what was happening and tried to think what a toddler might do in such a situation. He groped for the watch, never quite able to catch it as Clem flicked it away every time his little hands got close.

Then Clem let Chris grab the thing. Chris hadn't accounted for that and was suddenly nonplussed. He looked at the watch then looked at Clem. A normal toddler might sit and play or even try to chew the thing. Chris checked the time and then looked at the clock on the wall.

Clem turned his head to see what Chris was focussed on.

Oops!

He thought of dropping the watch but recognised it as a family heirloom and decided not to risk damaging it. It was now getting quite awkward.

"You see that, Edith; he knows that the watch is the same thing as that clock. He recognises the similarity!"

"You think so Clem?"

"I do."

Edith was now getting very interested in the goings on, but Chris wasn't. He'd made three major blunders in the last few minutes and was now feeling panicked. His mind was flustered and he was worried he'd be caught out again. His grandfather was very crafty indeed.

"Try something else," urged Edith.

"Right then Chris. Look at me."

Chris obediently looked at his grandfather, gently placing the watch on the carpet.

"Interesting," said Clem observing the care Chris took. He then held up two fists, "Pick one!" he ordered.

Chris had him now and he ignored the request.

"See Clem, he's just a baby. He doesn't know what you mean."

"Give me a second Edith," Clem urged, "Come on Chris, pick a fist!"

Chris looked at both fists and back at his grandfather's face, grinning widely.

That should put him off.

But Clem wasn't backing down, "ok, we'll try something else."

Clem left the room and came back a few minutes later with a glass and a bottle full of liquid.

Chris read the label, Dettol!

"What are you doing Clem?" Edith enquired.

"Just watch," Clem replied as he unscrewed the cap and poured some of the antiseptic liquid into the glass, "OK Chris, drink up," and he pushed the glass to Chris's lips.

"No! Clem, don't make him drink that!!"

"I don't intend to Edith, just watch!"

Chris recoiled but Clem just pushed the glass in his face again. Chris again recoiled and rolled away. Clem pursued him and picked Chris up in one arm, cradling him tightly, "One more try Chris," and he brought the glass up to Chris's mouth.

Chris panicked, this would be mean if he was a real baby, but he knew that his grandfather was testing him. No malice but mean all the same. He pushed the glass away with his hands. Clem just put it back to his lips, resisting Chris's efforts to reject him.

Chris knew a normal baby would probably just accept the drink, totally trusting the person making the offer. He did the opposite.

"Oh Clem, you'll upset him!"

"And yet, he's not crying is he. He's just resisting."

Damn!

Again, the glass came at Chris and again he tried to deflect but he was too weak to fight back. Clem lifted the glass and the liquid rose to the rim almost touching Chris's lips. As much as he tried, he couldn't stop it. Now it was a game of chicken!

If I wait, he has to back off, surely.

But Clem didn't back down, the liquid lapped the rim of the glass and licked Chris's lips.

"No more Clem, you'll poison him!"

"I don't think so Edith," and he tilted the glass some more.

Chris tightened his lips as the liquid surrounded his mouth and breathing through his nose, he smelt the familiar pine fragrance that he'd known all his previous life.

If he pulled away, antiseptic would be all over him. If he opened his mouth he'd take a full dose, so he just sat there holding back the tide as his grandfather watched.

"Well Lord be praised. Look at that," said Edith.

Clem withdrew the glass, capturing the antiseptic as it flowed back off Chris's face. He still kept his mouth sealed because his face was wet with the stuff.

Clem grabbed a clean handkerchief from his pocket and wiped Chris's face and Chris relaxed and took in a deep breath, tasting the antiseptic air as it went down.

"There you are Edith; I think the boy can read!"

"No. He just didn't like the taste."

"But he didn't taste anything. He was resisting before I picked up the glass. He knew what it was straight away," Clem insisted.

"How can, you be sure?"

"Do you know any child this age who would refuse a colourful drink?"

"Well, perhaps not," Edith said in resignation.

"Right, so I think he can read! And it makes me wonder what else he's capable of."

Chris could tell his grandfather wasn't going to back down and wondered what to do next. He was certain the next test would be just as revealing. Should he resist?

But before he could think his grandfather had vanished with the Dettol and the glass and returned with a box of matches.

"What now Clem?" asked Edith.

But Clem said nothing. He took a match from the box and struck it on the side, igniting the tip. He them moved it quickly towards Chris's face but before Edith could muster a cry of anguish, Chris blew the match out.

A stunned silence was followed by, "Well glory be!" This time it was Clem, "Did you see Edith?"

"Yes" she whimpered.

"He couldn't have known what matches or flames are; he just knew how to deal with the problem," Clem explained.

Chris sat and looked at his grandfather. He wasn't smiling and he wasn't angry. He was defeated.

"I'm going to try one more thing, "announced Clem.

"No! Please don't!"

This time it was Edith and Clem who were completely silent as they stared wide mouthed at the baby boy who looked at them scornfully,

"No more tests, you've got me. I know everything you think I know and more."

The secret he'd been keeping for so long was now in the open and he felt relieved,

"You don't know how long I've been waiting to say something. It's been so hard keeping quiet for all these months," said Chris.

His Grandparents were still sitting like stunned mullets, entirely shocked and speechless.

Chris looked at their expressions and realised he had to break them out of the trace, "Look Grampa, you're right. I'm not normal. I'm different in so many ways. You were right but you didn't expect this, I'm sure. It's not that I'm advanced. It's more than that," Chris explained.

"Wha, what are you?" asked Edith, "Are you possessed?"

"I'm your Grandson, truly I am. I was born just like everyone else and I'm one-year-old and I'm normal except..." Chris hesitated.

"Except what?" asked Clem despite his disbelief.

"Except for the fact that I'm fifty-three years old!"

Clem and Edith again fell silent. They couldn't comprehend what was happening.

"How is this possible? What do you mean?" asked Clem.

"I was sitting in a bath and the Sun, it spiked me and I fell through a tunnel and came out the other side, fifty-two years earlier. I was born with all the knowledge of a lifetime; a life I've already lived."

"Impossible," retorted Clem.

"And yet here I am, talking to you like an adult. Ask me anything, anything at all."

"What pray tell?"

"Ask me any question you like Grandpa, try another test," urged Chris, "But no Dettol!"

Clem couldn't wipe the astonishment off his face, "Ok, how old am I?"

'You're 62. You were born in 1900, September 2nd to be exact. You retired two years ago after a long and fruitful career as an Accountant and you had one daughter." Chris answered,

"Edith, I mean Grandma, was born in 1903 and was a nurse until she met you Grandpa. You both love gardening, particularly vegetables and you hoped for a better life for your daughter. You think Robert is a loser and isn't good enough for Mum." The silence was deafening, "Sorry, did I say too much?" Chris asked.

'Um, ah, I... I don't know?" replied Clem.

"Sorry. I know it's all a bit much to take in but if you can get it together, I can explain," Chris said.

"Um...ok?"

Chris set about explaining as much as he could about what he thought happened to him; the way the Sun spikes appeared in 2014 and the way he ended up coming back and starting life again with all that future packed into his mind.

His Grandparents listened intently, and Chris was careful to leave out the information about his mother's death and when his Grandparents would pass away. He stuck to the basics.

"But how do we know you're telling the truth Chris, "asked Edith.

"You don't I suppose, but we're having a conversation which in itself must seem awfully strange. I'm an adult in a child's body," Chris explained.

"Well then, tell us something that's going to happen, then we might be able to satisfy ourselves that this isn't just some strange dream," suggested Clem.

Chris thought for a moment, "Neil Armstrong."

"Who?" asked Clem.

"Remember when you were talking to Mum and Dad about the speech that John F Kennedy made about going to the Moon? You asked who would be dumb enough to go there. The answer is Neil Armstrong! It'll happen in 1969."

Clem looked at him, not with shock but with doubt this time, "Poppycock!"

Chris laughed, "You always said that when you didn't believe people!"

"Clem's face softened a little, "That's true. Tell us something that'll happen sooner than that."

"That's not easy, because before, when I was a kid last time, I didn't have any retained memory. I can only go on what I learned later so I don't have all that much detail," explained Chris.

"What about the war? Vietnam," suggested Clem.

"Oh, we lose...in 1975 we leave Vietnam and hand it to the Communists. Thousands will die, around five hundred Australians. It's all a real mess!"

Clem didn't flinch, "So, they turn their attention on us after that? We're over-run?"

"God no! It gets really messy for a while, but they eventually get it together. Peace and order are restored, and it becomes a popular tourist destination. Thousands of Australians go there every year for their holidays."

"My God!" Clem blurted.

"That's said, it was just one of many wars to come I'm afraid. But..."

"What," asked Edith.

"I don't know how much I should tell you. If I say something out of place it could change the World in years to come. I don't know what the effect might be."

"Would that be a bad thing?" asked Clem.

Chris thought about that for a moment, "Probably not, knowing what I know. The World is pretty messed up in 2014."

"Maybe that's why you came back Chris. Perhaps God is trying to make it right," suggested Edith.

Chris hadn't even contemplated such a deep theological possibility. What if that's exactly what was happening?

"I don't know Grandma; I'm still trying to figure it all out."

"Ok, that's all good and well Chris, but you still haven't proven anything. What's going to happen tomorrow?" asked Clem.

"I honestly don't know Grandpa," replied Chris.

Clem looked at Chris for a moment then said, "Well we have to tell you parents about this."

"Why on Earth would you do that? I've just explained I'm an adult. You're treating me like a baby. Yeah, sure on the surface that's what I am but in here," Chris tapped himself on the head, "I'm 53 years of age and every bit a mature human being. Don't tell them anything. I'll do it when the time is right."

"And when will that be?" asked Clem.

"When I think they can handle it. Please, promise me you'll say nothing."

Clem and Edith looked at each other then turned back to Chris having somehow agreed without a word, "OK, we'll keep our mouths shut, for now."

"Thanks Grampa."

"So, Chris," enquired Clem, "The future; what goes wrong?"

"It's a long and complicated story and I don't know where to start."

"Try...please."

"Alright, but you'll wish you hadn't asked," he paused, giving Clem and Edith one more chance to maintain their innocence, "OK then, well you know about Vietnam; it's a disaster. Then there's terrorism, political assassinations in the US and other parts of the world, two or three stock market crashes, the Falklands War, the Gulf War, two wars in Afghanistan, the attack on America, the dismissal of the Prime Minister, the Boxing Day Tsunami and another in Japan and, we lose the Ashes to England!"

Chris looked at his grandparents. They sat in stunned silence again, mouths agape. It took several seconds before Clem finally managed to speak, "We lose the Ashes?"

Chapter 5

Over the next few years Chris learned much about a childhood that had been all but extinguished from his memory in his first life experience.

He confided in his Grandparents and somehow kept any such knowledge about his consciousness from his parents, but it was very hard work.

Everything he'd told Clem and Edith about the future unfolded exactly as he predicted; the nuclear tensions between the West and the Soviet Union which deepened the Cold War, the Kennedy assassination, the deployment of troops in Vietnam and the rise of the protest movement. The sexual revolution and flower power, the Beatles and Rolling Stones and the Civil Rights Movement.

Chris spent a great deal of time talking to Clem, discussing the World and where it was headed. It was troubling for Clem to hear such horrors, and he could see that Chris was struggling with it too.

"Do you think I should tell someone about the things I know Grandpa? I mean the authorities?" Chris asked.

"They wouldn't believe you Chris and you'd probably get your parents into trouble. There's a lot of distrust and tension in the World because of Vietnam. I don't think it's a good idea."

"But what if I can stop things from happening. Terrorism is going to make the World a horrible place for everyone. I can't just watch, knowing what will happen."

"I understand Chris; I really do but who do you tell? How do you prove it? No-one will accept it and if you tell them something that does happen, they'll implicate your parents. They'll just say you overheard something you shouldn't have."

Chris thought for a while, 'What if we write a letter? They won't know where it's from. The technology to track us down doesn't exist yet."

"They can do that?" Clem asked.

"I'm afraid so, they know everything in the future, well almost."

Clem shook his head in disbelief, "A letter might get to the right people but again, I don't think they'll take it seriously. They probably get umpteen letters from cranks every day."

"You're right of course. I'll have a think about it a while longer," Chris said.

"You said it yourself Chris. If you do something that changes the future, what kind of impact might that have? What if they kill, what was his name? Bin Laden: what if they get him before 9/11? What if that doesn't happen?" Clem suggested, holding Chris's gaze, "That might just mean someone else, perhaps more terrible will rise in his place. You just don't know."

"Well, yes, I see your point, but I can't really think of anyone more terrible, and it might just end terror in its tracks. We might just be able to stop it."

They continued to debate the pros and cons of revealing the future to someone powerful but the more they talked the more complicated it got. In the end Chris agreed he'd do nothing for the time being and perhaps that would turn out to be never.

Then Clem looked at Chris out of the corner of his eye but before he could say another word Chris cut him off, "I know what you're thinking Grandpa and it's not fair to ask me."

Clem nodded knowingly while Chris toiled with the question his grandfather was so desperate to ask.

"Oh, stuff it. If I can't help family, what's the point? The truth is you and Grandma both have many years left. You'll both live to a ripe old age,"

Clem smiled as Chris continued, "but I always wondered if you might have been here longer if you gave up cigarettes!"

Chris looked Clem in the eye as he pondered his next remark, "Then again, and this is a bit difficult to say, you have to size up the prospect of extra years against the idea of who goes first."

"What do you mean?" Clem ask, genuinely confused.

"You're the first to go Grandpa. Grandma is around for a few years more. If you quit the cigarettes well, you may close the gap or find you're the one left alone. It's something you need to consider." Chris explained.

Clem was somewhat shaken by the revelation, "I see. That's quite a dilemma. I'll think on it. We never really discussed anything like that. I don't suppose many people have an opportunity to make any such decision."

"You're right," replied Chris, "It's truly odd, but I'm glad I told you. Looks like you're stuck with me for the long haul."

Clem smiled, "That's fine with me. Thank you."

Chris looked at his grandfather again, "It must be nice Grandpa?"

"What's that?"

"It must be nice to know that you're not going to drop off the twig for a long while. We all think about it and worry we'll go too soon or perish in some terrible disaster. You have something now that no-one ever gets" Chris explained.

"That's true. I hadn't thought of it that way and yes, it feels pretty good. And..."

"And what?" Chris asked.

"You have it too! You know you won't get sick or anything like that for the next 50 odd years at least."

Chris realised that Clem was right and smiled, "What a strange feeling it is, but of course that means maintaining the World as it is, no changing anything that could disrupt anything. Any ripple I or we cause now could tip over the apple cart."

"Indeed, just like to ripple we just created perhaps?" replied Clem.

"Perhaps," replied Chris, "But it's worth the risk."

January 1967, Chris emerged from the bathroom after brushing his teeth and dressed himself before returning to the kitchen where Rob and Sandy were finishing up their breakfast,

"Oh, don't you look handsome. Look Rob, Chris is dressed for his first day of school!"

"I see. You look good sport. Are you all set for your first day?"

"Yes Daddy!" Chris said, faking his childlike innocence as always.

Over time he'd cleverly increased his vocabulary until he was having conversations with his parents, both oblivious to his depth of knowledge.

While they understood that he was showing greater ability than everyone else of his age, they didn't think for a moment that it was unusual. They were simply proud.

"Right then, let's get going," suggested Rob.

Sandy gave Chris a big hug and a kiss on the cheek and Chris felt a wetness and realised his mother was crying, "What's wrong Mummy?"

"Oh nothing, I'm just going to miss you."

Chris remembered his first school day from his prior life but not in much detail. He recalled his father took him and Sandy stayed at home. He never understood why, "Come with us Mummy!"

Sandy looked at him, "Oh I've got lots to do. I have to make the beds and do the washing and it's on the way to work for Daddy. No, I'll stay here but I'll be thinking of you."

Chris suddenly understood. Sandy was losing her baby and couldn't face watching him go through the school gates for someone else to look after, "Its ok Mummy. I'll be fine."

She hugged him again, "I'll see you after school. You have a good day," and she smiled.

"I will Mummy," and he walked to the car and was soon on his way.

When they arrived at the school the place was a sea of people with Mums, Dads and kids everywhere. Chris felt strangely apprehensive as he walked through the gate and across the dusty, war-torn grounds of the school.

Children stood like lost cattle, some weeping, others wrapped around a parent's legs while many played with friends or relatives. The noise from the playground was deafening and Chris's memory was running overtime. It was like a waking dream.

"Come on sport," said Rob, "Let's find someone who knows what to do."

They made their way to a throng of people who were lined up at a table waiting with new arrivals. Chris saw real fear on the faces of those around him and recognised quite a few that he hadn't seen in a great many years. Sharon Johns, Rebecca Phillips and his best childhood friend Rob Dennis were there.

Wow!

Finally, they got to the front of the line where an older woman sat, her brown hair with wisps of grey rolled up into a beehive and a pair of black framed horned glasses delicately balanced on the end of her nose, magnifying her cheeks.

Mrs Priestley!

"Good morning," she announced with half a song in her voice.

"Ah yeah, g'day," replied Rob. "I'm Rob Parish and this is my son, Chris. It's his first day."

"Indeed, it is. Have you pre-enrolled?" asked Mrs Priestley as she took a long hard look at Chris.

"Yeah, his Mum did that awhile back."

"Well now, let's see," she said as she pawed over a pile of enrolment forms and plucked one from the middle, "Parish, Christopher, here we are then." She paused to read the form. "K2, you'll be in my class Chris. How do you feel about that?"

Until now Chris had remained quiet. As he recalled last time, she scared him and he'd recoiled and hid behind his father's legs. Rob hadn't taken that well. He thought boys should show courage no matter what. This time it was different, and Chris stepped up to the table, "I'm looking forward to it Mrs Priestley."

She nearly fell over, as did some of the other teachers and parents who overheard his rather mature remark, "Well, you certainly have a good grasp of speech for your age don't you?"

"Yes Maam," Chris replied having a bit of fun at her expense.

Again, she shot a look of surprise in his direction but quickly gathered herself, writing his name on a piece of card and thrusting it towards Rob with a safety pin under her thumb, but before Rob could take it Chris intercepted.

He took the name badge, eased the pin through the top and stuck it to his left breast pocket with all the dexterity of a grown up. Again, the adults were stunned and Rob was quick to notice them, "He's always been busy with his hands."

"Indeed. Well then, "added Mrs Priestly still surprised, "Over there, that's my classroom. Say goodbye to Daddy and find a seat. Can you do that Chris?"

He simply replied, "No worries," and walked off confidently with Rob.

Mrs Priestly shook her head in disbelief and Chris heard a few adults muttering to themselves as he moved off. Chris just smiled.

They climbed the wooden steps of the classroom, with its banister flaking blue paint and was suddenly overwhelmed with an avalanche of thoughts. He remembered sliding down the railing many times and being scolded by his mother for coming home with flecks of blue paint all over his shirt.

He walked across the wooden decking and spied the bench that was bolted to the outer wall where all the school bags were stored. As he stepped into the K2 classroom he was overwhelmed by the strong smell of linoleum, pencil and crayon, pausing as a dozen little faces stared back at him from their little seats and little desks.

'Ok mate, time for me to go," said Rob, "You be, ok?"

Chris turned and looked up at his father remembering this moment from before. He'd screamed and cried like he was being abandoned. His father had to tear him away that time and hand him to a teacher before making a break for it. Chris realised it would have broken Rob's heart to have to do that, "I'll be ok Dad, don't worry."

"Good to know," Rob hugged his son, a rare display of affection, and left. Chris was sure he had a tear in his eye.

He watched his dad walk off then turned back towards his new, or was it old, classmates and spied his desk and chair making straight for them. He knew exactly where he should be and didn't see any reason to sit anywhere else.

The fear on the faces of the others was palpable, and he could feel the tension in the room. None of the kids spoke. Some were crying as their mothers tried to calm them, others just sat looking confused by the upheaval of normality while another teacher, Mrs Smyth as Chris recalled, sat at the big desk and watched over them without a word.

As Chris sat quietly, he watched more students arrive one by one, taking their seats. Then, a kid that Chris instantly recognised stepped through the door.

Eddie Bolton!

Eddie was a bully pure and simple, even at age 5. He gave Chris Hell for years through Primary and High School and Chris never forgot it. He wondered if things would be different this time.

Soon the class was full, and Mrs Smyth stood and waited while Mrs Priestley hustled the last of the parents out and dismissed her colleague.

She stood at the front of the room, the huge green dusty chalk board filling the wall behind her as she looked around the room.

"Good morning children," she sang.

Chris immediately responded, "Good morning, Mrs Priestley," at which point several children giggled.

"SILENCE!" screamed Mrs Priestley.

There she is.

"Whenever I say good morning you will do as, "she paused to read the name on the card, "Chris just did. Let's try again. Good morning children."

A few in the group whimpered out a response, "Not good enough. AGAIN!" demanded Mrs Priestley as she slapped the top of her desk.

"Good morning, Mrs Priestley," came the chorus.

"Very good. Now let's begin."

The first lesson was revealed. Mrs Priestley unrolled a colourful chart which hung from the top of the chalkboard and Chris suddenly realised that he was going to be over-run by boredom. The chart revealed all the letters of the alphabet with a corresponding object next to each letter, A a and a picture of a red apple, B b and a picture of a book and so on.

The next hour and a half dragged as they recited each and every letter in capitals and phonics. He was very relieved to hear the bell for recess.

"I hope you brought your play lunch children. You have half an hour so go outside in the sunshine and come back here when you hear the bell," explained Mrs Priestley.

Chris noticed that everyone got up and left except for a kid that he recognised as Mark Johnstone. Chris wondered what the problem might be, straining to remember but he didn't wait around to find out.

Outside he grabbed his bag, rummaged around for his lunchbox and retrieved a packet of chips. He munched away as he sat on the bench and looked out over the playground, recognising more kids and a few teachers too.

He spotted Mr Randolph, a charming old soul and was saddened by the thought that, in a few years from now he'd be dead after a car crash. Then there was Mr Quincy LeBrock. What an arsehole. He loved bullying kids and playing mean tricks on them. Chris had been a victim of that too and he decided to be vigilant when LeBrock was on playground duty.

After eating, Chris joined the throng in the playground. He kept to himself until he noticed Eddie Bolton pestering a little girl, out of sight of the duty teachers. Cindy Fletcher was crying and Chris hesitated before deciding to intervene.

He walked up on the pair and caught a few words from Eddie, "Give it to me!"

Cindy was terrified as Eddie tried to tease a lolly out of the small white paper bag that she had crunched in her tiny hand. She started to raise the bag and was about to reluctantly offer the contents to Eddie.

"Don't do it Cindy," called Chris.

The girl jumped and Eddie wheeled around to see who dared interrupt the transaction.

"Off you go Cindy," added Chris, "I'll deal with this."

Cindy didn't need time to think and scrambled away as fast as she could. Eddie leered at Chris but didn't say anything while Chris sized him up, "OK, listen up Eddie. You're a bully, just like your dad and I know you'll always be that way BUT if I ever see you picking on anyone, I'll flush your head in the toilet. Got it!?"

Chris had been a victim of that punishment at Eddie's hands too many times and decided to use it against his foe in a pre-emptive strike, "And while I'm at it. You come anywhere near me I'll..." Chris suddenly went blank unable to quickly think of an appropriate punishment but then..." I'll poop in your school bag!"

Eddie was mortified and, without uttering a word ran off crying. Chris thought it went well until he saw Eddie homing in on Mr LeBrock who quickly looked up at the screaming kid, listened to his complaint while a finger was pointed in Chris's direction.

Oh crap!

LeBrock frowned and beckoned Chris towards him with his index finger. LeBrock pinch gripped the top of Chris's left ear and marched him to the Deputy Principal's office where he sat down in a little wooden chair and waited. He was nervous but had time to build a defence. The door burst open and in stepped Mr Patterson, a tall, thin wisp of a man with a mop of grey, greasy hair barely covering his bald spot, "Well young man, you've had quite a first day. Mr LeBrock told me what happened."

"I can explain, "replied Chris to which Mr Patterson balked.

"Please, tell me all about it," teased the Deputy.

"Eddie was picking on Cindy Patterson."

"Is that so? He said you punched him! Did you?"

"Of course not. Are you kidding? He's 5 years old," Chris blurted.

Mr Patterson was shocked at such a mature remark, "Well er, what happened?"

"I just told him to leave her alone and he didn't like it. He made her cry."

"And you made Eddie cry."

"Yeah well, he deserved it," Chris muttered under his breath.

"What was that?"

Chris realised he'd probably overplayed his hand and should just shut up before too many more questions were asked, "I don't know."

"Alright then. Stand up and turn around."

Chris balked, Jesus, really?

He sat there a for a moment as the Deputy's face crumpled with impatience, "Come on, stand up and turn around. I won't ask again!"

Chris reluctantly obliged and stood for what felt like an eternity and then THWACK. Pain reverberated through his bum as the sting of a yard ruler did the Deputy's bidding. Chris flinched but rather than bursting into tears he gritted his teeth awaiting a second blow.

The Deputy paused, "Have you learned your lesson son?"

"Yes Sir." Chris replied and pretended to be upset.

"Alright then, go back to class and I hope I don't see you in here again."

Chris left the office, refusing to rub the ache. He walked back to Mrs Priestley's room where he knocked on the door. The teacher looked at him strangely as he took his seat, but she didn't say anything. Cindy smiled at him as he scanned the room for Eddie, who seemed oblivious to everything.

Dickhead.

He then noticed Mark Johnstone was wearing a pair of brown corduroy trousers and he smiled to himself as he recalled how Mark had shit himself on the first day of school. He would never be allowed to forget either.

The class was now watching the teacher doing some drawing. She was filling the blackboard with lines and colours, slowly creating the image of a butterfly. Its orange wings and dark body covered in white spots, "Now who can tell me what this is?" asked Mrs Priestley.

A chorus of children all screamed out, "A butterfly."

Mrs Priestley, who had seemingly tempered her aggression after the early morning power trip reminded the children that they shouldn't yell, they should raise their hands and wait until they're invited to answer, "Now, who can tell me what this is?" She scanned the room as a score of little arms pointed upwards, "Chris? What do you think this is?"

Chris hadn't raised his hand and wasn't ready to be called upon. He was used to blending into the background and having all the other kids do the work, at least that's how he remembered it, "Um, it's a butterfly."

"Well yes and did you know there are many different kinds of butterflies? Do you know what this one is?"

It was an odd question to ask a 5-year-old and Chris suspected his teacher was playing games with the kids just to stimulate herself. He didn't care and was thrilled to be able to think for a change.

He looked at the picture again, "It looks like a Wanderer butterfly Maam, also known as a Monarch. They're found as far west as Australia and Asia and across the Pacific east to the Americas." It was just something he'd remembered from a documentary.

Mrs Priestley's jaw dropped and the white stick of chalk she held fell from her fingertips and broke into three even pieces on the floor. Even a few of the children realised the oddity of the response.

Damn it!

Mrs Priestley gathered her thoughts and picked up the broken pieces of chalk, placing them on the sill of the blackboard ignoring Chris's comments. She simply moved on to the next task.

Chris didn't know whether to be relieved or worried but decided to let it slide. Perhaps he'd dodged a bullet.

The rest of the day went without incident, Chris keeping mostly to himself as he tried to get his head around this bizarre situation. He never anticipated how strange and difficult school would be again.

At 3 O'clock Sandy arrived to collect her son. She was directed to his classroom and mingled with the other mothers as the bell rang. Kids started streaming out of classrooms all over the school, except for K2. Mrs Priestley was much more disciplined and made the children stand, "Good afternoon children."

"Good afternoon, Mrs Priestley," came the impish response but because the parents were nearby Mrs Priestley didn't push the point.

"OK, we'll work on that," she said, "See you tomorrow children," she added as she cast a quick glance at Chris.

The boys and girls ran outside and into the arms of their Mums and Dads. Chris too was very relieved to see Sandy waiting for him. He ran over and gave her a crushing hug.

"Hi Chris, how was your first day?"

"Good," came his uncustomary short reply.

"You can tell me about it on the way home," but before they could take another step,

"Mrs Parish?" It was Mrs Priestley, "I'm Chris's teacher. May we talk?"

Uh oh!

Mrs Priestley motioned them to the classroom. Sandy responded, taking Chris by the hand and walking up the steps.

"Good afternoon, Mrs Parish, I'm Mrs. Priestley." After the courtesies were complete, she asked, "I need to speak with you privately please? Chris can sit here," and she pointed at the bench outside the classroom.

"Is there something the matter?" asked Sandy.

"Oh no, not at all but I do think we should talk," suggested Mrs Priestley.

With that Sandy entered the classroom and Chris took post on the bench wondering what might happen next but deep down, he knew he'd gone too far on his first day.

Sandy was offered a chair and sat next to the big desk while Chris pressed an ear to the wall to pick up the conversation.

"What's this about?" asked Sandy.

"Well, I don't quite know how to put this, but I think Chris is a special child. I've been a teacher for many years Mrs Parish and I can't recall a childlike Chris in all my years," she explained.

"What do you mean special? Is he a spastic?!" Sandy blurted in sheer terror.

"Oh gosh no, I mean gifted Mrs Parish. He's incredibly intelligent. I've seen him do things today that are extraordinary and I've heard him talk quite fluently. He's also well advanced socially. He even defended a little girl from a bully today. I saw it with my own eyes."

Gee thanks for having my back, not!

"Really?" said Sandy, not quite sure what to say next.

"Yes really. And I fear he'll not do well here. He'll be bored and I doubt he'll thrive in this environment. He's much too clever," suggested the teacher.

"I don't know what to say. I mean we never really thought much about it?" Sandy suggested.

"Surely you've noticed this at home and how he is with other people?"

"Well yes, we know he's bright, but we didn't think it was anything unusual. My husband and I had no siblings, and Chris is an only child too. It never really crossed our minds to be honest."

"Are you sure? Nothing at all stands out?"

"Well, maybe a few years ago, when he'd sneak the newspaper into his room and look through it. And he did teach himself to walk very young," explained Sandy.

Mrs Priestley was gobsmacked, "And you didn't think it odd?"

"Well, yes and I took him to a doctor but after a while the doctor wrote it off as a coincidence. He must have thought I was exaggerating so he never pursued it."

"I can assure you Mrs Parish that he isn't at all normal, and I mean that in a good way. He is incredibly advanced; far more knowledgeable than any child I've seen. To be honest I think he's already a decade ahead of the other kids," said Mrs Priestley.

And then some.

"Really?" Sandy hesitated before asking, "So, what do we do?"

"OK, let me talk to the principal and we'll try and come up with some ideas. But I can tell you that he will need stimulation or he'll fade away very quickly. If he's as clever as I think then we shouldn't let him fall through the cracks."

"OK, thank you. I'll talk to his father as well."

"You do that and we can chat again tomorrow."

"Yes, thank you."

With that the two said their goodbyes and Chris looked back at Mrs Priestley as they walked away. She stood at the top of the steps with her arms folded, the look on her face suggesting she had a puzzle on her hands and she did. Chris felt uneasy.

On the way home Sandy looked at Chris but didn't reveal the conversation to her son, "So, how was your day, Chris? Did you have fun?"

"It was ok."

"Did you make any new friends?"

"No," he decided to keep his responses short and simple, just like a 5-year-old.

"Oh, why not?"

"I don't know. I'm hungry."

"OK, we'll make you something at home."

Chris had cleverly deflected her enquiries, and they got home without any further questions.

That night, after dinner Sandy and Rob sat down for a chat. Chris conveniently placed himself near enough to catch the entire discussion.

"They say he's very bright, too bright for that school," Sandy explained.

"So, what do we do?" Rob asked.

"I don't know. The school is going to try and figure something out."

Chris didn't know how to feel about the situation. His memories were filled with early school, Primary and High School. What if none of that happened as before?

"Maybe we should see what the school suggests and decide from there," said Rob.

"I agree. Let's see what they think but you know we can't afford to pay for private school or tutoring or anything like that."

"I know," replied Rob.

Chris pondered the situation; what to do? Would it be so bad to go to another school? He could still make things happen the way they needed to after that. It wasn't like school had steered him down his career path or towards meeting Judy. Maybe this would be good.

The next morning both Rob and Sandy drove Chris to school. They walked him to the principal's office where Mrs Priestley was waiting.

After a quick greeting all were shuffled into the office of the Principle, Ron Dillon. He sat behind his dark, wood-stained desk puffing on a cigarette, reading the local paper.

Chris read the headline, "First American soldier dies in Vietnam." He was about to shake his head but quickly took stock to avoid another demonstration that may raise more suspicion.

As Chris and his family walked into the room Mr Dillon folded the paper down and peered across at the trio, who were quickly joined by Mrs Priestley and Mr Patterson, the Deputy.

"Well, here's the man of the moment," cried Mr Dillon as he stood to greet the family, "Sit, please sit."

After the greetings, handshakes and shuffling of chairs, everyone took their seats,

"So, we appear to have a child prodigy on our hands," suggested Dillon, "We don't see too many of them to be honest. Bright kids yes, but a prodigy? Very rare. How long has he been reading?"

There was an awkward pause until Sandy took the lead, "Oh well, I suppose he was reading or pretending to since before he turned 1."

"Struth! Really? That's astounding. How about his speech? Has he developed a vocabulary?"

"Yes indeed," Sandy was starting to feel proud and began opening up, "He can talk about many things, and he loves watching the news on TV too."

"Is that so," said Mr Dillon as he kept a bead on Chris, "Tell me more."

"Well, I don't know what else to say. Chris toilet trained himself and he even helped me balance the cheque book one day!"

How the Hell did she know that?

"I didn't actually see him do it, but the handwriting wasn't mine or Robs' and no-one else touches the cheque book. It had to be Chris," Sandy explained.

The room fell silent for a moment. Chris was worried, how could he hide the truth now? He had to think fast.

"Well, we'd better take a look into this further," suggested the principal, "I have some advanced reading and problem books here, do you think he'd like to try and solve a few puzzles? They're like IQ test questions. Would you like to try that, Chris?" asked Mr Dillon.

All eyes fell on Chris as he decided on a tactic, "Yes."

"Excellent. Now these first few are oral questions, so we won't need to write at this stage. So, let me ask you..." Mr Dillon opened a textbook and flicked through a few pages, "Here we are. Chris, which of these is a prime number? 4, 11 or 20."

Everyone looked at Chris expectantly, and without hesitation he replied, "11."

"That's right," There was a gasp from everyone in the room, except Mr Patterson.

"How about," Dillon turned another page, "Here we go. There are two ducks on a pond and seven ducks standing on the grass. Three more are flying overhead, how many legs can you see?"

Again, Chris didn't hesitate to answer, "20."

"Right again," Mr Dillon grabbed the other textbook, "Try this. Which letter is missing from this sequence, D, H, P, T?"

Chris had to think about this one and said the letters over and over in his head. As he did, he counted the variations and realised they were sequential in units of four and announced the missing letter as, "L."

"Yep, he got it again."

The inquisition went on for a while. The tests involved problem solving, written tests, grammar, mathematics and general knowledge. Chris decided to throw a few questions just to be on the safe side. Finally, the Principle called a halt, "Well I'm impressed. Your son exhibits very high levels of knowledge, ability and awareness, far beyond any child, and I'm not just talking about kindergarten kids, he's showing High School capability at the least. He's a prodigy, I have no doubt."

Ron and Sandy had no idea what to say, they were in shock. Dillon continued, "He needs much more stimulation than we can offer but there aren't many schools that could cater for him either. Might I suggest something?"

Chris's parents nodded.

"What if we keep him on here, and work with him. I'm sure I can convince the department that this is worth investing in. He's a great asset for the future, whatever it is he decides to do with his life."

Again, silence from the adults for a moment before Sandy asked a question, "What about what Chris wants?"

"I'm sorry?" replied Mr Dillon.

"Well, if Chris is so aware and gaining knowledge like you say, perhaps he's capable of making the decision for himself," she added.

"Well then," Principle Dillon turned to Chris, "What say you Chris, would you like to come to school and work with a specialist teacher?"

Everyone in the room looked at him, anticipating his response.

Chris pondered the possibilities, "Well Chris? What'll it be?" asked Dillon.

"Yes, I think so," he replied.

"Oh, come on, this is ridiculous, "suggested Mr Patterson, "He's not even five yet, not for what, a month or two? How can he make a decision like this?"

"He's very bright Mr Patterson," added Mrs Priestley, "I've watched him closely and he has a mind like none I've come across."

"You determined this after one day? Give me strength. He's a small child and a bit of a larrikin to boot. His first day also saw him sent to my office for fighting, did you forget that?"

"It wasn't a fight," explained Priestley, "He confronted another boy who was trying to tease a little girl. He defended her. The other boy accused him of something he didn't do," she explained turning to Mr Patterson.

Wow!

"Well, he didn't exhibit anything to suggest intellect when I spoke to him," retorted Patterson.

"You heard his test answers, didn't you?" asked Mr Dillon.

"He could have been coached! No, I'm not convinced."

"Very well, what do you suggest?"

"We need a psychological examination. We need an official analysis to be certain that this child is something other than normal," explained Patterson.

Sandy asked, "And who would you do that?"

"I know a man who has recently started working with children. He was a doctor, but he took on child psychology. He could look at Chris. Then we'd know once and for all."

"And who might that be?" asked Mr Dillon.

"Dr William Chamberlain."

Oh crap, him again.

After much more discussion it was agreed, Dr Chamberlain would assess Christopher Parish.

Chapter 6

Dr William Chamberlain smiled as Chris was led into his office. He'd spent the last few years retooling his career and had become quite accomplished, working with children under all kinds of circumstances, "Good to see you again Chris."

Chris didn't answer.

"Mrs Parish, nice to see you too. How has Chris been?" asked Chamberlain.

"Quite well thank you."

"Better than that according to this report from the school," suggested the doctor as he handed Sandy the document.

"Yes, I've seen it. What happens now?"

"Well, it's quite simple. We'll test Chris using a process that is well regarded and determine his mental age."

"Mental age?" Sandy was confused.

"It's the age of his mind rather than his body. He's 5, right? But his mind may be 15. These tests will tell us where he sits."

"Oh, I see."

Dr Chamberlain turned back to Chris, "So Chris. When I saw you last you were a baby and to be honest, I didn't take you very seriously. I'm starting to think you may have tricked me somehow. Is that right?"

Chris simply shrugged which the Doctor could read any number of ways; a 5-year-old being shy, dismissive or he was being coy. Chris left that for the doctor to decide.

"I have to be honest Mrs Parish. Chris was something of a watershed for me. I enjoyed working with him so much that it inspired me to pursue a specialty in child psychology. It's been quite rewarding."

"Oh, well I'm glad to hear it." Sandy blushed.

Chris was taken back a little too. This was one of the things he'd always worried about. Had he changed this timeline because of Dr Chamberlain? Or had the doctor become a psychologist in the prior timeline anyway? There was simply no way of knowing.

"Alright Chris, let's get down to it," suggested Dr Chamberlain, "Mrs. Parish, if you could wait outside. Chris can't be distracted."

"Oh, of course." With that Sandy went back to the waiting room.

The first tests were simple, and Chris had no trouble with them. In fact, the big danger was that he might lose his concentration because of boredom and he'd lose his train of thought.

Next came problem solving and again he revelled at an opportunity to work his brain a bit. He didn't think about what it might mean to do these tests and excel at them; he just felt satisfaction with the stimulation of it all.

An hour went by and Chris showed no sign of fatigue, which didn't go unnoticed by the doctor. Very few 5-year-olds can concentrate for ten minutes, and Chris was going strong well into his second hour and hadn't taken a break.

Chris realised this was probably going to result in some extraordinary report, but the school had opened the door of his being a prodigy and that served him well under the circumstances. It might just give him some leeway, and he could relax a bit, knowing that he was a documented brainiac.

After a few hours Chris realised that he was really enjoying himself and that Dr Chamberlain really knew his stuff. He'd never felt so motivated in this life or the one he'd lived before. It was indeed gratifying.

Four hours went by and the tasks had reached a highly intellectual level and Chris found he was struggling. He'd reached his limits and he knew it.

"OK Chris, we just have one more test. Are you ready?"

Chris was feeling mentally drained by now, but he'd been having such a good time he excitedly gave a nod of approval. He didn't realise he'd dropped his guard...

"Right here we go. Can you name all the planets in the solar system?"

Too easy

Chris rattled them off without hesitation, "Mercury, Venus, Earth, Mars, Jupiter, Saturn, Uranus and Neptune!"

Dr Chamberlain hesitated, "And?"

Chris was confused for a moment, "And what?"

"There's one more isn't there?"

"No. Pluto isn't a planet," Chris suggested.

"Really? Why not?"

"It's a part of the Kuiper belt, it's been redefined as a dwarf planet, just like Charon, Sedna and Quaoar."

As soon as Chris said that he realised his mistake. He'd been so caught up in the process he forgot himself. That information wouldn't be known for decades in this timeline. Chris had recalled the data from his late-night love affair with astronomy on the radio and now, perhaps he'd revealed his hand. He hoped Dr Chamberlain would be none the wiser.

"Fascinating Chris, but I don't understand. Pluto was discovered in 1930 and is a planet. As far as we know there's nothing beyond. Why would you say otherwise?"

Oh Crap!

Chris had to think fast. He was in a corner now and only a perfect explanation would get him out of trouble. His mind raced and he panicked,

"I must have made a mistake," he said. He couldn't believe that's all he could come up with.

Dr Chamberlain looked at him with a doubtful expression, "I somehow don't think so Chris. You said names I've never heard of and seemed very certain of your answer. I think you really believe it. I think your mistake was telling the truth!"

Chris was mortified and didn't know what to do next.

"I wonder what else you know Chris?" asked Dr Chamberlain, "Hm?" The doctor looked excited for some reason.

"I don't know anything really."

It was starting to feel like an interrogation now and Chris's joy quickly evaporated.

"Look Chris. I don't mean to scare you, but I do want to investigate this. You're very clever, no doubt, but I'm looking at your answers here and it would appear that the majority of your ability is based on general knowledge," the doctor explained. "As far as the more advanced questions are concerned, you didn't fare too well, so tell me, how do you know what you know?"

Chris was in a bind. Had he been duped by the doctor or was this just someone grasping at straws? He couldn't be sure, but he wasn't going to give it all away without a fight.

"I don't know. I just know what I know."

Dr Chamberlain was unconvinced, Chris could see that and then the doctor dropped a bombshell,

"Who shot John Lennon?"

"What?"

"You heard me. In 1980 John Lennon is assassinated in New York. Who did it?"

Chris couldn't believe his ears and sat, wide-mouthed and in shock.

"I'll give you a moment to get it together. Four years ago, you were too clever for me," suggested the doctor, "but when you started talking today, I hoped you might drop your defences, and I could throw you a curveball. You did just that."

Chris ignored the remark, "But how could you possibly know about John Lennon?"

"Ah ha! You couldn't know that either, unless you were..." Chamberlain didn't finish his sentence and changed tack, "I initially thought that you were more than a prodigy and then, as we continued you answered things in a way that demonstrated life experience rather than learning experience. It was subtle but it was there."

Dr Chamberlain looked at the report in his hand and then back at Chris, "To be honest Chris, I don't think you're a prodigy at all, better than average, but no prodigy. I don't mean that as an insult, but I do think you've got a lot of knowledge that gives the impression of advanced ability. Would that be accurate?"

Chris looked at the doctor and realised that he wasn't going to shake him off, not now, not ever.

Ribbit?

It wouldn't work here, not this time.

"Mark Chapman."

"I'm sorry, what was that," asked Dr Chamberlain.

"Mark Chapman shot John Lennon in the doorway of Lennon's apartment, or at least he will in just under fourteen years," explained Chris.

Dr Chamberlain said nothing and began packing up his papers and reports.

"Your turn to explain Doctor, how could you possibly know about John Lennon?" asked Chris.

"Let's just say I can't breach privilege."

"Who's privilege?"

"Ah, that would be a breach in itself," said the doctor.

Chris realised he was never going to reveal his source or client or whoever it was and changed the subject, "So what happens to me now? You could blow the lid off this situation if you wanted to."

"To what end? You're not here to hurt anyone and you certainly didn't come back on purpose or with ill intent, right?"

Chris realised the Doctor knew much more than had been revealed in answering test questions, "I'm not sure what you mean," suggested Chris.

"I think you do, but you're right to be wary. With what you know there are many who would exploit it, if they found out."

Chris again caught the doctor's gaze, "Let's assume you're right, would you exploit my supposed knowledge?"

"Of course not. I'm old, alone and independently well off. I don't have delusions of grandeur, and I don't want to be filthy rich, but I'd be in the minority. Just be careful Chris. You have to learn to curb your excitement and guard every word. It's your biggest weakness."

"I know it, but sometimes people just piss me off."

Dr Chamberlain laughed, "You don't know how funny that sounds coming from a 5-year-old, but tell me honestly how old are you, really?"

Chris suddenly felt he could trust this man and with a surge of relief said, "In real terms I'm about to turn 57!"

Dr Chamberlain didn't seem at all surprised, "Well then. You have quite a dilemma, don't you? The burden of so much history yet to occur, it must be frustrating."

"Tell me about it. I don't know what to do."

"I get that," said Dr Chamberlain, "But if I could suggest you lay low, that would be the best thing to do. The wrong attention won't auger well for you, I fear. Better the Devil you know."

"Maybe you're right. My grandfather said the same thing," Chris noted Dr Chamberlain's surprise, "Yes, he figured me out too but not with as much prowess as you."

"Does anyone else know?"

"My Grandmother and your client."

"Well, it might be best to leave it at that. The more people who know, the bigger the danger and I don't think I need to explain myself, do I?"

Chris shook his head. He knew what the doctor meant, "You still haven't told me what happens now."

"Oh, I'll give the school the report they want. They're right about one thing; you'll be bored with the kindergarten kids. I can at least give you something more riveting to do by suggesting you're a few decades ahead of your time. But I doubt it'll make the next several years any less mind numbing."

"Thanks Doctor. It's good to know you're on the right side."

"You're welcome and if you ever need to talk, you can see me any time."

Chris smiled and acknowledged the offer.

Sandy soon popped into the room and the doctor explained his findings, which delighted Chris's mother who beamed with excitement. When she wasn't looking Dr Chamberlain gave Chris a wink.

As the doctor's office door closed behind them Chris looked back just in time to see Dr Chamberlain picking up the phone. He felt suspicious for a fleeting moment but soon let the thought slide.

Back at school Chris and his parents sat in Ron Dillon's office as the principal pawed over the report,

"As I suspected, he's quite an advanced child. Dr Chamberlain is recommending he be placed in his own class."

"How does this work then?" asked Sandy.

"We have to run it by the school board and arrange funding but given these results I doubt there'll be a problem. It might just take a few weeks, if you can be patient," replied Dillon as he cast and eye at Chris who shrugged.

"And what will this cost us?" asked Rob.

Ron Dillon was a little taken back by the question, "What do you mean?"

"We're not rich and to be honest I don't know how he turned out like this. We're not scholars and we can't really afford to pay for advanced education," Rob explained.

"I see your point. I'd be lying if I said there won't be some costs, for textbooks and materials but I'm going to ask for special funding to cover most of it. They should provide a teacher or re-task someone here. We do have one qualified candidate."

"And who's that?" Sandy asked eagerly.

"Quincy LeBrock!"

Chris cringed immediately. He didn't like LeBrock. The man was a bully of the highest order. In his former life, Chris had never attended any of his classes, but he knew students who had, and they never said anything positive about the man.

As well as intimidating children, he had a bad temper and was a liberal user of the cane with older students. He was simply mean.

"Well then, we'll be guided by you Mr Dillon," suggested Sandy.

"Excellent. I'll begin making the arrangements," concluded Dillon.

For the next few weeks nothing changed. Chris expected the bureaucracy would do what it always did and get around to something in a few months but somehow the funding was found and by the end of February, Chris was in a class of his own, and his teacher was Quincy LeBrock.

Chris hadn't really connected with any of the kids in the mainstream class, not even those he'd previously known as friends. Everything was different now and, despite his apprehension, he was actually looking forward to some stimulation.

The new classroom was tiny. No sense wasting an entire room for one child it seemed. There was a tiny blackboard on an easel and two desks, one for LeBrock and Chris's little desk and no window. Chris was sure he could smell chemicals which suggested it may have been utility closet in the very recent past.

Chris's parents introduced themselves and after hearing LeBrock explain his extensive credentials, which he did with great delight, they said goodbye to their boy and left.

"So, Mr Parish, what do we do with you?" asked LeBrock rhetorically as he turned toward his pupil.

Chris didn't respond.

"I've looked over the report and spoken with Dr Chamberlain," Chris looked up in surprise, "and we discussed some strategies. He suggested you may have your own ideas. Do you?"

"No sir. I'm in your hands," replied Chris causing LeBrock to raise an eyebrow.

Chris looked at the man and took in his chiselled features. He had a rather squarish head and a granite-like jaw. He remembered the older students gave him the nickname Rockjaw and it made him smile. LeBrock had the lightest of blond wispy hair which barely fell past his ears and eyes that were blue, bordering on grey which matched a sickly white complexion. He was 35 years old.

LeBrock smiled, "Ok then, let's get started."

Chris felt his stomach knotting up. This wasn't going to be at all fun.

"We'll start with an assessment and build a plan from there. Is that ok with you Mr Parish?"

Chris didn't know if this formal approach was LeBrock's way or if he was just being a dick, but Chris thought it best to play along for now,

"Very good sir."

"Excellent!"

The rest of the day was spent testing, probing, talking and generally learning about Chris and each other as it turned out.

After a few days Chris started to feel interested and after a few weeks inspired. He even began to like this LeBrock. The man who had cornered him in the playground in the previous life and offered him a ten dollar note while laughing out loud before snatching it away seemed to have softened in this version of events.

And there was another fascinating side effect. LeBrock was being nice to all the other kids too. The specialty role he'd been given was obviously reaping benefits for everyone as it turned out.

Chris felt satisfied that in this timeline at least, he was able to curtail the suffering of a great many children, albeit it indirectly.

That only got Chris wondering again about the one thing that worried him most, what might the effect be in terms of the future. Would a change in attitude by a teacher lead to anything that could ultimately change the future as he'd known it?

Again, only time would tell.

Chris completed the first semester at school and he was feeling good. LeBrock had done a great job of learning his capabilities and quickly had him working on high school level mathematics, science, geography and English. They even started on a little Latin and French, just to keep Chris from getting bored.

In his former life, Chris could best be described as a drifter. He had trouble concentrating and never studied. His school results were average or worse, and he was always told he'd do much better if he applied himself. And while he had an incredible memory for facts and figures he'd wasted that talent on counting cards at casinos and impressing his friends with statistics from a variety of sporting events.

Now, he was willingly absorbing information and gaining knowledge that had passed him by before. It was like an awakening and he felt good.

As the months rolled on things only got better. Chris simply loved school, but he loved the holidays more. His parents would take the opportunity to spend some time away, occasionally taking Chris with them but he preferred to spend that time with Clem and Edith having long discussions about the world as he knew it and what was to come.

He trusted his grandparents unconditionally and felt no qualms about being open about everything he knew.

As his first school year came to a close, he sat his exams. For all the other Kindergarten children, that involved colouring and reciting their ABCs. For Chris it was algebra and advanced English.

His test scores were outstanding and he felt incredibly satisfied. His parents were very proud as were Clem and Edith despite their knowledge.

Everything was going so well that Chris was beginning to believe that his life would be so much better. What could possibly go wrong?

On his last day in kindergarten, he arrived with his parents for school presentations and prize giving.

He'd hardly stepped through the gate when a raft of photographers and TV reporters pounced.

" What the Hell?!" blurted Rob Parish as they were stopped in their tracks.

Journalists surged forward firing questions so fast, they sounded like a gang of turkeys.

"How do you feel about being the parents of a prodigy?"

"How long has Chris been gifted?"

"Has your son decided to be a doctor or a lawyer?"

Chris shrank behind his parents, shocked at the sudden exposure that he had been so careful to avoid.

How do they know?

Sandy reached for Chris and gathered him up instinctively, dragging him close to her while Rob stepped forward to shield them both,

"Who are you, what's this about?"

"Your son Mr Parish, how advanced is he?" came another question.

"What? This is private family business, none of your concern."

"So, it's true, he's a savant?" asked another.

"Yes...No! What do you mean?" Rob was getting more and more flustered.

"Can we talk to Chris?"

"No! Not on your life!" Rob yelled.

Rob felt his anger welling up when he spotted Principal Dillon followed by three men in suits,

"Sorry we're late everyone. Please if you could make room!"

The journalists stopped firing off questions for a moment as the four men took station beside the Parish family. Principal Dillon introduced himself,

"Good morning and thank you for coming along today. We're very lucky to have with us the New South Wales Education Minister, who would like to share his thoughts on the great success of the Advanced Schooling Program we've been trialling here this year. Please make welcome the Honourable James Spicer..."

No one reacted. Journalists were used to politicians cashing in on success stories, particularly during an election campaign, and this was a perfect opportunity.

"I'm very proud to be here today and would like to congratulate Principal Dillon and his faculty for this outstanding achievement. It's not every day that we find ourselves in the presence of greatness but from all reports, young Chris Parish here, "he waved vaguely in Chris's direction, "is the next Albert Einstein!"

Chris suddenly realised what was happening and looked up at his parents. Their faces were ashen and they were clearly confused by the attention.

The minister carried on, "Of course such a success could never have been achieved without the full financial backing of this Government!"

Chris looked down to hide his anger and frustration, knowing that many inquisitive eyes were upon him. Perhaps they'd think he was just shy.

The speech went on and on and on and one of the journalists finally cracked,

"When do we hear from Chris?"

"Alright, I know you're anxious to hear from the man…er, boy himself. Perhaps we can encourage him to say a few words. Now where is the little rascal?" asked Spicer.

Chris remembered Dr Chamberlain warning him to keep a lid on things, but clearly someone else had decided to go public and he hoped it was just the school puffing its chest out. Even so, he scolded himself for his ill-discipline because now he was going to pay for it with more attention than he could ever have anticipated.

"Come along Chris, meet these nice people," encouraged the Minister.

Sandy hung on tight and Chris looked up at her and saw terror on her face, "It's ok Mum. I'll do it."

Sandy looked at her boy, "Are you sure Chris?"

"Yes Mum. It's fine."

Sandy gently slackened her maternal grip and Chris stepped forward, joining the Minister and his minders. He looked up at the man who he immediately recognised. Spicer would make news again in years to come when his corrupt practices came to light, but for now he was towing the party line and working to win his own seat.

James Spicer held out a hand and Chris shook it with slight hesitation, "Congratulations lad. I hear you've finished with top scores in all your subjects." He turned to the journalists again, "Chris Parish has achieved A levels of High School standard at the age of 5. I'm sure you'll agree that the Government's support of the program that made this possible has been well worth the one-on-one approach. And I'm happy to announce today that we will further fund…"

And he went on like that for ten more minutes, making sure Chris stayed close while cameras clicked and whirred.

Eventually the Minister ran out of words, "Are there any questions?"

It was like throwing money at a crowd of paupers. The questions came thick and fast and they were all directed at Chris.

Rob stepped forward, again a protective gesture, but Sandy grabbed his hand and pulled him back. He looked at her, confused that she would stop him intervening, "Let him speak," she whispered.

The Minister held his hands up to the group waving them in an effort to hush the crowd, "One at a time folks, please, give the boy a chance." The group hushed, "That's better. OK, who's first? Ben!"

"Yes, thank you Minister," He looked at Chris, "When did you realise you were different from all the other children?"

Chris didn't answer straight away. He pondered for a moment and thought about how to deal with the interrogation, "What do you mean different?"

"Well, your intelligence. You know? How clever you are compared to the others."

Chris had to be careful here. He didn't want to drop a bombshell that would open more doors and more intense questioning. He'd been tricked by his grandfather and then Dr Chamberlain. He would have to be on guard for the next few minutes.

"I dunno?"

"OK? Um, do you know what you want to be when you grow up?" asked the reporter.

"Um, No."

The reporter's line of questioning suddenly dried up, and the Minister called on the next journalist, "Mary!"

"Hi Chris. Your parents must be very proud,"

"I think they are. Are you Mummy?" and Chris turned to Sandy.

The journalists laughed at the cute response, but they didn't see Chris wink at his mother, who was slightly astonished but recovered quickly enough to respond, "We're very proud of Chris, yes."

The tactic worked with the reporters turning their attention to Sandy and Rob. Chris didn't want to put them in the firing line, but he knew that a proud mother would ultimately give them what they wanted. She just needed to be eased into it.

"When did he show signs of being so bright Mrs. Parish?"

Sandy set about telling stories of how soon he walked, his reading and so it went on. The reporters were all mesmerised by the amazing development of the boy who stood before them and were more than happy to get the story from a third party rather than from the horse's mouth.

The questions lasted quite a while before the Minister asked if there were any more.

There was dead silence from the crowd, and everything appear to have wrapped up when a voice from the rear of the throng piped up,

"When's the next stock market crash going to happen?"

A few people laughed but Chris wasn't amused.

"Yes, very funny," suggested James Spicer. "Thank you all."

He posed for a few pictures with Chris and his parents before the press conference broke up. The Minister slid past Chris and introduced himself to Sandy and Rob, "We didn't expect you to be so early."

Sandy wasn't sure what to say, "Sorry. We didn't know..."

The Minister cut her off, "And Mr Parish. You must be very proud."

"Well, yeah, we are."

"Good, good. Well, we must be off. Lots of people to see; an election to win you know?" And with that he vanished as abruptly as he arrived.

Chris was annoyed at being used to help someone win an election and they would win Chris recalled. He felt bad for his parents who were ill equipped to deal with this kind of attention, but he was also proud of them for dealing with it so well.

Sandy and Rob spoke to Principal Dillon and finally everyone made their way to the school hall for presentations where Chris gained a fistful of sashes and certificates, most created for him alone because there were no pre-existing categories for his level of scholastic achievement.

Several journalists who decided to sit through the monotony of the ceremony were rewarded with a few pictures for their respective media outlets.

After the official ceremony students and parents mingled, chatted and finally began to leave.

Sandy, Rob and Chris were relieved to have made it through the whole morning virtually unscathed when a lone figure approached, a man none of them knew.

He was about 30, well dressed with short black hair and an olive complexion. He strode quickly up to the trio, pausing and casting a quick glance around before addressing Rob and Sandy,

"You have no idea what this boy is. You're clearly oblivious. Watch him closely. There are people who would use him for unscrupulous reasons. Be careful."

Chris and his parents were dumbfounded,

"What are you talking about," demanded Rob.

The man looked at Chris, "They have to know what you are. You have to tell them everything. Their lives and your future depend on it!"

And with that he walked away, his head twitching left and right like he was being overly suspicious.

"Hey, what's this all about?" called Rob but the man didn't look back as he climbed into a shiny black car and drove off as fast as he could.

"What on Earth," Rob said to himself.

Sandy looked at Chris, "Do you know that man Chris?"

"No mummy."

"What did he mean when he said we don't know what you are?"

Chris didn't answer immediately. Things were seemingly coming unstuck and he didn't know if he could maintain the charade much longer.

"Let's go home. I think we need to talk," Chris said.

Both Rob and Sandy's jaws dropped and they followed Chris to the car. As they drove away Chris asked,

"Can we go to Grandma and Grandpa's before we go home?"

"Sure mate," said Rob and he glanced at Sandy with a dumbfounded look on his face.

Edith boiled the kettle and made everyone some tea as Clem sat in his favourite chair with Sandy, Rob and Chris filling the settee,

"You all look worried, what's going on?"

"I don't know what to tell ya," suggested Rob but then Chris jumped in,

"Dad, it's time I set the record straight."

Again, Rob and Sandy were dumbstruck with their son's sudden maturity.

"What's going on Chris?" asked Clem.

"Well, it looks like someone's let the cat out of the bag. Mum and Dad need to know the truth."

"I see. Do you want to tell them or should I?"

Sandy couldn't stand it, "What's happening? I don't understand any of this."

Chris turned to his parents and looked at them straight. They could tell something was very different. The child they thought they knew had vanished, like someone else had taken over their son's body,

"Mum, Dad. I'm not a child. I'm a grown up and I have been alive for nearly sixty years."

"What? That's ridiculous," suggested Rob.

"Listen to him Rob, "said Clem, "Go on Chris. Tell them everything."

Sandy looked at her father, "You know what this is all about?"

"Most of it; Edith too. Chris came to us a while back."

"What is this Chris, what's happening?" Sandy demanded.

"Calm down Mum. You and Dad need to listen and listen carefully. I was hoping I wouldn't have to tell you this way, but things have changed."

She couldn't believe the words that were coming out of her now, five-year-old son's mouth, "What are you saying Chris. I don't understand. Who are you?"

Rob was fuming with frustration and was about to burst, "Who was that guy at the school?"

"I don't know," said Chris, "But he knew about me and that means other people do too. That's why we need to talk."

"He knew what about you Chris," Sandy demanded.

"Give the boy a chance to explain. Things will be much clearer after that. BUT be prepared for a shock," Clem suggested to both Sandy and Rob.

They didn't answer and just sat there in hesitant expectation.

"Right, here goes," said Chris, "In 2014 I was thrust back here, effected by some kind of time shift phenomenon and born again in March of 1962. I came back with all the knowledge I gained through my life and am here now, living my life over again but I knew what was going to happen for the next 53 years."

"What?" exclaimed Sandy

"Listen Mum, just listen," insisted Chris.

Chris continued to explain everything that had happened to him. His life, his wife, his good times and the bad. He left out key information like his mother's death and the effect it would have on Rob. He went into as much detail as he could, giving examples where possible. He spoke continually for almost half an hour before concluding his story,

"So, I've been living a lie since the day I was born and I've duped both of you into believing I was just a normal kid. I did it to protect both of you but now, someone else knows so there's no point keeping it a secret. And that's it, you know everything."

Sandy and Rob sat motionless, not sure how to react but then Sandy looked up at Chris,

"I should have known all along. I always thought something was unusual. Those little moments when I saw you doing things that seemed out of the ordinary but then you'd mess it up or just stop. You knew I was watching and were hiding from me. I should have known."

"What?" said Rob, "I had no idea. I still can't believe it! It sounds like some huge joke to me."

"Well, it's not," said Clem, "It's very real and you both need to take it seriously."

"Or what?" demanded Rob, his gaze fixed on Chris.

"I don't know Dad; I have no Earthly idea but if people know about me and the knowledge I carry, then they would see me as a very profitable commodity, and I doubt these are people who we ever want to meet. Do you understand?"

As Rob and Sandy nodded Chris could see how worried they now were but he had no choice but to come clean.

Chapter 7

With the school year ended, Chris's parents decided on a holiday to escape the attention. Chris was certainly on board with that.

None of them, including Chris, had anticipated the sort of scrutiny they might face, and all were regretting the fuss. Chris in particular was kicking himself for a lack of discipline, which ultimately got him noticed. He should have played dumb, but a lifetime of habit was hard to curtail.

They went to the North Coast and spent several weeks in seclusion on a houseboat meandering around the Myall Lakes, only catching up with civilisation for fuel and supplies.

It was expensive and really ate into the family budget, but they needed the time to think about what was happening and how to deal with it.

Chris had also put his "future changes" concerns aside for the time being and decided to use some of his knowledge to build the family a nest egg.

He and Rob discussed it and Sandy reluctantly agreed to the idea. Rob would bet on the races and other sports on Chris's advice, based on years of stored data that was yet to unfold.

They'd have to be careful, because if it were noticed that Rob was winning more than his share, they'd be banned or worse, gain the attention of the racing authorities who didn't take kindly to any kind of fix; not to mention underworld figures who were well known to have interests in the gambling industry. They'd simply have no way of explaining it. Losing big on purpose a few times along the way should cover their tracks to a degree.

Chris would continue to study hard and work through school. The major concern was the fact that he was exposed; the papers had certainly guaranteed that. People knew about him now, but who? He'd been warned but what was the danger? There were too many questions and too few answers.

They discussed moving away or going into hiding but the more they talked the more they realised they didn't even know what they might be hiding from. Eventually they decided to go back and live normally, while remaining vigilant. What else could they do?

After some glorious weeks of fishing, swimming and relaxing, they all looked forward to going home but as the car turned into the driveway, they saw police tape draped over the front fence and gate.

"Jesus," shouted Rob.

"Oh my God!" added Sandy.

Chris felt his stomach twinge in nervous anticipation.

Rob didn't bother to get out of the car to investigate and immediately reversed the car and drove to Clem and Edith's place, screeching to a halt out front, barely missing the gutter. They all rushed to the door and were met by Clem,

"You best come inside," he said and they sat in their customary positions in the lounge room.

"What's going on Clem?" asked Rob.

"Well, the Police say it looks like a robbery. I'm afraid the place is in disarray." He explained.

"This is worse than we thought, "suggested Chris.

"Looks that way," added Clem.

Sandy was in tears and too distraught to say a word. Edith tried to calm her daughter down, but it wasn't working.

"Who was it? Do they have any idea?" asked Rob.

"Nope," said Clem, "The Police are truly mystified."

"I suppose we'll have to talk to them about it, even though it won't solve anything."

Chris was deep in thought and looked to his parents,

"I'm really sorry about all this. If I'd been more careful none of this would have happened."

"It's not your fault Chris," Sandy finally said, "You couldn't have hidden forever."

Chris smiled, relieved that his mother wasn't blaming him.

"We need to find out who this is and why they're doing things like this," suggested Rob.

"We know why," Chris remarked, "They want my knowledge. They've probably turned the house over, looking for anything we've written down like dates and times of events or something. What else could it be?"

Clem agreed, "Sounds logical. Chris has a mind full of knowledge, and it was worth a fortune to a great many people. Stands to reason that they'd consider it to be written down somewhere."

"God, I never really thought of it that way," Sandy replied, "What if they try to hurt you, Chris?"

"I'm sure it won't come to that," but he'd already considered it, "Someone leaked, even before the school presentation day. That man who confronted us wasn't a parent and couldn't have known about me, unless someone told him. I'd bet it was Dr Chamberlain."

"Dr Chamberlain?" Sandy was confused, "Why him?"

"He asked me a lot of questions the day of that appraisal; questions he couldn't have known to ask yet. It was very odd," Chris explained.

"Jesus Christ, why didn't you say anything?" demanded Rob.

"I don't know. He seemed honest. I trusted him."

Chris turned to Clem, "He was clever like you and got me in a corner. I gave myself away to him as well. He knows, but..." Chris hesitated.

"But what?" asked Sandy.

"He knew what he was doing from the start. Now that I think about it, I'm sure he was aware of me before I arrived that day. Someone must have tipped him off."

"Was there anything else?" asked Clem.

"Yes, he said to call on him any time, if I needed someone to talk to," Chris added.

"Oh great," exclaimed Rob, "I'll go see him and demand an explanation."

"I don't think that would be wise," Clem said, "He's a clever man and a confrontational approach might well give us nothing. I have a better idea."

Clem explained his plan to everyone, and all agreed on the strategy.

Sandy picked up the phone and called Dr Chamberlain's office. He agreed to see Chris the next morning.

"Right then, not much we can do now. Perhaps you'd all better stay here for the night," suggested Edith.

Sandy agreed but Rob wanted to deal with the break in and decided to go back to the house and look around before talking to the Police.

He told everyone not to worry; he wouldn't be telling them anything useful.

He didn't know much anyway but more attention, particularly from the authorities, could just make things that much worse if the papers got wind of whose house was trashed.

Rob would treat it like a simple break and enter incident and hope that's what the Police thought too.

When he returned a few hours later, he reported that everything went as planned, the Police were clueless.

"Was anything taken?" asked Sandy.

"Not that I could tell, it's just a mess. They turned the place upside down. They were definitely looking for something."

"OK, so we now know for sure that someone wants my knowledge. Let's see what tomorrow brings," added Chris.

That night, sleep was difficult as he rehearsed the charade they'd planned with the good Doctor.

Next morning Sandy and Rob Parish drove their son to the clinic to see Dr Chamberlain.

They planned to use a psychological approach to get under Chamberlain's radar, just like he did with Chris and see if he let something slip.

It was a long shot, but they had to try but when they walked through the clinic door something was off. The receptionist was on the phone and crying openly. There were no sign of the doctor and no patients in the waiting room. Chris listened to the woman on the phone, hoping to pick up on what might have happened,

"He was fine when he left yesterday. I don't understand," she uttered, "How could this have happened? What do we do now?"

Whoever was on the other end of the phone spoke at length, but Chris couldn't hear a word.

The receptionist just sobbed and nodded her head, reacting to the remarks on the other end of the line.

Chris looked at Sandy and Rob,

"I think the doctor is dead," he whispered.

"What?" blurted Sandy, "How do you know?"

"What else could it be? There's something going on and we're part of it. I just wish I knew who and why."

"We'd better leave," suggested Rob.

"Not yet, this might just be the chance we need to find out what's happening," replied Chris.

So, they waited while the call went on and on, the girl behind the counter barely speaking.

Eventually she said a few final words and then goodbye to the person on the phone and hung up,

"I'm sorry," she said to the family as she wiped the mascara off her cheek. Her eyes were bloodshot, "What can I do for you?"

"Um yeah Chris Parish to see Dr Chamberlain," said Rob.

"Oh, I'm afraid we can't help you today. Dr Chamberlain is...unavailable."

"Oh," replied Sandy, "I only called late yesterday, is he ok?"

Well done, Mum.

But before the girl could answer she burst into tears again.

Rob and Sandy looked at each other then at their son.

Chris frowned at Sandy and nodded for his mother to go over to the receptionist.

She immediately understood what he was suggesting and went around the counter,

"There there, what's the matter? It'll be fine, I'm sure."

"I'm so sorry, this is very unprofessional. The doctor..." she was cut off by another blubbering explosion.

Sandy didn't say anything and gave the girl a hug, patting her back.

"I'm sorry, it's...it's so sad."

"What is dear? What's happened?" Sandy urged.

"Dr Chamberlain is dead!"

"Oh my God!" Sandy couldn't help the reflex comment but quickly recovered, "What happened?"

"That's just it, no-one knows. He was at home, watching TV and fell asleep. They think it was a heart attack. There was no sign of a break in or a fight, he just died!"

The girl started blubbering again while Sandy tried to calm her down.

Chris turned to Rob, "This was no accident," he whispered.

"How do you know?"

"He knew something or someone and they've decided he was a risk or no longer needed. He was dealt with I'm sure of it," Chris suggested.

"No, that can't be right," whispered Rob.

"Think about it Dad. He asked me things he couldn't have known and now he's dead. Someone wanted him to stay quiet."

Rob looked really worried and Sandy too.

The girl calmed herself and apologised again, "I don't know what happens now. We have to contact Dr Chamberlain's lawyer."

"Is that what they told you on the phone?" Sandy asked.

You're getting good at this Mum.

"What? Yes. But how..."

"It doesn't matter. Who was that anyway?"

"His business partner, "said the girl.

"Business partner? I thought he worked for himself," Sandy suggested.

"Well, he used to, but when he made the decision to change to a speciality..."

"Child Psychology," Sandy added.

"Yes, that's right. He needed help to cover costs while he studied because he couldn't work full time."

"I see, and who is this business partner?" Sandy was pressing now.

"I don't know a name. I've never met them."

"OK, I see. That's alright."

Sandy turned her head to Chris, her expression saying she had no idea where to go next.

Chris didn't either but then he had an idea and nodded again to his mother hoping she'd get the message.

Sandy looked confused for a moment but then the penny dropped,

"Can I get you a cup of tea dear? Would that help?"

"Oh, don't trouble yourself," the girl said.

"No trouble. We have time..." but then she bit her tongue knowing the rest of the remark might upset the girl some more, "Let's go to the kitchen and make a cuppa."

"OK, that's lovely. Thank you."

When Sandy disappeared Chris turned to Rob,

"Watch the door."

"Where are you going?"

Chris didn't answer and vanished into the doctor's examination room making straight for the desk.

Rob looked at him with apprehension, but Chris didn't care, he had to see what he could find.

The desk was very tidy, not much to see so Chris tried the top draw. He had to climb on the chair to look inside but all he found were pens and paper clips with a few medical writing pads and a packet of chewing gum.

The next draw didn't yield anything either and Chris turned his attention to a filing cabinet.

He pushed the wheeled office chair across the vinyl floor and climbed up being careful not to propel the chair back across the slippery floor in the process.

He tried the top draw, finding it unlocked and slid it open.

There he saw lots of manila folders with their standard buff colouring, some brand new but most dog eared and grubby.

Staring at the front Chris flicked through the names hoping against hope that something would stand out.

He got to the back of the draw and was frustrated that none of the names were familiar, but he was only up to J and so slid the draw closed and opened the next one.

Again, he peered at the names, ever wary that his mother wouldn't be able to keep the receptionist at bay for long.

K and L drew a blank and he stared through the Ms'

Makeham, Michaels, Milne, Monash...

Wait a minute.

Something twigged in Chris's memory.

He went back one file and pulled it from its suspension folder, looking at the name again.

The name was familiar but why?

He opened the manila folder and looked at the doctor's notes, reading as fast as he could.

Just then he heard a voice. The receptionist was coming back.

He scanned the paperwork quickly, trying to figure out the connection.

When he turned the page his eye widened as he read the last few lines,

Holy Cow!

He couldn't read any more, he had seconds to get out.

Chris slipped the file back, slid the draw closed and was halfway off the chair when the receptionist walked into the office,

"What's all this!?' she exclaimed.

Chris looked up at her looking as guilty as a little boy could look, his feet barely on the floor and his stomach draped over the seat.

He smiled at her and gave himself a good shove and rolled across the floor, faking a giggle as he went.

Sandy was right behind the receptionist and saw Chris,

"What are you doing," she demanded trying to sound angry.

"It's alright," said the girl, "no harm done. He must have been terribly bored."

Chris slid off the chair and ran to his father, pretending to be shy now.

"I'm so sorry," said Sandy.

"Forget it, he's a little boy. He was just having fun," the girl smiled.

"Well, we best be off. I'm so sorry about Dr Chamberlain. I hope it all works out for you," Sandy said.

"Thank you. I hope so too. And thanks for...you know, the tea."

"My pleasure."

With that, Sandy, Chris and Rob left the surgery and hastened to the car.

Not a word was spoken until they were well on their way,

"Well?" asked Rob, "Anything?"

"I'm afraid so," said Chris, "I think I know who's after me."

"Who?" demanded Sandy.

"His name is Jason Milne. He was or will be a casino crime figure. Big time mob ties I heard!"

"But how is he here, what does he want?"

Chris remembered some of the news stories about Milne from his former life and none of it was good; money laundering, intimidation, unsolved disappearances, paying off police. He was very bad news.

"He wants what I've got, knowledge," said Chris.

"But how is he here," asked Rob.

"Maybe he was swept back like I was. That's the only explanation!"

Sandy started to cry, "How did he find out about you?"

"I don't know, he just did. Maybe the good doctor said something that tweaked a thought in Milne's mind. He was a client there," Chris suggested, "that would explain why the doctor asked me questions he couldn't have known anything about."

"Well, that's just great!" exclaimed Rob.

There was a brief silence as they absorbed the information, and then Sandy had a suggestion,

"Maybe we just tell him what he wants to know. Just come clean. What do you think?"

"We could do that, but I don't trust him. Let's just say he wasn't shoplifting, he was moving millions of dollars and probably hurting a lot of people in the process. Who knows what he was into, but it was very grubby, real underworld stuff," Chris explained.

"What was in his file?" asked Rob.

Chris explained it was the last sentence in the file that shocked him, "Up until then the notes seemed normal, just like he was a regular patient. I assume that's how they met and the records were all average stuff, you know, comments about sleep problems and nightmares but at the end there was one obscure line, a question really."

"What was it?" asked Sandy and Rob in unison.

"Dr Chamberlain wrote, 'Ask him about the murder of John Lennon'," Chris said.

"What? That doesn't make sense. Lennon is very much alive!" Rob blurted.

Chris looked at his parents, "He is now but he won't be. He will be murdered, by a crazy fan in New York in 1980."

"Oh my God," Sandy said.

"But how does that relate to you Chris," Rob added.

"Chamberlain asked me that very question last time we met. That's how I know Milne is the...."

Chris's comment was cut short; The car suddenly shunted hard, hit from behind.

"What the?" exclaimed Rob.

He looked back and saw a large sedan riding on his bumper.

The car accelerated and gave them another hit.

Sandy screamed.

"Go Dad, just go!" yelled Chris.

Rob had already slammed the accelerator to the floor and pulled away from the sedan.

The trailing vehicle fell back but was soon increasing speed and making up for lost ground and would be on top of them again in a few seconds.

Rob swerved and hooked his car into a hard right turn, cutting across traffic and into a side street where the pursuers had little chance of getting beside them.

He kept his foot down and hoped no-one would suddenly cross their path from any of the alleys or cross streets. The sedan was still in pursuit and closing fast.

There was nothing Rob could do but maintain his speed and keep driving until they came out the other side, but the sedan had better acceleration and, in a few moments, rammed them again.

"Jesus!"

Rob saw the main intersection ahead, a stop sign clearly visible but he didn't slow down careening through into the cross flow of traffic.

Screeching of tyres, car horns and howls of abuse came thick and fast but Rob didn't back off, clearing the mayhem without as much as a scratch.

When he looked in the rear-view mirror, he felt deflated. The sedan got through too.

"I can't outrun them, Chris!" shouted Rob.

"I know, let me think for a minute."

"We haven't got that long," said Rob as the car shunted them again.

There was a clatter of metal on tar as the rear bumper tore loose and tumbled along the road causing the sedan to swerve and lose ground again.

Rob floored the accelerator in an attempt to break away, narrowly avoiding other cars as he flashed by them.

The pursuers weren't giving up and were soon behind, then beside the family.

Chris popped up to the side window to look.

Two men were in the front of the vehicle while the rear seats were empty.

The road dipped suddenly and elevated everyone off their seats for a brief moment then the cars crunched again as the sedan driver tried to force Rob off the road.

Rob fish-tailed but managed to regain control.

No-one said another word; they were much too frightened now.

The sedan came again, flicking the right rear mudguard of Rob's car. This time they felt the car begin to slide. Rob tried to correct but he was going so fast he had no hope of overcoming the situation and they slid sideways then flipped.

They rolled over and over for what seemed like an eternity, the grinding sound of metal on the solid road surface drowning out the sound of traffic screeching to avoid the mayhem.

Rob, Sandy and Chris were tossed around like beetles in a glass jar being rolled down a hill.

Sandy screamed then suddenly went silent.

Chris heard Rob yell in anguish before he too was instantly quiet.

Then with a huge crash of metal on concrete the car abruptly stopped and crumpled around Chris.

He immediately felt a searing pain at the side of his head and watched as the light faded and he was swept off into a black void.

Chapter 8

Chris Parish slowly but surely gained consciousness, not remembering much of anything.

His thoughts were muddled as his eyes flickered to life.

There was commotion all around, a multitude of voices all yelling and talking but Chris couldn't understand a word.

As he tried to open his eyes, he was blinded by lights and only saw very blurry faces hovering over him.

Chris drifted from darkness to light and back again for quite some time, but it seemed the commotion around him was continuous.

As his awareness improved, he could hear strange beeping sounds and the hissing of machines, but he was failing to make sense of it all.

Darkness enveloped him again but then he woke with a start, like waking from a nightmare.

The memory of the crash suddenly hammered its way out of his brain, and he flailed wildly as panic overwhelmed him.

"Someone hold him down or he'll hurt himself," came a voice.

Hands quickly clasped his arms and legs and held on till he stopped struggling.

Chris thought the gripping on his limbs felt odd for some reason, but they didn't feel like adult's hands wrapping around a child's arms.

He realised his throat was sore and when he tried to call out was stymied by something in his mouth.

He tried to take a breath but felt like he was choking and began to convulse.

"Get that tube out, he's trying to breathe on his own!"

Someone lifted him up into a semi sitting position, which they managed to do quite easily it seemed,

"Mr Parish, can you hear me?"

At first Chris didn't respond.

He felt someone shake him as they asked again, "Can you hear what I'm saying Mr Parish?"

Chris lifted his head, which felt so very heavy and tried to look at the person who was speaking, his eyelids feeling like lead weights as he attempted to open them.

He nodded to the individual that he had heard him, but he couldn't understand why he called him Mr. Parish,

"That's good, really good. Now listen, we're going to remove the tube so you can breathe, ok?"

Chris nodded again,

"Right, I want you to take a deep breath through the tube and when I count to three you need to give us a big, long cough, ok?"

Chris understood and nodded one more time.

"Ok, here we go, take a breath...hold it! Right, one, two, three!"

Chris exhaled heavily and felt the tube sliding up his oesophagus and out of his throat and mouth.

He coughed a deep, raspy cough as the gag reflex kicked in and vomited up a huge wad of phlegm.

"Well done Mr Parish, you can breathe easy now."

He was laid back into a pile of pillows as another person wiped his face.

He took a few deep breaths and was soon feeling a little more relaxed.

A small sting in his arm caused his eyes to widen suddenly but he couldn't make much out and was soon drifting off to sleep.

It was hours before he woke again and as his eyes flickered open, he heard another voice,

"He's back, oh thank God, he's back!"

He knew that voice, it was Clem, his grandfather.

"Chris, can you hear me?" Edith was there too.

Chris nodded and tried to speak but couldn't make anything more than a wheezing sound.

Edith started crying and Clem grabbed Chris's hand and gave him a reassuring squeeze.

"It's ok Chris, it's going to be ok," Clem said.

Chris tried to smile but he was so weak he could barely move.

A nurse told Clem and Edith that she'd get the doctor to look Chris over and perhaps explain what might happen next.

Chris suddenly remembered his parents and wondered if they were nearby.

"Hi Clem, Edith," someone said, "How's he doing?"

"He's seeming much better thanks Doctor," said Clem.

"Good! Let's take a look."

Chris felt the doctor's stethoscope on his chest and then a reflex hammer struck his knees and arms. It hardly had any effect.

"Will he..."

The doctor didn't let Clem finish his question, "It's too early to say, but the fact that he's awake is much more than we could have expected. It's really a miracle that he survived let alone woke up."

Chris could hear what was being said and wanted to ask about his parents but just couldn't break out of his semi-conscious state.

"Will there be long term effects?" asked Edith.

"Well, he suffered extensive injuries as you know and the head trauma was quite a concern. He may have suffered brain damage, but we won't know until he wakes; if he wakes fully."

If?

Chris was getting frustrated, he was remembering more and more with each passing minute, he just couldn't find the strength to articulate his thoughts.

"When do we tell him Doc?" asked Clem as Edith began to weep some more.

"Not now, he doesn't need another shock. Give him a few days and let's see where things are. We can decide what's best after that," explained the Doctor.

Tell me what?

Chris was anxious now. It was like he was there, but no-one could see him. It was horrible to be having lucid thoughts in what was essentially a useless body again. He couldn't even scratch himself.

Despite the questions in his head and the dire need for information, fatigue beat him and he was soon asleep.

The next time Chris woke he could see more clearly. Clem and Edith were gone but a doctor was checking his chart,

"So, what's the story Doc," he growled, still recovering from a sore throat.

Dr Simon Gribble was a young man, but quite brilliant and had been working closely with Chris,

"Do you remember anything?"

"Flashes of the accident, but mostly nothing," Chris explained, still confused by the strangeness of his voice. It was breaking up and down like a teenager, but he put it down to the swelling from the tube and yet he felt strangely odd. Something was different.

"I must say I'm very impressed by your recovery, we didn't really think you'd come back."

"What do you mean come back? Was the accident that bad?"

"Oh yes, you suffered significant head trauma. No-one thought you would come out of the coma," explained Dr Gribble.

"Coma? How long?"

"Well, this is the hard part, I don't know how to prepare you for this Chris," the doctor paused but Chris was still processing, "You've been asleep for a very long time."

"How long Doc," Chris demanded, getting more frustrated.

"It's been years Chris, around seventeen years!"

The news stunned Chris to his core, and he felt a huge knot tie him up inside. He looked down at his hands and arms and realised they were those of an adult. He felt his face and noted soft stubble. He struggled to lift the bed sheet, his mobility quite impaired by years of inactivity and saw a long slender body and legs.

Oh my God!

Until now he'd not had the awareness to pick up on even the most obvious signs of the time that passed.

"Seventeen years, that can't be. What year is it?"

"1985," came another voice.

Chris looked over to the door of his Intensive Care ward and saw Clem as the doctor excused himself.

With his improved vision he could see how much Clem had aged and he knew that it was no lie.

Chris was very confused, "What's happened, what's going on?"

"I suppose we need to talk and get you all caught up," Clem suggested.

"I suppose so."

"But I'm afraid you're not going to like what you hear," added Clem.

"Where's Grandma?"

"She couldn't come mate. She's too upset."

"Why? I'm back, surely that's good news."

"It is, it most certainly is Chris, but Edith has really struggled with everything that's happened."

"You're talking about Mum and Dad, right?"

Clem didn't answer straight away but Chris could tell by the look on his face,

"They were killed instantly Chris. They died that day!"

Chris felt the knot tighten inside and gritted his teeth but then the revelations hit their mark and he began to cry.

Clem went over to the bed and cradled Chris in his arms,

"I'm so sorry Chris, so very sorry."

A flood of memories cascaded into Chris's head, probably opened up by the shock of the situation,

"It's my fault. If I'd been more careful, maybe they'd be alive."

"You can't blame yourself. Things were out of control. Who knows why anything happens. It wasn't anyone's fault," Clem suggested trying to be reassuring.

Chris sobbed for a long while before he finally gathered himself, "They didn't suffer," he told Clem, "I remember the crash, well parts of it. They just went quiet; there was nothing to it. It happened very quickly."

Clem didn't respond and just nodded.

The pair sat for a while before Chris broke the silence,

"You look old Grandpa!"

Clem smiled and looked at Chris, "So do you!"

They both laughed.

"You better get me a mirror so I can see how I look at...what is it? Twenty-two?" Jesus! I am old!"

"There's a bright side to all of this Chris," Clem suggested.

"What's that?"

"I don't have to tell you what's happened over the last seventeen years!"

The irony made Chris laugh out loud again, which hurt his throat incredibly.

Then Chris had a thought, "One thing's changed Grandpa."

"Oh, yes? What?"

"You, You're still here!"

Clem was clearly surprised by the remark but realised what Chris was getting at, "I gave up the cigarettes, about fourteen years ago."

Chris smiled, "Good for you. I guess I'm stuck with you for a while yet?"

"You are indeed. I'm as fit as a horse! Edith too. We decided to get fit, well as fit as one can get at our age, eat healthy and try to be around in case you woke up. Good thing we did."

"I'm very glad to hear it."

Chris and Clem chatted for a while and despite feeling fatigued, Chris wanted to carry on. The discussion was proving valuable and opening up all sorts of memories and more questions,

"This place must have cost a fortune, how did you...."

Clem cut Chris off, "Your parent's estate. They were very savvy as it turned out and had good insurance. They left you quite a legacy, which Edith and I have been looking after. You're ok financially, not rich by any means, but you'll have a nest egg to get you going when you leave here."

Chris was pleased to hear it and so very proud of his parents. They'd never told him, but they had the foresight to know that things could go bad at any time.

Still, Chris was deeply saddened by the fact that he never got a chance to save his mother. In fact, Sandy died sooner than the first time around which he regretted. He couldn't help but feel responsible.

As for his father, Rob didn't have much of a life after Sandy's death in the life before and probably would have gone down the same road again. Chris somehow felt eased by the fact they went together but it was only a fleeting thought.

Then Chris asked, "What about the men responsible, what happened to them?"

Clem looked glum again, "They disappeared and haven't been seen since."

"What?" Surely there were witnesses."

"Sure, there were, but the plates were fakes and the car vanished. They covered their tracks and the Police had nothing to go on. The investigation went away after a while."

Chris was angry but not surprised, "Those guys are dead and the car a block of metal in the ground somewhere!"

Clem was shocked.

"I'm not kidding Grandpa. If the man I suspect was responsible, he would have dealt with the evidence and any potential witnesses," Chris explained.

"You know who it was?" exclaimed Clem.

"I'm fairly certain. That day, at Dr Chamberlain's, I found a file with a name and something that connected him to me. I'm 99% sure it was Jason Milne."

"I know that name, he's been on the news. Some young highflyer, rich, successful. Yeah, him I'm aware of! So, what's the connection?"

Chris explained the whole affair and how he found the evidence connecting them,

"I'm guessing he was thrust back in time like me and it seems he too had a head full of future information to work with,"

"I suppose so," replied Clem.

"What's he been doing?"

Clem didn't hesitate to explain, "He's into everything. Real estate development, lots of union ties, waterfront and shipping and who knows what else. He's a big gun."

"And he hasn't tried to find out about me, see what happened, anything like that?" asked Chris.

"No, nothing at all. Only the press for a while after your school success but that faded away rather rapidly," said Clem.

"Curious," said Chris, "Milne must have thought I was as good as dead and gave up on me. We can't let him know I'm back. It might start again."

"I agree with you there!" said Clem.

The pair discussed life after hospital, but it would be many months before Chris was well enough to leave.

For now, he'd have to begin rehabilitation and gain his strength.

He had to learn to walk again for starters. Most of his muscles had atrophied after years of stillness and it would take a lot of work to get back to normal.

How he and Clem would keep his awakening quiet would be an even greater challenge.

It took a very long time indeed for Chris to reach a level of fitness that enabled him to move well enough to leave, but leave he did and move into Clem and Edith's place where he could hide for the time being.

They still lived in the same house, and it seemed that very little had changed over the years.

With money in the bank and another thirty years of future knowledge to work with, he started to create a plan for his life, unsure what form it might ultimately take.

The one thing that did have him deeply worried was meeting his wife, Judy.

So much had changed, his life leading up to the time he met her originally simply hadn't happened this time.

How would he create circumstances so that they would meet again and have her fall in love with him?

He knew her intimately, but she wouldn't have a clue who he was, which could make things awkward if he let his guard down.

He felt immense pressure and anguish at the prospect of failure, but he knew this was the very first thing he had to sort out.

He kept up his exercise regime and slowly gained strength.

Having been near six years old when the accident happened, his body hadn't grown normally, and it took extra effort to get the desired results.

There were much pain and frustration, but he was focussed, thinking only of Judy.

After many months of dedicated effort, he ventured out. The one thing he knew was that he would have to meet Judy very soon, so the timing was right for their relationship to build, to get married and to have Caleb. He'd woken from the coma in the nick of time as it turned out.

Chris easily gained his driver's licence, bought himself a used car to avoid appearing too conspicuous and started looking for a job.

Sadly, the career path that enabled him to meet Judy hadn't happened, so he would have to find another way.

At this point in time, she should be living back in town, and he couldn't help but drive by her house to take a look.

He remembered the little cottage and smiled at the terrible shade of green that her father had painted it.

It certainly stood out from the rest of the homes in the street with their various shades of drab fibro grey.

Chris drove slowly, hoping to catch a glimpse of his bride-to-be.

It was a Saturday afternoon, and a hot day, so he knew Judy should be home but was disappointed to see the family car wasn't there and realised they were probably visiting relatives, something they did quite often on weekends.

It was probably a good thing. Meeting her now would be too soon and he didn't want to risk getting it all wrong but not working with her like he did before could prove a major issue.

She wouldn't get to know him as a work colleague like before and Chris suddenly recalled there were other suitors during that time.

The dilemma was tying him up mentally and he couldn't think straight.

Suddenly a car horn blurted behind him.

Chris looked in the rear-view mirror and realised it was Judy's family arriving home.

He was blocking the driveway and, being so focussed on the house, was oblivious to the traffic.

Oh shit.

Chris couldn't afford to get caught but panicked, dropping the clutch and stalled the car.

The horn sounded again as he retched at the ignition to restart the vehicle. The starter turned over but the engine wouldn't fire.

After a few more seconds, the grind of the starter motor slowed and then stopped. His battery was dead.

Chris was so consumed with his dilemma he didn't notice the man standing by his door who knocked on the glass which startled him.

He wound the window down as he turned a deep shade of red.

The man, who he immediately recognised as his Father-in-law, leaned on the door,

"Flat battery I reckon son."

"I think so too sir, I'm sorry about this," Chris replied.

"Yeah well, no harm done. Would you like a push?"

"I suppose so. Thanks."

"OK, slip her into neutral and steer it to the curb. I'll give you a shove."

With that, Chris made ready and David, his father-in law, who didn't have the slightest clue who he was, took up position at the rear of the vehicle.

Chris looked back and noticed that Judy, her sister Kathy and mother Frances were all now standing on the nature strip watching the whole fiasco.

His embarrassment was worsened by the fact that Judy was laughing and must have thought him a total idiot.

She always saw the lighter side of life, which he loved about her but then remembered how he gambled all of that out of her.

That wouldn't happen again.

Chris felt the car rock then move slowly forward and he steered it to the gutter, bumping the tyre into the cement as he straightened up, just to add insult to injury.

David came back to the window as Chris yanked on the hand brake,

"You got roadside assistance?"

"I'm afraid not."

"Oh well, never mind. I can try and jumpstart you if you like?"

"OK, thanks."

By now Judy and the rest of the family had grown bored with the spectacle and gone inside the little green house.

Chris didn't know whether to be relieved or disappointed but then he noticed Judy taking a peek through the blind and she smiled at him, probably more out of sympathy than anything else.

David drove his car up and around the street then nosed it up to Chris's little bomb.

They popped the bonnets and David attached the jumper leads,

"Righto, give it a try," he yelled.

Chris turned the key and tried to fire up the engine, pumping the accelerator a few times but it only turned over once and then died again.

"Whoa up young fella, I think you've flooded the engine."

Chris felt worse than before if that was possible.

His mechanical abilities were never a strong point and David always used to have a bit of fun with him over it.

"Never mind. You best give it time to settle, and we can try again in half an hour. Why don't you come inside for a cuppa," asked David.

"You've been too kind. Perhaps I should wait here."

"Don't be daft! Come on, I won't bite!"

"OK, thank you," said Chris.

"I can't say the same for my daughters though," added David with a wink.

He was always a cheeky beggar.

Chris followed David up the driveway and into the back door.

He immediately recognised the odour, a welcome combination of fresh baked biscuits and air freshener.

Frances was a great cook and Chris's mind flooded with memories of his previous courtship with Judy.

"Take a seat son. Coffee?" asked David.

"Yes sir, thank you David."

In Chris's confusion he hadn't even introduced himself and suddenly realised that he'd used a name that he shouldn't have known.

"Well then, it seems you know who I am, how about telling me a bit about yourself?"

Chris felt a surge of adrenalin and started to sweat.

He couldn't tell the truth, they simply wouldn't believe it,

"Um, well, I like your house and I'm looking to buy in the area. I was just looking when you came home."

"Well, there are two things wrong with that. One, the house isn't for sale and two, who'd want to buy a green house?"

"I must have been confused with the address," suggested Chris.

"Maybe, but I'm not aware of any homes available around this part of town," added David as he concentrated his stare on Chris.

Chris was again on the verge of panic but then realised he could solve the whole thing with one actual fact,

"I'm sorry sir. I didn't mean to lie. It's your daughter, Judy. I was hoping she might like to go out with me. I've seen her around and finally tracked her down to this place. Creepy I know, but there it is."

David looked at him sternly, then his face relaxed and he suddenly burst out laughing,

"Oh, thank God! We thought she'd never meet anyone decent! JUDY!!!" yelled David, "Look, I don't know who you are, but I reckon I'm a good judge of character and for some reason I have a good feeling about you...JUDY!"

Almost immediately Judy bounced into the room, "What's up Dad?"

"Judy, this is..." David paused, "What is your name son?"

"Chris, Chris Parish sir."

"Nice to meet you Chris," and David gave him a firm handshake, "This is Judy. Why don't you tell her what you told me?"

This was truly embarrassing.

"Hi," he said to Judy

"Hello," she said with a slight tinge of pink in her cheeks.

He suddenly got his first close up look at her, again, and she was truly beautiful.

He hardly remembered those amazing blue eyes, her perfect bronze skin and blonde hair that was cut just above the shoulder.

If there was one thing Chris knew about Judy, it was her love of style, something he knew she gave up when things got tough for them before.

But here he was, with a new opportunity and she was indeed a catch. He always thought her out of his league.

Chris gathered his thoughts and quickly formulated his next remark.

He had to remember she wasn't fifty; she was twenty and barely an adult and therefore, still somewhat immature.

If things to this point had gone as he'd known them in the other timeline, then she'd have come out of at least two dreadful relationships by now, with thugs and football stars who only wanted one thing, and it wasn't a long-term relationship.

He also knew that Judy was looking to settle down and here they both were, staring at each other expectantly, or at least he hoped so.

But before he could speak, Judy frowned and looked at him like he was some kind of problem to be solved,

"I know you. Your name is very familiar?"

"Um, I don't know? Maybe we met once," Chris suggested, remembering the day they crossed paths unexpectedly in the library when they were toddlers, but she couldn't have remembered that.

"No, that's not it," she said.

Chris knew she would figure it out, she had a great memory, just like him.

"That's it. You're that kid in the coma!" she blurted.

"What? I mean, yes! How did you know?"

Judy's parents and sister were gobsmacked!

Judy smiled; pleased she'd figured it out, "I heard them talking about it at work just the other day. I've got one of those memories you know. I remember names and places easily."

It was true, she did.

"That terrible crash and your parents...." she cut off the rest of the remark.

Chris saw that she was embarrassed, "It's ok, don't worry about it."

Despite the fact that he'd only known about his parent's deaths for the last six months or so, he managed to hold back his sadness,

"I miss them very much, but I really haven't had time to absorb it you know?"

"Why? When did you wake up?"

Judy was full of questions while her family just watched, like it was a soap opera,

"Well, it's only been a few months," Chris explained.

"Really!? Wow, did you hear people talking to you?"

"Judy!" scolded her father.

"Sorry."

"No, it's ok, I want to talk about it but maybe...." Chris looked at David and Frances then back at Judy, "Maybe we should discuss it elsewhere, like over dinner?" The opportunity was perfect. She knew who he was and wanted to know what happened and he wanted to tell her, "I know it's a bit weird. You don't even know me, but I would like to ask you out Judy," suggested Chris.

She only baulked for a moment but then said something that Chris thought was profound, "I don't know why, but there's something familiar about you and I don't mean that you were all over the news for a while. I can't put my finger on it, but I will! So yes, dinner would be lovely."

Odd

"Thank God that's over with, now can we have a cuppa, please?" asked David.

The five of them sat and chatted for a while, drank coffee and ate all the homemade biscuits.

It was a strange way to meet his wife and future family, but he wasn't surprised by their hospitality, that's just how David and Frances were. Chris also realised that it didn't really matter how they met, he'd won Judy's heart before and now he'd do it again.

He also knew Judy's favourite places, favourite foods and more importantly what she hated, he was overjoyed with the possibilities and this time he'd get it right.

Chapter 9

Chris and Judy went out for a meal, more than once.

As Chris had hoped and ultimately expected, Judy took a real shine to him and then started to fall in love. It was an odd experience for Chris who didn't go through the bonding process as before because his connection had already been established. It was almost like Judy was playing catch-up in their relationship. He did, of course, have a great advantage which he exploited for her benefit.

He took her to places he knew she loved, particularly the beach and rock concerts. He avoided the failed attempts to impress like that terrible sci-fi film that he wanted to see but she hated and the day down by the river that was ruined when the car broke down on a causeway and they had to wade to the bank and then walk a few miles to get help. In short, he constantly surprised her,

"It's like you can read my mind," she exclaimed more than once.

Chris had to be careful not to overplay it, just in case it became too weird, but he seemed to be doing just enough to win her over.

In the meantime, he had to watch his money, which was adequate for now, but he would need a job soon.

He had a lot of experience in banking but much of his knowledge was very rusty and oddly, not feasible in the current climate.

Most of the systems he worked with in middle age just didn't exist, like online and mobile banking. When he was working, bank computers were very basic, single terminal systems which only batched data. Even the humble ATM was only new technology.

Still, he might be able to weasel his way into the industry if he played his cards right, but he would soon have to make some quick cash and recalled his idea of betting on sporting events.

It would be easy cash given the fact that he knew just about every major horse race and football result for the next three decades.

Chris did his sums and decided to wait a few months until the Melbourne Cup where he'd put a huge bet on that one race.

It wasn't uncommon for someone to place a large bet, and it wouldn't set off alarm bells.

It was November 1985 and he remembered very clearly how the Melbourne Cup went down that year. He'd bet on about five horses in the previous timeline, but as the race was about to begin, the odds started to shrink on a horse he'd never heard of. It didn't particularly bother him until it bolted home and he recalled being livid!

When the day finally came around and the entire nation stopped to watch the race, Chris clutched the ticket tightly in his hand sweating on a bet of five thousand dollars to win.

The attendant at the betting agency was a little shocked at someone so young with that amount of cash but they were so busy, the transaction was processed without a word.

He was nervous as race time neared, and he sat in the car with the radio on, waiting for them to jump.

Chris could feel the sweat dripping from his armpits as the clock on the dashboard clicked away the seconds and he couldn't help wondering if he'd made a terrible mistake.

What if changes in the current timeline cause the outcome to alter?

He hadn't considered that when he placed the bet, but it was at the forefront of his mind now.

"RACING!!!!!......."

Too late

The 3200-meter marathon would take a bit over three minutes and Chris knew that this bet might make him a fortune or he'd go bust.

The time dragged as the horses and jockeys diced for prime positions.

It was impossible to know if things were unfolding as they had previously, Chris just had to hope it would work out.

As they started turning for home Chris could hear the thunder of hooves over the radio and the caller amplifying the excitement as the crowd cheered,

"And here comes Kiwi out of the blue," screamed the announcer.

"YES," cried Chris.

Kiwi, a chestnut gelding from New Zealand crossed the line first at ten to one, very generous in terms of Melbourne Cup odds.

Chris was overjoyed but couldn't help feeling a twinge of guilt having double-crossed the Universe with his inside knowledge.

Still, he didn't hesitate to hand in his winning ticket, which caused much discussion behind the steel bars of the agency counter.

Eventually they drew up a cheque and handed Chris the money,

"Well done young fella. Don't spend it all at once," said the cashier.

"I won't," Chris replied and left for the bank.

He'd transferred all his money to the branch where Judy worked, the office where they first met in the former timeline in fact. When he walked into the building, he saw that the staff had done a great job decorating the counters with jockey silks, saddles and all kinds of horse racing paraphernalia.

It looked rather splendid and Chris smiled as he caught Judy's eye. He also recognised former co-workers that now had little clue about him beyond the fact that he was Judy's boyfriend.

The whole atmosphere of the bank was festive with glasses of champagne and finger food all over the office desks.

It was the one day of the year when workers could let their hair and their guard down without drawing the wrath of their bosses.

Judy met Chris at the teller's counter,

"How did you go?" she asked.

"Pretty good, what about you?"

He was savouring the moment.

"I came third in the sweep and won five dollars," she said.

"Hey, good for you!"

"And what about you? How much did you win," Judy asked.

"A little bit more than that," he beamed.

"What do you mean," Judy asked after seeing Chris's face, "Show me!" she giggled.

Chris handed Judy the cheque, "Will you deposit that for me please? And add your five dollars if you like," he suggested with a smirk.

Judy looked at the piece of paper and went silent for a moment then gasped, "Holy Shit! Fifty thousand dollar," she screamed. The entire office went quiet, "You won fifty thousand dollars," she repeated.

In a few seconds Judy was surrounded by co-workers,

"Bloody Hell," came some remarks and a few other choice words were thrown into the mix.

Thankfully Chris was the only customer in the bank, so no-one was scolded for overstepping their bounds.

"How? I mean what happened," Judy asked as he accepted handshakes from a few of the male bankers.

"Just lucky I suppose. I heard someone talking about that horse and thought, why not," he explained knowing it was a lie.

"You can buy a house with that much," Judy said.

"Great idea, why not?"

Judy smiled.

The deposit really bolstered his bank balance, and he realised that he may not need to get a job so soon, but he'd have to be very careful. Gambling was a dangerous business if you made too many waves or if you won too much or too often or both. It wouldn't go unnoticed and there was also the question of his addiction, which he was all too aware of. He had demons ready to burst out and had to control his urges.

That night Chris took Judy out for dinner at an exclusive restaurant.

They'd been going out almost every night for a few months now and everything felt right.

Things were happening faster than before though and he wasn't sure what to do about it.

In the old timeline, they hadn't started seeing each other at this stage but blundering into her the way he had, accelerated their romantic connection by a few years.

Did it matter? He didn't know but it didn't seem so.

Chris was much more mature than before and a straight thinker and Judy was incredibly bright and always knew what she wanted, that's what he really loved about her, so he decided there and then, in the middle of dessert to do something out of character.

"Judy?"

"Yes? What is it?" she asked as she lifted a medium rare morsel of prime rib to her lips.

"Will you marry me?"

It took a few seconds for the words to take hold in Judy's mind but then her jaw dropped, her face flushed and the fork fell to the plate with a loud clang.

Chris eased himself out of the dining chair and took a knee,

"Judy, I love you more than you can possibly know…will you do me the honour of being my wife?"

For the second time that day, Chris had silenced a group of people with all the restaurant patrons stopping to watch.

Judy blushed as she said, "Yes," and cried to the applause of the other diners.

She stood and met Chris beside the table, giving him a crushing hug and a smouldering kiss.

He couldn't have been happier.

"I'm sorry, I didn't get a ring. I didn't know I was going to do it. It just seemed like the right moment."

"That's ok, I'd rather pick it myself anyway," said Judy and Chris smiled knowing that's exactly what she would say.

She smothered him with her lips once more.

They spend the next few months working out dates, venues and all the finer details that go with a wedding.

Chris again drew on existing knowledge to help out and again, surprised Judy with his understanding.

"You'll have to tell me how you do it one day Chris," Judy remarked.

She was joking of course, but Chris realised he might just need to have that conversation at some stage, but he didn't know when or how to bring it up.

The wedding was a small affair, just family and a few hand-picked friends. For Chris it was also a bit strange. The events in this timeline meant he didn't know any of the people who were close friends before, so his side of the church was sadly devoid of witnesses.

Clem and Edith represented Chris with Clem as Best Man, which certainly had some people wondering. Still the day was perfect and there was no denying their happiness.

They jetted off for a honeymoon in Fiji, something Chris had suggested which Judy was overjoyed about. It sure beat Tasmania, which is where Chris insisted, they go in their former life. She never let him forget because it rained for two solid weeks and they were both so very bored.

Chris was certainly taking advantage of a great deal of hindsight now.

When they returned, Chris and Judy moved in with Clem and Edith. It was only temporary as they set about finding their own house to begin life together.

Within a few months they were settled in a home to call their own, just around the corner from Clem and Edith, but, of course, Chris knew more than he was letting on.

He paid cash for the property and had a little bit left over with which to rebuild his nest egg.

Still, he realised that if he was going to blend into society properly, he'd need a job and started looking at the newspaper classifieds. Thankfully it was a good time to find work.

The country was prospering, the stock market booming and interest rates were at an all-time high, which was great for an investor and he certainly planned to be that.

He knew the current situation would last two more years before the crash of 1987 and the recession of 1990 so he had plenty of opportunities to insulate against it.

He applied for banking positions, finance company jobs, clerks' positions and a myriad of other clerical roles but, as the knock backs started rolling in he realised it wasn't going to be as easy as he thought.

His qualifications were non-existent after the time lost in a coma and so he decided to go back to school and gain a degree.

He applied to several universities and eventually gained a position as an adult student with the University of New South Wales Business School.

It wasn't that difficult when they realised he could pay for his tuition in advance.

Chris studied while Judy worked at the bank. He knew she was desperate to start a family but had convinced her to wait until he'd finished University and got a job.

He kept their income supplemented with the occasional sure thing, but only enough to keep them afloat and, more importantly, to avoid unwanted attention from anyone, including Judy.

He found university study stimulating although, much harder than anything that he'd done before but he had knowledge that no-one else could tap into and many of his papers were regarded as insightful and clever.

Quite often his ideas caused debate in the faculty and gained him attention he really didn't need but if this worked out, he could write his own ticket.

After only a year of school he was already well through the course, leaving his peers behind. After 18 months he was done and received his degree with honours in a small ceremony with little fuss, just the way he liked it.

"Congratulations babe," Judy loved nicknaming everyone, "So, as soon as you get a job we can...."

She didn't finish the sentence and Chris knew she was hoping he would fill in the blanks.

Chris suddenly realised that to have a baby now would most certainly mean that it would not be Caleb.

He had to put her off until the exact date of conception, which he knew would be New Year's Day in 1989. He remembered it clearly because they had a raging fight at the New Year's party and made up the next day. That wouldn't be for another 19 months. How would he keep her at bay for that long?

He was, once again, in a position where he had no answer.

There was really no reason to reject her and, unless he spilled about who he was, she wouldn't accept a denial. His hesitation was clearly obvious,

"What is it Chris? What's the matter?"

"Hmmm?" he murmured snapped out of his self-inflicted trance, "Oh nothing. I'm just trying to imagine what our son or daughter might look like!"

Judy squealed with delight. She took that response as a yes and Chris wasn't in any position to correct her now. He'd committed to the idea but the caveat was getting a job and he was going to take that nice and slow.

He played the part well, buying the papers every day and going through the vacancy ads.

Again the difficulty of the situation became clear when he realised just how many jobs were starting to appear for people like him. He knew he'd get a job easily if he simply applied himself.

Just have to wait a few more months

The University didn't help either, publishing their top graduates and Chris was first on that list but he couldn't blame them for wanting to boast about their successes. The phone was ringing off the hook for interviews.

He filtered the offers and didn't much like any of them. It led to an argument with Judy and he realised she couldn't be kept at bay any longer.

"Ok, I'll seriously look at a few," he conceded.

"Good," she snapped and the argument was over.

Next morning, he sat and pondered the job ads. They were all ok, but he didn't really feel at all thrilled by them, some of which were huge commutes and he wanted something closer to home. At that moment the phone rang.

"Mr Parish," the caller asked.

"Yes, who is this?"

"My name is Michael Sunderland and I represent a client who is very interested in your skills."

"Oh really? Who would that be," Chris enquired.

"Well, as much as I'd love to say, it wouldn't be prudent at this point. They're a big organisation though and they want me to talk to you on their behalf."

"I see."

The caller continued, "They outsource their employment and I send them a short list or a recommendation. In your case it would be a recommendation. "

"OK, so is this a job offer?"

"Yes and no. We get the University lists and pay particular attention to them. If we see someone who might fit in with a client's needs, we call and so, we're calling you."

"I see, well I'm flattered, I guess," explained Chris, "What would the job be then?"

"It's a newly created position, a kind of futures opportunity."

Chris thought the terminology a bit odd and wondered if it was a financial role and began to get interested.

"You'd be working in their main office in the city, and looking at opportunities, creating them really. We looked over your thesis, and it really made us think. You have a good mind for where things in the business world are headed and our client needs that," said Sunderland.

"Wow! Well then, I'm interested. What now?"

"We meet, here at my office."

"Sure, that'll be fine."

Chris took down the details and felt somewhat excited about the idea of this role but couldn't help wondering what kind of organisation he might be working for, if it all worked out.

When he told Judy she was thrilled,

"This could be huge," she squealed.

Chris certainly hoped she was right.

Next day he went to the office of Frankston Recruitment, an intermediary for large corporations looking for specialist staff.

The plush styling of the office suggested they were very good at what they did and were paid handsomely but that could simply have been a clever facade.

He checked in at the front desk and announced himself and was told to take a seat. He was the only person there.

Within a few minutes a man in a slick grey suit exited a lift and walked straight towards Chris. He instinctively stood and met the man who stretched out a friendly hand,

"Hi Chris, Michael Sunderland...welcome."

"Thanks, good to be here."

Sunderland was tall, well-built and handsome.

"Coffee?"

"Yes please."

"Rebecca? Coffee for two please, one black and one white, two sugars, right Chris?"

"Um, yeah."

This guy is good.

"Two sugars for Chris, ok?"

"Yes sir," replied the receptionist.

"Ok, let's go to my office," suggested Sunderland.

They entered the lift and started up to the fifth floor.

"It's a big operation you have here," Chris remarked.

"Yes, well we're international and there are a lot of head-hunters looking for good minds."

"I suppose so."

"Here we are."

The lift opened up to a huge office.

People sat in cubicles as the buzz of telephone chatter filled the air. He could see across the room to a floor to ceiling window that gave a panoramic view of the harbour.

"Wow!"

"Yes, it's impressive. I quite often forget we have the best spot in the city."

"The rent must kill," Chris said.

"Oh, we own the whole building. People pay us rent," explained Sunderland.

"Really? That's amazing."

"Yeah well, we're good at what we do. And it helps to get a piece of every pie we bake."

Chris nodded his understanding.

They walked a little way, and Sunderland opened his office door, inviting Chris inside.

If Chris was mesmerised by the view of the harbour, he was equally impressed with Sunderland's office layout.

The carpet was white and spotless, as was the leather lounge against the side wall.

The window showed the same harbour view and the backdrop to Sunderland's desk was a saltwater tropical fish tank that took up the entire wall.

Chris was impressed but bit his tongue this time.

Even so, Sunderland smiled, having noticed Chris's gobsmacked expression.

"Sit, please Chris, take a load off."

"Thanks," and Chris sat in front of Sunderland's heavy wooden desk, no doubt an antique or something with a story behind it.

Sunderland noticed Chris scanning the wood.

"It's a table from the HMAS Melbourne, out of the officer's mess. We bought it from a collector and paid double its worth, but we liked it. See that dent," Sunderland pointed to the corner of the table as Chris nodded, "That's where the table smashed into the wall when the Melbourne collided with the Voyager."

"Holy shit, really," Chris had forgotten himself for a moment.

"True...it's a great piece of wood."

"Indeed, it is."

Just then the coffees arrived, "Thanks Rebecca. Would you like something to eat Chris?"

"Oh, no thanks, I'm good."

"That'll be all Rebecca."

"Thank you, sir," and she left, casting a quick glance at Chris as she passed.

Sunderland took a sip from his coffee cup, "So, we have a client who is very keen on you. They believe you can help them with a few projects that will be worth a fortune if they can win certain contracts. And they need ideas."

"Sounds interesting, who are they?"

"Well, we'll get to that, but let's just say they know how to take care of people. They have offices all over the world and they specialise in several areas, but let's just say, they know what people want," Sunderland explained.

"Ok."

"And they take care of their own. As well as an attractive salary, you would get a licence fee for anything that bears fruit in the marketplace and in some cases, royalties which continue for life."

Chris liked that and given his knowledge he was sure he could be very useful, if he knew exactly what it was, he would be doing.

"That's the good news Chris but like all deals, there are a few things you need to consider."

"Sure, I understand."

"You would have to sign an exclusivity contract. That would mean you couldn't take ideas and use them for yourself, sell them to someone else or hold back on potential ideas to use later. If you left the company you'd be out of the business for ten years!"

"Ten years? Why ten years?"

"That's the standard length of a patent Chris."

"I see. That makes sense. But ten years out of work?"

"I'm sure it won't come to that," Sunderland suggested.

"Ok?"

"I know it's a lot to take in and we've only just started talking but I don't want your answer today, or tomorrow. I want you to really think about this, talk to Judy and make a fully informed decision."

"I understand," replied Chris.

"So, shall we continue?"

Chris nodded.

Sunderland explained how the company was created to foster big ideas and turn them into cash. He gave an overview which was clearly devoid of details.

"The owner realised there must be other people with bigger, better ideas but had nowhere to turn, so we started looking for them and brought them all together and now this is one of the richest companies in the world," Sunderland said, "We've been working for them now for over ten years and we are very good at finding the kinds of people they want, like you."

"And who are they," Chris enquired.

"I'm not prepared to say just yet. They pay us well so why would I want to risk that by shooting my mouth off," replied Sunderland.

"I see your point."

"I'm not arguing with their methods, and they go to great lengths to keep out of the limelight. That's why they won't list the company on the stock exchange."

"Are they legitimate? I mean is this legal?"

"As far as we know they pay their taxes and all their bills and are squeaky clean. No-one has ever questioned their methods or business practices."

"I must confess," Chris said, "That this is all a bit odd."

"True," said Sunderland, "I suspect the owner is living it up on an island somewhere and raking it all in while everyone else does the hard work," he laughed.

"If they're anything like you say, and you haven't said much, an island is last place you'll find them, "Chris suggested.

"And there it is!"

"What?"

"The exact attitude we want. You know what hard work is, how to solve problems and what a good idea is, and you know how the people who think like that, think. Your university work was exemplary, and we liked what we saw. You are perfect for this role."

"And what is the role exactly?"

"I don't know."

Chris practically scoffed, "Wait a minute. I'm being interviewed for a job that you can't tell me anything about?"

"Yep, and you'll be doing it for this," Sunderland handed Chris a folded piece of paper.

"What's this?"

"Your offer."

Chris opened the slip of paper and looked at it. It didn't immediately register but then he counted the zeros,

"Wait a minute. This has to be a joke."

"No joke Chris, that's a genuine offer. We get 15% of course but that is your starting salary."

"Starting salary?"

"Yes, you'll start at the bottom and go from there. Oh, and we get 15% of your salary as it increases including licences and royalties."

"This is a one million dollar offer!"

"Yes, it is and that's the starter for new employees of your ability. Some people are on ten million a year with the kinds of success they've achieved. Licence fees can be very lucrative it seems."

"Holy shit," Chris was embarrassed at the expletive, "I'm sorry. It's a bit of a shock."

Sunderland laughed, "Believe me Chris, some people aren't as calm as you."

"What if I suck?"

"Then you suck and we end the relationship, no harm. It has to work for both you and the company."

"What if I want to leave in a few years?"

"That's fine, but the contract still applies. You cannot foster ideas outside the company."

Chris was in deep thought.

"Like I said, you have to think about this. Give it a week or more if you like. Think of questions and we'll get the answers, if we can. It's totally up to you of course."

"But, if I'm so good at what they think I'm good at, what's to stop me saying no and simply going out on my own?"

"Nothing whatsoever, BUT you haven't got the resources to make the kind of money we're offering, not in the short term and by the time you get there, you could have been on ten times the salary you are being offered now. It's a win win."

"Maybe, but you're right, I need to give this a lot of thought." Chris noticed he was shaking with nervous tension.

"Good! I see too many people glaze over when they get the offer and that's the end of them. You've passed your first test."

"Really. It was a test?"

"Yes and no. The offer was genuine, but the company was certainly interested in your reaction, and they'll be pleased with my report.

"Ok."

"Chris. It's natural to be suspicious or alarmed or even frightened by what seems like an overwhelming offer but let me tell you that the people we've put into these jobs are happy. Rich and happy!"

"Righto. I'll talk to Judy and think about it. How do I get in touch with you?"

"We'll call you next week Chris. No rush though. If you need more time, just say so and we'll hold off a little longer."

"Ok, sounds good."

The pair exchanged handshakes and Sunderland led Chris to the door,

"Rebecca will show you out. We'll speak soon."

"Thank you, sir."

"My pleasure Chris."

Sunderland closed the door just as his phone rang but Chris was long gone before he could hear anything. Something in his gut told him the call was about him.

The receptionist said nothing until they were at the front door,

"Goodbye Mr Parish."

"Bye," he replied as he left the building and headed home in a state of utter excitement and confusion. Who was that guy, and what is this company?

This is just too weird.

Chapter 10

Naturally Judy was over the Moon with the job offer but Chris, despite the money, had some misgivings.

The contract clearly stated that he would be unable to use any new ideas of his own, no matter what they were, for a decade after leaving the job.

He wasn't even sure it was legal but to challenge such a contract in court would probably cost him more than it was worth in any case.

Of course, if he stayed there for a while, he wouldn't need to worry about money for the rest of his life but principally, it really bugged him.

Judy kept on about the opportunity and how the company was simply protecting its property and Chris knew that, but something was nagging at him and his mind kept going back to Jason Milne.

What if he was the brains behind this operation?

It certainly seemed like something he could do, cashing in on pre-existing knowledge for personal gain.

Perhaps he'd become wise this time, paying handsome dividends for information that he knew was worth billions.

But when he boiled it down Chris was in no way interested in working for the man who was most likely responsible for the death of his parents.

He had no proof of course, but the circumstantial evidence connected him and Milne through Dr Chamberlain.

That couldn't have been a coincidence and now, suddenly, there's a mystery corporation trying to buy him off.

Judy couldn't understand his reluctance,

"What's the matter Chris? It's a dream job. A million dollars a year to think. Why is that so hard for you to accept?"

"Because it is Jude, I can't explain. You wouldn't understand."

"Why don't you try? Please, help me to understand," pleaded Judy.

Chris looked at her as despair creased up his face,

"What is it Chris, you can tell me," Judy asked again, "I know there's been something on your mind for a long time, almost from the day we met. What is going on?"

"I'm not sure you want to know or will believe me when I say it. It's so beyond my comprehension, I can't imagine you'll accept it."

"Accept what?"

Chris hesitated, not knowing how to start the conversation or even if he should.

Ignorance is bliss as they say and he was more than happy for Judy to be blissfully ignorant, but now it was becoming a problem, but he realised the conversation had already started,

"I'm...we...I don't know how to explain," Chris said.

"Just tell me Chris. Just say it!"

"Ok, I was married to you before."

Judy looked at him in astonishment, shaking her head.

"What? You've been married before! Is that what you said?"

"No, I was married to you once before! To you Judy."

"I don't understand. That's crazy! What do you mean?"

Chris sighed heavily knowing that this was going to be very difficult,

"I know this sounds weird, so just listen and I'll tell you everything and then you can ask me anything you like. No matter how strange this sounds, you need to listen ok?

"Ok," Judy said but he could tell she was very apprehensive.

Chris took another deep breath,

"Right then. When I was 52, we were married and had been for 27 years, but it wasn't going well. Money was tight, I'd lost my job and I had a gambling problem...."

"What," The look on Judy's face was one of utter confusion.

"Just hear me out...then, one day, there was a lot of news about strange activity on the Sun. Spikes of light that were causing some disturbance, possibly with time. I never got the full story, but I suspect I was struck by one of those things and here I am again and I have all the memories of my entire life before," Chris explained.

Judy's eyes were wide and she blinked multiple times in exasperation, "You're saying you went back in time?"

"Exactly, and I'm living my life over again, but I can still remember everything from before but more to the point, I know what's going to happen for the next 30 odd years."

"I don't get it. This is insane!"

"I know it's a lot to take in but I'm not making it up. I've already taken advantage of what I know," Chris added.

"Taken advantage? How?" Judy asked.

"The Melbourne Cup. I knew the winner because I'd seen that race before."

Judy was suddenly silent, her eyes still wide and her mouth now agape.

"I'm sorry I never said anything before, but I thought it best to say nothing. I mean, how could you possibly think of me as normal with a story like this," Chris suggested.

"Wait a second. You knew what you were doing when you came to our house. You knew who I was and...."

Judy stopped mid-sentence,

"Yes, I did. You were my wife for 27 years and I knew I had to find you and be with you again. It was my one and only goal in this new life, or whatever this is."

"But it's not the same, is it? Things have changed."

"So, you believe me?"

Judy nodded, "Oddly enough I do. I had this strange feeling the day we met. It was like I knew you. I felt so comfortable with you. I can't explain it."

"That's strange because in the previous timeline,"

"Timeline?"

"Yes, that's what I call it. Anyway, before, we hadn't even married at this stage, my dad didn't die but my mother did, but not this soon. Things I've done have changed the timeline and caused other events that shouldn't have happened," Chris hesitated then said, "There's one more thing."

"What's that?"

"I'm not the only one who came back."

"What?"

"I'm not alone here. There's one more; one more that I know of anyway."

"Who?"

"The man who I think owns this company they want me to work for."

"Oh my God! Are you serious?"

"I'm pretty sure."

Chris went on to explain everything from Dr Chamberlain, the connection to Jason Milne, his knowledge of his criminal activity before and what happened to his parents."

"Holy shit!"

"I know right? So, you can understand why I can't take this job."

Chris finally made his point, and Judy had all the information on the table, mulled it over for a moment then said,

"You have to take the job."

"What? After what I just told you?"

"Yes, you have to. What's that old saying? Keep your enemies closer? Besides, you don't know for sure it's him, do you?"

"Well, no. I'm just going on a hunch really, a feeling and what the doctor asked me that day about John Lennon."

"John Lennon?"

Chris explained the questions Dr Chamberlain asked about his apparent intellect and how he'd been caught off guard by the question about John Lennon's death.

"Oh my God, how could they have known that," Judy asked.

"Exactly!"

"So, you saw this Milne character's name in a file? Are you sure it's exactly the same individual?"

"Yes, pretty sure, there was a note that said, ask him about John Lennon in that file. Who else could it be?"

"The doctor could have been tied up with someone completely different, couldn't he? It may be another Jason Milne, or he dropped the note in the wrong file, right?"

"Yeah but, if it looks like a duck!"

"A what?"

"It's him, I know it."

"But Chris, here's an opportunity that will set us up for life and you're worried it might involve this, Jason Milne. If it is, then you can keep tabs on him. If it's not, then what difference does it make?"

"But he's probably a killer!"

"He was before, right? You don't know that he is now. You don't even know if it's the same guy for sure! You have no evidence whatsoever, except for a file in a doctor's office, which might just be a coincidence," Judy suggested.

Chris absorbed Judy's argument, "I'm so confused. So much has happened and to be honest, I can't really tell what is real and what isn't any more. I'll have to think about it."

"You do that, but know that I'll back you no matter what decision you make, ok?"

"Thanks, but I thought once you knew the truth you'd run for the hills."

"Believe me, I thought you were nuts when you started talking but, on reflection, you clearly have knowledge that is impossible to have, right?"

"Yes."

"So why did we buy this particular house and don't tell me because it's close to your grandparents."

Chris smiled widely, "Because I know there's about to be a huge jump in property values here and we're going to double our money."

They both laughed but then Judy looked at him strangely,

"Did we have any kids, you know, before?"

Chris was caught completely off guard, "I'm not sure that's something we should discuss."

"Oh, but it is, because if we had children then we need to make sure we do it right in this timeline. Am I right?"

It was Chris's turn to be nonplussed.

Judy continued, "I know that the circumstances of your life are drastically different compared to before, but we can assume certain things like when our children are conceived, right?"

"Yes, and its child, singular."

"What?"

"We only had the one."

Judy was stunned,

"Why?"

"Um, me, money. I messed up."

"Oh."

"But that's not going to happen this time, honestly. It's all so different and I know when we need to, you know, do it?" Chris blushed.

"You do?"

"Yes, it's...."

Judy cut him off.

"Don't tell me. Not yet. Let's keep it as a surprise for now."

"Are you sure?"

"Yes. Let's spend the next couple of years getting our lives sorted, however you want to do that and then we can...." This time it was Judy who went red in the cheeks.

"Actually, it's not that long and yes we can."

Chris smiled and hugged his wife, relieved that she understood what he was trying to explain.

It was easier than he expected in the end and it cleared his mind completely. He felt an immense weight lift, having come clean.

Chris looked at his beautiful wife, "And you know what? I think I'll take that job."

"Good decision," Judy said and they kissed passionately.

"Careful, we don't want to go too far," she said.

"Very funny," Chris replied smiling broadly.

Chris didn't wait for the call, he phoned Frankston Recruitment and announced his decision to Michael Sunderland,

"That's great news Chris; you won't regret it and neither will our client, I'm sure."

"About that, who will I actually be working for?"

"Parallax Corporation."

"Never heard of them. What's with the name."

"Well, they fly under the radar. Most of the business they're involved with is well known because it's up front, but Parallax is a holding company and strictly off the grid, so to speak," Sunderland explained.

"Of course. What does it mean, Parallax."

"I have no idea to be honest. I've never thought to check."

"Never mind," said Chris, "What now?"

"Well, we tell the client you're a goer and they'll sort out some paperwork, and we'll get you back to meet them and go from there."

"Great, so I'll be hearing from you?"

"Yes indeed" said Sunderland, "In a week or so. Is that ok?"

"Fine."

"Great, we'll be in touch, and congratulations. You've made the right choice."

"Thank you."

Chris hung up the phone.

Parallax?

He grabbed a dictionary and started flicking through the pages,

"Ah, here it is," he said to himself, "Parallax, an effect where an object appears to differ when observed from different directions. That's weird." He read more, "A displacement or difference in appearance along two lines of sight."

Chris pondered that for a moment.

"Jesus. Milne. It has to be Milne. That's too strange to be a coincidence!"

When Judy got home from work, he told her what he'd learned,

"So, you think Milne is behind Parallax," she replied.

"He must be. Look at what that word means. Who else would think of something like that, other than someone who has existed on two separate planes?"

"True, but it could also be about what they do, right? You're being asked to come up with new ideas. Couldn't that include creating something from a new perspective?"

Chris looked at Judy, "You always have an answer, don't you?"

"Ah, yeah, that's why you love me," and she giggled.

Chris lunged at her, "Come here you," and he swept her up in his arms, "You're the best thing for me...all over again."

"I know."

They kissed then Judy asked, "What exactly went wrong, you know, before, with us?"

"Lots of things but it was all on me. I was out of control, and I forgot what was really important. And then, when Caleb, came along..."

"Caleb?"

"Oh shit! Sorry, I let the cat out..."

"No, that's ok, I love the name. In fact, it's one of my top picks. So, he'll be our son?"

"Well yeah, he will."

"What's he like?"

"He's great. Just like his mother. Bright, handsome, witty and a bit insular in his teenage years."

"So, I'm handsome and insular, am I?"

"No, I mean, he got the good stuff from you," Chris spluttered.

Judy laughed and they hugged again.

"Caleb," Judy repeated, "I can't wait to see him."

"Yeah, me too. I miss him terribly."

"That must be so strange."

"It's certainly not normal. I can't believe it myself even after all these years."

"What if we don't time it right," Judy asked.

"I know exactly when it happens, believe me."

"Yeah but...."

"Stop worrying. You can't control it and neither can I? Will it happen exactly the same way again? There's no way of knowing but we can only give it the best possible chance. Right," Chris suggested.

"Yes, I suppose so. And there's plenty of time, right? No need to bother ourselves now," added Judy.

"Look, we could go nuts trying to figure it out but it's better we take a relaxed approach."

"How so?"

"Well, they've worked out that stress can impact on a woman's ability to conceive, or they will work it out."

"Holy cow! You really are from the future."

"I know, it's a gift!"

Or a curse.

Judy and Chris chatted for hours about the future, the past and the possibilities.

They didn't realise it immediately, but their bond was growing around a completely different set of circumstances and objectives.

They were literally living for the future, a future that they should be able to influence and control to suit themselves, that is if nothing came along to mess with it.

Chris was back at the recruitment office within the week.

He and Michael Sunderland waited in the meeting room for the company representatives to arrive.

He didn't realise he was sweating heavily until a cool drip of perspiration from his armpit caused a minor flinch as it dripped on his skin.

"You ok Chris," asked Sunderland.

"Yeah fine, I just hate waiting."

At that moment the door opened and one of Sunderland's secretaries invited two people, a man and a woman, to go in.

Michael Sunderland stood and straightened his jacket before meeting them halfway across the room, shaking hands with both.

Chris was on his feet too and watched as they approached the table.

The man was young, quite young, about Chris's age and very fit it appeared and definitely not Jason Milne, but then he wouldn't be doing this grunt work.

His features were chiselled and strong and his dark hair matched an olive complexion.

The woman was around thirty and quite stunning. She was a brunette, wore a tight business suit and her hair was tied back so tightly it looked like she had it glued on.

They both looked at Chris as Sunderland introduced them,

"Graeme Leach and Jane Harper, this is Chris Parish, the one I told you about and the one who has agreed to come on board."

"Hello Chris," said Graeme offering his hand.

"Hello, nice to meet you."

"We're very hopeful about you Chris," added Jane as she too shook his rather sweaty palm.

"Well, I hope I don't disappoint."

"I doubt that very much. Michael here has an eye for talent. That's why we pay him so well, "suggested Jane and the trio laughed.

"So, shall we do the honours?" asked Graeme.

"Sure," replied Chris.

They all sat and Jane took the contract out of her briefcase.

"These are not standard contracts Chris. You should really look them over and ask any questions that come to mind, no matter how trivial," Jane explained.

"Do I need a lawyer?"

"That's up to you. They'll say that the contract is quite demanding, but the remuneration is generous and that one balances against another; at least that's what our other employees have fed back to us."

"Ok, but can you break it down for me in simple terms."

"Sure," said Graeme, "Our company is involved in business concepts all over the world. They vary from real estate, to owning sports teams and casinos and everything in between."

"Ok" said Chris still pondering the casino angle.

"We need people like you to keep the ideas flowing. To look at different ways of doing things, things that we haven't considered, no matter how strange or bizarre."

"Like what?"

"For example," Jane added, "We own and operate a charter air company in California, and we've increased profits significantly by catering for more exclusive clients such as celebrities and sports stars who don't want to be stuck on commercial flights. That idea came from someone like you."

"I see and what kind of person am I in your eyes?"

"An ideas man, a thinker, someone with vision. You can look at something ordinary and make it extraordinary," explained Graeme.

"How do you know?"

"Because Michael said so!"

"Ok and whatever I come up with is all yours?"

"Yes, but you will be paid a truckload for it. There is a payoff for making us successful."

"I see. Well, I told Michael I'm in, so I'm in. Where do I sign?"

"Right there," and Jane flicked to the back page of the contract pointing to the bottom of the page.

Chris was handed what looked like an expensive pen and hovered it over the signature box, then hesitated,

"Just one more question?"

"Shoot," said Graeme.

"Is Parallax owned by Jason Milne?"

There was a pregnant pause before Jane responded, "Sorry, who was that?"

"Jason Milne?"

"No, never heard of him. Parallax is run by a woman," added Graeme.

"Oh, sorry, I must have been mistaken."

"No problem," said Jane.

Chris felt great relief at the news and signed the contract.

"Fabulous! You start Monday. Be at the office at 9AM sharp. The Monday morning creative think tank starts at ten," explained Jane as she handed Chris a card and an information pack, "Everything you need to know is in there."

"Thank you."

"No, thank you. You're going to be very happy working for us," Jane said.

"I'm looking forward to it."

All parties shook hands and the executives were shown out.

"Well, you're all set," said Michael.

"I guess so."

"You probably won't have need of my services again. My job is done. Congratulations."

"You too I suppose. You'll get another fat fee right?"

"Oh yes. My tropical fish are high maintenance."

They laughed, shook hands and said their goodbyes.

Chris drove home feeling greatly satisfied with his decision and started to believe his life, this version of it, was finally turning out for the better.

First day on the job Chris arrived on the dot of 8am, an hour early and went to the reception desk.

If the recruitment office was ornate, the Parallax office was the Taj Mahal! The foyer was completely encrusted in white marble from the front step to the counter. Even the seating was made of the stone with live gardens in every corner.

The centre of the foyer featured a fountain, made of marble of course, filled with giant carp of all colours in crystal clear water.

By the time Chris got to the reception desk, his eyes were practically popping out of his head.

He craned his neck skywards as he realised the centre of the building was open up to the very roof, around twenty-five stories. The building simply surrounded this void giving people views into or out of the building. All the offices, as far as Chris could see, were walled in thick glass. It was for all intents and purposes a crystal tower.

"Takes your breath away, doesn't it?" came a voice.

"What? Oh yes, it's amazing."

"You must be Chris Parish."

"Yes, how..." Chris didn't need to ask, this company had already proven to be very good at finding people, so it was clear they were expecting him, "...and you are?"

"Julie Briggs, receptionist."

"Nice to meet you," said Chris as he focussed on Julie.

She was indeed a stunning young woman and certainly someone who would turn heads. It was obvious why she was tending the front desk.

This company was all about displaying a professional image and making sure people knew how successful they were. Julie was front line and perfectly suited to the task.

"Welcome Chris. Being day one, you need to do some paperwork, get sorted with security and go through your orientation. It sounds worse than it is, but once it's over, you practically have the run of the place,' she explained.

"Sounds good."

She showed him to a room off to the side of reception where he went through all the company requirements and watched an introductory video which was very professionally produced. He noted there was no mention of the founder of the company. The woman's identity remained a mystery.

When the presentation and paperwork were complete, Julie escorted Chris to the elevator, handing him a pass key.

"This is your electronic key. It's new technology and you only need wave it over the sensor to gain access," Julie said as she pointed at a little black box near the elevator door.

Interesting

Chris didn't think it at all amazing but then remembered that kind of technology wasn't common for another decade at least. He took the card and waved it over the sensor, opening the lift doors.

"You're on? Level 17, already on your way up the corporate ladder I see," she smiled as he stepped inside.

"Where do I go?"

"Oh, they're waiting for you Chris. You'll be looked after," Julie replied as the doors closed silently.

Wow!

Chris was very much impressed with this organisation and excited to get down to work, whatever form that might take.

There was a very slight bump as the elevator halted on the 17th floor and the doors opened to an office where dozens of people sat and typed, read or talked.

The place seemed very casual at first glance.

"Chris?"

"Yes sir!"

The man greeting him was tall, thin, probably in his mid-twenties and dressed in what appeared to be an expensive suit.

"Welcome. I'm John Rhodes and I'm the building supervisor."

"Nice to meet you."

"Anything you need before we get started?"

"No, I'm fine thanks."

"Good. Ok, so I'll show you around, introduce you to everyone and give you time to get settled before the 10am meeting. How does that sound?"

"Perfect."

"Great!"

Chris was led from desk to desk, meeting his co-workers and learning the basic layout.

"It'll all be a bit strange for a while, but you'll get to know how we work and find your niche soon enough."

"Ok."

"And this is you," said John who was pointing to a desk next to the internal glass wall, "I hope you aren't afraid of heights?"

"What? Oh, no this is great!"

The workstation was perfectly laid out and had everything he would need. Chris was surprised to see a computer on the desk, which he hadn't anticipated.

John noted his reaction, "We all have them and they're networked, so we can communicate better."

"This place is really ahead of its time," Chris suggested.

"Well, that's what we do Chris. We make the future and from what we hear, you're a perfect fit, so welcome again. Get settled and we'll see you at the meeting, just down there."

John pointed to the end of the office where two large doors separated the office space from what he presumed was a boardroom of some kind.

"Ok, sounds good."

"Coffee or tea over there, toilets that way etc. You'll figure it all out. Oh, and the canteen is on level 10 if you get hungry."

"Great, thanks again."

John walked off as Chris scanned the office, noticing a few faces looking in his direction.

He gave an awkward wave and got a smile or two back, but everyone kept their distance.

Chris sat down and switched on the computer.

It whirred and coughed to life and the green screen eventually warmed up revealing the words, "Welcome Chris."

A nice touch.

He soon noticed that the computer had functions that were years ahead of what he remembered, word processing, an internal messaging system and email.

None of it was at all familiar, it wasn't Windows or Apple based technology, so he decided not to muck around at this stage.

He had a bit of time before the meeting and decided to get something to eat.

The canteen was impressive, with lots of options and a wealth of healthy foods, again something that wouldn't have been too common before.

He ordered a milkshake and a sausage roll.

As he sat and consumed the goodies he was approached by another man,

"Mind if I join you?"

Chris looked at the fellow, a slightly portly gent, around thirty whose shirt was untucked on one side, revealing a hairy navel.

"No, not at all," Chris replied.

"I'm Simon. Simon Galway."

"Chris Parish."

"Nice to meet you, Chris. Welcome to the future," Simon added with a bit of a laugh.

"I still don't quite know what I'm doing here."

"Yeah, that's normal. None of us did at first, but you'll get it sorted out fairly quick."

"What do you do Simon?"

"I'm working on a computer project at the moment. They're hoping we can nail down a patent on miniature drives so we can take data around in our pockets, can you imagine that?"

Chris almost choked on his food, "No, sounds like science fiction." He had to lie of course.

"Yeah, I reckon, but the drive technology we've managed to develop so far has been amazing, so I don't doubt we'll crack it."

"Really? Wow, that's impressive. How long have you been here Simon?"

"Oh, a year, I think. I'm so busy I haven't thought about it."

"So, they work you hard?"

"Yes and no. You can choose your hours; work at your own pace, things like that. It's a very relaxed place."

"Like Google," Chris added without thinking.

"Like what then?"

"Oh nothing. So, you're making good money?"

"Holy cow! Yeah! It's really lucrative. I've achieved two major patents for them and get the licensing fees on top of my salary. I never thought I could make this kind of money."

"I see, what did you develop?"

"Well, we, a team of us, created a drive for computers which dispensed with the need for floppy disks. They also carry much more data; the latest version can store 500 megabytes."

"Half a gig, impressive." Chris tried not to smirk.

"Yeah, right? Who knows what the future might hold eh?"

Chris couldn't help but smile this time but Simon was oblivious to the truth of the reaction.

"So, what happens at these meetings?"

"Oh, they're never to be missed. The Monday brainstorm we call it. We all report our progress while others start on new ideas. The Boss often divvies out tasks, it's pretty intense."

"The Boss?"

"Yeah, we call her that, just Boss really. No-one knows her name. She likes to keep her distance," Simon explained.

"I wonder why?"

"Dunno, but who are we to challenge her methods, we're all making a squillion."

"So, she retains the majority of the income?"

"Sure. She provides all the resources, development and manufacturing. It's a massive operation and I honestly can't tell you how big it's really become."

"I'm getting that."

"So, don't miss the meeting Chris, she'll kill you," said Simon as he pointed his double-barrelled finger gun at Chris.

"Ok, understood."

Simon slurped down the last of his coke and a donut, "See you up there."

"Sure, thanks for the info."

"No problem."

Chris was intrigued by this company.

So little in the way of information and everyone, so far, seemed to have a very limited understanding of what it was about. They didn't care either, the money was outstanding, and that was clearly built into a very dynamic business model.

Chris finished up the sausage roll and milkshake and went back up to the 17th floor.

Everyone was making for the boardroom and Chris followed, not sure what to do.

He waited for everyone to settle and took the only spare seat at the end of a huge, oval table.

Chris counted twenty-five people, including his supervisor, John Rhodes who was fiddling with some device in the middle of the table.

He pushed a few buttons, and a green light came on before he spoke.

"Good morning, Boss, everyone's here."

A female voice beamed back and sounded somewhat thin, like it was a phone connection, "Good morning, John, good morning, everyone."

"Good morning, Boss," everyone replied except for Chris.

"And I see we have our newest recruit on deck this morning? Hello Chris and welcome."

There was an awkward pause until Chris responded, "Um, yes, hello Boss."

Everyone chuckled at Chris's expense.

"I know this must all seem very strange Chris, but believe me, you'll get the hang of it, won't he everyone?"

"Yes boss!"

Chris felt like he was in one of those evangelical churches with the doors locked.

"OK, let's get started. Simon, how are you going on those thumb drives?"

Chris was very alert to the use of the term thumb drive. That kind of name hadn't surfaced until the late nineties from what he could recall and yet they were talking about it seventeen years ahead of its time.

"Well Boss," said Simon, "a few hitches on coding and we keep running into corruption issues with the samples. Then there's the hardware interface, we're having problems with drive ports ..."

There was silence on the line as Simon explained the pitfalls and some of the progress he'd made.

When he concluded the Boss replied.

"Ok, Simon, thank you. I'll be emailing you some thoughts on a different coupling system between the device and the computer. Just keep working on what you're good at with the code. I'm sure you'll nail it. By the end of the month, ok?"

Simon gulped but agreed on the deadline.

The Q and A went around the table as each person or team leader updating "The Boss" on their various concepts.

One team was working on developing very efficient solar panels, while another was creating an alternative fuel for motor vehicles without having to change the engines. A third group was focussed on wireless technology that sounded very much akin to Bluetooth, but he wasn't sure.

The more he listened the more he realised that all the ideas were way ahead of his old timeline and were no doubt going to accelerate the world technologically.

But it didn't stop at technology.

Someone suggested a new approach to advertising breakfast cereals, and another was working on animal husbandry techniques through cloning.

It was extraordinary to Chris that such advances were all in the same room like this and so far ahead of what he understood in the old timeline.

He concluded that much of what they were talking about could only have come from someone like him, another who had flashed back with knowledge from a former life, unless all of these people were re-treads too, but that was very unlikely.

He again thought of Jason Milne and felt a twinge of regret at his decision to join the company.

As the meeting wound up, The Boss made a few final recommendations before dismissing everyone but then added, "John, I'd like you and Chris to stay on a bit longer please and shut the door when everyone leaves."

Chris didn't think anything of the remark as he was new and expected some kind of formal discussion with the company director or whatever this person was.

The room was clear fairly quickly and the door closed.

"Hi Chris, sorry about outing you a bit at the start, I hope you weren't too embarrassed?"

"No, not at all. I'm still trying to settle in."

"Good, good. I wanted to hold onto you for a few minutes just to go over a few things. As you know we have head-hunters looking for people with special skills, so when they sent me your name I was intrigued," The Boss explained.

"And why was that," Chris asked.

"Well for a start, you're nothing like the others I employ. They're all very capable, don't get me wrong, but I have to spoon feed them. You on the other hand seem to have the insight I'm looking for."

"Ok, I'm thrilled but I still don't know exactly what you want from me."

"Simple, I want you to oversee all the projects we're working on and offer your own ideas to the mix on each one. You have general knowledge, broad knowledge from what I can glean and that can help the teams greatly."

"They all seem very capable to me; won't I just tread on toes?"

"Probably but they live in little cocoons, which I find makes progress slow. Take Simon for example. He's nearly there but he's been plodding along for weeks on the interface issue. He should have solved it by now. I think if you look over his prototypes, you'll nail the problem and voila, we go into production. See what I'm saying?"

"Yes..." Chris hesitated.

"I can hear a 'but' in there Chris."

"Sorry, it's just that I'm not sure I can help. I mean, I don't know anything about alternative fuels, solar energy or advertising."

"Oh, but you do Chris, you've seen it all in action right?"

It took a moment for the penny to drop

What the Hell?

"Is he still there John? It's all gone quiet," asked The Boss.

"Yes Boss, but the look on his face...."

"I can see," she added.

"Who are you?" asked Chris.

"Someone who is trying to make a buck and help the World at the same time. Someone like you who is giving the world a chance not to spiral into oblivion."

"I don't get it. I'm not doing that."

"You will though Chris because you know what the future has in store. Believe me, I fully intend to take every possible money-making venture the world has seen and make them mine and make a global fortune in the process. I'll tie up every conceivable idea and lock them down so they can't be copied, bought, sold or traded except on my terms. Then I will fix this planet before we hit the wall...again."

Chris was stunned but then he had a kind of an awakening, "That explains the secrecy. If you stay off the grid, it's harder to stop you. You're already pissing off powerful people, politicians and probably the military and they want to find you and stop you and...."

"You see John, I told you he'd get it."

"You sure did Boss."

"So, Chris, what do you say?"

"I've signed the contract; what choice do I have?"

"Stuff the contract. You're unique. I need you more than anyone else here. I've been looking for you for a long time."

Chris hesitated. He had only one thought in mind, "So?"

"Yes Chris, you can ask me."

"I'm like you, you say?"

" Yes Chris."

"So, you..."

"You can say it Chris," The Boss implored.

"You're a flashback?"

"Well, I haven't heard of that reference before but yes, that's what I am. Just like you."

"How? When?"

"Oh, the same as you I expect. I was minding my own business watching a midday movie when "whoosh" I'm coughing up amniotic fluid and screaming blue murder."

Chris was intrigued, he wanted to know so much more, "When did you come back, what was the date?"

"My same birthday, June 16th, 1941"

"So, it spits you out at exactly the same moment you were born?"

"That appears to be so Chris."

"Are you aware of any others?"

"No, you're the first I've come across."

Chris wanted to ask about Jason Milne but decided to keep that ace up his sleeve but he didn't know why.

"So, you have all the knowledge I have and more really. That explains everything. All this new tech that shouldn't exist yet."

"Indeed, it does but I'm doing it right this time," the Boss explained.

Chris was in shock. For the first time, someone who had been through the same thing had made themselves known to him. It was liberating and exciting and she seemed to be doing the right thing for humanity with all this knowledge.

"This must be too strange on all kinds of levels Chris," the Boss added.

"Tell me about it."

"Well, you're not alone anymore."

"Yes, but I don't know who you are."

"And I'm afraid it has to stay that way, Chris. My isolation from the network keeps us safe."

"I see that."

"Who knows Chris, maybe one day we'll meet but you will hear from me regularly. You can count on that."

"Ok."

"John will fill you in on the rest. He's been fully briefed. I have complete trust in him."

"That seems odd to me," suggested Chris.

"I get that, but he's my son, so I'm not all that worried. Right John?'

"Yes Mum."

Chris was completely nonplussed now,

"Is he? I mean, was he?"

"No, not before. I didn't have children last time."

"Oh, you've adapted well. Better than me."

"I hope to change that for you Chris."

"Um, thank you I guess."

"And Chris, just so you know how special you are to me, you are the only one that knows John is my son. None of the other employees has the slightest clue. They think he simply in charge and that's how I want it to stay."

"I understand and thanks for the vote of confidence."

"Hey, we're kindred spirits Chris. I'm so pleased to have found you," said The Boss, then she added, "Look, take some time to get your head around all this and we can talk again tomorrow, ok?"

"Sure, thanks again."

"Look after him John," and with that the green light on the communicator went out.

John briefed him on his new role and after more than an hour behind closed doors they emerged.

"Attention everyone." John announced, "As you know, Chris Parish has joined us today. The Boss has asked him to work with all of you on everything we're doing on the 17th floor."

There was a united groan.

Great

"No need for that," John said as he scowled at everyone,", The Boss is expecting your full cooperation and won't tolerate a rebellion. Don't forget who pays you. Chris will meet with all of you daily and offer advice. That's all."

John turned to Chris and said, "Good luck."

Chapter 11

Chris settled quickly into his new role and the other workers slowly accepted him as a team leader. His general understanding of the concepts they were working on did help as it turned out. Simon's issues with the thumb drive were solved within a week when Chris suggested a universal serial bus that could easily be adapted to a multitude of devices, from computers to motor vehicles. His suggestion that the animal husbandry team should focus on sheep for their cloning experiments hit pay dirt as well.

He was also able to give others a few ideas to work on as if he were simply speculating on possibilities rather than drawing on actual knowledge which he'd retained quite well to his surprise. New teams were created, and people employed to work on ideas that he offered. Chris started a team focussed on fibre optics which resulted in a patent on a new data delivery system, tying up the concept for future users which ultimately meant Parallax would be paid handsomely for the technology. Fuel cells, despite his lack of understanding, spawned a team of experts to work on the idea and it was likely a prototype would be ready within a year.

Most of his ideas centred around technical advancements but a big push was made on hemp plantations for the creation of future manufacturing materials from clothing to paper and even building products. "The Boss" was particularly excited by the idea and even though she'd heard of it in her and Chris's original timeline, it hadn't really crossed her mind again until Chris came along. She had the money and the power to sway politicians and trial crops were in the ground decades ahead of when Chris knew of in his old life.

Before long Chris's salary rose steadily as things developed. He almost felt guilty, like he was cheating on exams, but the ideas kept coming and the company kept growing, much to everyone's delight and all in a few short months.

"Chris, I'm so thrilled. You've delivered just like I'd hoped. Congratulations," said the Boss via her wireless intercom.

"Thanks Boss. I'm really enjoying the work."

"That's good but Chris; It's time for a change. I think we need to have you focus on something for yourself. A big project. You've got the team thinking for themselves, so let's get you re-tasked."

"Ok, that sounds good, what did you have in mind?"

"Well let me see. How do you feel about sport?"

"Are you kidding Boss? I love sport, even though I know all the results already," and he laughed.

"That's good, because I hate it and have never understood it. So, I'd like you to see about creating a global franchise for making money out of sport."

"Um? I'm not sure what you mean. You own most of the world's best teams or players in the big leagues, what's left to do?"

"I haven't got the; what did we call them? Punters. I haven't got the punters!"

"You mean gambling, creating a gambling system?"

"Yes, exactly. There's a fortune to be made in it and I want to take the lead before it gets outsourced."

Chris nearly choked, this was his greatest weakness, and he'd avoided it for a long time. The Boss noted his silence,

"What's wrong Chris?"

"Oh, nothing. I'm just thinking that the Government has it stitched up pretty well with racing and football and are making a lot in taxes. They won't be keen to let anyone else in."

"You don't need to worry about the politics. I have people for that side of it. We got hemp going right?"

"True."

"So, are you in?"

"I do have one concern."

"What's that Chris?"

"Gambling is a major social problem, or it will be on a much greater scale when deregulation happens, which I'm sure you know. I'm not happy to fan that flame," Chris explained.

Chris had been in that hole and knew very well what it might cost people. The idea of adding to the misery of anyone who got caught up in sports gambling was abhorrent to him.

"Ok, I get that but I'm not really asking Chris. You are employed and you are required to follow instructions, right?"

"I understand that, but I have a moral objection to this."

"Fine. I understand. What if we give half the earnings to charity or better still built gambling centres for those who fall off the rails?"

"You would do that?"

"Yes of course. I'm about fixing things not messing up lives and if we don't go down this path, someone else will and your fears will come to fruition in any case, right?"

"Yes, I suppose."

"So, why are we fighting about it? You do your thing and I'll look after the rest. You have my word," said The Boss.

"You're right. Ok, yes, Let's do it."

"Great! Start working on a draft plan immediately. I want a report in three weeks."

With that the intercom clicked off and she was gone.

Chris was both excited and apprehensive about the idea, but he was well qualified to work out a series of proposals and put them to The Boss. He immediately started racking his brain and writing notes. He was in his element and the ideas trickled out at first but then the floodgates opened. He was so focussed on the job he lost track of time and before he knew it, it was midnight.

Jesus!

He decided to pack up and made for the lift. Heading down to the carpark he smiled at the idea of using gambling for good. He wasn't kidding himself though, he knew there would be problems and people would get hurt financially but if the Boss came through, and he didn't have any reason to think she wouldn't, they and their families would be taken care of, wouldn't they?

He took the lift all the way down to the sub floor car park, walked out the door and fumbled for his keys. He didn't quite have hold of them as he wrenched them from his pocket and they flew from his fingertips and dropped onto the exit lane. As he leaned over to pick them up, the lights of a vehicle came on blinding him momentarily.

"Who's there?" he yelled, feeling a bit silly, like he was in a bad detective film.

There was no answer as Chris stood and tried to focus on the windscreen through the glare. He couldn't see who was at the wheel as the engine cranked. The deep throated woofing of the engine made it clear this was a high-performance vehicle with plenty of grunt. Chris gulped.

"What do you want?" he yelled again, only to be answered with a more intense rev of the motor.

Chris looked around but the lift doors had closed. There were no other exits nearby and very few cars in the lot besides his own, which was further away than he liked. He calculated that if the car started towards him, it would take around five seconds to reach the point he was standing. Running would be useless but could buy him a second or two if he had somewhere to go but before he could finish making his plan, the engine died, and a brief silence returned. The car door opened, and a figure stepped out and stood beside the vehicle, lights still ablaze.

"Hello Chris," came a voice that was utterly unfamiliar

"Hello? Who are you?"

"You don't know me Chris, well not personally. You may know of me though, from the world before," explained the mystery man.

Chris was mortified. Who was this? How did he know Chris? And what did he know about 'the world before'? Chris decided the best course of action for now was to play dumb.

"What world before? That sounds a bit crazy," Chris suggested with a half chuckle.

"Oh, come on Chris. We both know that you know what I'm talking about. You were born again and I'm not talking the religious way. You're living your life over again with all the knowledge from the first time around, just like me," explained the man.

"That's, that's just ridiculous," Chris replied not sounding at all convincing.

"To anyone other than you and your employer perhaps it would be, but you know better don't you Chris?"

He had no answer this time and thought about running and looked towards the ramp which led to the street. He didn't have a chance of making it out before being run down and both men knew it.

The stranger continued, "Come on Chris, there's no way out of here and I only want to talk."

"About what?"

"About how we can help each other. We're both smarter and wiser I think, and we know where we both went wrong in the time before this, right?" explained the intruder.

Chris still didn't quite know where this was going but realised it couldn't be anywhere good. He decided to push back, "OK, I'm listening, but I won't agree to anything until you tell me who you are."

"Haven't you figured it out yet Chris? I'm Jason Milne!"

Chris stood there stunned for a moment, the silence seemingly lasting eons until he finally woke from his trance, "Milne, it's really you?"

"Of course it's me, did you think I was mythical or something?"

"No, I mean, what are you doing here? How did you get in?"

"Too easily really, security here is farcical and let's face it, money can get you through almost any door, am I right," Milne explained.

"I suppose so, but…" Chris was starting to clear his head, "How did you find me. More to the point, how do you know about me?"

"Jesus Christ, it's not rocket science. Once I realised what was going on, I started looking for people just like me, people who have come back."

"How?"

"It's simple really, I just looked for odd situations, mainly in newspapers. You've made the headlines many times over the years haven't you. Having my people go through microfiche copies of newspapers at the library really paid off," said Milne.

"But why? What do you want with me?"

"Well, let me say it's not you personally I'm interested in, it's just people like you and me and anyone else who came back after that Sun shit happened. So let me ask you something, how did it happen for you Chris?"

"Um, well, I was in a hotel room, in the bathroom and got spiked there." Chris thought it best not to mention the casino.

"Spiked? I like that. Makes sense. I'll use that from now on. You wanna know my story?"

"Um, I don't know. Yes, I suppose so."

"Well, I was in my brand-new Lexus, screaming along at some ungodly speed when it all went white. I thought I'd hit a tree or something and was dead, you know seeing the light and everything but then, out I popped in that shitty hospital in Italy. Fucking weird. What a trip! eh?"

"Yeah, I guess so. Italy?"

"I was born there, moved to Australia when I was 2. Learned the business from Poppa and built an empire but you probably know all about my previous business life, right?"

Chris blushed, "I suppose so, you had something of a reputation."

"So true, but I've been more careful this time, MUCH more careful. In fact, I haven't needed to step outside the lines very much you know? Knowledge is indeed power."

"Is that why you've tracked me down?"

"Yes and no. No disrespect, but you're not the powerful one around here, am I right?"

"Um no, I just work here."

"Thought as much and you're selling off your knowledge for a pretty penny I'll bet?"

"I'm doing ok," Chris didn't feel right. These questions were starting to get uncomfortable, and he started to worry, more than when the conversation started. He decided to change the subject, "So, you'd know about my parents then."

"Yeah, tough break and all that time in hospital. That must have been a bitch."

"It was. So did you kill them," Chris asked bluntly.

"What? Fuck no. Why would I need to do that?"

"Well, someone wanted me out of the picture. I don't know why. I thought I was minding my own business when all Hell broke loose."

"That's usually when it hits the fan, Chris. Look, I can understand why you accused me but hand on heart, I didn't do it. I didn't need to then and still don't need to do anything heavy. In fact, I very much want you in the picture," said Milne.

"Wait a minute, if not you then who?"

"Stuffed if I know, someone with a bone to pick, I guess. I'm telling you it wasn't me. I was only a kid then, just like you. I had nothing to gain from it."

"Well, I was there, and it looked like something you might be capable of. No offence."

"None taken. Look, I don't know how else to say it, but I wasn't involved Chris. I promise you that."

Chris looked at Milne through the glare of the car lights, "Then why this cloak and dagger crap, why the revving engine and the headlights?"

Milne laughed, "I guess there are some habits I can't break, not even in my second coming, I'm sorry about that," Milne switched off the lights, "Truth is I need your help."

"What kind of help?"

"Simple really, I want you to find out who your boss is!"

"What? Why? How?"

"Well, if I knew that I wouldn't be asking, would I?"

Just then the lift doors opened and a colleague of Chris's emerged having worked back late too it seemed.

"I gotta go," said Milne, "I'll be in touch."

With that he got back in his car, fired up the engine and put his foot down, the tyres screeching slightly on the cement before gaining traction. Milne disappeared up the car park ramp, lights still turned off and was out of sight in seconds.

Chris was dumbfounded. He realised he was being asked to act as a corporate spy for a man who he knew, historically, had been a power player in the Sydney underworld, had probably killed and who knows what else.

"Everything all right Chris?"

Chris looked up and noticed Gwen Matthews who had just popped out of the lift.

"Oh yeah, just thinking about, you know, stuff."

Gwen laughed, "Yes, I do. Who was your friend?"

"Oh, I dunno, didn't recognise him," Chris suggested, hoping Gwen hadn't seen anything more than the car moving off.

"Oh OK, well I've got to get going. Getting fed up with these late nights, but they do pay off you know?"

"You're right about that," Chris said, "See you tomorrow."

"Sure thing. Bye Chris."

Chris waved as he moved to his car, got in and started the engine and was soon on his way home thinking hard about what had just happened and what he should do about it. He could discuss the conversation with Judy of course but that would just make her worry. Maybe he should tell the Boss? He just didn't know what to do. One thing was certain though; he wouldn't be doing any dirty work for Jason Milne.

When he got home Judy was asleep, so he sat and watched a bit of TV without really taking much notice. His head was still spinning, and he was wired, so sleep was impossible but lucid thoughts were proving difficult as well. He felt very much cornered and at odds.

Just then a light came on and Judy emerged from their bedroom, "Hey baby, you still up?"

"Yes, can't seem to wind down."

"Anything wrong?"

"Yes and no. Work issues, nothing to worry about."

"Are you sure," Judy asked.

"Hmm? Yeah, it's fine. Hey, I got a new project today," Chris said trying to divert Judy's suspicion. "I'll explain in the morning, it's a bit late and I'm not in the mood to go into detail."

"OK, I understand, but hey congratulations. I'm sure it's exciting," Judy replied.

Chris didn't really hear her, "You know what? We need a holiday. I'm going to get this project sorted out for the Boss then ask for some time off. How much leave does the bank owe you?"

"Not sure, several weeks I think but you won't have any leave built up yet, will you?"

"It doesn't work like that at Parallax. They have a very flexible approach. If you need a break, they give it to you because they know how important it is to keep your batteries charged and a break, I think."

"Well, you have been working long hours, and I know you're invested in, whatever it is Parallax is doing," Judy giggled.

"True, so I'll tie off this project, and we can take a trip. Where do you want to go?"

Judy didn't hesitate, "How about Paris?"

"Paris huh? You got it."

"Really?"

"Really. Call a travel agent and make the booking, we're going to Paris! Oh, and make it First Class all the way."

Judy squealed with excitement and now neither of them felt they would get any sleep tonight.

"Oh, and book with Qantas, ok?"

Judy looked puzzled for a moment, "Why?"

"Believe me, it's the safe option knowing what I know."

"Oh, ok, I see," and Judy smiled.

Next day Chris continued working on his gambling project ideas. It proved to be much easier than he expected, his inside knowledge and understanding of the industry making for some brilliant concepts.

He worked with one of the company's mathematicians and together, they created several models to present to The Boss covering a multitude of sports. Multi betting; multi-sport combinations; betting on individual players and athletes; betting on statistical outcomes; first scorers; cash back options; opt out options. There was no end to the possibilities.

So far, in this timeline, the gambling world was very basic, mainly because it was all wrapped up in Government red tape. With the kind of control, the Bureaucrats had there was no need to be elaborate about process or to develop any new ideas, so basic gambling was all that people had at their disposal legally, mainly on horses and dogs. Gambling outside a Government agency or through a non-registered bookmaker was illegal. Betting on football was only brand new and very simplistic, and the only other form of gambling was lotteries which again were strictly Government controlled and nothing more than a glorified raffle. Even the Lotto systems that existed were basic and the odds were terribly bad for players which raked in billions for respective provincial Governments.

Of course, there was a lot going on underground and that kept the authorities busy. Chris guessed that the Boss would use that as leverage to get the industry deregulated and his work would lead to a whole new level of gaming and of course, divert those billions to a private operator, like Parallax. Chris wondered if The Boss might be treading on any toes in the criminal world and his mind jumped straight to Jason Milne who did indeed have a history in gaming and didn't mind hurting people along the way. He dismissed the thought for now.

Over the weeks that followed Chris fine-tuned his concepts and calculations until he had working models for The Boss.

"I'm impressed Chris; this is wonderful work. I mean, I don't really understand gambling or why so many people feel compelled to do it, but I can see that these ideas can work magic for us. Well done," said the Boss.

"Thank you, Boss. It wasn't really that difficult."

"Well, I appreciate the hours you put in and of course I expect you to register the patents for all these ideas. They are inventions, right?"

"Well, yes, I suppose they are."

"There'll be quite a lot of money in it for you in that case, just as soon as I can wrangle the Government into deregulating the market on gambling, which I expect will take some time."

"I can imagine but of course you can pitch it in a way that makes them see dollar signs. Increasing the taxes on gambling to help with addiction, that kind of thing, seeing as that's your main motivation for controlling the industry, right," Chris suggested, "Sell it to them like they're doing the public a favour."

The Boss was quiet for a moment, "You see, that's why I hired you. You are a lateral thinker. You know how to work a problem. I might just take that idea and use it to our advantage. Money talks, particularly with politicians but giving them something to win votes is even better."

"Very true," then Chris added, "And you hired me because I have inside knowledge."

The Boss laughed, "Yes I did, and a good thing too."

In his short time with Parallax Chris thought he was getting to know The Boss, despite not really having a clue as to her identity. They seemed to gel and often had long conversations about their other past, The Boss occasionally revealing a little more about herself. Nothing significant though, she was very careful about details. He understood her need to be anonymous given the high stakes games she was playing in so many industries. There must be a lot of people who hated what she was doing simply because it was costing them millions or even billions in lost earnings. He already saw the effects with major corporations from the previous timeline simply not existing in this one while others he knew were big players now only cottage industries. The world was not anything like he remembered before. It made him worry a little. He also wondered if he should tell The Boss about Milne's appearance.

"There's something else I need to discuss Boss."

"Sure, what is it?"

"I need a holiday. I promised Judy a break and well, she wants to go to Paris, and I could use a break. I know I haven't been here long but..."

"Say no more, you've done a splendid job, and you deserve a breather. Take as long as you like. Your office will be waiting for you when you get back," explained The Boss.

"Thank you. I really appreciate it."

"I'll even throw in some bonus cash for the trip, how does that sound?"

"Really? That's terrific, but unnecessary. I'm doing ok and I think you know that."

"Of course I do, but as I've said many times, I'm not here to get mega rich. I'm here to save the planet. Throwing you some extra bucks for a holiday isn't an issue for me but it is an investment. I want you to be comfortable here; happy. You are my best asset, and I can't do without you. Do you understand?"

Chris's ego started to swell as he absorbed the words, "Wow, no-one has ever said anything like that to me before. That's so kind of you."

"Well, it's true, so get going, enjoy your trip and give me a call when you get back to town and we'll pick up where we left off. I'm guessing you'll come back fresh and brimming with new ideas."

"I hope so. thanks Boss."

"And get those patents in for registration before you leave, they're too valuable to have lying around."

"Will do," and he spent the afternoon doing the paperwork, making sure the mathematician wasn't forgotten and had the documents couriered to the patents office with a cheque to cover the fees.

Hmm, I'll have to look into electronic banking, I think.

With that Chris packed up, said goodbye to his colleagues and headed home. He felt very happy, thrilled even and couldn't wait to pick Judy up from work and pack for Paris.

Chapter 12

The flight to Paris was uneventful and Judy was swept away with the romance of it all. It was simply the best time that either of them had experienced and they absorbed everything about the French city. They visited all the major attractions, The Louvre, Eiffel Tower, Cruised the Seine and basically took in the culture. They found little eateries off the main roads, relaxed and talked a lot about their future together. Money was no object, and The Boss was very generous with that holiday bonus.

They hired a car and did a week of travel through the French countryside visiting historic sites including some famous battlefields, then drove up to Belgium, across to Germany then doubled back to Holland, where Judy's family originated. They even found some distant relatives and stayed with them for a few days despite an obvious language barrier.

Where's Google translate when you need it?

After driving back to Paris, they spend another day in France before taking a train to Calais and then a ferry across the channel, spending a couple of weeks in England, Scotland, Wales and Ireland.

The trip was amazing but soon Chris felt the pangs of needing to get back to work and Judy was just about out of leave time anyway, so they changed their plans and flew home out of Heathrow instead of Paris, Chris making sure they were on a Qantas flight again.

Chris looked at Judy as they settled back for the 24-hour transit and smiled. She smiled back then gave him a smouldering kiss, "Thank you. I've had the most incredible time."

"Me too and we can do it again any time you like. We have money now; it's all going to be great and…" Chris hesitated.

"What is it?"

"Well, I was just thinking, we can start trying soon. I mean it's really not that long before the conception date for Caleb."

Judy beamed with excitement, "I still can't get my head around how certain you are about it. I mean I believe you, but it seems so strange to be talking about a certainty when nothing is ever quite certain."

"Well, I am quite sure about it. I was there."

"Yes, I know but what if we do it, like an hour early or something, won't that affect our chances?"

"Maybe, but you will deliver that one egg, the same egg as before I'm sure of that. The only uncertainty is which of my sperm wins the race and there's no way of knowing that. I...."

Judy smiled, "I know what you're trying to say. It might be a totally different outcome."

"Exactly and with so many things having changed for me this time, it's simply impossible to calculate but I have to believe that something else will make it happen."

"What do you mean something else," Judy asked.

"Well, I'm talking about faith. If there is a God and that children are born according to his will, then this will be Caleb's time regardless of the variables."

"WOW, I wasn't expecting that. You're not religious."

"I know right? But I have to believe that this will happen. I can't think about Caleb not existing. I saw him born, I watched him grow, and I helped him with maths homework, played soccer occasionally. I..." Chris suddenly choked up.

Judy cupped Chris's face with her hand and turn his head toward her, "I can't imagine what you must be feeling. I know I was there too, but I have no memory of anything before. It didn't exist for me, but you, you have memories of a whole other world with me, Caleb and your parents. It must be horrible sometimes."

"It is and to be frank I was a shitty Dad." Chris took Judy's hand and gave it a gentle squeeze, "I did so many things wrong. I hurt you, Caleb, everyone. I was a messed-up guy."

"And yet, you have a second chance now. You can right those wrongs and create a whole new life. You're doing that already. Paris? That was amazing. I'll bet that didn't happen before?"

Chris laughed, "Certainly not. I think we went to Nelson Bay one time though?"

They both laughed and they continued to talk for what seemed like hours until they were too exhausted to talk any more. They managed some sleep, tried to enjoy airline food and, after a stopover in Singapore, finally landed in Sydney, utterly exhausted.

After breezing through customs, they caught a taxi and within the hour they were home. Jetlag was taking its toll and despite the time being just after 9am, they felt compelled to go to bed for a good sleep.

They decided to grab a few hours and then force themselves up and ride out the rest of the day. They both had a few days before they were back at work so they should be able to brush off the time difference by then. Chris and Judy were unconscious before they hit their pillows and soon in a deep sleep, waking some hours later feeling, not much better.

Bloody jet lag!

They spent the next few days adjusting to local time, catching up with family, sharing stories and showing off their photos and souvenirs. Clem and Edith were quite elderly now and very frail, but they were thrilled to hear about the trip. For Chris it was indeed time well spent.

As they drove home, they felt so very happy and content and Judy said, "These have been the best weeks of my life Chris. Thank you."

"You're welcome. I love you so much."

Judy kissed him on the cheek and snuggled into his shoulder as they passed through the city on their way home. Chris caught a glimpse of the Parallax building and wasn't surprised to see the lights on. Sundays, Mondays, it didn't matter at Parallax, the people were so committed they worked anytime they wanted to and there they were on a Sunday night, doing whatever they could to improve the world. Chris smiled and felt a surge of excitement about going back to work.

Next morning Chris rose, showered and dressed. He saw that the towels were changed since last night and thought it odd that Judy would do that. He also noticed a few other odds and ends weren't where they were before, like the toothpaste and that Judy had suddenly changed brands of perfume and shampoo.

Weird

Once he was shaved Chris met Judy in the kitchen where she was preparing breakfast for them both, "It's going to be hard to get back to work after such a lovely break. I mean I'm looking forward to it but it's always a bit odd going back after time away, don't you think?"

Judy didn't answer which was strange because he was sure she heard him, "Jude, did you hear me?"

"Yep."

He recognised her tone. She was angry, "What's wrong?"

"You don't remember? Typical," Judy said.

Chris was confused, "What did I say?"

"Last night you told me how much you hated work, and you wanted to leave and here you are again saying how hard it'll be to go back. Why can't you just commit to the job and stop whining?"

Chris was utterly flabbergasted, "I have no idea what you're talking about. We spend a lovely day with your parents and Clem and Edith yesterday, there was no such fight."

"Oh really? Well, I remember it clearly and you seem to have chosen to pretend it didn't happen. And we haven't seen Mum and Dad for a week, your Grandparents passed away years ago and that excuse for a holiday was months back, so can we please just get past it?"

Chris was mortified, his grandparents, Dead?

"What on Earth are you talking about? Clem and Edith are fine, and we've only been back from Paris for a week. Nothing you're saying makes sense."

"Paris," she scoffed, "We went to Nelson Bay and stayed in a beach house. That's all we could afford. Where did Paris come from? You really are losing it Chris. We could never afford to go to Paris."

Chris had to collect himself, something was off, but he couldn't understand what or why. Judy was very hostile towards him and talking about things he had no memory of.

Think! What could this mean?

"Ok, sorry, I'm just thinking it would be nice to visit there sometime," Chris said hoping to calm the waters.

"Well, if you ever committed to a job and stopped spending every Saturday listening to the races, then maybe we could go to Paris!"

"The races?"

"I mean your gambling Chris. You're going to bankrupt us one day. I just wish you'd stop!"

This time he recognised the subject of the discussion. It was like someone had flipped a switch and he'd been transported back to his original life. The only thing was that this was all happening too soon, much too soon in their relationship. In fact, it shouldn't have been happening at all. They were well off, wealthy even. How could they be struggling? Chris decided it would be best to play along for now, until he could figure out what was happening, "I'll stop No more gambling. I promise."

"Yeah sure, I've heard that before."

"Seriously, it's no longer an issue," Chris urged.

Judy seemed to soften a little, "Ok, well we can discuss it later, we have to get to work," she said as she gulped down her breakfast and the last mouthful of coffee.

"Sure, have a good day and I'll see you tonight," and he moved to give Judy a kiss.

"What? Where are you going?"

"Parallax of course. Why? Where do you think I'm going?"

"Parallax? Never heard of it. You really are acting weird. Come on, we have to get to the bank, we're going to be late."

Chris was feeling incredibly confused and had no idea what was happening, "Um ok,"

They jumped in the car and Chris started towards the city. As he looked around things seemed normal at first but as they left their suburban street, he noticed that this wasn't the city he saw yesterday. It was Sydney all right, but not as he knew it. Things had quite literally changed. There were different buildings in different parts of the city that weren't there yesterday. Skyscrapers that he hadn't seen before, even the cars were oddly different, like someone had just snapped their fingers and like magic, changed everything, "What the Hell!"

"What's the matter," Judy asked.

"My building, it's not there."

"Your building? What building? We work downtown at the State Bank. We've never worked around here. You really are off today, Chris."

As they drove past the place where Parallax should have been he saw instead an old facade in convict brick, a building that had been there for at least one hundred and fifty years. It appeared to be an office block with a variety of occupants from lawyers to accountants. No sign of the amazing steel and glass concave structure of Parallax which dominated the skyline the day before.

What the blazes is going on?

Luckily Chris knew of the State Bank building and where it was. He drove into a parking station near the bank where he knew all the workers in the downtown area parked. Judy said nothing which, under the circumstances, was a good sign. He stopped at the boom gate, waited for the machine to spit out a ticket then found a space and parked the car. Nothing made sense. He hadn't forgotten what Judy said about Clem and Edith either and hoped that this was just some nightmare he would soon wake up from. Surely, they're not dead but deep down he knew he wasn't dreaming.

As Judy got ready to pop the door Chris stopped her, "Listen Jude, I have to talk to you."

"Later. We're so late. We'll get our butts kicked! Come on!"

"No, listen to me, please. This is important."

She huffed and fell back into the passenger's seat, "OK. One minute, what is it?"

Chris decided he needed to tell his story over again, just like before when he met her accidentally in the new timeline and hope that her reaction was the same; with some underlying knowledge or understanding of who he was, "I don't know how to begin, so much has changed."

"You can say that again."

"No, I mean overnight. Today the city isn't what it was yesterday. My world is totally different, and I mean literally and physically. I worked for a company called Parallax. We had a building right over there," and he waved vaguely up town, "and now it's gone. You tell me I work with you, at the bank? I never have worked at the bank, not in this timeline anyway…"

"You're making no sense at all Chris. In fact, you sound like you're off your tree. What's gotten into you?"

"Listen Judy, please, I'm telling you the truth. I was struck by a Sun spike caused by what might have been a black hole in the year 2014 and thrust back in time and started my life over again. I'm here now with all my former life's knowledge. I had a great job, and we had money; we were happy right up until yesterday and now it's all changed. Something has shifted in time and space, and I can't explain it," Chris said with urgency in his voice although it was bordering on desperation. He couldn't seem to get the message out the way he wanted, and it sounded disjointed at best.

Judy looked at him with a face he knew well from the life before, utter disdain, "You're kidding me. I've heard some real crap come out of your mouth before, but this is way out of the ballpark. Just stop it ok. I'm not in the mood for jokes."

"It's no joke. Seriously, I'm telling you the truth."

"Save it. I'm late and so are you. Let's just get inside before they sack both of us."

"No. I'm not going in. I have no idea about banking. I haven't done it for over 25 years."

"What? You're kidding. You were in there on Friday and for the last, who knows how many years. I think you're losing it big-time Chris. Now cut the stupid jokes."

"I've already told you I'm not joking. Everything I'm telling you is true."

She looked at him harshly, "Fine, whatever. I'm going in and you had better do the same. We can't afford to lose either job. Have you looked at our account balance lately?"

Chris chose not to stoke the fire. Clearly something wasn't right, and he had no idea what was happening. It was also clear that Judy wasn't going to accept his story a second time, "You go, I have something to do. Tell them I'm sick or something."

"What? No way! Get your arse out of the car and come to work!"

"I said no! I have to sort this out. You go in and I'll call you later."

"Fine, do what you want but if you're off to the track or something, don't bother coming home!"

With that she slammed the door and stormed off without looking back, vanishing through a car park exit.

What on Earth has happened?

Chris pondered his situation but the more he thought about it the more disturbing it became. Then he had remembered Jason Milne. It's likely he has witnessed the same thing. He had to find Jason Milne. With that he drove off, leaving the car park and headed for the most likely place he'd find Milne, the casino. After all, that's what he did before any of this started. It made sense to start there, and Chris had no other leads.

As it turned out one thing hadn't changed. The casino was exactly where he hoped to find it although it looked much newer than during his last visit when he won all that money just before his life suddenly changed. Now it had changed again, and he needed to see if anyone else had been impacted. Jason Milne and The Boss were his only connections with the world as he knew it. With Parallax gone, he had no idea where The Boss might be or how to trace her. He didn't even know her name or what she looked like, but he knew Milne. Chris parked the car and got out, striding for the entrance. He walked straight in and went to the first staff member he saw, "Hi, I'm looking for Jason Milne."

The waitress looked at him with wide eyes, "Um, well he's here but he's not seeing anyone."

"This is an emergency and I'm sure he'll want to see me. Tell him it's Chris Parish."

"Ok, wait there. I'll see if I can find…" the girl didn't finish her sentence, looked around and then rushed off intercepting a security guard. She spoke quickly and waved in Chris's direction as the guard turned his head. Conversation over, the muscular brute headed towards Chris,

"What's this about?"

"I'm Chris Parish and I'm here to see Jason Milne."

"He's seeing no-one today."

"I realise that. The girl said so, but he'll talk to me. Please, it's urgent."

The guard eyed Chris suspiciously but Chris didn't budge, "Wait here."

The man walked to a nearby cash counter and grabbed the receiver of a wall phone. It looked like a toy in her meaty hand. He dialled and waited, said a few words and hung up the phone. He then turned to Chris and motioned him to follow. Chris hustled across the foyer and followed the man into a corridor and to a lift door which opened almost immediately. They stepped inside and Chris recognised the ornate interior.

Some things never change.

The guard used a key to activate a panel in the lift then pressed the very top button. The lift went up and didn't stop on any floor until they got to the top. The door opened and the guard urged Chris to step out, which he did. With that the door closed and the guard was gone.

Chris stood for a moment and listened. He could hear what he thought was a TV then a voice, "In here Chris."

Chris walked down the hall which opened into the most amazing penthouse. The furniture was all white and practically glowed as the sun streamed through the floor to ceiling glass windows. The view was captivating, and he could see ferries and boats meandering here and there on Sydney Harbour with the Opera House and Harbour Bridge dominating the centre of the view, "Wow!"

"Yeah, pretty amazing huh? You'd never get sick of looking at it, right?"

"But the bridge? They've…"

"Built another one, yeah. Two of them now, hard to believe, eh?"

"That's for sure," Chris snapped out of his trance and turned to see Jason Milne sitting on a single seater lounge wearing a dressing gown and slippers holding a glass of what was probably scotch, "Hi Jason."

Milne continued his remarks like Chris wasn't there, "Of course I'm as mesmerized as you because I haven't seen this view in many years. When I woke up this morning, I was in that room," he pointed to a door through which Chris could see a vast and elaborate bedroom, "and I haven't slept in that room for over two decades," Jason concluded.

"You too? I woke in my house but that's all that was the same. My building is gone, my job is gone, even my money is gone. Everything is different. What happened?"

"If you've come here for answers, you've come to the wrong place. I have no stinking idea. Yesterday I was someone else doing something else and trying to get my foot in the door with Parallax and now, this."

"And what is this exactly?"

"It's my old life essentially and it ain't pretty. I mean, it's like it was before, sort of. I think you know what I mean."

"So, the crime, corruption, pay offs, the heavy handedness...."

"Yeah, yeah, you get the picture, don't rub it in but I wasn't like that yesterday. When I came back, I had knowledge and I tried really hard to keep on the straight and narrow, I really did. Sure, I took a couple of minor shortcuts, but for all intents and purposes, I was on the plus side of the life ledger, if you know what I mean?"

Chris nodded.

"And now, here I am, back in the shit and looking over my shoulder. I feel jilted. And of course, the authorities are barking mad and want to bring me down. It's like...."

"A nightmare," Chris added.

"Exactly. Now I don't know what to do. I never wanted to come back to this. I was living a decent life. Doing good really. You never believed me, and I don't blame you, but I was making things right with the world. Now that's all gone."

"I believe you. I didn't before but after what's happened, why would you lie to me?"

Jason gave Chris an understanding nod, "So what now? What happens next? You got any ideas about what might have happened?"

"No, but I think I know someone who might be able to help us. Or at least have some theories."

"Who?"

"Doctor Fred Wilson at the Australia Observatory."

"Who's that," Milne exclaimed.

"He's an astronomer and in the previous timeline he had a theory about those Sun spikes and what they might mean. He's in Canberra and I think we need to talk to him."

"Let's go!"
"What? Right now?"

"Yeah. I don't want to be here anymore than you do. I need answers too."

"OK, I'll have to call my wife and explain."

"Sure, go right ahead, the phone is over there," and Jason pointed to the kitchen, "I'll go change while you talk."

"Ok, thanks," Chris said as he picked up the phone and dialled the number, after having to look it up in a phone book.

"State Bank Sydney, can I help you."

"Um yeah, it's Chris Parish, can I talk to Judy Parish please."

"Oh, hi Chris, how are you feeling?"

"Ah, ok I guess."

"Oh, that's good. We were all so worried. The way Judy told it, you were in pretty bad shape."

Chris realised he was supposed to know this person and that Judy was covering for his not being at work, "Oh, well yeah, it's been a bit of a struggle. Listen I'm at the doctor's and need to talk to her. Can she come to the phone?"

"Oh, ok Chris, get better soon; Judy it's for you," and the call went on hold.

Errrrr Greensleeves.

"Hello"

"Judy, it's me."

"What do you want?" She was clearly still very angry.

"I have to go to Canberra. I can't explain and you wouldn't believe me anyway. I'll be gone a day or two."

"Are you serious," she said in a sort of shouting whisper.

"Yes, and I know you think I'm crazy and this is all some joke, but I have to know what happened and I think I know someone who can help."

"Well, it better be a psychiatrist," and she hung up hard!

Jason Milne appeared at that moment dressed like he was headed to a wedding, "What do you think?"

Chris hung up the phone, "Um, yeah sure, whatever you like."

"What? Too much?"

"Maybe a little."

"Ah what the Hell, you only live once, right," Milne said.

Chris looked at him and managed a smirk, "Well actually."

"Yeah, yeah very funny. Let's roll."

"Your car or mine?"

"Jesus, mine of course, Milne exclaimed, "It's gotta be better than whatever shit heap you've got."

"You're probably right."

Chris and Jason went down into the basement car park where Jason was met by the attendant, "My car," then he paused, not recognising the man and added, um…good fella."

Chris realised Jason had no clue who the guy was and smiled.

"Right away Sir," the man replied.

"That was close," Jason said as he winked at Chris. Chris almost laughed. He never took Milne to be so amusing.

A few moments later the attendant drove up in a Rolls Royce Silver Ghost.

"Holy Shit," Jason exclaimed which certainly confused the car park attendant, "Thanks Jeeves!"

Jason slipped into the driver's seat and Chris into the passenger's side and barely had the door closed when the car squealed off with a shriek, "Road Trip!" Jason screamed.

Chris wondered what the Hell, he'd gotten himself into.

"Shouldn't I call Dr Wilson before we go," Chris suggested.

"Probably, but I'm bored sitting up there wondering what the fuck happened overnight, so we're going regardless. That ok with you?"

"Yes, of course, I'm as confused as you."

"And shitfully poorer by the sound of it. The opposite happened to me. I suddenly woke up with a bank account full of dirty money. Not sure who's worse off."

Chris hesitated at the question on his lips but then decided to throw it out there, "So, did you kill people? I mean before?"

"What," Milne blurted, "You think, or thought I was a killer?"

"Well yeah, most people did. Your reputation was um, well, you know."

Jason didn't respond immediately but then said, "Yeah it was. I was a thug and while I did play hard and put the heavy on people, I never killed anyone and I never arranged any killing. Do you believe me?"

"Honestly, I'm not sure but you aren't demonstrating the kind of persona that I would expect of a killer. I mean, initially you freaked me out a little but then you just became annoying."

Jason laughed, "Demonstrating the kind of persona? That's priceless."

Chris smiled, "So no killing?"

"No, not once. Never!"

"But you said dirty money."

"Yeah, I did that. Look, it's not something I ever talk about, for obvious reasons. Loose lips etcetera, but I feel I can tell you and you won't turn State's evidence. The money I made before and again now after whatever changed overnight is dirty, but not from killing. It's laundered, mainly to avoid tax. Under the table stuff, you know?"

"So, you're Al Capone?"

'Something like that."

"Ok, I get it. That's a relief to be honest. Not as dirty as you could be."

"Gee thanks."

As they drove, they talked endlessly. They discussed their lives before and now and tried to make sense of the sudden change of circumstances. The miles just cascaded away as they chatted, only stopping once to refuel and get something to eat. Chris felt much more relaxed around Jason the more he learned about him and even started to like the guy. Under the gangster facade he was just a regular guy who happened to have been born into a life of organised crime. He never really had a chance to be anything else. His second coming changed all that until the night just gone.

"So can I ask you a couple of things that have been bothering me," Chris asked.

"Sure."

"What's your connection with Dr Chamberlain?"

Jason said nothing at first and seemed to tighten up in his seat somewhat, "I remember that guy. It was my mother's idea. Pride drove my father and he thought that I was insane because I stupidly talked about the future and what was going to happen. But then my mother decided a shrink was the best thing for me," Jason explained.

"I see, and the John Lennon remark?"

"The what?" Jason asked with a guilty tone in his voice.

"I saw Chamberlain too and he told me about the death of John Lennon years ahead of when it happened. I saw your file, well to be totally upfront, we took it upon ourselves to look at Chamberlain's files and there was a note in yours saying he should ask me about John Lennon, why would you do that? And how did you know about me back then anyway?"

"OK, I was so bored I started looking for people like us as soon as I could move about and found the articles about your super brain long ago. Then, coincidentally, I was at Chamberlain's office, and he had files on his desk. He didn't try to hide them. Probably thought I couldn't read, and I saw yours. I told him to ask you about the death of John Lennon. He kind of freaked out when he realised, I was reading confidential information," laughed Jason.

"You still haven't explained why," repeated Chris.

"I wanted the doctor to believe me. I didn't want to be alone in all of this. I was a stupid kid. It was not my intention to blow the lid on you, I just saw your file and said, ask him about John Lennon and told him the story of Lennon's murder. He didn't believe me of course, but he must have asked you and, well, when you said what I said, I'm sure he shit himself."

"He sure did. Thanks for that."

"Sorry."

"So, did it work? Did he believe you?" asked Chris.

"I don't know. Not long after that I stopped seeing him. Dad tore strips off my mother for letting someone else into our affairs. They had a raging fight about it. Mum's not meek."

"Did your father hurt Chamberlain?"

"I don't know; I never knew much about that side of Dad's business. He died while I was still young, and Mum took over. She was tough but not mean, if you get my drift."

"I think I do."

"But I think Chamberlain must have said something that upset my father, so I guess something went down after that. Probably told him I was a psycho or something. Dad would have freaked. You don't disgrace family; you know what I'm saying?"

"Yeah." Chris paused then said, "Chamberlain died, very suddenly and unexpectedly. That sound like your dad?"

"Perhaps. He never discussed the bad stuff in the open. But I wouldn't put it past him. He was a tough dude."

"How did he die," Chris asked Jason.

"Who? Chamberlain? I don't know."

"No, your father, how did he die?"

"Heart attack. Heavy drinker and smoker and a dicky ticker. Dead before he hit the floor, in both timelines."

"I'm sorry."

"Don't be. It was better for all of us in the end. He was a prick in both timelines; to my mother and to me and to everyone else. He probably would have been bumped off eventually anyway," and Jason forced out a laugh.

"One more question if you don't mind," Chris asked.

"Go for it."

"Milne doesn't sound Italian?!"

"My mother's idea of a fresh start. The family name was Milano, so we altered it to sound more innocent. She was an Aussie, so it made sense."

"I see that. Thanks for being up front. And your mother?"

"Retired from the business, but then after last night, who knows. Haven't had a chance to check, given everything you and I have been dealing with since we woke up."

"Fair point."

"I hope you got what you wanted," added Jason.

"Yeah, I did."

Chris was now convinced that Jason Milne was not his enemy and never had anything to do with his parent's deaths but that still left the question of who killed his parents and the mystery man at the school the day the media pounced on him. Did it mean anything? He didn't have a clue. Maybe they were just quirks of fate. It was too long ago now and whatever happened overnight had changed his personal history anyway, so did it really matter? While it was all part of his memory it wasn't now part of this timeline. Chris was so very confused and desperate for some kind of clue as to what was happening.

After about four hours they were in Canberra. Jason drove straight through the city and up the winding road through the Brindabella Ranges to Australia Observatory, "So here we are, time for you to do your stuff!"

"My stuff?"

"Yeah, chew the fat with the star man and see what shit went down last night."

"I'll do my best," Chris said, and he knew exactly how he would start the conversation.

Chapter 13

Chris and Jason hastened to the front desk inside the observatory, where a receptionist waited, "Can I help you?"

"Yes, I'm Chris Parish and this is my friend Jason Milne. We're here to see Dr Fred Wilson. Is he available? we're not expected."

"May I tell him what this is about?"

"Yes, tell him we're visiting astronomers, and we have a theory about inter-dimensional space, and we feel Dr Wilson can help with our theory. I know we should have called first, but we had a few hours before our flight, so..."

Jason's expression was one of astonished confusion. Chris just winked as the girl picked up the phone.

"I'm sorry, where are you from?"

"Sydney," Chris replied which told the girl nothing.

"Just a moment please," said the girl professionally as she dialled, "Hello Dr Wilson. There's a Chris Parish here to see you. He wants to talk about inter-dimensional space," There was a pause then, "Yes, ok sir. Thank you". She hung up the phone and looked at Chris, "He'll be right down, please take a seat," and she waved them toward a row of chairs near the sidewall of the foyer.

Chris and Jason just stood waiting; they were too agitated to sit.

"Where the Hell did you come up with that intermodal crap just then," Jason said under his breath.

"Inter-dimensional space. It's one of his personal theories, so I used it to get his attention."

"Ah, good thinking," Jason added.

Chris looked around, noticing the photos on the walls, all kinds of nebula, planets, stars, the Moon and the Earth as seen from the Space. Some were prints of original photographs like the ones taken by the Apollo missions while others were artists impressions, he was sure. Either way, they were spectacular.

A few minutes later a tall, thin, balding man appeared, around 40 years of age. He wore a long sleeve business shirt that looked like it was in dire need of ironing, with coffee stains around the top two buttons and his trousers were grey slacks that looked at least two sizes too large and flapped over his well scuffed leather shoes, "Hello, I'm Dr Wilson, you must be Chris Parish?"

"Yes sir, it's a great pleasure to meet you. This is Jason, my...colleague."

"Wonderful to meet you Chris and Jason," and he offered his hand which they both shook, "Please come this way. Can I get you something? Coffee? Tea?"

"Oh yeah, coffee would be great," answered Jason.

Fred looked at the girl who was already on the move, "In my office please Tracey."

"Yes Doctor," she replied.

The trio worked their way through a myriad of corridors and offices. There were people here and there, but Chris thought it was oddly vacant, "Not many people here Doctor?"

"No, we're Government funded and that generally means we suffer through budget cuts like so many other Government institutions. Science doesn't really rock their world I'm afraid, but we do our best with what we've got."

"Well, I can tell you it will get better in years to come," Chris replied which caused Doctor Wilson to look back with an odd expression, "Sorry, I will explain," Chris added.

"I can't wait to hear about your theories on Inter-dimensional space. It's one of my pet subjects," said the Doctor.

Jason looked at Chris clearly impressed by his astronomical prowess.

They finally reached the end of another corridor, and the Doctor popped the lock on a door, and they all entered an office that Chris thought was way too small and messy for someone who was trying to unlock the secrets of the Universe but then he wondered what kind of office someone like that would need?

Doctor Wilson moved two chairs to the edge of his desk and offered them to Chris and Jason while he swung around to the other side and took his own seat, "So, here we are," Fred announced trying, to break the ice.

"Yes indeed," said Chris and there was an awkward silence which left them all feeling a little embarrassed.

"So, tell me about your ideas on my Inter-dimensional theory," asked the Doctor.

"Look Doctor Wilson, you're going to think my friend and I are crazy", Jason announced, "We aren't astronomers or anything like that." Jason noticed Fred's sudden uncertainty so he kept talking, "What we have experienced is nothing short of sensational and probably would be better placed within the realm of science fiction, but I can assure you we're here to tell you the truth. In fact, we need your help. We know things; things that people just shouldn't know and it's not, like mind reading or anything. It's because we've been through it all before. That's why we needed to talk to you. We need answers!"

Chris looked at Jason in total astonishment. He was ready to lead the conversation, but Jason just took control and the ice was well and truly broken, albeit in a very confusing way.

Doctor Wilson was clearly taken aback too, "So you're not here about inter-dimensional space?"

"Yes and no Doctor," said Chris, "Look, maybe I should start at the very beginning, tell you my story and, well Jason can tell his, then you can decide whether we're freaks or if there really is something to what we say. I know how this must sound right now and, well, I'd probably think us both mental cases too. All I'm asking is for you to hear what I have to say and whatever you decide I will accept," Chris explained looking at Jason who nodded in agreement, then added, "And being a man of science and someone who looks into the unknown every day, I'm sure you will be opened minded enough to at least hear us out."

Dr Wilson peered at both men, clearly sceptical and probably ready to call security but then said, "I honestly have no real idea what you're talking about or why you're both here, but I confess you have my attention and you're right, as an astronomer I agree that we know so little and see so much that cannot be explained. I must concede that point, so I will listen to your stories. Go ahead."

"OK," Chris said as he took a deep breath, "In 2014 I was swept back in time by what I believe was a Sun spike created by a miniature black hole. Jason here had a similar experience. We came back and began our lives again with all the knowledge we gained in our former timelines and have been living like that for over two decades but that all changed last night."

"Wait a minute. You went back in time?"

"Yes, I believe so. At least that's what we think happened but we're open to other ideas which we're hoping you may be able to shed some light on."

"And what happened last night," Dr Wilson asked.

"We don't know but it was like something changed in the current timeline which distorted our reality and everything we knew. We somehow transitioned into an alternative timeline...again. My job, the company I worked for, no longer exists and Jason woke up in an alternative reality which was like his previous life. We just woke up and our lives just didn't exist anymore; well not like they were yesterday. It's hard to explain."

Dr Wilson was listening, but Chris couldn't tell whether he was interested or thought they were just stone-cold nuts!

"This must all sound so weird, but I assure you it's true. These Sun spikes were happening all over the world or will happen. You were on radio talking about them and had a theory that they were caused by small black holes hitting the Sun releasing the spikes and potentially distorting space and time."

"But I've never been on radio."

"Not yet Dr Wilson, but you will. I know how hard this is, but please you have to listen to us."

Just then Tracey turned up with their coffee and a tray of biscuits, Family Assortments; no expense spared in a government facility it seemed, "Thank you," said Fred, as Tracy turned and closed the door as she left.

With coffee served and everyone settled in Fred sat back and looked Chris squarely in the eye, "Right then future boy, tell me everything from the start; both of you and let's see if we can't get to the bottom of this."

Chris started again and left out nothing. He told him about winning at the casino and the penthouse suite where he took a bath and was suddenly thrust into a dark tunnel and when he came out the other side, he was a newborn and it was 1962, but he had all the memories and knowledge he'd gained in the fifty-two years he'd already lived. He took his time, spelling it all out right up to the previous evening when he went to bed with his wife and then woke to an augmented reality with the life he knew totally extinguished, except for his memories.

Jason's story was much the same and he took less time to explain with Chris doing most of the heavy lifting.

As they talked through their respective journeys the Doctor sat quietly, listening intently, taking in every word.

It took them both about 45 minutes to explain everything they knew, "So that's the story Doctor, what do you think," Chris asked finally.

Doctor Wilson sat up and clasped his hands together and rested his elbows on the desk, "Well I have to say I don't know what to think. I mean it sounds so fantastic."

"Do you believe us?"

"Oh yes, yes indeed. Who could make up a story like that," Dr Wilson replied.

"I'm so relieved and I know it's probably impossible right now, but do you have any ideas about what happened and what seems to be happening again?"

"Maybe. The Sun spikes theory, I can buy that and, well, here you are living proof so I must have been right or will be. What confuses me is the time shift. I have always believed that if time travel were possible, you could only go forward, not backwards but you appear to have done just that."

"Yes, that's indeed the case," Chris confirmed, "But what if it wasn't time travel but a shift between parallel universes?"

"Now that is fascinating but almost impossible to prove. Multiple Universe theory is, well, just that, a theory. We have no proof that there are other Universes."

"Not yet, but in 2014 there are you were starting to put it together and lots of scientists were starting to believe it was likely that multiple universes exist."

"Really? How interesting. Well let's assume for a moment that there are multiple Universes, why would a Sun spike that disturbed time send you into another Universe? It doesn't add up to me. The spikes happened within this one Universe, so I would theorise that you are still in the same Universe."

"Yes, but if the Sun spikes were caused by black holes, would it be possible that these spikes were in fact wormholes? And if they were wormholes, couldn't they link different universes?"

"Honestly Chris, I wouldn't dismiss anything, but you have combined several theories into one concept which stretches the possibilities into an improbability in my opinion. There are just too many unproven options going on there."

"You think so," Chris asked.

"I do. You have been thrust backwards somehow and because you have lived and gained knowledge before it simply came with you. You and Jason are somehow repeating your lives over again in the same Universe, I think. It makes more sense to me than crossing a Universal threshold. What says the other Universes are carbon copies of our own? The probability is they are not at all like ours. Assuming they exist, it's likely they're as different to ours as the planets and stars are different from our Earth and our Sun. Unless of course these multiple universes exist within each other rather than existing side by side but still the Sun spikes shot out and struck the planet which doesn't suggest any break in the fabric of the Universe."

"But if I know you like I think I do; you cannot be totally sure."

"That's true, it is indeed possible that things aren't cut and dried and things are happening that we can't possibly comprehend. You may well be in some weird Universe that looks like ours, but when you break it all down, you must go with the simplest explanation probably being the right one," Fred explained.

"Occam's razor," Chris suggested.

"Precisely!"

Jason just sat there with his mouth agape and was clearly losing track of the conversation.

Chris continued, "That's a relief because I was starting to think that my wife and I weren't, you know, each other's original partners, if I'd jumped from one Universe to another. Does that make sense?"

"Hmm, I never thought of that. I can see that would be something of a traumatic revelation, if it were true but I suspect we're still all on the same plane. This is your Universe. It has to be. Everything that happened occurred in this Universe. You have simply slipped back in time somehow."

"OK, let's go with that for now. What about last night. How is it we were living one life and suddenly, it's all gone. Today, this world isn't the same as the one we were in yesterday. Another Sun spike maybe?"

"Unlikely," suggested Dr Wilson who then paused to let his mind tumble with ideas.

"What are you thinking Doc," asked Jason

"Well again, just a theory but you both got hit by Sun spikes we think, so you got jumped back in time to your respective birth dates, right?" Both men nodded, "OK, so what if it happened to someone else after you but they flashed back to a time before you were born again in this timeline. They could have conceivably disrupted what was normal for you and set off a chain of events that created the world you woke up in today."

Both Chris and Jason were stopped dead in their tracks. It hadn't occurred to either of them that their worlds could have been altered in the past and thus not exist now despite them experiencing it for all of their second lives,

"So, if that's true, how is it we remember everything about both our timelines and life experiences and the people we know, don't," Chris asked but before Dr Wilson could say a word Chris had another thought, "And these Sun spikes happened around the same time for all of us so how could we have lived our new lives for so long before someone else got jumped back. It doesn't add up."

"That my friend is the sixty-four-thousand-dollar question," said Dr Wilson, " however, you don't know if those Sun spikes didn't come and go for years after you were flashed back."

"But that then suggests time as we know it is all wrong and that our old timeline is still running. Wouldn't that mean we are in a different Universe or a different time frame, independent of another?"

"I still don't believe so. I think it's more likely that time is not a constant, that we can live within one timeline but at different points. That everything is happening in time all at once." Dr Wilson could see the confusion on both their faces, "OK think of it this way. You are living now but, if I'm right, all the people in history are living their respective lives now at different points in time. For you Napoleon is dead but he's still alive right now, but in the 1800s. Does that make sense?"

"Jesus!" blurted Jason.

Chris ignored the remark, "That's starting to sound as complex as my multiple universe theory which you yourself debunked a few minutes ago. What about Occam's razor," Chris suggested.

"I see your point but let me ask, which of you came back first?"

The pair looked at each other, "Me," Jason said pointing to himself.

"Ok consider this," suggested Dr Wilson, "It wouldn't make sense that getting spiked back suddenly meant that your old timeline stopped being, otherwise you Chris would have vanished from existence when Jason was flashed back, you see my point?"

Chris absorbed the idea, "So the timeline has to exist within itself and we're just travellers caught in a fluke event and someone else got flashed back well ahead of us and changed something to create another reality, which only we are aware of," Chris announced.

"Precisely!" added Dr Wilson.

"Wait a minute," Jason said, "Does that mean that someone else could be spiked back sometime in the other reality's future and change things again in the now?"

"Well, yes, I do think that's indeed possible, assuming these Sun spikes keep or kept on happening but there's really no way of knowing if they lasted a few weeks or a few years or longer," explained Fred.

"Yes, there is," Chris said excitedly.

"How?" asked Jason.

"We find the person who created this variation of our new timeline and ask them!"

Dr Wilson looked at Chris, eyes wide open, "That could work, but how do you find them?"

"Easy, we just look for the richest and most powerful person on the planet that we'd never heard of yesterday," suggested Chris.

Dr Wilson pondered for a moment, "It does appear that being spiked somehow made you immune to any of the memory changes after an alteration in the timeline, however it also means that when things changed again, the reality you are in now wasn't part of your life, so everything is suddenly alien. It's all so very odd and very confronting."

"Spot on Doc," suggested Jason and the three sat silently for a few moments as the possibilities swirled around in their collective minds.

"Thank you, Dr Wilson," said Chris as he reached out to shake hands.

"My pleasure Chris, good luck to both of you. And call me Fred, I think we've reached a point where we can use first names."

"Ok, thank you Fred, I promise to keep you up to date with everything, assuming something doesn't change that wipes this meeting from your existence," and they both smiled knowingly.

Chris turned to leave then paused, "By the way Fred, The International Astronomical Union is going to debate the status of Pluto in years to come. In 2006 it will be reclassified as a Dwarf Planet. You might want to see what else is out there. Just saying," Chris suggested with a smile.

This time Fred was speechless with a gaping mouth.

"Goodbye sir," said Chris as Jason waved and they left the office and headed down the corridor.

"Why did you tell him that," Jason asked.
"He deserves to make a discovery. I just gave him a helping hand. It's the least we can do. He helped a lot today."

"He did?"

"Yes, we know what to look for now."

"And what is it we're looking for?"

"Someone rich and powerful. Someone who didn't make the papers yesterday, but you can bet they're all over them today."

Jason wasn't as sharp as Chris, but he was no idiot and he understood what Chris was saying, "Shouldn't be too difficult but once we find out who it is, what then?"

"We arrange a meeting. I'm sure they won't mind talking to people with the same experiences as they've had."

"Well, if they do have an issue, I can sort them out."

Chris shot a scornful look at Jason.

"I'm just kidding Chris, chill Man."

With that they were out of the building, in the car and headed home.

They agreed to start the search the very next day and see if they could find the person who came back and changed their world.

When they finally got back to Sydney both were very tired. Jason dropped Chris off to collect his car, and both agreed to talk in the morning,

"I'm going to have some explaining to do when I get home," suggested Chris.

"Anything I can do to help?"

"No, she doesn't know about you at this stage, so I'll tell her and hopefully I'll convince her that what I'm saying is real."

"Ok, good luck with that. See you tomorrow."

"Right, bye Jason."

With that Jason Milne screeched away in the Rolls and vanished into the bowels of the casino. Chris got in his car and headed home trying to think how he might be able to persuade Judy about everything that had happened. It wouldn't be easy, but he had to try.

When Chris got home Judy was sitting in front of the TV, "Hi, I'm home," he said.

She looked up at him, "There's food in the fridge if you're hungry."

Chris was relieved that her mood seemed to have eased to mild irritation and even though he was exhausted he was determined to have the conversation he needed to have, "I'm not hungry, had something on the road."

She didn't look up from the TV.

"How was work," Chris asked.

"Oh, everyone was worried about you. Including me," This time she cut him a scornful glance.

"Yeah, sorry about that. Look we need to talk and you're not going to like it, but you have to listen...please."

"Chris, I don't know what happened this morning. You acted like you were from another planet. You've never taken a sickie before. What's going on," The scowl on Judy's face unmistakable.

"You're going to find this hard to believe and you're going to still think I'm a fruitcake but everything I'm going to tell you is true. All I ask is that you listen and then decide whether or not I'm a crackpot. Can you do that," Chris asked while his stomach churned.

She looked at him closely, "You look like my Chris, but I don't know for sure. My Chris wouldn't dump his wife on the curb and rack off to wherever you went. For the record I'm still angry and I think you skipped work to go to the races, just so you know. But ok, I'll listen."

"Thank you," Chris said, and he drew a deep breath.

"Oh gee, this must be serious. How much did you lose this time?"

"What? Nothing! I wasn't at the track or at the casino." Chris hesitated, "Well I was at the casino, but I didn't bet. I was there to see someone."

"Yeah right. You're off to a great start with this explanation."

"Ok, I can understand your speculation but I'm not the guy you think I am. Up until yesterday we were blissfully happy, and we were very well off, rich in fact and ready to have a baby."

That remark saw Judy's head whip around again, this time in total shock. Now she was interested.

"Right, so here's the thing…" Chris began.

He started from scratch just like he had with Dr Wilson and like he did with Judy when they met previously in this timeline. He went into every detail and was careful to spell it all out so that Judy would hopefully understand. He wanted so much for her to believe him again, like that first time when she said she just knew about him, but it didn't feel the same this time. She'd had, as of now, several years of the old Chris to reflect on. The liar, the gambler and the lazy shit who didn't help around the house. If he failed here, he didn't know what he would do.

After what seemed like an eternity he finished.

"So that's the story. Dr Wilson thinks that this timeline has been altered by another like me and like Jason who came back before us and changed everything somehow. We woke up this morning retaining everything we knew only to find that what we knew didn't exist anymore and you have clearly lived a life that I have no recollection of whatsoever. I am not the man you think I am and I do not gamble, not anymore. I had something great going. I was working for a very advanced organisation, and we were doing good things and now that's all just disappeared. I still can't get my head around it. That's it, that's the whole story," Chris concluded.

Judy sat silently through the whole presentation without uttering a word or giving away any hint of an emotion. She'd listened intently from go to woe absorbing the information and was now crunching it in her head. Chris didn't push, he just let her think it over anticipating the best but fearing the worst,

"So, this Dr Wilson, what did he say when you told him all this?"

"He said it was too complex a story not to be true. He believed me. He saw it from a scientific perspective and worked through some theories. In his line of work, these are things that are plausible."

"And this Jason Milne. You said he was a thug, a bad man in the other time you, lived before being, what was it? Spiked?"

"Yes and no. He owns the casino, several casinos and had a reputation for being a crook, but after spending time with him and his choices he's made in this timeline, I've changed my mind. He and I are in the same boat, and I think we need each other right now."

"I see and what about The Boss of Parallax. What do you think happened to her?"

"That's a good question but I suspect that whoever came back and caused the changes probably made her redundant. She's probably out there somewhere, making do with the knowledge she has but if someone got a twenty-year head start on her, then she probably didn't have the opportunities she had before BUT like me and like Jason, I suspect she woke up this morning in shock; thrust into an alternative life without any idea what happened or why. She must be as confused as us," Chris added.

"Right, so you're telling me you lived a shitty life, with me and at 52, poof, you got zapped back and started again, knowing everything you knew in the first timeline, right?"

"Yes."

"So, when you came back you made amends with me, your parents died but we had a good life?"

"Yes."

"And we were going to have a baby?"

"Yes."

"And overnight that all just evaporated and you woke up to this life, something like it was the first time around when we hated each other and fought and were bankrupt?"

"Um, yes, that pretty much sizes it up."

"And you expect me to believe this whole story?"

"I hoped you would. I have everything pinned on it. You are the only person I can really trust."

"What about Jason," Judy said with a look of disdain this time.

"I don't absolutely trust him just yet. I just know we both need to work together to find whoever caused this. They're probably oblivious to what they've caused. Only people like me and Jason, The Boss and anyone else that got spiked back, if there are any more, would be in this position but you are the one I love and trust. It's just you, it always will be," Chris said sounding more desperate than ever.

Judy was thinking again, "I don't know Chris. You've blown it so many times. How do I know this isn't just some elaborate snow job?"

"I'll prove it."

"How?"

"I don't know yet, but I will. How much do we owe on the house?"

"What?"

"How much?"

"In round figures? About eighty thousand, give or take…"

"OK, I'll have that paid off tomorrow."

She looked at him with a face that clearly suggested he was off his tree, "Yeah right!"

"I mean it. I can make our debts disappear in a day."

"How?"

"I have knowledge. I know things that no-one knows. I can make that work for me."

"You mean gambling, right?"

"I'm afraid so. It's how I got started before and it worked but once I got things where I wanted them, I stopped. It no longer controls me, I…"

"STOP! I don't want to hear it. I want to believe you but it all sound so ridiculous. I can't accept it; I just can't and now you want to gamble again; to prove you're not a gambler. It's sounds like a complete fabrication and exists only in your mind. That's what I think."

Chris was devastated but wasn't going to let up. He had one more ace up his sleeve, "Ok, I understand. I've let you down, again and you're right to be angry and in the future, I'll let Caleb down too."

Chris had kept the baby's name out of his explanation, hoping it would be the key to getting through to her if he needed it, and he needed it now.

"What did you say?"

"I said I let you down."

"No, not that, who's Caleb?"

"Our son, or he will be in about a year from now, assuming we time it right."

Judy sat, eyes wide open, totally shocked, "How could you know that name. I was only thinking about names the other day and that was one of my favourites, but I hadn't told you anything or anyone else. I hadn't even written anything down."

"Quite unlike you, I know how you love lists, but there it is. I know because we've been through all this before. I'm telling the truth, I really am."

"It makes no sense. It's not possible," Judy said still perplexed.

"I know, but it's entirely true, everything I've said, including us having a boy and naming him Caleb. If we time it right."

"What do you mean time it right?"

Chris again found himself explaining the timing of conception and the probabilities and Judy listened again but this time she was on the same page and when Chris finished this time,

"Oh my God!"

She thrust herself up off the lounge and gave Chris a crushing hug, "I'm sorry I doubted you. I must have been a real bitch."

"It's Ok, how could you have known and living these last few years with a total prick, well I had my work cut out."

"Even now I can see you're different. There's something more mature about you. I didn't see it before."

"Why would you? The Chris you knew yesterday wasn't like me. This is all so weird."

"Yeah, it sure is."

Judy and Chris talked for several more hours, both exhilarated by the conversation and thrilled to have a fresh start, again in Chris's case. He didn't tell her that this could all happen again at a moment's notice. He didn't think it worth worrying her, but it certainly bothered him. Eventually fatigue got the better of both and they went to bed. Just before Judy went to sleep, she asked, "So you'll pay the house off tomorrow?"

Chris smiled to himself, "Sure, why not!"

Chapter 14

Next morning Chris went to the casino to meet Jason Milne. He was sent straight up to the penthouse, no questions asked. When he stepped out of the elevator and walked into the main part of the living area Jason was nowhere to be seen, "Jason?"

"Just a tick mate, getting dressed."

Chris looked towards the bedroom where the door was ajar and spotted two naked women on the bed and Jason zipping up his fly. He spotted Chris and winked cheekily before making his way into the kitchen.

"I see you've settled back into your old life very quickly," Chris suggested.

"Yeah well, it did have its perks. Hey, they're still up for it if you want to…."

"No thanks, happily married."

"Ah so you got that sorted out, eh?"

"Yes. It took some hard talking but we're on the same page again, which is quite a relief."

"Coffee," Jason asked.

"Yeah great. Thanks."

As Jason prepared the coffee he chatted about the events of the day before and what might be the best course of action, "I think it's a good idea to look into whoever caused all this and meet them if we can, but I wonder what will come of it?"

"What do you mean," Chris asked

"Well think about it. If they're unaware of the changes they've caused, then why would they care and what could they do about it? In real terms there's nothing that can be done. What has happened is a new reality so the world we're in now isn't going to switch back to the way it was before; like never!"

Chris was a little surprised by Jason's train of thought. Maybe he was sharper than he seemed, "I know that, but I think meeting this person might open some doors for us. We have a lot to offer, we have knowledge. I don't know about you, but I'm broke…again and I want my new life back. I loved what I was doing and the money I was making, and I owe it to Judy."

"I get that, but what if they see us as a threat? Did you think of that?"

Chris didn't say anything for a moment, "Um, no, I didn't."

"Well, that's the kind of thing I have to consider all the time in this line of work," and he motioned around the room, clearly indicating his empire, "And people who are mega successful tend not to like to share their toys. Maybe we'll be more of a problem than an opportunity. We don't know anything about this person. It could be a minefield for us."

"So, what do you suggest?"

"Well, we should track them down for sure but not meet until we've learned more about them. We must know who we're dealing with. Make sense?"

Chris had to concede Jason's point of view, "Yeah, it does."

"Ok, good," replied Jason, "So how do we find this guy?"

"Well, we can start with newspapers, business sections; probably the financial publications and papers with more of an upscale target group, there'll have to be something there. We just have to look for a corporation that we've never heard of that is an economic giant."

"Well, that should be easy. The papers are over there, got delivered an hour ago. Have at it."

"You haven't looked?"

"I was a bit busy," said Jason and he winked again.

"Right," Chris said with a smile as he headed for the kitchen table. He grabbed a paper and started thumbing through the pages. Nothing much stood out at first, just regular news on the first few pages but then he spied something odd, "Hey, this looks interesting. Aussie company on the Verge of AI breakthrough, it's in their technology section."

"AI, like artificial intelligence. It's 1987, that couldn't be happening yet. It's like…" Jason pondered.

"Thirty years too soon. Could just be journalistic licence but I suspect not."

"Who is it?"

Chris scoured the text just as Jason handed him his coffee, "Jesus Christ!"

Jason balked, spilling the coffee on the floor, "What, who is it?"

"It's not the who, it's the what?"

"Eh, what do you mean?"

"It's Parallax!"

Jason stood motionless for a second or two, "Are you kidding?"

"No, it's there in black and white," and Chris read the passage aloud,

In what technicians have described as a technological breakthrough, the Parallax Corporation claims to have developed the very first quantum supercomputer with artificial intelligence. A corporation spokesman says the company has been working on the project in secret for ten years and has made huge strides in supercomputing during that time. Parallax says this technology will change the lives of people around the World because the computer will be free thinking and will be able to learn, making its own decisions. The company hopes to create a worldwide network of supercomputers designed to learn from each other. The hope is that these machines will give companies and individuals a new way of analysing everyday problems and find solutions to things as small as the household budget right through to international relations and medicine. Parallax is planning a demonstration at its international headquarters in Sydney tomorrow.

"Does it say who is behind all of this?"

"Nope. The Parallax I knew always associated an announcement with the developer and they tended to be put up for interviews and comment, mainly department heads. The place was an open book when they wanted things to be known although The Boss never did any of that for obvious reasons, she valued her anonymity. It protected her from potential threats, so she said."

"Makes sense but she could never have predicted what happened two nights' ago."

"That's true."

"What else does it say?"

"Nothing much, just the address and time. It's an open invitation, so they're obviously keen to show off their new toys to anyone who wants to go along. Odd though, I don't recognise the address."

"Great, I'm guessing we'll be there?"

"Damn right we will," said Chris.

"Cool, so that means we're free and clear until tomorrow. What do you want to do," Jason asked, nodding towards the bedroom with a smirk on his dial.

"God no! I promised Judy I'd pay off the house. I wanted to prove I was telling the truth."

"And how were you going to do that?"

"A few well-placed bets but it's Thursday so I don't have much to go on."

"Don't worry, I'll spot you until you can win some cash."

"Oh no, that's not necessary."

"I know, but I want to. Look, we got off to a rough start, but I think we're on the same page now. Let me do this. It's a loan and you can take as long as you like to pay me back. I'm serious."

"And you won't send the boys after me?"

Jason laughed very loudly which stirred up his two companions in the bedroom, "Of course not. The heavyweights are only window dressing, most of the time. I want to do this, to seal our friendship. Besides, I've got more money than I can shake a stick at. You don't think those girls are in there because of this face, do you?"

Chris was apprehensive but he did feel that the two of them had bonded given their circumstances, "Ok, I accept."

"Awesome! Um, how much do you need."

"About a million, give or take," Chris suggested.

"Ok, no worries," Jason replied without a hint of hesitation.

"I'm kidding, it's eighty thousand."

"Ha, good one. In that case, consider it a gift. It's chump change. Take it."

"You're acting all weird Jason. This doesn't feel right. I can't just take your money."

"Let's just say that living a second then a third life has opened my eyes somewhat. If I can't help you, then what's the point. And you know what, it feels good."

"If I didn't know any better, I'd say you're on something."

"Oh Chris, don't spoil the moment man. Let me do this, please. I've never really had any friends in my life. My circumstances didn't allow it. Just hangers on and, companions," again he nodded to the bedroom where the girls were sitting up in all their glory much to Chris's embarrassment.

"I get that, but gifting money is too friendly Jason. Let's just call it a loan, ok?"

Jason looked at Chris and nodded, "OK, a loan. Zero interest and a lifetime to pay me off."

Chris realised there was no arguing with Jason about money. His pillow was probably stuffed with million-dollar notes anyway. The deal was done, and the pair spent the rest of the morning scouring papers for any more information about the 'new' Parallax. Similar articles were in a few papers but there was nothing substantial to help them learn anymore and no photos either. All very peculiar.

Later they arranged for the loan money to be wired to Chris and Judy's bank with instructions to pay off the debt and release the title deed to Mrs Parish once the legals had been taken care of. Chris felt great but then realised he would have to lie, "How do I explain this to Judy?"

"I've got an idea Chris," Jason blurted.

"What's that?"

"How about you come work for me, as my personal advisor or something."

"Firstly, that's a bad idea, secondly, Judy would never go for it given my gambling history and thirdly, what could I possibly advise you on?"

"Whether to jump the blonde or the brunette first; I don't know but you need a job, and I need you. It's that simple."

Chris was mortified, "Geez Jason, you know what they say about friends becoming work partners?"

"No, what do they say?"

"I can't remember but it never ends well."

"That's just some crap you read in a fortune cookie or something. Look, you need a job and I'm giving you one. Take it or take it," he said with a smile.

"And how will I explain it to Judy?"

"Normally I'd say, not my problem but how about you tell her I want you for your brain, to help me develop new ideas for the business beyond my casino empire. Make something up. I'll pay you handsomely."

"I don't know Jason; I need to think about it."

"Well, the offer is on the table. And I won't take no for an answer."

"Gee thanks. You do know that's not how friendship works right?"

"How would I know that," Jason said with a laugh.

"Good point. I'll talk to her after work. Now that she realises, I'm genuine, she might go for it. She doesn't know your history as such, so that might help. I can't believe I'm getting into bed with you."

Jason smiled, "Hey there are worse things and besides, who else have you got in this World?"

"That's very true."

"Come on, lunch is on me, then we can discuss your new job and work something out to tell your wife."

"OK, sounds good."

"As they headed for the lift Jason called to his other friends, "Make yourselves at home girls, I'll be back later. Call downstairs for anything you want."

"Thanks Jase," came the weary reply.

"They'll probably sleep all day; they had a busy night."

"I've heard enough," Chris said.

"Ok, no worries."

That night Chris went home, armed with the proposal that he and Jason hatched about the fictitious job. Judy listened to what Chris had to say and when he revealed the salary, she was stunned, "He's going to pay you how much?"

"Two hundred thousand a year, for starters."

"Just to help him think?"

"Well yes, that's what I was doing before and I was earning ten times that much, but that was another life and another time. I've had to start again and, well this is it."

"And you're sure you can trust him?"

"I do have some misgivings but we're both in the same boat. He just happened to land in a boat full of cash. I lost everything and I almost lost you, again. He didn't have to do anything for me. We're kindred spirits I guess, so yeah, I trust him just enough."

"And what if he tires of you or decides he doesn't need you anymore?"

"That happens all the time in the business world, I'll deal with it. I'm sure I can use my talents elsewhere, if I must."

"I suppose so. Well, it's a lot of money and we could sure use it," Judy said.

"Oh, and the house is paid off. I guess they didn't tell you. It's done."

"Really?! You, did it?"

"Well Jason and I did it. I decided not to gamble. It's an advance really, so I suppose I do have to work for him for a while at least."

"No doubt about you. You said you would do it. I guess you found a better way, sort of," suggested Judy.

"True and you once said keep your enemies closer, so I took your advice."

"I said that?"

"In another life."

"Oh," both laughed, "You know, a day ago I thought we were headed for a divorce, but you are nothing like the old Chris. It's strange, I miss him, but I like the new model so much more. It's like the best of him just came to the surface and shut the rest down," Judy explained.

"That's probably true in a way. As for how it happened, we have a lead on that," Chris explained what he and Jason had learned about Parallax and their demonstration, "So we're going to see what they're all about. I wonder if I'll know anyone. It'll be so strange, but the weirdest part is that Parallax exists at all. I can't really understand it, but it must be more than a coincidence."

"Well, I've never heard of them but why would I? That's way above my pay grade," said Judy making them both laugh.

Once again, they chatted the night away, filling in some of the residual gaps in their lives, more for Judy's benefit than his but he felt it was important to strengthen their bond knowing that it could all vanish in a flash. Chris explained more about his two previous lives and Judy listened intently. It was such a thrill to have her on his wavelength again.

Despite that Chris slept restlessly, constantly fighting a repetitive dream where he vanished down a dark hole as Judy receded from his view. As much as he fought, he couldn't reach her, and she looked like she didn't care. He woke in a cold sweat, his stomach in knots as he realised that it was all just a nightmare. Still, his subconscious reacted to what it perceived as fear and sadness.

It was early but Chris decided to get up. He showered, dressed and was preparing breakfast when Judy woke, "You're up early."

"Yeah, wanted to surprise you."

"Mm, I am really loving this new guy in my life. Please don't go away."

"I'll try not to but it's in the lap of the Gods really," Chris noticed Judy's face sink a little, "Hey, don't worry, I'm not going anywhere." He gave her a hug and a kiss on the lips, "Come on, breakfast is done, burnt toast and shitty coffee."

Judy laughed, "Sounds great."

After they ate, Judy got ready for work and Chris drove her into the city, "We'll have to get a second car," he said.

"I guess so," she replied as he dropped her at the car park.

"Can you give this to, whoever is my boss in there," and he handed Judy an envelope, "it's my resignation."

"Oh! Right."

"I hope it's not awkward for you, me not giving notice."

"It'll be weird, but what can they do, sack you?"

"That's the spirit. Don't catch the train home, I'll pick you up, ok? 6 o'clock?"

"Really? That's sweet, see you then," and she blew him a kiss.

Chris drove away to meet Jason who was waiting outside the casino. He jumped straight into Chris's car.

"What a heap of shit," Jason said with a laugh.

"Yeah well, it's from a former life, so ease up."

"Oh, we have to do something about this," Jason suggested.

"What does that mean?"

"You're getting a company car, and one for the missus."

"Oh no, enough Jason, really!"

"Ok, just one for you then."

Chris was about to protest again but Jason put his hand up, blocking Chris's attempts to reject the offer, "We better leave if we're going to get to Parallax in time for their big reveal," Jason urged

"What do you mean, we've got almost two hours."

"Yeah, but we're in this thing!"

"Ha ha."

"Seriously though, park this heap and we'll take the Rolls."

"For once I agree with you."

After changing cars, they headed across town and Chris asked, "Why are we going so early? We'll be there way too soon."

"All part of my evil plan Wilson. We're going to case the joint and see what we can see."

Chris looked at Jason wide eyed, "Wow, you know that's a good idea!"

"Of course it is, Mindy suggested it."

"Who?"

"The blonde."

"Oh, ok. Enough said. No, wait, you told her?"

"Well, not everything, just that I was looking into this AI stuff to see how the casino might take advantage."

"Clever," said Chris.

"Thank you"

"I meant Mindy."

"Very funny!"

Both men laughed.

As the Parallax building came into view Chris was speechless. It was almost the same as the original Parallax building except for one or two things, "This is getting curiouser by the minute."

"You're not wrong. That's almost a replica of…"

Jason's words trailed off as they drew closer and took in the scene, "It's bigger, almost twice as big as before," Chris said.

"It definitely is!"

Jason drove straight up the main ramp towards the central foyer entrance.

"What are you doing? Way too conspicuous," Chris suggested.

"Relax, we're in a Rolls. Watch and learn!"

As they stopped a little man in a tidy maroon uniform and maroon cap opened the driver's door. Jason stepped out and Chris followed suit. The valet gave Jason a ticket, stepped into the car and drove off, "We're in."

Chris stood there in disbelief, "It shouldn't be that easy."

"That was the easy part truth be told, now you have to get us inside," Jason added.

"Me?"

"Of course. You are the former Parallax employee. Use what you know."

Jason was right. If this was the very same Parallax that he knew, then he should be able to get to someone significant but there was no telling who that might be.

They walked into the foyer. It was bustling with people. He recognised many of the building's features; the steel pylons and the thick plate glass panelling and that incredible vacant centre which reached the sky. Extraordinary to say the least and twice the height of the building he knew and had grown to love, which in real terms he'd only been in a few weeks before.

They walked towards the wide marble reception desk where two security guards eyed them suspiciously. Chris ignored them and made straight for one of the receptionists. The combination of tailored business attire, perfect hair, manicured nails and sublime make-up suggested she should be a world class model and not on a reception desk, even one as ornate as this. Chris noticed she was wired for sound and looked around. It appeared all the employees wore these little earpieces.

Bluetooth?

"Hi, I'm Matilda, how can I help you Gentlemen?"

"Yes, hello, I'm Chris Parish and this is my, um, boss Jason Milne. I'm hoping to talk to someone in charge. I used to work here, sort of."

The look on Matilda's face was something between shock and fear, "Chris Parish?"

"Yes, that's right!"

The girl immediately reacted to the confirmation of Chris's identity, "SECURITY!"

Before Chris could utter another word, the guards were all over him with what appeared to be Tasers, "Don't move!"

"Wait a minute guys," suggested Jason but they weren't listening.

One of the brutes tapped the thing on his ear and mumbled a few words, waited for a response and nodded as he received instructions. He then looked back at Chris and Jason as he lowered the Taser, "Wait here, someone's coming down for you."

"Who," asked Jason but no-one was talking.

Chris looked around and noticed several cameras in the lobby, too many for security only, they were eyes. One was pointed straight at his face, and he tried to look normal and smiled. He felt stupid.

A few moments later a young man approached. He was quite thin and had a spring in his step. His suit, despite the grey colour was practically glistening and almost outshone his black dress shoes but it was his tie that got Chris and Jason's attention, bright pink on a white business shirt which was no doubt silk.

"Gay," Jason whispered.

Chris just smiled.

As the man reached them, he held out his hand as if to shake in greeting but, then started waving his disapproval at the guards, "Oh please boys, no need to be rough, put those Tasers away." He looked towards Chris, "So hard to get good help these days," he said as he eyed the pair, "Mmmm very handsome. Better than I expected."

"You know me?"

"Sure love, everyone knows of the infamous Christopher Parish. I'm surprised you had the audacity to show your face here again."

"What? Look, I don't know what you're talking about. I've never been here before."

The man raised his hand to his chin, crossing his other arm over his chest and scrutinised Chris a bit more, "I find that incredibly hard to believe. To be honest we thought you were gone for good."

"Who's we? Are you in charge?"

"Oh God no, I'm just a roustabout, I answer to the Big Cheese."

"Ok, then I want to see him, or her."

"Oh my, forgotten already, have we? That just won't do. Come on, you have a lot to explain."

"Where are we going?"

"As if you didn't know," and the man walked away expecting Chris to follow.

"Told you, gay," whispered Jason again.

"Not a good time Jason," said Chris clearly agitated.

"Right, sorry."

They followed the suit to the elevator with the security guards on their heels. As much as Chris wanted to run away, he was keener to find out what the Hell was going on.

The doors of the lift opened, and the suit stepped in, followed by Chris and Jason. The security guards were about to do the same, "No! Back to your posts boys," said the suit and the duo retreated just as the doors closed.

"Aren't you worried that we'll beat the shit out of you," Jason asked.

"Oh Jason, if you try, I'll kill you with a flick of my wrist."

"How, how do you know my name?"

There was a slight shove as the lift began its ascent.
"Are you kidding? Don't play dumb, it's beneath you."

"I'm not playing dumb, I really have no idea what's going on," Jason exclaimed.

The suit just clicked his tongue emitting a tisk.

The lift was racing upwards at an incredible speed now, so much so that Chris could feel his body weight pressing into the balls of his feet. As it neared the very top, he felt it slow rapidly, and his weight momentarily reversed causing a flutter in his stomach.

"We really must get that fixed. These electromagnetic elevators are supposed to be so much smoother than that," said the suit.

The lift stopped with a very slight bounce and the doors opened. Chris and Jason stepped out closely followed by their chaperone, "This way," he said as he took the lead.

They followed him past a foyer where another receptionist sat, as well manicured as Matilda. She gazed at Chris as they walked by. The suit opened a secure door with some device on his wrist.

Smart watch?

They all entered what was a board room, "Please take a seat boys, she'll be with you shortly."

"Who is she?" they both asked in unison.

"Oh, you are funny, Abbott and Costello," he said and then the suit left.

As the door closed and the lock clicked Chris again did a quick scan, no cameras and no communications device on the table.

Before he could think on it further another door clicked and opened at the opposite end of the room and a little old lady in a wheelchair coasted into view, pushed by a middle-aged man. As they approach Chris looked at her closely, but he couldn't guess the woman's age and certainly didn't recognise her but the man pushing the wheelchair was vaguely familiar.

"Hello Chris, good to see you again," said the old lady. She looked at him closely, utter surprise briefly apparent on her own face which vanished very quickly.

"I'm sorry, but I don't think we've ever met."

"Oh, but we have and there's no sense pretending otherwise. Now where are my blueprints?"

"Um, blueprints?"

"Oh, stop it. You took them, I want them back. No point denying it. Now, where are they?"

Chris was totally confused and had to think fast. Given everything that had happened in the last couple of days, his timeline being extinguished and accusations that were clearly real to his hosts he considered a possibility, "Wait a minute. I'm probably not who you think I am; not the Chris Parish you know anyway. I woke up in this world of yours and I don't know much more than that. I have never seen you before Madam and never been here before."

"I see. I hoped it wouldn't be necessary, but I suppose we need to persuade you," and she tapped her wrist.

A second later another man entered the room with a briefcase which he raised then laid on the board room table. He popped the electronic locks with a wave of his wrist and the contents were revealed; several syringes and vials of various sizes with coloured liquids, blue, yellow and a deep red one that looked like blood.

"These will make you tell the truth," said the old lady.

"Ok, to be honest I have no issues with telling the truth because I know my truth but if you let me tell my story before juicing me up, you might not need that stuff," Chris suggested.

The woman mused at the remark for a moment, "Alright, you have five minutes. Talk!"

Chris realised he'd piqued her interest and decided he would tell his entire story from start to finish, making it as clear as possible that whoever she thought he was, he certainly was not the Chris Parish she had somehow encountered.

Like Dr Fred Wilson and his own wife, he took a great deal of time and care to put the story together. He was in dire need of a glass of water when he concluded which the middle-aged man was quick to realise, much to Chris's relief.

As he gulped down the ice-cold liquid the woman pondered, peering at the light blue carpet, which was astonishingly clean, Chris noticed.

Finally, she spoke, "So if I get the good doctor here to pump you with this stuff, we're going to hear a somewhat drunken version of the same story, right?"

"Yes," answered Chris.

"I see, well in that case we'll corroborate with your partner in crime," and she looked at Jason.

"Whoa, wait a minute, I'm the innocent party here. I've never had anything to do with Parallax. He and I only came together very recently, because of the circumstances he has so accurately regaled."

Regaled, Chris smiled inwardly despite the circumstances.

Jason continued, "So I don't think anything you do will change that story."

"And that's what I need to find out."

With that she tapped her wrist, and four men of gorilla-like stature came in, "Hold him," said the woman as she pointed to Jason.

Before he could flinch, they were on him and had all his limbs locked down tight while one held him in a headlock. The doctor or whatever he was took a large syringe and vacuumed up some of the dark red liquid, then added a touch of the blue which mixed into a purple cloud. He walked to Jason, smiled and then jammed the long needle into Jason's temple injecting the liquid directly into his brain. Jason was unconscious in a split second.

"Jesus," cried Chris, "Is he dead?"

No-one answered.

Chapter 15

When Jason came to, he looked around and the first person he saw was Chris.

"How do you feel," Chris asked.

"Like someone stabbed me in the head!"

Chris laughed, "Well that would be fairly accurate. Do you remember anything?"

"Not really. Has anyone got an aspirin?"

"Your headache will ease shortly Jason," said the old woman, "I'm sorry we had to do that, but I wanted to be certain that Chris was telling the truth."

"And was he? I mean did I back his story?"

"Well let's just say that what you know about Chris does indeed match his claims. It's impossible to lie with what we just did," said the lady.

"And what was that exactly," Chris asked.

"It's like a truth serum, which people have been using and developing for years, but ours was created right here and it's much more, how do I describe it? Liberating."

"So, I noticed."

"What did I say?" asked Jason.

"You pretty much told your story and the parts where we were both in the picture together confirmed what I said earlier. You did good Jason," explained Chris who then turned his attention back to the old woman, "So, now that we've cleared up some of your concerns, who are you exactly?"

"Well Chris it's complicated. I'm The Boss, or I was?"

"That can't be, The Boss was older than me, that's true but she wasn't..." Chris hesitated.

"A geriatric?"

"Well, yes, I guess so." He turned to the middle-aged man, "So, you must be John?"

"Hello Chris."

"Holy shit! You got old, I don't understand. When I saw you last which was only weeks ago, you were, what? Maybe 30," to which John simply smiled.

The Boss then interjected, "You didn't know everything we were doing at Parallax Chris. You worked on your projects and anything I asked you to do, but we were big, global in fact and some things were way above your pay grade, which is why we have this situation right here."

"What situation is that," Jason asked.

"I'll get to that, but first I need to know what you know about your version of Parallax. What were we doing with you Chris?"

"That's a weird question."

"Maybe, but you'll understand once I've heard what you have to say."

"Ok."

Chris began yet another story, explaining how he was head hunted and employed by Parallax. He explained how he oversaw several minor projects before being assigned the task of creating a working document to develop several concepts for use in the gambling industry. After that, the holiday and then wham, all gone. Chris didn't beat around the bush and told the story in plain and simple terms having been over much of this ground with her already, "...and when I tried to come back to work, there was no Parallax, not as I knew it anyway."

"I remember," she said, "but what if I told you that you did come back to work that day? Everything was normal and you slotted back in like everyone expected. We worked together for many years and made some great things together. You became my very best employee and got very rich in the process. It reached a point where I trusted you implicitly; I even told you my name," she explained.

"I don't remember any of this because it didn't happen."

"There's more. We were working on a major project, something that was going to change the World in ways that no-one could imagine but you weren't convinced that we should pursue it at all. It led to disagreements."

"What project?"

"We'd been working on solving the issue of the, what did you call them? Sun spikes. We wanted to see if they could be recreated and harnessed so we could use them. It took us some time, but we were on the cusp of success," she explained.

"Jesus! That was a very bad idea."

"Was it? Controlling time would be the ultimate tool and would enable us to save the planet, save the people, stop wars and assassinations, the World would be better off."

"Well, that could very well be debated until the end of time but I'm guessing something went wrong."

"Yes, you! You went wrong. We'd been working on the project for years but somehow you got wind of it. You stole the blueprints to the Parallax machine and disappeared."

"Me?! When did I do this?"

"In about 20 years from now."

"What?! I have no recollection of anything like that. I'm 25 years old and haven't lived my next twenty years yet, well not in this lifetime anyway. It can't have happened, can it?"

"It did happen Chris. I knew you as a colleague and friend of 20 years. I knew your wife, your son, Caleb and Jason here."

"Caleb?" "Me?" exclaimed Chris and Jason in unison.

"Yes."

"Wait a minute. If what you're saying is true, then how come you're back here now? What happened," Chris demanded.

"Well, that's where it gets messy. A few weeks ago, we fired up the prototype, intent on going back to where we could intercept you, so that the plans were never stolen. We were almost ready for a test anyway. You created the first real opportunity."

"You actually made a fully operational machine?"

"Yes, in secret of course. Only the necessary people knew about it or were supposed to know about it," she explained while firing a laser beam look at Chris then continued, "We set the machine to take us back 54 hours so we could stop you taking the blueprints, but…"

"It failed?"

"Yes and no, it did something, but it didn't take us back like we expected. It sent out bursts of energy which had some kind of effect on certain individuals."

"Which individuals?"

"The people I recruited for the project, Flashbacks like you, they vanished right in front of us one by one as the machine spooled up. It was like time ripped them away. The only theory we have is that they were sent back into their old lives again and started over."

"Bloody Hell," cried Jason.

"How many people are we talking about," Chris asked.

"27 in total."

"My God, how big was this machine?"

"Huge. We built it in seclusion, away from any potential physical impact points, at a place we knew was untouched for hundreds of years so that when we came back, we wouldn't merge with something in the past and end up like the Philadelphia Experiment. It's in the desert on a large tract of land that I own."

"I get it, out of sight, out of the Government's mind," Chris added.

"Yes, and it was big enough to carry people, equipment, cars, you name it. In simple terms it was designed to move us through time but not space, like a mirage in the desert."

"That's amazing," Jason blurted.

"Yes, and we were well prepared. We took spare parts, other equipment, computers, fuel cells and around 50 of the best minds I had, just in case," explained The Boss.

"Risky, but it makes sense. Flight of the Phoenix, sort of," added Chris.

"So, we tried to go back, but instead there was some kind of effect that caused those 27 people to vanish."

Chris looked at The Boss, "What about you? How come you didn't get sucked back, like the others you lost."

"We stopped the machine before I could be affected. The rest of us were relatively ok. We don't know why some vanished and not others. Probably an individual time variance of some kind."

"Jesus Christ," yelped Jason.

Chris too was utterly shocked, "It might have been better if you had let it run its course. Maybe you would have been sent back too and avoided this. It would have meant starting over perhaps but then, who can be sure?"

"That's why I want the blueprints. I need the machine working again. If I can go back to my birth, everything that went wrong will be undone."

"What about me and Jason here. What might happen to us if you do this again," Chris asked.

The Boss didn't answer but continued with her explanation, "I've been trying to work with the remnants of my team, but the missing people were critical to the project and without them we couldn't be sure of it working the same way. We altered things somehow which clearly changed many lives."

"It changed things alright. Jason and I hardly recognise this world, it isn't ours. What I can't understand though is why we simply woke up and everything was different but only for people like us, Flashbacks."

"Probably the effect of another time distortion."

"What does that mean exactly?"

"A few nights ago, we tried again."

"What?! Why would you do that? What happened?"

"It worked but again, not as expected. It didn't do the same thing as before. This time there was a vortex, a time distortion of some kind we think. It surrounded the machine and brought us back alright, but instead a few weeks as we planned it was twenty odd years," she said looking very sad, "We still haven't figured out why. It was only supposed to be 54 hours plus the extra weeks after the first attempt.".

"I don't believe it. It's impossible."

"And yet, here we are Jason," said The Boss as she turned her attention back to Chris, "The evidence is clear. You never did meet me in person, but you met John. You can't deny it's him."

"I know; I mean I see that but it's still too fantastic. And this effect it grabbed me and Jason, but we didn't age for some reason."

"You weren't in the machine when we came back, but the pulse must have sent a wave around the world and that's what impacted on you and Jason. Somehow you were reset in the here and now and your next twenty years evaporated. I'm sorry Chris," said The Boss.

Chris wondered if she was sorry for him or just for herself, "It must have created a lot of effects. It erased time for me and Jason but you keep that time and knowledge. Being in that machine must have been the difference. How many others were shifted for example, why aren't you at the old building site? It doesn't make sense."

"We owned this land before but hadn't developed it. Somehow the change altered something in the past too, and this building simply existed when we arrived, right down to the staff. I still can't get my head around it. We were originally going to build this, but that other building was available, so we decided to start off small. Somehow that option was removed, and we came back to a building that was only ever an idea."

"I'm just trippin here. This is cloud cuckoo land," blurted Jason.

"Maybe the vortex swept back through time even after you 'arrived' here, that could have changed things, changed people, other Spike victims. It might explain why there are so many differences. You couldn't have done all of this yourself, right," Chris suggested.

"True, and we thought the same thing. The vortex may well have kept flashing back and made changes while it travelled, like a Sun spike."

"Jesus," cried Jason.

There was a pregnant pause as Chris and Jason absorbed the possibilities, "So, what now," asked Chris.

"I want you to come work for me again," said The Boss.

"Why? To help you fix things?"

"Yes, if we can replicate the original effect, I think it will time shift me into a restart."

"And what if you're wrong? What if it just deletes you from existence or something. Have you considered that? Those 27 people vanished completely, didn't they? As you said, you haven't found anything of them, right?"

"Nothing. No trace at all."

"So, what's worse? Living out the rest of your life or trying to go back and get reborn and maybe get blotted out of existence in the process? What happens to John? He fails to exist too. Chances are there are 27 people that no longer exist after what you did."

The Boss didn't have an answer for that. She just sat in her wheelchair looking as glum as an old woman could. The deathly silence in the room was palpable. No-one spoke for a long time but then she looked up with a beaming smile, "You said you were switched into this timeline along with Jason when we fired the machine a few days ago, am I right?"

"Yes."

"And then you said, 'how many others."

"True," Chris said when a revelation hit him, "oh wait, you think?"

"Yes, I do, the missing 27. Assuming it was a global effect, they may all be in this plane right now, snatched across like you two, back from wherever they went. It may well have reset everyone who ever lived for that matter." she turned to John, "Start another search immediately."

"Yes Mother," John began tapping frantically on his wrist device.

Chris's brain was running at a hundred miles an hour now. The very thought that he may have given The Boss a way of completely rebuilding her contraption was a stunning possibility and he didn't know how to feel about it. He and Jason had seen what kind of effect it could have. Their very world ceased to exist in a flash and now she was going to try again. He thought of Judy and how she had changed and his ordeal in trying to win her back. He didn't want to have to do that yet again. And who knows how many others she'd wrenched from their own 'normality' who were now facing the same dilemma but with the added burden of not knowing why, "I don't want to come back again. I can't help you with this because I'm morally against it. It will create changes again that will impact on more individuals and who knows how much of the world? I can't be a party to it. And if you're right and it did reset everyone who has ever lived, then this is the 'new' normal. Best left well enough alone, don't you think?"

The Boss lifted her eyes from the wrist device and looked at Chris again, "I understand but I haven't accepted my plight willingly and I don't really care what you think Chris. I'm doing this with or without you!"

"I realise that, but I have to think about my wife. I've already had to win her back twice. If you do this and are successful, I may have to go through it all again. And that would apply to Jason here and those other people. Can't you see the problem," Chris pleaded.

"A reset is just an inconvenience for you, that's all, but for me it's an imperative."

"Why? Because you don't want to die? It will probably just kill you anyway. And you seem to have forgotten what you were doing all this for. You wanted to save the World from itself. I admired that; I was in that with you, but now? I don't know. You're lost."

The Boss's face softened a little, "I remember why I was doing this, and I still want that, but I can't start again in this time at this age. If I die now, or anytime soon, this will all crumble. No disrespect to any of my employees or to John, but they need me at the helm for a good while before I can pass it on and be confident that it will survive for the long-term benefit of everyone. Don't you see?"

"I can understand your frustration but that doesn't mean you're right to try and fix it. Parallax can go on without this machine and still do great things."

"Parallax was on the verge of doing what I set out to do, but it took another twenty years, and I was in charge. If I'm not there in twenty years' time, it will fall apart."

"From where I sit," Chris said, "it's already falling apart. Have you had a good look around? The World isn't anything like the one we all knew. I don't think you can even account for all the alterations, right? You did this, not me and you should leave well enough alone before it causes more problems."

"Well, that's disappointing Chris. I really wanted you, both of you, on board with this," she suggested.

"Me," blurted Jason in surprise.

"Of course. You came on board with Chris around this time and became a huge success for us. You were as much a part of the team as Chris. You perfected his gaming protocols and developed many other areas of my sporting and gambling franchises," explained The Boss.

"Really? That's all I ever wanted. Chris knew that but I didn't live those 20 years you talked about. None of what you claim has happened, I have never been a part of Parallax."

"Well as far as I am concerned you were and you can be again Jason," suggested the Boss, "You can be a big part of it all. This is where you met your wife. You had a beautiful daughter. You really can't afford to say no."

"Jesus! My wife? In my original time we met at a party. Is it the same girl? I don't want to meet the wrong one."

Chris was gobsmacked, "You're married?"

Jason ignored him.

The Boss answered, "It's the same girl. We arranged to employ her so you two could meet and we can do that again. It's not just about big business and control here. We value our people, and we did what we needed to do for you Jason and your wife Stacey and daughter Jenny!"

Jason just sat with his mouth agape, lost for words.

The Boss looked at Chris, "and for you too Chris. We can make this work together, I'm certain of it. What'll it be?"

"You only want me on board so you can keep control of me. I don't have the skills or knowledge you need. Your motives are selfish. I just can't. I won't," Chris said.

"What about you Jason?"

"Um, well, I don't know," He looked at Chris then The Boss, then at Chris again, "I'm so confused."

"Well take some time to think. No pressure, and come back and see me when you've decided," suggested The Boss.

"And what happens to me," asked Chris.

"That depends, will you try and stop me?"

Chris didn't answer.

"I'll take that as a yes." She paused giving him another chance to respond.

Chris changed tack, "You know, when you came in the room and looked at me, you were surprised. Now I know why, I wasn't the 45-year-old that took your blueprints. You knew I was telling the truth all along. Am I right?"

"Maybe."

Then Chris turned to Jason, "This also means that what happened a few days ago was not a natural event and is avoidable."

"Um," was Jason's only reply.

The Boss, seeing Chris's defiance, decided it was time to break up the reunion, "Ok, well I'll send you on your way Chris and that will be the end of it. As you say, I don't need you for this project. I'll certainly miss you being around but it's too risky given your feelings about the matter. Goodbye Chris," then she turned to Jason again, "You though, you can still be a part of my future if you want to be. I'll expect your call."

With that she had John wheel her out of the room without another word. Chris and Jason were escorted out of the building. The valet brought up the Rolls, and they were soon on their way back to the casino.

"Holy fuck," exclaimed Jason.

"I have to stop her," Chris said.

"Whoa, wait a minute. She's willing to help us, make us rich, employ my wife and did you hear? I'll see my daughter again and you, your son, you can't just say no!"

"For starters Jason, you're already rich and as for my son, I know I'll see him again and I'll do it without her involvement. You can too!"

"True, but I also have the police and the authorities breathing down my neck. I don't need that."

Chris didn't really hear him, "This world, the one before, it doesn't matter if I have Judy, and I have her now. We can make a life without all this crap. Right now, I have a clean slate, and I don't want to start over again. It's too hard and too risky."

"Well for me it's the answer to everything. Life on my terms, no heat from the authorities and I get my wife and daughter back? Just in case you don't understand me, I've already missed that window because of what's happened. She can set it right."

Chris heard him this time, "I understand Jason, I really do but I can't do it again, not for you and not for her. She's a bitter and twisted old lady now. Time has corrupted her and even if she resets and starts again, she will carry the corrupt knowledge with her into the next timeline. She won't be the same person regardless. I just don't trust her anymore."

"Well, I really must think about it. She has offered me a much better future than I could have imagined. No strings. I want to do this I think."

Chris was disappointed but understood Jason's reasons, "That's up to you Jason but if you go with her, I won't be there. I'm sorry but she's wrong. She's just wrong."

"What are you saying, we're through? We were only just starting to be friends, I mean real friends, something I have never had in any of my lives."

"I know and I hate to do this, but I must think of Judy first. And I won't hold up our friendship as a bargaining chip. You must decide for yourself. Just know, if you go with her, you go it alone."

"Ok, but when she asked if you would try and stop her you didn't answer. So, will you?"

"I don't know how. She's got that placed stitched up tight. I can't see how to get past all that. I guess it will be impossible even if I really wanted to."

"You're right about that. Well, I haven't fully decided but...." Jason left the thought hanging in the ether.

They drove into the car park of the casino and stopped near Chris's shitty car. He got out and turned to say goodbye, "Let me know what you decide."

"Sure, seeya," said Jason and he drove into the underground parking area.

That evening Chris picked Judy up from work as promised. He drove her home with little to say.

"What's wrong," She asked.

"I'll tell you at home. It's hard to explain and you're going to need to listen carefully."

"You're scaring me."

"Sorry, I didn't mean to."

They drove for another fifteen minutes without saying much. After Chris heaved their clunker into the driveway, they went inside, where Chris cracked open a bottle of wine and poured two glasses. They then settled on the lounge.

"Right, what's going on Chris. I'm worried."

Chris explained what he knew at length, detailing what might happen if Parallax was successful in creating a restart.

"You mean to say that people like you, who have been through this Sun Spike effect and been rebirthed, are affected by anything that they might do?"

"Exactly, which is why I woke up the other day in a new world, with you hating me and us broke. A day before we were happy and doing well."

"But I don't understand. How will this happen?"

"If they finish building this machine, like they did before, they'll try to replicate the conditions that saw those 27 technicians vanish. In doing so, all those who flashed back originally like me will reset, perhaps in another plane, the ones in the machine will be reborn and live their lives over again, at least that's what they think could happen."

"Oh my God!"

"There's more. It's possible their latest attempt to rip through time, the effect that brought me into this reality, may have brought those missing 27 technicians into this timeline. It's just a theory because of what happened to me and Jason. I can't be sure really and I have no idea who they are."

"And what happens to people like me?"

"You wake up without any memory of the 'me' that's talking to you now. You will have lived some other life, probably with another me and I'll have to try and convince you all over again. Just like three days ago."

Judy was dumbfounded with fear written all over her face.

"Judy," Chris said, "You won't know a thing about it, if it happens. It just won't be a factor in your life. I know that doesn't make you feel better but…."

"I understand what you're saying but for you, it's a living nightmare."

"It's starting to look that way. The only thing I can do is stop her somehow."

"How?"

"Well, I clearly tried before when I supposedly took the blueprints. I guess the only option I have now is to try and talk her out of it or…destroy the machine."

"Would that end it?"

"I think so, it took them twenty years to get it right last time and if they had to start from scratch, I doubt The Boss would see it through, she's so old now. There'd be no motivation to keep the project going."

"But they'll probably kill you if you get caught, won't they?"

"Yes. They're huge and powerful now, more so than I could have ever imagined and her mind is completely closed. She's bitter and angry and nothing is going to stop her."

"Where's the machine?"

"In the desert, but where exactly, I cannot say."

"How do you find it?"

"I don't know yet."

Judy was chewing on a fingernail, and she was considering everything that Chris had told her, "There's another option."

"What's that?"

"You do nothing and hope they fail."

"I thought of that, and you may be right but it's a risk. If those 27 are found and the project is fully revived, they will succeed, eventually."

"I'm so scared Chris. I don't know what to do."

"Frankly neither do I," Chris said, and he put an arm around Judy's shoulder to be reassuring, "but I'll figure something out. I have to."

Chapter 16

After another, Chris got up early, made breakfast and sat staring into his coffee as Judy wandered into the kitchen.

"Good morning," she said, almost as if there wasn't a problem.

"Hi," Chris replied as he pushed a plate of scrambled eggs across to Judy and flicked the switch on the kettle to make her a coffee. She sat on the counter stool and picked up a fork, "Sorry if it's a little cold. I should have waited for you before I cooked it," Chris added.

"That's ok babe, I'm sure it'll be fine," but he saw her wince as she took her first swallow.

"You don't have to eat it you know?"

"Just a coffee then," she said with a smile.

"Coming right up."

Judy could tell that Chris was distracted, "Couldn't sleep?"

"Nope! I just don't know what to do. This whole situation is out of control. If I do nothing, any number of things could happen assuming they get that machine operational again."

"Can't you go to the authorities? Get them to shut her down?"

"I thought of that, but they'd just think I'm a nutter with a fantastic story. I could prove my case I suppose but I expect they'd write it off as a trick or worse, take me away somewhere for 'questioning'," he made quotation signs with his fingers, "I don't trust them to deal with it, even if they believed me, who knows how long they'd take to make a decision either way?"

"I see your point. What about trying to talk to her again?"

"I love the way you see the good in everyone, but she's not the woman I started working for originally. She's a pinball machine at full tilt and the steel ball is rolling."

"What?"

"I'm just saying that she is dead set intent on making that machine work and 'fixing' all the problems she caused but mainly she's looking to recover her youth. She resents the lost years because she came back to this time. No-one will stop her. Even her son, who stands to be evaporated from existence, isn't willing to save himself. It's crazy."

"Is there, or was there anyone there you can trust?"

"Not really and it's clear that even The Boss doesn't know for sure how things turned out the way they did. The new building in a different location, that's truly odd and I don't think she or her people were even clued in on some of the tech they were using. It's like the Parallax here isn't the one they created. Quite bizarre."

"Sure is. Any ideas on how things changed?"

"Only that when she tried to make the jump back, she changed something. Maybe one or two of those 27 missing men and women got zapped back far enough to change things so that Parallax couldn't become what it was before. Maybe one of those people tried to stop them from existing? I really don't know."

"Gosh, it's so hard to understand. It really messes with my brain."

"Yeah, and you just see the aftereffects. I've had to live through it, twice now."

Judy sipped her super-hot coffee while Chris crunched on his egg laden toast staring at nothing. Both were deep in thought when the phone rang. Judy snapped up the receiver, "Hello?" A few words leaked from the earpiece, but Chris couldn't pick up more than a male tone. Upon hearing the message, Judy's eyes flicked up at Chris, "I see. Uh huh. Ok. Yes, he's right here," and she offered the phone to Chris.

"Who is it?"

"It's John."

Chris's eyes bulged and he grabbed the receiver, "John?"

"Hello Chris. We need to talk. Can we meet in an hour or so?"

"I'm not sure. Is this some kind of trick?"

"No, I assure you. Mum doesn't know I'm calling and if she found out…" John didn't finish the sentence.

"Ok, where?"

"I'll pick you up. See you soon," and the phone cut off with a click.

Judy was staring at Chris as he handed the receiver back to her, "So that was John, The Boss's son?"

"Yes. He wants to meet."

"Hmmm, maybe he's not sitting back and waiting to be erased after all."

"Maybe. He'll be picking me up soon. He wants to talk."

"Well, it can't hurt, can it?"

"No," Chris said, "but it also suggests that The Boss is losing control of her people. If he is trying to save himself, there may be more that aren't happy about what she's got planned. There may be some hope yet."

Judy didn't answer which caused Chris to look her way, "What's wrong?"

"I was just thinking, why don't you want to try and get back to where you were before this? You say we had it all and were happy. This must be horrible, being here, losing everything."

"But I didn't lose anything. I have you. That's all there is. Money, success, all the 'stuff' that I had before isn't what I wanted, not without you. It doesn't matter where or when that is, as long as we're together."

Judy smile, skipped around the counter and gave Chris a huge hug and a smouldering kiss, "You always know what to say."

Chris smiled, "It's a gift." He looked at the clock, "You better get to work."

"Oh shit, I'm late," and she raced off to the bedroom, dressed and made herself up and was out the door in a shot, "Tell me everything tonight, ok?"

"Sure will. Bye baby," Chris yelled as she cranked the car over.

Judy waved as she drove away leaving Chris to think about John and what he might want to discuss.

Chris decided to wait on the step, and it wasn't long before John rolled up in a late model Ford, white with no standout features. It was a very average car which surprised Chris a little bit. He trotted down the step, out of the gate and opened the passenger door and took his seat, "Good morning, John."

"Hi Chris, how are you?"

"Apprehensive."

"Understandable. My call must have been a surprise."

"Yes, it was. Where are we off to?"

"Somewhere we can talk," John noticed Chris's expression, "I know, it seems to be all cloak and dagger. Sorry about that but I will explain."

"Righto. I'm in your hands," said Chris as John pulled out from the curb and headed down the street.

At first very few words were exchanged during the drive and Chris had time to look around at the features of the city, taking in some more of the abnormalities. Of course they were only abnormal to him. To everyone else, including his wife, this would all be normal. These buildings, parks, bridges, roads and other infrastructure would have evolved over time and been accepted as the natural state. For Chris and John, it was far from that, "I hardly recognise the place," said Chris.

"Me either. I mean a twin Sydney Harbour Bridge? That was eye catching," added John.

"Indeed, that caught me off guard too and the water taxis and ferries, they're all so modern!"

"Yes, and if you look closely at Sydney Tower, it's actually taller."

"No kidding! You have a keen eye. I'm guessing some of the technology you have is a bit different too," added Chris.

"You noticed huh? Yes, we've had to fake it until we can make it. Some of it was easy but there's tech in the building that is way out of our league. Funny thing is we invented it, or at least this version of Parallax did. This era is certainly very different."

"I know. I saw the airport from a distance and there are aircraft that I've never seen before. Huge passenger planes, double decker jobs with six engines. They look like they could circumnavigate the planet non-stop. There's certainly been a technological leap here but no mobile phones, which I find odd."

"No, we think they skipped that and went straight to implants. They have them in their heads. Didn't your wife mention it?"

"No?"

"She probably couldn't afford one and assumed the same for you, given your previous circumstances financially."

"They're still our financial circumstances John. I came into a dark time in our marriage. It's only these last couple of days we've been able to reconnect."

"I know. That must have been tough. I'm sorry."

"It's ok, I mean, it's not ok, but it happened and that's that I guess."

"You're taking it well."

"Only because of Judy. If she wasn't here or some event had seen her with someone else or she hated me so much that we didn't get back together, I think I'd be a mess."

"That would certainly change your mind about another reset, wouldn't it?"

"Eh? Oh clever. Is that what this is all about?"

"In part. We'll talk about everything soon, I promise."

John steered the car down one of the new freeways that neither of them had ever seen before.

"How the hell do you know where to go," Chris asked

John explained that the car was synced to the city's road system and that the illuminated intelligent signs made navigation easy, "This car might seem standard, but I found out that if you just tell the car your destination, the smart signs on the road help you. It's an overall navigation net. Quite amazing."

"Holy shit, really? That's too crazy."

"Watch the sign."

As Chris focused on the high-res street sign he heard a soft tone in the cabin of the car that sounded like a xylophone note and then an instruction appeared on the sign, Hi John, take the next off-ramp in 2 kilometres.

"My God! How does it do that with so many cars on the road? It must cause so much confusion."

"I think it's a combination of factors, various Wi-Fi frequencies and an active windscreen that interprets messages for me alone. Other drivers get their own messages which I can't see. It's quite amazing."

"You're telling me, and much better than mobile sat nav."

"Very true. Also beats a heads-up display, because you're more inclined to keep your eye on what's happening outside. Much safer in general."

"What about suburban streets though. I didn't see these signs in town."

"No, the car provides VIM."

"VIM?"

"Voice integrated messaging. It's like sat-nav but it's a network system. Nothing like the sat-nav systems you know. You just start the car, tell it where you want to go, and it talks you through it. It tells you about traffic, accidents all in real time. It's a cut above anything that you and I ever used."

"I haven't heard a thing though."

"That's because you're the passenger, but I can hear it. Quite incredible."

"Wow, do you have an implant?"

"No, I can just hear it. It's like a subliminal thing for the driver I guess."

"That's years ahead of its time. In fact, way ahead of anything we ever saw developed in our previous timelines. I assume it's a Parallax system?"

"Indeed, it is. Most of the tech is. We have a lot of catching up to do."

"Is anyone, you know, suspicious of your ignorance John?"

"Yes, but they are also our most trusted people. They are helping us get up to speed."

"That was lucky."

"Yes, it really was," replied John.

He took the off ramp and was soon back on suburban streets. He drove around like he'd done it a hundred times, but he'd never been in this world or on these streets ever before. After a few more minutes he pulled into a retail district the likes of which neither of them had ever seen. A super multiplex shopping precinct of epic proportions. It was easily ten stories high and looked to have a rooftop forest, with waterfalls; shops merged with nature and yet, very high tech it appeared! It was truly stunning.

"Holy shit," cried Chris.

"What you said," replied John.

He maneuverer the car toward a car park entrance and suddenly let go of the wheel.

"What's happened," Chris asked.

"I think it's parking itself?!"

"Jesus, what next?"

As John suspected, the car simply drove itself up the ramp and circled its way to the top floor and moved into an executive car space right near a private entrance. It slid in seamlessly before shutting itself down.

"Here we are, I guess."

"Where's here," Chris asked.

"You remember the big Shopping Centres in our time?"

"Yeah."

Well, welcome to the Parallax Multiplex."

"No way!"

"Way!"

"I have got to see this place," Chris said with much excitement.

The pair quickly got out of the car and John waved his wrist at a small black bubble next to the door, which immediately slipped open revealing a series of offices and cubicles. People were everywhere but very few took much notice of John and his guest.

"I guess I must have come here a lot given that reaction," suggested John quietly, "That's a relief I suppose."

"So, you've never seen this before?"

"Nope."

"Weird."

John nodded and headed for what could only have been an executive's office. A few people acknowledged him with one or two others saying hello but mostly he was left alone. Waving his wrist device across another bubble, the executive door clicked open and both he and Chris stepped inside without incident."

"It seems I was expected. They probably didn't know who you were Chris, but being with me, no concerns."

"Maybe," Chris added.

As John sat at his desk, the computer came to life automatically, "Good morning, Sir," it chimed.

"Bloody Hell!" blurted John and Chris in unison.

"Is something the matter sir?" asked the computer.

"Um, no, all is well, carry on," said John which made Chris smile.

"Another first time experience I gather?"

"Yes."

"Is that one of those new Quantum computers you revealed to the World yesterday?"

"I'm suppose so, we have them at the main building as well, but this is the first time I've really been close to one. To be honest, this is way above my pay grade. Well, it's not but you know what I mean."

"I think so. The changes in this world, the computer systems and the other technology have been developed by Parallax much sooner, compared to your original timeline and now we're in a place where things are decades ahead of when they should have been developed, right?"

"True. We were only just tinkering with this kind of tech."

"Why do you think the World is so advanced now?"

"Well, I think that we, Parallax, have been operating in this timeline for a lot longer than you and I suspect. The company has had much more time to develop new ideas."

"But how? And without you? It doesn't make sense."

"Actually, it does. In talking to the people we employ, we, as in me and Mum and others, have always been a part of it. Our impromptu arrival the other day only changed what we knew and not what the company had done."

"And your ages? Aren't people wondering about that?"

"Well, we haven't aged to them. I don't really know how that can be."

Chris pondered the situation for a moment, recalling a conversation with Dr Fred Wilson, "Well I have a theory. I spoke to an astronomer recently and the idea of multiple Universes was discussed. He said he didn't think we were moving from one Universe to another unless the Universes were overlapping. What if that's what we're experiencing?"

"You mean; this World really isn't ours. We're infiltrators?"

"Could be. The people are the same, mostly but the technology varies due to fluctuations in the events that shaped reality."

"You've really been thinking about this," suggested John.

"Yes, well I've always been fascinated by astronomy. I think when your mother and I were first reborn, we went back in time, within our own Universe but this last event, I think that was different. You have moved across a threshold and in this place, you were already older for some reason. Maybe there are other machines within each Universe, and they connected and open windows between worlds. All just theory of course," Chris explained.

"Maybe. Anything's possible I guess."

"Well, I could be wrong of course. I'm just making this up as I go along."

"I should hope so," added John.

"BUT if your 27 missing scientists went back and were reborn and you with them in this timeline, that would explain this World being as far ahead as it is. Right?"

"Well," John said with what appeared to be feigned surprise, but he didn't offer any more comment.

Chris's gut told him that John was holding back, "Wait a minute, you're not arguing at all, and you don't seem to be too overawed by the whole situation John. I wonder, did you have any luck tracking down your missing people?"

John looked across at Chris and could tell he wasn't going to be discouraged, "Ok, I'll be straight with you Chris, they're here, or they were when we checked after your unexpected visit yesterday. It seems they're all fine and working for us as we speak. They did come back, and, as you suggested, they were reset with all their prior knowledge and came to Parallax years ago in this timeline and continued where they left off, all of them," suggested John.

Chris's stomach twisted with the news, "So that means I was right?"

John looked at Chris's face, "Yes."

"And you knew? You figured it all out?"

"We did, except for the Multiple Universe thing. That may well be the missing piece of the puzzle. It's certainly something to consider."

"And the machine? Surely you don't need it now" asked Chris

"It's been made top priority."

"Jesus! You know it'll ruin my life and Jason's. I told your mother how I felt and why this is such a bad idea and if I'm right about multiple universes overlapping, then you're opening Pandora's Box!"

"I doubt that. We can factor in just about any variable now because we have much more to work with, the technology available now, the quantum computers for example, they will make certain we won't fail," John suggested.

"Never say never John, but regardless of what you do, it will destroy my timeline if your mother goes ahead and resets."

"Unless you come with us."

"Jesus John, I've already said no."

"I know that but, there's another option that you may not have considered."

"And what's that?"

"Bring Judy with you. She gets reset too and wakes up knowing what you know and that will ensure your future together."

Chris was dumbfounded. It had never occurred to him to have Judy reborn. He shook off the thought, "But as I told you all yesterday, you don't know for sure what will happen. You may simply be deleted from existence. It's too risky!"

"I agree, there's a risk, but the technicians have had years to perfect their calculations. They know what went wrong before and they know what to do about it. They can make the machine work this time; I assure you."

"And when will this happen?"

"I'm not sure. We must do a lot of work on the machine before it's ready."

"And what if your mother, you know?"

"What if she dies in the meantime?"

"Yes."

"That hasn't been discussed," John said.

"I see. So, let's assume she doesn't pass away before you get the machine up to spec, what's stops me from destroying it? I mean, you must be thinking I will try."

"I'm hoping you won't. I want you on board. You were always so dedicated until…"

"That machine came along?"

"Yes, but now we can do it properly."

"That's what you say but have you looked around you? This isn't our World. This isn't right. You have tampered with reality and now, this," Chris said pointing at the computer.

"If that's how you really feel, then why do you want to stay in this World? You've contradicted yourself!"

"It's not about staying or going; it's about being with Judy. If I must stay in this world to be with her, that's what I'll do. I may not feel this is my World but it's what the World is, so I must accept it, why can't you?"

"I was robbed of time, like Mum. I came back to a prior time with extra miles on the clock. It feels bad and I don't want to be an old man before my time. Don't you see that?"

"I do; I mean sort of. It must be so strange to be 50 when you should be 30 or whatever age you should be, but you did it to yourselves." Chris was determined to make his case, "And there's one more thing you may not have considered in all of this, besides being disappeared forever."

"And what's that?"

"If you do reset your timeline what's to say you won't fast forward development and technology even further? What if your mother jump starts quantum computing by another decade or more? Every reset changes something because more people go back with their knowledge."

"True."

"And what if one or two of them go rogue? They could take what they know and start their own version of Parallax, and your mother and you might not be of any use in the next timeline? Does that make sense?"

John looked at Chris intently, "We have already thought of that, and the risks are worth taking as far as we're concerned. We trust these people; they are dedicated and devoted. Bottom line is we want our lives back regardless. We need to be in sync again. Don't you see that?"

"I get it; I really do but I don't see why I should pay the price for your mistakes. It's just not fair."

"I know it's not fair but if that's all you can put up as an objection, then I'm afraid you have no argument."

"Then why did you bother to call? You should have known I wouldn't go for this."

"I thought that offering a reset to both of you might change your mind. Can you at least ask her? I promise you it will work this time."

"This World is all that she's ever known. It's normal for her. Why would she even consider it?"

"Why won't you? You can save your parents, your grandparents, you know what can be done with all that knowledge of yours."

Chris hadn't had much time to think about Rob and Sandy or Clem and Edith for that matter but in this World, they were indeed dead. He didn't know how or when or why, but Judy made it clear that they'd all passed. That's one thing he may be able to fix.

"And have you considered that the Judy here, might not be your Judy? If you're right about the multiple universe scenario, then she's not yours, period. Just think about it Chris. That's all I ask," added John.

Chris was visibly taken back by the potential of John's remark but not overwhelmed because it had indeed crossed his mind too. He just didn't want to believe it, "Ok, I will consider your 'offer'. But I can't give you any guarantees."

"Thank you," said John.

They remained silent for a moment more, then Chris said, "So, are you going to show me around this shopping centre of yours?"

"Sure, if I had any clue where to go," and they both laughed.

That night, when Judy got home, Chris explained what happened. He told her all about the plans to fire up the machine and do another reset and there would be nothing he could do to stop them.

He then explained how this world was so different from where he'd been before, "But that doesn't matter as long as we're together. I know this is a world you know and understand. This is normal for you."

"I'd never really thought about it. I mean from where I sit, you grew up in this World with me. It never occurred to me that you were in an alien environment," Judy suggested.

"Well, not alien, just advanced. In my original timeline we didn't have any digital technology or communication implants or quantum computers. In fact, computers were barely capable of adding up in my original 1987, so technologically this is a weird place to me."

"Wow, I mean…Wow," Judy said without having to elaborate.

"I know and if, or when, they do it again, the world as I know it now will change again, but for you it will be normal, no matter what form it takes...unless…"

"Unless what?"

"Well, they're going to do this regardless, and I am steadfastly against it, but I know I don't want to have to restart either way," Chris said.

"What do you mean either way?"

"Well, if I do nothing and they fire up that thing, I lose you and have to get you back again. If I go with them, same thing but, if you come with me…"

Judy took a moment to absorb what Chris was suggesting, "You mean, I go in the machine too?"

"That's one option and if you do, and I'm not saying you should, but if you do, then you will reset and be born again on your original birthday with all your knowledge for this life. It will be a restart like the one I have experienced."

"You actually sound like you want to do this Chris," Judy suggested.

"Well, I was totally against it right up until John brought up my parents and grandparents. What if I can go back and save them. I don't know what happened to them in this timeline and I've lost them twice before, well my parents anyway. What if…"

"Ok, but what if the Universe is trying to tell you that their time was over regardless? You may never save them. And what about my parents? They're still here. I can't just leave."

"You wouldn't be leaving. You would just be restarting. But as I said, I don't want to force you. I don't even know how I feel now. Part of me feels wrong but I also feel an urge to save my Mum."

"And what about Caleb?"

Chris looked Judy in the eye, "I know we're very close to that moment, when we can conceive our son, but if we reset, we still have that opportunity. It's not a write off, it's just delayed. I know that's true. It's a huge ask though, I understand that."

"Probably more so for you. I haven't met him yet, you have. So, I don't feel the bond, if that makes sense. Can you wait another twenty-five years Chris?"

"I don't know. I really don't."

"Well, I don't think we should decide right now. We need to look at this from every possible aspect, weigh it all up and see what's best for both of us. What do you think?"

"I agree."

"Good," then Judy added, "I really can't believe we're talking about this. It's totally off the planet!"

"It is indeed," Chris said, and they both had a laugh.

Chris decided not to tell Judy about his theory that she wasn't his original partner and that he was an imposter in another Universe. For one thing, he wasn't entirely sure it was true. Second, she seemed utterly the same so he couldn't convince himself that she wasn't his original Judy and third, he didn't see any logic in adding another concern to their already muddled lives. His head swirled with possibilities, and he had to work hard to hide his reactions so that Judy didn't get any more frightened.

With everything that was happening and, what could happen, sleep proved very difficult for both of them that night.

Chapter 17

Over the coming days Chris and Judy discussed the pros and cons of doing a flashback and starting their lives again. For Chris it would be a double restart in real terms, taking the knowledge of two life experiences with him. For Judy this would be a first, if indeed they decided to go ahead with the venture.

Both felt confident that if they did this, they would find each other and be together again. That wasn't the question. The sticking point was the fact that life was good right now, they were together and could soon be parents to Caleb, so why risk it? Even though the world was nothing like Chris knew, he was with his wife, and they were happy. The rest he could figure out in time.

On the other hand, not going might mean a shift of some kind anyway, once The Boss got the Parallax Machine running again and that appeared to be a fait accompli. The only way to stop her would be sabotage and that would most likely cost Chris his life. The Boss wouldn't let him do it without a fight and she clearly seemed to be willing to circumvent the law if she had to and he had a strong impression that murder wasn't beyond her now that her mind had become so corrupted.

The other option of course, was to go it alone, flashback without Judy and hope they were somehow reunited, but that was a bigger risk in both of their minds.

The more they discussed it, the clearer the answer became.

"I'm going to talk to Jason. I think I need to clear the air with him, is that ok," Chris asked.

"Of course, you don't need my permission," she replied with a smile.

"I know, but thanks anyway."

Chris drove into the city, parked in the casino public lot and went in through the main entrance where he was immediately intercepted by a security guard, "This way sir," he demanded.

"I'm only here to see Jason Milne, there's no need to worry."

The guard ignored him and walked towards the now familiar elevator but this time the guard accompanied him into the penthouse and right up to Jason who was standing at his window taking in the panorama of Sydney Harbour with its twin bridges. He said nothing for a moment then turned and looked at Chris through suspicious eyes, "You took your time coming to see me. I was ready to give up."

"Sorry."

"It's OK," said Jason and he waved a hand to dismiss the guard who vanished back down the corridor to the lift, "So what are you going to do Chris? Blow up the machine?"

"No, not at all, Judy and I decided to flashback together, we're in!"

Jason's face softened a little but then his suspicion returned, "Really? Or is it a ruse to get at the machine?"

"No, it's not a ruse, we both agreed that it's the best decision. If we don't then as soon as that machine fires up, I'm disrupted anyway. Do I really have a choice?"

Jason thought for a second, "I suppose not. I'm glad to hear it though."

"Why the security guard?"

"Oh, paranoia, I guess. Last time we spoke you were ready to destroy it all, I didn't know if you would come back and if you did, what your intentions might be, just…"

Chris interrupted, "I get it, well I was still right, The Boss is off her tree, but she also has the power and the technology to do it and I can't stop her, so I guess I have no recourse."

"No, you don't but it can't be just that can it? You were clear on stopping her."

"True, and I will confess that I have happiness with Judy again and I'll be risking that but this place;" Chris waved out the window, "it isn't home. It's alien. It's wrong."

Jason looked Chris in the eye, his face softening some more, "I know, I feel it too, there's something off about it. I can't put my finger on it, but I feel like I'm here but not really here, you know?"

"Yes, I do. This is not our World."

"What does that mean?"

"When we spoke with Dr Wilson, we discussed multiple Universes and I asked if I could have been shifted from one to another and he said no...unless..."

"Unless what?"

"Unless the multiple universes overlap each other. Most people seem to think they probably exist next to each other and that you would have to travel to the end of our universe to reach the next one but what if they all co-exist on different planes? That could mean we shifted into another realm, and this really isn't our original Universe."

"Jesus, are you serious?"

"It's just a theory. They only think there are multiple universes, but no-one knows for sure. It's all speculative. This could just be a more advanced version of the World we came from because of Parallax," Chris added.

"Well, I'm open to any possibility. I mean look at us, reliving our lives. We're both, what, around 70 or 80 years old in real terms, that's just way out there!"

"You're right, hard to absorb really."

"So, your decision, it's based on this place not being our place?"

"Yes, to a certain degree, and the fact that I think I'm better off going rather than staying and suffering another 'effect' and Judy has agreed to do it too."

"I think it's the right call, when you size it all up," Jason added.

"It's still a huge risk; they could mess this up again and who knows what happens this time. We could all simply be wiped from existence."

Jason didn't have anything to say about that but the look on his face said enough. Then his expression changed again as a thought manifested itself, "If you're right about layered universes...then Judy, she..."

"I know, she might not be my Judy, assuming the theory is right. I hope I'm wrong."

"Me too, but if she isn't your original Judy, what will happen to her if she does come with us?"

"I assume she'll flash back to this reality."

Jason looked at Chris closely, "Tell me the truth Chris. What gives?"

Chris pinched his bottom lip between two fingers, mouth slightly agape as he prepared his next statement, "If I'm right about multiple overlapping Universes, and we shift back to where we came from, then she will go back to a life of poverty and be living with a loser version of me BUT if she is reborn with her life knowledge, then she's better off with or without me…"

"Christ, you really have been thinking about this. You want to save her from a shitty version of you!?"

"Basically yes."

"This is all too weird," said Jason.

"Very weird. I know. Look, for all intents and purposes she IS my Judy, she's exactly the same. So, if I'm wrong about the multiple Universe theory, we both win. If I'm right, she's better off."

Jason absorbed the concept and finally conceded that it was a good plan essentially, "I had no idea that your mind was so complex. Your foresight is remarkable."

"Thank you."

"So, we're doing this then? What do you think will happen to us if you consider all the possibilities that are now on the table," Jason asked pensively.

"Well, if we've been shifted into a Universe that isn't ours, then who knows where we might end up. We could simply stay here and start over; we could be put back where we came from, or we could end up somewhere else. I'm making assumptions that nature, God or whatever, will make a correction, but it could be that none of that holds true and we're simply subject to the laws of physics and that could result in a multitude of possibilities."

"Or it could be that this is our universe and it's simply been corrupted by that machine."

"That's also possible but my gut tells me otherwise. I can't put my finger on it except to say I just feel out of place, all the time."

"Me too, it's strange but it's there every moment, even when I'm asleep," Jason suggested.

They chatted for another hour before deciding to visit Parallax and tell The Boss they were both in.

On arrival the scene at Parallax was not as expected; an ambulance was parked awkwardly across the main doorway to the building. As Chris and Jason approach, a gurney exited the building with a white sheet covering a body.

They rushed up just as The Boss's son, John appeared, his face flushed and flooded with tears.

"John," cried Chris, "what happened?"

"It's Mum. She's dead."

"Oh God! I'm so sorry. How did it happen?"

"A heart attack they think. It happened so fast. She was just talking and then she was on the floor."

"Chris put his hand on John's shoulder, "I'm truly sorry."

"Thank you." John was about to jump into the ambulance when he turned back toward the pair, "We should talk, tomorrow, 10 o'clock here?"

"Sure John, no problem."

With that the ambulance sped away followed by John's car and a driver.

"What now," asked Jason.

"I'm not sure. It could mean everything is scotched. I guess we'll know more tomorrow."

"How do you feel about that?"

"It pretty much solves itself. I stay here with Judy, and we live out our lives. What about you?"

"I'm in the same boat I guess, but with the law after me. Given the history of my 'business dealings' I suspect I'll have to do a bit of time sooner or later," Jason suggested.

"You can't make good and avoid jail?"

"I doubt it. There's too much water under that bridge. Tax avoidance to the tune of millions, criminal charges, intimidation, money laundering, drugs; it's nasty stuff," explained Jason.

Chris smiled, "Minimum security?"

"Very funny and highly doubtful! But I have protection inside, so it might not be too bad. I guess I'll find out."

"So that's your real reason for wanting to flash back huh? To get out of all that?"

"Yeah well, you can't blame me, right?"

"Not at all," Chris said, "Hey, you want to meet Judy?"

"Really?"

"Sure, why not. Come over now, have dinner with us."

'Well? Yeah sure, I would love to meet her."

With that they were in Jason's car and headed for Chris and Judy's place.

"I never saw us becoming friends Jason," Chris confessed, "I had so many preconceived ideas about you."

"Well don't be too hard on yourself, for a good while I was exactly what you thought of me, to a certain degree. Heavy handed, ruthless, greedy, all of that but time tends to change people, and I've had plenty of time to think and change. I can see after all these years that I was not a good person and was going to end up killing someone or being killed, so I changed all that with my second stint at life. Now I've fallen back into it."

"Must be tough."

"Yeah, I'm also used to it though. I know the game, but I don't want to play, if that makes sense."

"It does," Chris said.

In a very short time, thanks to Jason's high-tech car, they arrived. Chris led Jason into the house, "Judy? Are you here?"

"Yeah baby, in the kitchen."

Chris led Jason up the hall and into the kitchen and dining area, "Judy? I've brought a visitor; this is Jason Milne."

Judy swung around and was about to say hello when her jaw dropped, "Holy shit! Don't I know you?"

"Um. I'm not sure. Maybe," Jason answered.

"How could you know him Jude," asked Chris.

"Years ago, my father was visited by a man, I don't know why, but you were there too," Judy suggested.

"My father I would guess. They must have done business of some kind."

"And my dad was never the same after that. He was quiet and serious a lot of the time. I was very worried about him. His business seemed to thrive but somehow, he wasn't happy and we never seemed to have much money, does that makes sense to you Jason?"

"I'm afraid it does. That sounds a lot like my father's business model."

"Business model? He was a thug and a bully. He fleeced my father and left us with nothing. Get the Hell out of my house," Judy demanded.

"Wait a second Judy, this is Jason Milne but not THE Jason Milne you remember. He's like me, a flashback, remember? We're both different people, like I'm different to the man you married. Don't you see," Chris explained.

"It's true," added Jason, "I have no such memory, and I have never met your dad that I'm aware of. It was another version of me I guess."

Judy absorbed the words for a moment then looked at Chris, "I'm sorry. I've never really gotten over it," then she turned to Jason, "So, you're not that Jason?"

"No, I've just sort of landed in the mess my father created. I won't say that I wasn't like that before, but it was a long time ago. When the shift happened recently, I just fell back into it and I'm as unhappy about it as you are, really, I am."

"OK, I guess I can believe that. I'm sorry."

"No need to apologise. These are strange times. I understand," and Jason reached out and shook Judy's hand, "nice to finally meet you."

"Thank you, you too," said Judy and she let a faint smile appear.

Chris was surprised by the story, "I have no recollection of your father ever having dealings with Mr Milne. That must have only happened in your current timeline and not in our previous timelines. Stands to reason I guess; this world is so different. What did your father do for a living?"

"He was or is an accountant. I'm guessing it was money laundering or something. He worked very hard, and it came at a cost. He's not very well these days and has semi-retired. The partners run the business now."

"I'm sorry I haven't been to see your dad since I arrived. A lot of other things to think about," Chris suggested.

"Well, he probably wouldn't recognise you in any case and he was pissed with you because our marriage was failing. He blames you of course."

Chris smiled as his cheeks flushed red with embarrassment.

Jason added, "If it's any consolation, I'd been planning to wind back those practices but it's a slow process and well, with the focus now on a flashback, I'm not really paying much attention to the business. It's running itself really. I'm not that invested to be frank."

"I understand and I appreciate the gesture but for Dad, the damage is done. He's just a shell of a man these days," Judy explained.

"Jesus Judy, I had no idea. Why didn't you say something," asked Chris.

"We were having our own troubles and when I learned you were different, I just didn't bring it up."

"And your mother?"

"Struggling. The pressure has made their lives difficult. They pretend everything is OK, but I know it's not."

"All the more reason to flashback with us Judy," added Jason, "You can put it right...we all can."

Judy looked at Jason then at Chris, "I know. It makes sense."

Chris realised that they all had good reasons to flashback now, Judy to help her parents, Jason to escape the law and run a legal operation and Chris could stop his own parents from being killed, but now that The Boss was dead, it may be for nothing, "We have to convince John to continue the project!"

"What do you mean? I thought it was on track," Judy asked, looking concerned.

"It was, until The Boss died," Jason told her.

"Oh my God! When? How?"

Jason and Chris explained the story and the fact that they would be meeting John in the morning.

"I'm coming too. There's too much at stake," Judy added.

"Agreed," Chris said.

Next morning the trio drove out to Parallax and were sitting in John's office at 10am sharp.

"Thank you for coming, I appreciate it," John said,

"I'm sorry about your mother John. I know we didn't always agree but in most of my dealings with her, we got along famously. It's the shift that drove a wedge between us," explained Chris.

"I know that. I understand it all now. That's why I wanted to talk to you. With Mum dead, the main reason for trying another flashback has primarily gone. It was supposed to give her back those years so she could carry on her work, but she's dead and I don't know if I can do it without her."

"So, you still want to," asked Jason.

"I don't know. I'm tired and, well I'm not sure about anything right now."

"You're in shock John," said Chris, "so it's going to take some time to get your mind straight."

"I know, I…" John paused.

"Let us help you," suggested Judy.

John looked up, "Really?" he turned to Chris, "I didn't think you were interested."

"Well things have changed. We have a lot we need to fix, so I'm in. We all are and Judy's right, we can help."

"You don't know how glad that makes me Chris, thank you."

"Think nothing of it John. We all have a lot at stake and there's another thing to consider."

"What's that?"

"A successful flashback will mean your mother will be alive again."

John's face froze for a moment, and his eyes glazed with tears, "In all the confusion it never occurred to me."

"Well, now we all have good reason to make this happen, don't we," asked Jason.

"Yes, we do!" John wiped the tears from his cheeks, "Right then, we should get to work."

"What do you need John," asked Chris.

"First, you need to sort out your personal situations, jobs etc. then we can get to it without any interference, agreed?"

"Well, I'm all yours now. I have no such ties," said Chris.

"I can quit my bank job. A week or two tops," added Judy.

They all looked at Jason, "Um, I don't do anything much as it is, so, it's all good. I'll tell them I'm on holiday and let the manager run the show. It can fall flat on its face for all I care."

"Great! You two might as well start now and Judy? You better get to work and hand in your resignation and nice to meet you by the way," John smiled.

"You too John," said Judy.

"Well now that everything's settled, where is the project up to John. How far off are we," Asked Chris.

"By my reckoning, we've got a few months' work ahead of us, a few more in testing so we should be ready to go in March if we don't hit any snags."

"March. OK," Chris said, his mind clearly distracted.

"What's wrong," asked Judy.

"Well, by then you should be two months pregnant."

All four of them stood silently at the thought. Everyone knew what Chris meant, even John who had heard the story before in another timeline.

"Perhaps you two need to talk but if you want my thoughts, it would be pointless to try, assuming we're successful. Of course, if we're not, then you miss your window. Tough decision," John said.

"First things first, I have to go quit my job," suggested Judy.

"Right. Of course, you go," said Chris.

"Take my car," added Jason as he tossed Judy the keys.

"Cool! Thanks. I've always wanted to drive one of those tech-mobiles."

"And scratch it up as much as you like."

They all laughed.

A few days later Chris, Judy and Jason were heading west, accompanied by John to the secluded and secure desert location where the machine was based. The trip was long, hot and boring, but the machine needed to be out of sight of everybody.

As they approached the facility Chris noticed that it didn't look anything like he anticipated. He expected to see something akin to a nuclear power plant or a space port. Instead, it simply looked like a huge factory or some kind of massive farm storage facility. It looked like nothing at all really. Just sheet metal panels and a slightly pitched roof. There were very few windows, but the huge metal doors were obvious although not unusual in the farming industry. The penny dropped quickly when he came to the realisation that it had to look ordinary to allay suspicion. At odds with the mundaneness of the facility was the massive level of security that could easily keep an army at bay if need be.

Upon entering the building his spaceport theory was more apparent. The exterior was simply a shell hiding the real deal, a mass of pipes, towers, electrical elements, conduit and high voltage wires by the thousands. There were also sections that didn't make any sense at all, great bulbs of glass like material and metal in a myriad of colours. Sheets of matt black graphite like material festooned on various walls and floors; heat resistant tiling like the Space Shuttle projects of his time and doors that sealed like those of a deep ocean submarine.

Inside the machine was a confusion of corridors, hutches and tech space. The computer rooms were crammed with a multitude of quantum computers, all networked and crunching numbers or being programmed to do so. Scientists and mathematicians worked side by side and looked a bit like surgeons performing a lifesaving operation. Dust free zones were sealed off from the general access ways. At the very centre was a circular room which rotated in any direction, controlled by huge electromagnets. The wall was covered in bubbles which turned out to be transport pods for everyone making the 'trip'. To access the pods, you walked onto a gantry and the wall simply rotated enabling easy access to each pod. The entire room was the size of a small stadium and could accommodate a thousand people. Another room of similar size was designed to encase equipment, spare parts and vehicles which were housed in larger pods.

"How does this all work? I mean when the time comes to push the big button, what happens," Chris asked.

"Honestly, I don't know for sure. It's like hypnotism really. We know it works, we just don't know why," John answered.

"You must have a basic idea?"

"Well sure. We have three main power units, all with different purposes. The first creates a bubble which envelops the entire facility, like a force field. Second, we charge those huge thingamajigs there," John pointed at four huge towers at the extremes of the facility's four corners, "They create the time vortex or wormhole or whatever you want to call it. When that's stable, we fire up the photon accelerator which we call The Spiker, housed under the facility. In theory it sends the bubble back in time through the wormhole. Simple," he said with a sarcastic smile on his face.

"Jesus," cried Jason, "And it works?"

"Not yet, but it will. We have much better power supply systems and better computers to work with this time. The calculations messed up the timing before, we think. This time will be different. Things must click to the millionth of a second. We just weren't capable of that before. Hindsight etc. but now we have exactly what we need."

"Good to know."

There was a definite lack of technical expertise amongst the newly appointed trio but as John explained, their focus would be primarily support and supervision, securing supplies and day to day running of the project. Between the three of them they had enough experience in that regard, and it meant they could maintain secrecy. The constant traffic flow could be hard to explain but the authorities hadn't made any enquiries yet.

Everyone involved in the reconstruction of the Parallax Machine would be flashing back, so all were motivated in some way to make it work. Chris found himself intrigued by how many people were involved, most not originally flashback victims but certainly affected by the more recent episodes. Their lives, regardless of cause, had been disrupted in some way.

The technology required to make the machine work was the stuff of imagination and many of the scientists found themselves giving components names from science fiction stories just for fun like the flux capacitor and the dilithium chambers although if they were actually made up of lithium batteries and designed to store a significant amount of energy which would be released at specific times during the various phases of the journey.

One major advantage they had was that this timeline was certainly advanced from a technological standpoint, so they were able to secure components and materials that were much better than the original machine contained.

After the inspection, Chris, Judy and Jason were shown the accommodation section of the facility, which was set up like a barracks with rooms for sleeping, a communal kitchen and shared amenities. It was basic, but it did the job and the food was pretty good under the circumstances.

Over a period of weeks, they worked feverishly as the new and improved machine came back together. Judy helped with logistics, Chris assisted around the machine itself, mainly doing labouring jobs to help the scientists. It also gave him more insight into how the machine worked while Jason used his extensive contacts to secure the more difficult components for the project.

It was hard work and was made more difficult by the extreme temperatures in the mid-summer desert. There was a brief pause to celebrate Christmas and then the New Year which was enjoyed by all the workers but for Chris and Judy it was the moment of truth. They still didn't know what to do about Caleb and the next morning was the time of conception.

"If we don't do it and this machine fails, then Caleb will be lost to us," Chris suggested, "However if we do...you know...do it, then Caleb may well be conceived but then if the machine works, well, I don't know?"

"What do you mean, you don't know," Judy asked.

"OK, suppose you get pregnant and then flashback, you will be reborn, physically reborn in 1962, but because another life form goes back too, I don't know what happens to him? Will he be part of you, will he start anew some other way, or will he simply cease to exist again?"

"Oh God! I never considered that. I assumed he would just not be. I mean if he isn't born until 1988, how can he exist at all in 1962?"

"I agree but he will effectively be flashing back because he's alive. He's inside your womb, but alive nonetheless, so I don't really know how things will go."

"So, we don't do it. It's that simple," Judy suggested.

"And if the machine fails?"

"Then we accept our fate, and Caleb's."

"That's easy for you because you've never met him, but I have. I knew him and loved him and nurtured him. I can't live with the idea that he will simply not be."

"It's an impossible decision," said Judy, "maybe we should talk to one of the scientists about it. What do you think?"

Chris liked the idea, "I'm open to anything but we must do it now because tomorrow is crunch time. My only concern is that everyone is quite drunk. I doubt we'll get a clear answer."

"What about her," Judy said pointing at a lonely figure sitting away from the crowd.

"Sure, why not?"

Chris and Judy walked up to the woman, "Do you mind if we join you?"

The startled lady looked up, wide eyed but then smiled and said, "Not at all, I could use the company."

"Great! I'm Chris and this is my wife, Judy."

"Nice to meet you," the woman said, "I'm Jennifer, but you can call me Jen."

At a guess she was in her late thirties, attractive but with her hair tied back in a brunette ponytail, no makeup and thick glasses she looked older. Even so, she was quite a lot younger than most of the scientists and mathematicians which probably accounted for her solo celebrations.

"What's your story Jen? How is it you're involved in all of this? Are you a flashback?"

"No, I was employed for the project as a computer programmer. I was a bit of a prodigy through school and Uni. I didn't have too many friends; it was all about study and work for me. When I joined Parallax, I had no idea what I was getting into, but it seemed very exciting and they were paying us a lot. But then I went through the same disruption as everyone else. I guess I'm kind of trapped in all this now. What about you two?"

Chris explained their situations and how he was the flashback while Judy was not. He talked about the more recent shift and how it disrupted his world and how he had to win back his wife's affections a second time. Jen listened intently,

"My goodness, that's extraordinary!"

"I know and now we have a dilemma we hope you can help with."

"Sure, what is it?"

They explained the situation with Caleb and the timing issues. They offered up their own theories while Jen listened. Chris concluded with, "So, the question is 'should we do it...in the morning, you know, try to conceive our son or not?"

Jen didn't answer immediately, and Chris could see her pondering all the angles. Finally, she said, "All of us working here talk about the time disruptions and movement through the years, backwards and forwards. We all have different theories but one thing we agree on is that going back resets everything, so bearing that in mind, Caleb would not go back, he would simply be erased and so I think you should do it. If this machine doesn't work, then you will have your son. If we succeed then he will, in my opinion, cease to exist in this plane and you will get another opportunity in the next timeline. That's my opinion but I have to say, I cannot offer any guarantees. This is all high-end science and there so much we simply cannot predict."

"We understand, and I feel as you do. I think it's worth a shot," suggested Chris. He then turned to Judy, "But it's really up to you Jude, what do you think?"

"Well, we have all the science and knowledge we could ever need but, in the end, it comes down to faith, doesn't it? You knew Caleb and clearly miss him. You know when he is conceived, and you know I believe you. So, I think we should do it."

"Really?"

"Really!"

"That's wonderful. I, I...I don't know what to say," Chris's eyes were watering pure joy.

"You don't need to say anything. He's our son, it's a no brainer when you really think about it. We must do it for him and for us, regardless of what happens with the machine."

Chris gathered Judy in his arms and gave her a huge hug and smothered her in kisses which resulted in Jen suffering the reddest of blushes, "Sorry Jen."

"Oh, no problem, glad I could help and congratulations, I guess."

Next morning Chris and Judy made love. Whatever happened next was down to fate.

Chapter 18

Weeks passed with Chris and Judy keeping their minds occupied working on the project. It was an impossible waiting game even so. In a short time, Judy started feeling ill and was off her food, particularly in the morning, and a quick examination by one of the doctors on staff at the facility confirmed that she was indeed pregnant. They could hardly contain their excitement. It was too soon to determine the sex of the child, but Chris knew in his gut that it was Caleb.

Around two months later, with Judy's baby bump showing slightly, the Parallax machine was declared complete and ready for testing. Of course, a dry run wasn't possible due to the functionality of the machine. Opening a time vortex probably wasn't a great idea unless you were ready to use it, so a series of diagnostics were performed on each element of the machine. All parameters were tested and the computer programs checked, re-checked and checked again again by each programmer and technician just to be certain nothing had been missed.

Like preparing for a manned rocket launch, the diagnostics took several days until everyone was happy. Reports were signed off and the project leaders handed their final approval to John, who accepted it with delight.

All were then assembled for the announcement, a total of 286 people whose lives were literally staked on the success of this machine.

"I just want to say thank you to everyone involved in this project," John said, "I know we've had some setbacks and for some of us the price has been too high. I can't tell you how much I appreciate your unwavering support and dedication."

A few tears were shed but mostly there were smiles and a lot of relief on the faces of the workers. They had pulled off something miraculous, essentially recreating a time warp machine that would kick them back to their very births and enable them all to reset their lives and start again.

"This time we will get it right! This time we will renew our lives, set things straight and make the world a better place. That's what Mum ultimately wanted and, God willing, we will now be able to deliver."

The group cheered!

"So, there's no point wasting any more time. I ask you all to do whatever you need to do to make yourselves ready. I want the jump to take place by the end of the week, come what may. Thank you again," John concluded.

Everyone cheered again before breaking up and making final preparations.

Chris turned to Judy, "OK, this is it. Are you ready?"

"I think so. It feels very strange though. It's not like going on a cruise or moving house, we're re-setting our lives!"

"I know. It's incredible. Even though I've been through this before, I still can't believe it."

Chris had told Judy all about what to expect and how her life might be once she came out the other side. They'd made a pact to find each other no matter what. There was no reason to expect that they wouldn't.

"What should I tell my parents? Should I, you know, show my hand," Judy asked.

"It's up to you. I didn't and it eventually caught up with me, so maybe you should. You'll know what to do. They're your parents, so they'll love you no matter what."

Judy nodded in agreement.

One of Chris's jobs in these months on site had been to lecture those who hadn't been spiked previously, so they too knew what was likely to happen. They asked the same questions as Judy and Chris gave them the same advice. A few were apprehensive because they were aware that their original births hadn't been easy and one or two had come close to dying. Chris tried his best to reassure them suggesting that what happened before would happen again and that they would come through it. He had to be honest though, this time they would be fully aware of the experience, and it would remain a strong memory, and they should be ready to face it. He also suggested that having an understanding might strengthen their resolve and they could overcome the disadvantage faster in some cases. He was only speculating of course but some accepted the idea.

A few scientists had been discussing the retained memory phenomenon following the Sun spikes and put it down to the synapses in the brain remaining intact during the transition enabling access to all memory functions. They speculated that the switch was physical and therefore, memory could be retained. Others thought it was simply a reset in time but not in mind and pure luck that someone could have an unconscious transference into a new mind and body. Whatever the reason, it was going to be a rough ride for some of those involved but they remained committed, nonetheless.

Most of the preparations were finalised in the next few days and the decision was made to fire up the machine at dawn the following day, Friday the 13th of May as it turned out. Being scientists, none paid much attention to the superstition.

The machine was ready, the people were ready, and the technicians were satisfied that all was optimal for the flashback to take place.

Chris tracked down Jason to wish him well. During their time in the desert, Jason had met his future wife, as The Boss had promised, and they were now very much in love.

"Great to see you two so happy," Chris said.

"Thanks Chris, it feels good, but now we have to go our separate ways again. Freaks me out."

"Understandable but we really had no choice I suppose."

"True," added Jason.

"Anyway, just wanted to say good luck and thank you for your support. I really underestimated you. You're a true friend," Chris confessed.

"No worries. It all worked out for the best, eventually."

Chris smiled, reached out a hand and they shook. I'll look you up some time."

"I'll hold you to that!"

Both men smiled and said goodbye.

At 4.00am on Friday everyone rose. The kitchen was closed; there didn't seem much point having a meal and leaving a mess. It probably wouldn't have mattered either way. Everyone simply woke, dressed and assembled at their respective rally points, ready to access the pods.

The Parallax Machine was programmed to operate automatically once all the travellers were safely on board. The lead scientists would simply push a button which would then signal the mainframe to begin the sequence. The whole process would take mere seconds in real time but the journey for each of them would be very much longer given what they were embarking on.

Chris hugged Judy, "See you on the other side Ray."

"What?"

"Ghostbusters? Never mind. I'll see you in a few years, at the library."

"Oh right. It's going to be so hard to live without you for that long."

"I know, but those first few years will be difficult enough. You'll have to work hard to train yourself and, well I've told you all this before," Chris suggested.

Judy let a tear roll down her cheek as she looked at her swollen tummy, "We're so close," she said as she rubbed her stomach.

Chris simply held on tight as they awaited their instructions. Soon enough the green light came on, and the first groups spread out across the gantry and entered their pods. Once secure the pod room rotated, and the next group did the same.

Eventually, Chris and Judy walked to their staging points on the gantry, looked at each other one more time and then stepped into their pods. Chris felt a pang of regret as soon as Judy was out of sight but kept on with the task of securing himself into the apparatus.

There wasn't much to the pod, it was simply a vessel that would be unaffected by the transition and come out the other side within the machine at the designated time. The technicians had created a two-phase operation, the vortex would flashback the people to their respective births while the machine itself would, in essence be sent to a specific time when they were all able to meet again at this same point in the desert, some years after being born. It would be a quick jump for the machine but years in terms of the travellers who, in some cases would live 60 or 70 years before the machine's re-emergence.

Chris's pod closed like a coffin. It has no window or porthole, it didn't seem necessary, there'd be nothing to see anyway and once the process was over, he'd be inside his mother's womb again, for the third time as it turned out. He shook his head in disbelief at the thought.

He lay on the vinyl feeling its cold surface on his back. The seat was like a basic concave chair, and he strapped himself in with seat belts across his thighs and chest. A few tally lights provided the only illumination. White light to see and coloured lights that were simple indicators of the process; currently amber saying that the loading wasn't yet complete. A green light would show all systems go, a red flashing light and buzzer would indicate an abort and evacuation, which no-one expected. Even so, they had done several drills, just in case. Chris wondered if anyone would have a chance to escape if there was a failure, given the power levels and everything else that was supposed to happen in exact millisecond bursts.

Chris felt the room rotate every few minutes as the next batch of the travellers entered their respective pods. He couldn't take his mind off Judy though and wondered if she was ok. In hindsight, having some kind of communications system might not have been a bad idea from a human standpoint.

The process seemed to take forever, a slight rotational movement, and then nothing, then the pod would move again. Eventually he felt his weight shift as his pod rotated to the upside of the room, suspending him on the belts. Ultimately the belts would do nothing as the pod room would soon be spinning and centrifugal force would pin him and the other passengers to their seats.

Around half an hour later Chris saw the green tally light brighten, all was in readiness. He knew that the lead technician was in place and would simply push the go button to fire up the Parallax Machine and in a few seconds, he would be reborn. He held his breath.

The first thing he felt was the pod room moving again but this time it didn't stop; it sped up and within a few minutes he was pressing back into his chair as the centrifugal force took hold. In a short time, the pod room reached full speed. It was a little uncomfortable but not significantly so. The constant hum of the pod room rotating was somehow reassuring.

Then the first of the machine's power banks fired up. Chris could hear the circuit breakers snapping into place, venting tens of thousands of amps of energy creating the virtual bubble, encasing the entire facility.

Chris couldn't see anything at this stage, but he kept an eye on the green tally light just in case of an abort signal.

Seconds later the quantum computers signalled the system to fire up the second set of batteries which would light up the photon accelerators and the vortex bulbs. Chris was struck immediately by a powerful feeling and the pod inexplicably flung open. He didn't know what to think, it wasn't mentioned in the briefings, and he was worried. He felt like he was suspended in a dark tunnel, floating for a moment then he emerged from the pod. He recalled people saying that no-one really knew how the process would work but most agreed the transference would occur in an enclosed pod, so this was odd. He felt a little uneasy but convinced himself that it was normal.

Any second now he thought, anticipating the emergence into his infant self and the birthing process as his mother's pelvic muscles pushed him into his next life. He closed his eyes and held his breath, remembering how he took a mouthful of amniotic fluid last time.

A few more seconds passed but nothing happened. It was like time had somehow been interrupted or stopped completely. He opened his eyes and could make out the shape of the other pods which were all now suspended in the vortex. They appeared like cigar shaped blobs which stretched in a circle up and down away from where he was floating. All were sealed, except for his and one other which appeared to have also opened and was emitting light. Now he knew something was wrong.

What the Hell?

As he watched, a figure appeared in the distance, floating like him. He looked about and saw no-one else. He checked Judy's pod, which appeared intact then turned his attention back to the figure, who had also spotted him. As if by will alone they started moving towards one another. Oddly there was little sound, just a dark void all around which they seemed to be suspended in

"I don't think this is supposed to be happening," called Chris to the unidentified individual.

A familiar voice came back, "Where am I?"

Chris's face crumpled in confusion, "Who are you?"

"Funny, I was about to ask you the same question."

As the pair came closer together, Chris got a glimpse of the man's outline. He seemed eerily similar to Chris, "What's your name?"

The figure was clearly analysing Chris as much as Chris was doing to him, "I'm Chris."

"Chris who?"

Just as he completed the question, the man came into full view, "I'm Chris Parish!"

Chris gasped and went white with shock, "You're...me?! That's impossible!!"

"I was about to say that exact sentence, what on Earth is happening? Am I dreaming?" The pair finally got close enough together to make out more detail. Chris couldn't speak for a moment as he looked at a carbon copy of himself; a living, speaking, breathing replica, "I must be dreaming or dead or something," said the second Chris.

"Where do you come from? How did you get here? I would have noticed my own doppelganger working on this project," Chris suggested.

"Yeah well, I hate to disappoint you, but I have no clue where I am. I was just snatched out of my bed...again!"

"Wait a minute, this happened before?

"Well not like this but sure, months ago. I was just living my life and wham! Woke up in a changed world overnight. I thought I was going mad. Still haven't been able to find out what happened."

"No way, so you were with your wife?"

"Judy? Sure, she was different though."

"In what way," Chris asked.

"She liked me for starters, and we were in love again and we were happy. Never thought I could get her back, but she was suddenly cool with me, so I went along with it."

Multiple Universes?

"Ok, this is going to sound crazy, but I wonder if we got swapped when that event happened and now it's happening again?"

"Search me?"

"What was the world like where you've come from?"

"To be honest, primitive compared to what I knew before, why? Where did you come from?"

"Sounds like I was shifted into your world and you into mine. Now we're somehow shifting back again...I think."

"Whoa, that's too heavy!! What do you mean shifting back?"

"Seems that the overlapping Universe theory was right. We switched Universes somehow and now we're in limbo."

"That's ridiculous!"

"And yet, here we are. Did you ever talk to Fred Wilson, the astronomer?"

"No, never had the pleasure but I've heard of him. What's that got to do with anything?"

"Doesn't matter," Chris was thinking at a thousand miles an hour now, "Look, I don't know how long we've got."

"For what," asked the second Chris.

"To go back to our real worlds!"

"Wait a minute. You're assuming I want that. My wife hates me there, if you're right about this Universe switch!"

"She used to hate you, but not anymore, I fixed all that, she's 100% with you," Chris pointed to Judy's pod, "See there? That's your wife!"

"What? You're lying. She's at home in bed!"

"Yes and no. She's right there and at home in bed. Look I haven't got time to go into detail, she's about to go through a time vortex and be reborn and you need to do the same!"

"Why?"
"Because she's pregnant!"

Just then Chris realised what he'd said. She was pregnant but not to the man he was talking to, it was his child she carried. And she wouldn't be pregnant in a few second because she was about to become a baby herself.

Jesus, this is madness

"Well, that's a hoot, my Judy is pregnant too!"

"What?!"

"Yes, she seemed to know when we needed to do it! Something about timing and having Caleb...so, she fell pregnant as planned. Her plan, not mine."

"New Years Day!"

"Right! How did you know...." Finally, the penny dropped with the second Chris, "Holy shit!! You're telling the truth!"

"Yes, I am!"

"This is real?"

"Yes!" Both hovered in silence for a moment but then Chris realised what he needed to do, "Look, you have to get into that pod!" he pointed to the one that he emerged from, "Somehow I think we being offered an opportunity to switch back and set things right."

"But what about the pregnancies? What happens with them?"

"Your Judy will be reborn, and you'll grow up and meet her again, I will do the same in my Universe. You must trust me on that."

"Well, I'm looking at myself, hearing all this weird stuff, why wouldn't I believe it?"

"Wait, were you spiked before. Were you reborn by Sun spikes in your original Universe in 2014?"

"No idea what you're talking about and 2014 hasn't happened yet. It's only 1988," said the second Chris.

"Holy shit! OK, something's going to happen, and I haven't got time to give you the big picture, but you are about to experience a rebirth. Not a biblical rebirth, a real one. When you get into that pod, you will go through a time vortex and be born again in 1962 and start your life over, but you'll remember everything from before...and I mean everything!"

The second Chris's face revealed only dismay, "Look, this sounds ridiculous and if I wasn't floating in some weird bubble room talking to myself, I'd think it was crazy or a dream, but something tells me this is really happening. It's too vivid to be a dream."

"Believe me, it's real," Chris said, "So you'll go?"

"I guess I have to. Where else can I go?"

"Good point. Go in there and I'll get to that other pod if I can."

That very second Chris seemed to levitate to the pod just as it was closing again. He looked back at Chris, "Thanks, I think."

"No worries," Chris said, "and one more thing?"

"What's that?"

"Treat her good this time. Lay off the gambling. You have a second chance, don't blow it!"

The other Chris smiled, gave a thumbs up and said, "You have my word." He slid into the pod just as the door sealed shut.

This is so weird

Chris should have been perplexed by the experience he just had but instead he felt driven to get to the other pod and take the opportunity before him. Still, he couldn't help wondering why this was happening and if there was some other influence in play? He dismissed the thought. He could try and figure that out some other time.

Chris then looked toward the second pod a short distance away and felt himself drifting towards it, moving by will alone. As he closed on his target, he could see that it was open and empty. He suddenly felt torn between the Judy he knew and the Judy he was leaving but he also knew it was right to switch back to his real world, where his real wife would be. He wasn't worried about the pregnancy because he knew that it would be erased, and they would try again in the next life. He resigned himself to that, so this new twist didn't really factor in. He was surprised by how calm he felt.

As he entered the pod and the hatch sealed him in a horrible thought came to mind, his Judy wasn't in this world, the one he was about to leave. She was still in the old world; would that be an issue? Too late now. A jolt then a fierce light split the pod and injected itself into his head and the headache he'd felt when he was originally spiked, again erupted in his brain and he vanished down the dark tunnel. The sensation of falling was also the same as before and he knew that next he would be surrounded by liquid and feel the pressure of birth any second but then the falling stopped, there was no pressure, no confinement, there was no emergence, there was just darkness. Chris suddenly blacked out.

As Chris began to awaken, he could hear muffled voices. He couldn't move his arms or legs and the noises around him were dull and indecipherable. He opened his eyes. There were bright lights, but his vision was blurred and he couldn't make out much. He was aware of figures moving about but nothing more. He tried to talk but the only sound that came out was a squawk.

"He's awake. Someone page the doctor in ICU, tell him we have the survivor!!"

ICU? This didn't happen last time??

Chris could feel himself moving along on a gurney, lights flashing overhead as he passed under them. He tried again to talk but he simply couldn't. The gurney crashed through a set of doors, made a swift turn to the right then crashed through another swinging door. A few seconds later he felt himself lift and then land on a soft surface, a hospital bed. He then realised he had a tube down his throat and felt air pumping into his lungs. He coughed.

A stern male voice then said, "Someone take that crap out of his mouth, he's breathing on his own."

He felt someone cup his head and a female voice said softly, "Sir, I'm going to pull this tube from your throat. On three I want you to give a big cough and keep exhaling," Chris nodded in the affirmative, "One, two, three!"

He coughed and kept blowing the air from his lungs as the tube slithered out of his throat and mouth. It ripped as it did so, the pain bringing tears to Chris's eyes. A second later it was over, and he took a long shaky breath, reinflating his lungs.

"Well done sir," said the voice, "Now relax. You need to rest."

Chris didn't want to rest though; he had to find out what was going on but struggled to talk. He felt pain now all through his body but still managed to spit out a few raspy words, "What happened?"

The female voice replied, "No-one knows Sir, a terrible accident of some kind. A terrible mess, but don't worry you'll be OK."

"My wife?"

"I don't know sir. Now please rest, you really shouldn't be trying to talk."

Before the woman said any more, Chris was unconscious.

Sometime later, Chris awoke. He had no clue how long he was out. He felt groggy and pain racked his entire body. His throat was of fire, and he felt an incredible thirst, "Water, somebody, water please?" he rasped.

He heard a clutter and footsteps, then a soft hand lifted his head, "Here, there's a straw." Chris felt the plastic hit his lips and he latched onto it and sucked furiously, "Not too much sir."
The liquid was cool and refreshing despite the sting he felt in his throat. He released the straw, "Thank you."

"You're welcome, Sir."

"Why are you calling me sir? My name is Chris, Chris Parish."

"Well...Chris. We didn't know who you were. You were without identification."

Chris realised, suddenly that he wasn't a baby. He could talk and he noticed now that he filled the entire bed and somehow knew it wasn't a crib, "How long have I been asleep?"

"Around 15 hours or so. It was a close thing for a while. Your body has been through something traumatic, but you're going to be OK we think."

Chris ignored the remarks, "What day is it?"

"It's Tuesday."

Tuesday? That can't be right.

"Don't you mean Friday? Friday the 13th?"

"No sir, it's Tuesday the 13th of May," said the woman.

Chris, despite the confusion and pain, considered another possibility, 'What's the year?"

"The year? It's 2014 sir."

Chris felt a deep swirling in his gut as the shock of the answer set in. It was the same feeling as being told of a death in the family and he began to cry.

"What is it sir? Do you need a doctor? I'll page one." The woman, a nurse it seemed, picked up a phone, "We need a doctor to ICU, STAT! It's the mystery patient," she hung up, "A doctor will be here shortly."

Chris didn't answer. The news of his arrival into 2014 was still grinding on his sensibilities.

What went wrong? What happened to Judy?

He wept uncontrollably. He was thinking about Judy and Caleb, Jason and everyone else on the Parallax machine? What had happened to them? Where were they? The thoughts rotated in his head uncontrollably.

Moments later he heard running feet in a hallway and then entering the room, "What's the problem?" demanded a male voice.

"I'm not sure Doctor. He woke and we talked a bit. He took some water then just had some kind of emotional breakdown."

"Hardly surprising after what he's been through. What did he say?"

"He thought it was Friday the 13th but I told him it was Tuesday. Then he asked the year, so I told him and he. Well, this," and the nurse nodded towards Chris as he now cried out hysterically.

The doctor turned to Chris, "Sir, can you hear me, Sir?!"

"His name is Chris," said the nurse.

"What," asked the doctor.

"He told me his name was Chris Parish."

"Right," said the doctor, "Chris, can you hear me? You need to calm down."

Machines were beeping and alarms were sounding off. He didn't know why but it was freaking him out even more.

"Ok, we'll have to calm him down or he'll go into cardiac arrest."

A few seconds later he felt a sting, followed by a coldness moving up his arm, then darkness again.

When Chris woke a different nurse told him he'd slept another eleven hours. He had nothing to say about that but physically he felt a bit better, although the pain was still significant, like his entire body had been slammed into concrete and every bone was shattered. He wondered again about the machine and why it had spun him forward and that he remained an adult. It didn't make sense, but he had no way of figuring out the reason for the failure. Maybe when he got out of here, he could learn more or maybe he'd never know the truth. For now, he resigned himself to the fact that it had indeed gone horribly wrong yet again. Perhaps it was a simple oversight in the programming, something they missed repeatedly. He remembered how the Russians made similar mistakes with their spacecraft when they programmed a rocket to go to the Moon with the distance in miles instead of kilometres. Rather than a soft landing on the lunar surface, the rocket hit the Moon at full tilt! Could it have been that simple? Probably, but then he thought, what if it was sabotage? He dismissed the idea.

Chris realised his vision was improving and he could see around the room. It was blurry but he noticed it was a room with a glass wall and door through which he could see a corridor. He imagined that there were similar rooms either side. There were no windows. Privacy didn't seem to be a factor and why would it be? Being in this place certainly meant you were on the brink. The other walls and the ceiling were light grey, and the back wall was a haven for sockets, dials and an array of fixtures to plug in anything from a respirator to a mobile phone it seemed. The trolley next to his bed had a heart monitor beeping slowly, which was a relief, and another held his saline drip with another dosing him up on who knows what, probably a painkiller. It wasn't working.

Chris remembered being in the same situation a long time ago, after the car crash that killed his parents. The thought again, fleeting, who was that in the car that hit them? He also wondered which realm he had ended up in after swapping pods with the other Chris and what had happened to him? He may never know that either. He decided to try and find out, "Excuse me?", he asked the nurse.

"Yes sir, how can I help?"

He could see she was young, brunette, late twenties, "Do you know what happened to me?"

"Not much sir. There was a terrible accident, some kind of collapse. It's all over the news."

"Oh…" Chris felt a shiver, "My wife? Her name is Judy."

"No idea I'm sorry to say. So far, you're the only survivor."

"Survivor of what?"

"I really don't know. Perhaps when the police arrive. They'll be wanting to talk to you when you're feeling better; they've been quite persistent," she explained.

"Thank you."

"Quite alright sir."

"Chris, my name is Chris."

"Of course, I'll write it on the chart, so people know."

"Thanks," Chris had one more thought, "Um, we're in Sydney, right?"

"Yes?"

"Ok, how did I get here? I was hundreds of miles away. Was I transported after the accident?"

"No Chris, the accident happened right here, in the city!"

My God, how?

Chris hadn't gained much knowledge from the conversation, Parallax was in different parts of the city in both the Universes he'd seen, so which was it? And how did he end up there and not just re-emerged in the desert. The machine wasn't supposed to move localities, just time.

"How much damage exactly," Chris asked.

"Quite a lot sir, the entire building was demolished, all 12 floors!"

12 floors?

In his original dimension Chris had worked on the 17th floor of the Parallax Building. He knew it had 24 floors in total. The Parallax building in the alternative Universe was much taller, so this was just another confusing factor. He didn't know what to think.

The biggest problem right now was the issue of the year, 2014. What had happened to those 26 years? Was Judy still around? Was he even part of the picture? So many questions and too few answers.

"Is there some way of contacting my wife?"

"Certainly, what's her name and phone number or an address if that's easier?"

Chris knew those details off by heart. Interestingly in both Universes, that hadn't changed. He told the nurse who agreed to make the call and contact Judy. He was feeling quite apprehensive, not knowing what might have happened but he also felt excited to a degree. Everything might be ok after all.

Before he could learn anything about Judy though, the Police had called, and he agreed to speak with them. They took no time to arrive.

"Hello Mr Parish, thank you for talking to us. I'm Inspector Keith Williamson and this is my colleague, Inspector John Summers."

"Hi."

"We'll keep this brief if we can. Are you able to tell us what you remember about that morning and the event that took place?"

"Event?"

"Yes, the event, the collapse of the Castlereagh bank building and the cause of it? I assume you worked there?"

Castlereagh bank building?

Chris recalled that there was an old bank building on the site where Parallax would be established after his first flashback. This must be his original universe, before anything happened but he wasn't certain. He let the thought go and turned his attention back to the question at hand.

"Well, it's a little more complicated than that. I worked there many years ago. I haven't been inside that building in years."

The two men looked at him with astonishment, "How then were you in the building yesterday?"

"I don't know. I wasn't even in the city yesterday."

The second inspector turned to the first, "Amnesia I think, he doesn't know what he's saying."

"Hello, I can hear you," Chris said cheekily.

"Sorry sir, but what you're saying makes no sense. You were pulled from the rubble of a collapsed building and yet you say you were never in it, or in the city at the time. So where were you?"

Chris suddenly realised that telling the truth would only confirm their suspicions, that he was crazy, but he had no way of explaining things to them rationally. He would have to lie, "Look, it's all very confusing. When I said I hadn't been in that building I meant as an employee. I have been consulting for them on and off, so I could have been there. I just can't remember." It was only a half lie.

"I see," said Inspector Williamson, "But you said you weren't even in the city?"

"Yes well, that's what I woke up thinking. I may have been remembering something else from weeks ago. I honestly can't recall."

Just then a doctor walked in, "Sorry gentleman, he's been through a lot and he's not going to make much sense for a while," and he pointed at one of the drip bags.

"That's true," added Summers sarcastically.

"I'm sorry," said Chris faking his desire to help.

"That's OK sir, we'll come back when things have settled down."

"Thank you," said the doctor.

But before the officers took a step Chris asked, "Were there any others? Survivors or anyone else?"

They looked at each other, then at Chris. Williamson's face looked grim, "I'm sorry Chris, but you're the only one they've pulled out. Funny thing is, you're the only one full stop. We haven't found a single body in the wreckage.

"Wreckage?"

Williamson realised he'd said something he shouldn't have, "Well," he spluttered, "the carnage, the rubble, call it whatever you like."

"I see. Thank you," Chris said but he knew the Inspector was lying.

As the officers left, the nurse from earlier poked her head it, "Mr Parish? Your wife is here."

Chapter 19

Chris felt a chill run through his body as he anticipated the reunion with Judy. He didn't know what to expect or what she would be like. What effect did all the time slips have on her life? He thought about the other Chris and the attitude he demonstrated. On reflection that version of Chris seemed arrogant and careless. Had he done any damage to the relationship? Was there any impact in the time between the machine's activation and now, some twenty-six years which, to him, went by in a flash. He only hoped that whichever version of himself had been in Judy's life during that time, he had treated her right. Now she was coming to see her husband who had survived some terrible accident, for reasons he still couldn't fathom.

He heard footsteps and looked through the glass of the hospital room. The blurriness didn't help. It was like losing one's glasses, the images were warped and featureless. Two figures appeared, but he couldn't make out any detail. Had they looked at him? No way of knowing. They stopped briefly and spoke to someone, probably the doctor before the door swung open and the pair stepped in.

As they approach there was a noticeable gasp. Judy came closer and Chris was now able to make out her features. Even though he'd only seen her, or a version of her a mere day or two ago, she was now a fifty something woman and it shocked him. He hadn't seen her like that in a very long time, since this whole crazy journey started and he wasn't expecting it.

"Oh my God, it really is you," Judy said sounding astonished.

"Yeah, it's me," came the croaky reply.

"Where have you been? What happened to you?!"

"Um, well it's a long story. I don't know where to start. What was the last thing you remember?"

"Well?" Judy paused, "God, this is so crazy. I can't believe you're here!"

For some reason Chris was starting to get a dark feeling. The way she was talking didn't give him a good vibe, "Judy, you saw me a couple of days ago. I mean a version of me to be more precise, what's with all the surprise?"

Judy frowned as Chris's words sank in, "Two days ago? Chris, you've been gone for 26 years!"

"What?" Chris was mortified.

"And now, you're back and you haven't aged a single day; I don't understand?!" Judy was suddenly crying and ran from the room, leaving Chris in total dismay.

Chris called out to her, pleading for her to wait but she was too distraught to listen. That left a lonely figure in the room who now moved to the side of the bed, "Hi Dad!"

Chris's head turned suddenly at the voice, "Caleb?"

"Yes Dad, it's me."

Chris was stunned for a few seconds and just sat with his mouth agape, "I...I don't know what to say. I've missed you so much! Come and give your dad a hug."

Caleb didn't hesitate and landed in his father's arms, sobbing uncontrollably, "We thought you died or something. Mum says you were just gone one day and never came back."

"I'm here now. It's ok." They held each other for a few minutes before things settled down, "Let me take a look at you." Caleb stepped back while Chris squinted to clear his vision. It was no use, but he didn't care, he could see that Caleb looked strong; a fine young man indeed, "You look well. How has everything been, you know since I vanished?"

"It's been tough on Mum. She was a single mother."

"Oh right, if what your mother says is true, I would have gone before you were born, I guess. I didn't think of that. Jesus, this is so messed up."

"Yeah, it is a bit. I'm talking to my dad, who I've never met and he's the same age as me."

Chris felt another jolt of shock, "Oh Lord, I can't believe that either. No wonder your mother freaked out."

"Well, I'm struggling too. This is some crazy shit Dad," Caleb added.

"I know it is and I'm sorry I haven't been around. It's a long story and one you'll find hard to believe."

"I can see that."

Chris hesitated but then asked, "What about your mother, has she moved on? I mean, I've been gone a long time, she must have found someone else?"

"There were a few men over the years, but nothing ever lasted. She never got over you really. She went through phases, anger, depression, that sort of thing. There were also periods of happiness, but mostly she just missed you," Caleb said.

"God, I'm so sorry."

"What happened Dad? Where did you go? And why are you still so young?"

"I think it would be easier to tell you both together. It wasn't a choice I made, it was just a freak event. I got caught up in a thing that no-one could have predicted. Sheer bad luck, wrong place, wrong time. That simple."

"You better do some fast talking then, because I can't understand why you left me like that?" It was Judy. She'd gathered her wits and was back in the room.

"Come here babe, please let me see you."

Judy walked up to the bed. It was still hard for Chris to get a decent picture of her, but clearly, she was his original Judy, "Tell me what you remember, please. I can probably fill in the blanks from there. I'll try to anyway."

Chris held out a hand and, after a moment he felt Judy's hand slip into his, her skin soft and smooth. He gave her a light squeeze and felt her skin slip over her knuckles as he rubbed them with his thumb. It was a reflex action, something he did many times when they were intimate and she recognised it instantly, "Oh God, it really is you!" Judy wept again.

"Talk to me Judy, I really need to know your side of it before I can make my story understandable to you. If that's even possible."

"OK, this is weird but here goes. Before you vanished, we were happy. We were expecting Caleb. Everything was great. I mean, we had some problems then. Money was tight and…"

"And what?"

"You were gambling; I know that now. I found a box of tickets and the bank account was next to empty. You nearly cleaned us out, but I didn't know that. I mean we were ok but then you were gone and I…" Judy stopped.

"Gone how? What happened?"

"I'll never forget it. It was Friday the 13th of May 1988. I woke up and you were just not there. Not in the bed, not in the house, nowhere. You didn't take anything either, your wallet, keys, clothing, nothing. It was all still at home," Tears were streaming down her face, eyes bloodshot now and she was shaking her head in confusion, "What happened Chris?"

Chris, in hearing the exact date of his vanishing, realised where Judy and Caleb fitted into his distorted time history and where he was too, so he could now tell them everything that had happened. The latest attempt to flashback had somehow converged with his original timeline and caused him to vanish much sooner than the Sun Spike had. It virtually eradicated the entire relationship with his wife and son. He knew they'd have trouble believing but he was determined to tell the truth yet again, "OK, you both better sit down, I've got a lot to tell you and it's going to be hard to comprehend."

Judy and Caleb dragged a pair of hospital chairs to Chris's bedside and settled in.

"OK, the first thing I say is going to be a big shock and you will not believe me but it's the starting point of a long and confusing story, so you have to trust that I'm telling the truth. Just hear me out and you can ask as many questions as you like after. Agreed?"

"Ok Chris," said Judy.

"Sure Dad," added Caleb.

"Right then. By my calculations I am technically 104 years old, but because of the jump I'm only 78, I think?!"

"What!!!? This is a bad joke," Judy scoffed.

"Please, let me explain. I'm not lying. Look at me, I mean, I'm supposed to be 52, right? But I'm lying here looking a 26-year-old very much, so give me a bit of latitude, if that's ok?" He tried not to sound too aggressive, but it came out harshly in any case.

"Sorry, it's just way too much to take in."

"I know it is, but it will eventually make sense, I hope?"

Both Judy and Caleb said, "OK" in response.

"Right, here goes. In 2014 I was struck by a natural phenomenon; we called it a Sun Spike." He could see the confusion on their faces, but they didn't interrupt, "Yeah, I know, it's currently 2014 but keep listening. The Sun spike created some kind of time distortion effect, and I was sent back to my birth in 1962 and started living my life again, literally. I consciously experienced my birth, and I carried with me all the knowledge of my original 52 years, giving me huge advantages, so I thought…"

Chris continued to talk, explaining how he met his parents and grandparents again and what became of them, how he met Judy, their marriage, the job at Parallax Corporation and how rich and successful he became and how great their lives were. He told them about The Boss and her plans to save the planet from itself though her control of advanced technology, amongst other things.

"Then, one day, it was suddenly gone. I woke up and the World had changed," he said and he explained how Judy again hated him, like everything they'd achieved had simply dissolved. He described the alternative Universe, Jason Milne becoming an ally and how it was basically the same place as this only more advanced and that he never felt quite at home there.

Chris went on to say how he discovered that Parallax existed in that realm too and how they had caused the second time shift through the creation of the Parallax Machine, but something went wrong.

He spoke as candidly and calmly as possible, told them how he met Judy again and how they fell in love yet again and started to live their lives once more. They were settling down when he learned of plans by Parallax to reinvent their machine and try to reset the World, mainly for the benefit of The Boss more than anything else and he explained how the machine had thrust her and the others back and she had aged considerably and wanted to fix her error.

He wanted to stop them but realised he simply didn't have the capacity to do so and agreed to help them instead, with Judy by his side as a part of the project. They would warp back together and start their lives over yet again, planning to meet in the future with all their life's knowledge and be together, with Caleb.

"And so, on May 13th, 1988, we hit the button, but it somehow didn't happen like it should have. During the transition I was ejected from my pod along with another passenger, who turned out to be the Chris Parish from that alternative Universe. I still can't explain it, but I think we were swapped when the Parallax Machine was first fired up and then the May 13 event somehow switched us back," Chris took a deep breath then continued, "I don't know what went wrong or why but something terrible happened and I'm back in 2014 instead of 1962 and yet I'm 26 years old, the age I was in 1988. I assure you that the story I've told you is true. That's it, that's everything."

Chris stopped talking and left them to absorb the information. His throat was sore from the strain of talking but he had to set everything straight. He couldn't really see their faces clearly, but he could almost hear the tumblers in their minds grinding away as they crunched the data.

"So, this other Chris Parish, did I meet him?" Judy asked.

"Well, yes and no. He certainly met you and he told me you were pregnant BUT from what you've told me, I was the one that vanished so essentially, no you haven't met him. His existence in this realm has been erased I think."

"Thank God," Judy exclaimed.

Chris was confused for a moment and then realised what she was thinking, Caleb was indeed his son and not the son of the other Chris Parish, "Oh, right! Yes, I'm Caleb's Dad, definitely."

"And this other Judy, what happened to her?"

"I have no idea. She must have stayed in her own Universe. You must realise that I didn't figure out the alternative universe was a thing until I met my other self and even then, I wasn't sure, not until I woke up here."

"I see, so why are you so young?"

"The flashback failed. Something went wrong. A computer glitch; maybe something else. I may never know. I don't know why I ended up here and not in the desert where the machine was due to reappear, around now actually. There must have been a mistake in the programming or in the destination files. I wasn't much involved in that side of it, so..."

"But she was pregnant?"

"Yes."

"To you?"

"Yes, I mean I thought she was you and we wanted to make sure Caleb was conceived so we set the date."

"New Year's Day, 1988," Judy said.

Chris smiled, "Yes, even though we knew the flashback would revert it all, we wanted a contingency plan in case the whole thing failed. That way we would still have Caleb, no matter what."

"And if it went the way you all planned?"

"We would meet again, grow up, marry and conceive Caleb just like before. That was the plan."

"And a well thought out plan. I…" she hesitated.

"What Judy?"

"I love how you both made sure Caleb was your top priority. You would have had to wait a long time to see him if things had gone as you expected."

"I know, but we had no choice. If we hadn't gone along with Parallax, they would have done it anyway and there would still have been a time shift, and I really don't know what would have happened. Better to start again on familiar ground."

"I see that. I even admire it. I don't even feel like you wronged me by getting another woman pregnant, even though she was me," Judy paused, "Wow, I just heard myself. This is truly out of my league. I can't believe what I'm hearing or saying."

"But you do believe me?"

"Strangely I do. Somehow, I just know you're telling the truth."

Chris let out a huge sigh of relief, "I've missed you both so much, especially you Caleb. I haven't seen you in such a long time. I'm just so happy to have you both back."

"Well let's not get too hasty Chris, there's still a lot of ground to cover. First, there's now a significant age difference and your son is the same age as you. How do we deal with that, let alone explain it?"

"I don't know and frankly I don't care. I'm not losing you two again. I love you more than ever Judy and that won't change regardless of any age difference. It might be fun growing up with my son too…"

"Oh shit," said Caleb, "Dad, I'm married, with my own son. I have a home and a job. I have a life. I'm all grown up already."

Chris lit up, "I'm a grandfather?"

"Yes Dad, his name is Clem!"

Chris way crying now, with joy, "Are they still?" He didn't finish the question.

"No," said Judy, "Clem, Edith and your parents, they all passed. I can go over all the details another time I guess, if you want to know."

"Of course I do, but I've seen it all before in one way or another," Chris paused, it wasn't surprising news. Then he turned to Caleb, "She brought you up well Caleb. I'm so very proud," Chris turned back to his wife, "He's a fine young man, you did a good job."

"You seem surprised!?"

"Well lets' just say that when I was around before, Caleb and I were not on the best of terms but that was my fault. Everything that happened to you both then was my doing. In some respects, you were better off without me, I can see that. He's a much better man than I made him."

"Well, I have no memory of that."

"Because, as of this timeline and what's transpired, it didn't happen to either of you. Only to me. You have lived an alternative life without me because of a freak event and then because of Parallax."

"So, what happens now," Judy asked.

"I suppose, when I get out of here, we try to rebuild our lives, if that's what you want?"

"When they told me you were here; I didn't believe them. I thought you'd died a long time ago, killed by someone you owed money or something horrible like that. Now that I see you, I'm in complete shock. You're so young. I'm not sure I can handle that."

"I understand, and I can't make you take me back, but you need to know that I never gave up on us and, from what I can tell, neither did you, so there's something we can build on, isn't there?" Chris asked, feeling quietly desperate.

"I don't know Chris. I hope so, but I need time to think."

Time? How ironic

Just then the doctor walked in, "Sorry folks, you need to wrap this up. We have to do some tests."

Chris ignored him, "OK, just think about it Judy. Come back tomorrow, please. We have to keep talking."

"OK, I will."

With that she gave Chris a soft peck on the cheek and walked out. He could tell she'd started crying again. Caleb looked at his father and gave a half smile, "I'll talk to her dad. See what she's feeling. It'll be OK."

Chris couldn't believe the man that stood before him and his heart swelled even more and he gave Caleb a reassuring squeeze on the upper arm, "Thank you."

"See you soon Dad," Caleb said as he walked out and caught up with his mother.

They'd hardly left the room when the doctor swooped in, "Right, sorry about that Mister? Mr Parish is it," asked the doctor.

"Yes, that's right."

"I'm glad we finally have a name, how are you feeling?"

"Tired, sore. What's wrong with me?"

"Well, there certainly has been some kind of trauma event, that's for sure, but we can't see any breaks or any damage to your organs, but something's not right, we just can't tell what it might be."

"That doesn't sound encouraging," Chris suggested.

"Yes, I'm sorry but that's all we have so far. We need to take some blood and do some tests, reflexes, neurological, the full kit really. And when you're feeling a bit better, stress tests, that kind of thing."

"You don't sound too certain of much Doc."

"Well to be frank, we're completely nonplussed. You should have been crushed in that mess but here you are, basically intact. It doesn't add up. Any idea what happened?"

"All I know is that I woke up here, I don't remember anything else," Chris was lying of course. He just didn't know who he could trust.

"Well, we'll look at your brain first, see what's going on there. Your memory might come back."

"Thanks Doc. Right now, I just want to sleep."

"Sure thing, after we do some of these tests," and the doctor scribbled on Chris's chart

Over the next few hours, he was wheeled from one end of the hospital to the other, poked, prodded, scanned and stung as they tried to get an idea of what was ailing him.

When he finally got back to his room, he was exhausted and before a few more seconds went by Chris was in a deep sleep and didn't wake for another twelve hours.

The next day Chris was roused by a nurse, "I'm sorry Mr Parish, but the police officers are back and want to talk to you again."

"That's ok," Chris said in a croaky voice, this time the result of being suddenly woken, "I'll talk to them."

"Would you like anything to eat or drink?"

"Sure, anything, I'm famished."

"OK, I'll get something sent up."

"Thanks," said Chris as the nurse waved the police into the room. He noticed that his vision had improved almost to normal. Things were clear now, not perfect but certainly better than the last time he was awake.

Williamson and Summers were at Chris's bedside at light speed, "Good morning, Mr Parish," uttered Williamson as Summers nodded a half-hearted greeting.

"Hello gents, nice to see you again."

Chris got his first real look at the two men. Keith Williamson was a tall, rather thin man of about forty, with a receding hairline and a pale complexion, bordering on pasty. His hands were almost white and blue veins popped out like little pipes. His suit was new and all his apparel matched well.

John Summers, on the other hand, looked like a slob. He was probably ten years older than Williamson, grey hair, several cuts from a hasty shave on his round face and stains on his striped, blue shirt which clashed badly with his tan jacket and navy trousers. He clearly scowled a lot too, judging by the furrows in his forehead.

"Gee, you don't look so hot, are you ok," blurted Summers.

Chris wasn't sure if the man was trying to get a rise out of him or if the question was genuine, but he decided it was the former so he answered bluntly, "I'm very hungry, so if you could make this quick?"

Summers was annoyed but let it slide, "Look, we really need your help. This affair is proving quite a mystery, and we need to know what happened."

"I really don't know how I can help. I just can't remember anything."

"I see, well it may help to know we've found a body. Did you know Jason Milne?"

Chris couldn't hide his shock at the unexpected name and had to think fast, "What? I mean, yes, the casino guy, right?"

"Yes sir, that's right. Did you know him, personally I mean?"

Chris wasn't quite sure where this was going but his relationship with Jason had to be spot on in this reality. He recalled that most of their friendship happened in the other Universe, "Well, I'd gambled at the Casino a few times but didn't have much to do with the man himself. I saw him around occasionally, but we hardly said a word to each other."

"So, you did speak to him," asked Williamson.

"Well, I'd call it a quick hello, how are you, that kind of thing but not a conversation." Chris was struggling to keep his emotional response to Jason's death in check, and it was being noticed.

"I see," said Williamson who was clearly chasing something, but Chris couldn't tell what, "And did he have cause to take issue with you at all?"

"Um? No? I did win a shitload from him some years ago, but it never came to anything. I mean, they gave me the penthouse for the night but that was it."

"How many years ago Mr Parish?"

"Um? I can't recall exactly, a few I guess..." Chris suddenly realised his mistake. That win hadn't happened yet in this timeline. He'd blundered badly and any back pedalling now would be a clear lie.

Damn!

Summers looked at Chris with an odd expression, "Mr Parish, did you kill Jason Milne?"

"What? No! Why would I do that?"

The officer's clearly noticed Chris was distressed, "For someone who hardly knew the man, you seem awfully upset Mr Parish," suggested Summers, "Maybe it's time to come clean. It'll make things a lot easier."

"Easier? For you perhaps, but not me. I want a lawyer!"

The two officers laughed then Williamson said, "We're not on a US cop show Mr Parish and we're only asking questions, so no lawyer. If you want one, that's up to you but for now we're just talking, ok?"

"Well, I think we're finished."

"If you say so Parish! BUT you realise you've opened a few doors here and things need to be explained. Are you sure there's nothing you can tell us?" asked Williamson.

"What do you want to know? Did I kill Milne? No! What caused the accident? I don't know. How did I survive? No idea! That's everything right there, that's all I can tell you, honestly."

"OK Mr Parish. We'll be back when you've had more time to think. Oh, and we'll be checking on some of the details," Summers said with a sarcastic wink.

As the officers left the room Chris called out, "How did it happen?"

"What's that Mr Parish?" asked Summers.

"How did Jas...um, Milne die, if it wasn't in the accident?"

The verbal slipup didn't go unnoticed either, "Had his throat cut, just before you reappeared after all these years. Sneak attack from behind by the look of it. Only found the body last night. Very messy."

"I see," said Chris. He didn't have any more to add, he was too shocked.

"You wanna know what I think?" asked Summers but he didn't wait for a response, "I think you owed Milne a lot of cash, a mother lode in fact and he was getting heavy with you. His reputation suggests that and he certainly didn't like people who were late paying him. Anyway, you were probably threatened and felt your life was in danger, so you made a pre-emptive strike. Then you heard about the accident at the bank building and dumped the body, banged yourself up a bit and voila, a perfect alibi, how does that sound Mr Parish?"

Chris put his face in his hands in anguish but didn't try to defend himself. It sent the wrong message to Williamson and Summers.

"Right then. See you soon Mr Parish," and the pair ambled off.

Jesus

Chris was feeling suddenly ill. With Jason dead he had no-one to call on. He wondered why someone would kill him. Regardless of the reason, Jason was dead, his only true friend in the World.

Chris was deeply confused. Jason's flashback and ensuing events were almost identical to Chris's, so why didn't he meet his alter ego and get switched back. But then maybe he did. When was he killed, before or after the jump? If it was before, then who and why? If later, it would have been almost immediately after they emerged, which was highly unlikely. None of it made sense and Chris realised he might never figure it out. For now, he had to get his own life sorted out, once again. Chris didn't notice the doctor walk in a few moments later, "Are you alright Mr Parish?"

"Oh yes, sorry, just got some bad news."

"I'm sorry to hear that. You probably don't need that kind of thing in your condition. Let's take a look at you, how are you feeling?"

Chris could be honest with the doctor, "Not so flash Doc. Aches and pains, general fatigue, that sort of thing and it's getting worse, not better," he looked at the doctors and noticed the man's expression, "What is it Doc, you look like you've seen a ghost."

The doctor quickly corrected his gaze, "Oh nothing, it's," but he couldn't hold the ruse, "My God!"

"Doc, you're freaking me out, what's going on?"

"Well Mr Parish, you look older than you did yesterday, and I mean, like a decade older!"

"What? Like I'm suddenly 36, not 26?"

"Give or take, but yeah!"

"How? Why," Chris asked. He already suspected the reasons, but the doctor clearly had no clue.

Chris was strangely calm about the aging phenomenon, possibly because his mind was elsewhere. He knew that things couldn't go on like they were and, with Jason's death hanging over him, he decided enough was enough. He would come clean, on everything.

Chapter 20

The doctor was clearly in shock, "If I didn't know better Mr Parish, I'd say you're aging and rather rapidly. Were you exposed to anything in the accident?"

"You could say that," answered Chris.

"And what might that have been?"

"I'm not sure you'd believe me."

"If something affected you, I need to know. Everything is relevant until we rule it out Mr Parish."

"Chris. Please call me Chris."

"Ok, Chris. Please, what were you exposed to?"

Just then Judy walked in, "Oh my God!"

Chris felt suddenly embarrassed, "Hi baby. Surprise," and he made a half-hearted grin.

"What happened? You look old!"

"Yep, I do," Chris said back to her then turned to the Doctor, "Why don't you tell her Doc?"

"Well, um Mrs Parish. We don't really know," but then the doctor got his wits together and turned it back on Chris, "Look Chris, people are talking, on the news, in papers, on the streets. That accident is the talk of the whole world. Witnesses are telling incredible stories, and the authorities can't contain them. And everyone knows we have this one survivor in the hospital who came out of there, and the networks want a piece of you. And from where I sit, knowing what the police have said about your missing persons case in 1988, you're too young to be, well, you. So, will you tell me what the hell is going on?"

"Wait a minute, what eyewitnesses? What stories? No-one's told me shit! I can't read the papers in here, watch TV, listen to the radio or access the Internet. Police orders I'm guessing, so quid pro quo Doctor then we might get somewhere."

The Doctor didn't hesitate, "People reported a bright light emitting from the bank building just before dawn and loud noises like a high-pitched whining. Then suddenly, something merged with the building, like it just appeared from nowhere, some kind of weird machine and then the whole thing collapsed, the building and the machine, into one massive pile of metal and concrete."

The doctor paused, looking at Chris who was anticipating there was more to the story.

"But that wasn't the strangest part, people emerged from the machine, hundreds of them. They were unscathed, perfectly ok except for the fact that they looked confused, even dazed. Some of the witnesses tried to talk to them but they ran off. They all just ran off. No-one knows who they were or where they came from, except for you Chris. You were found unconscious in the rubble, the only one. Why?"

Chris knew the protocol. If something went wrong and people found themselves stranded, there was a designated rally point. He assumed that everyone would have made for that place, although it was nowhere near where they emerged. He wondered what his colleagues did about that but then switched back to the conversation, "Well, you're clearly more informed than I was aware of. But before I say anything, answer me this, are you subject to privilege? Is everything I tell you confined to this room?"

Judy stood passively having heard his whole story the day before. The doctor looked at Chris, then Judy, then Chris again, "Well that depends. As far as your medical records are concerned, that's privileged information but anything to do with the police investigation, that's a grey area."

"How grey?"

"Well, I have to consider public risk. If you were exposed to something then that's not privileged, I must report it. The cause isn't the condition, if I'm making sense, so it's not something I can or indeed should keep secret."

"I see," Chris had formulated a little plan in his mind that he hoped would get the doctor on his side and keep his secrets for a bit longer but he didn't know if it would work, "Ok doctor, I was exposed to something but it wasn't a chemical, so you can forget that as a factor and it won't pose a clear and present danger now."

"How do you know?"

"Because I was part of the project that created a vortex that brought me here!"

"A what?"

"A time vortex, doctor. That was a time machine. That's what hit the bank building, and I was in it, along with hundreds of other people. It went wrong and poof, here I am."

"Why are you telling him everything Chris," Judy asked.

"Because I can't stand it any longer. There have been too many lies, too many deceptions and too many mistakes over too many years. This all needs to end!"

"Wait a minute, you're saying you travelled through time," suggested the doctor.

"Bingo," said Chris.

"Why, that's impossible! Isn't it?"

"I always thought so until it happened. Grab a seat doc, I have to tell you a story. It might just answer the question you want answered."

"And what's that," the doctor asked having totally lost his professional focus.

"Why I'm aging as quickly as I am."

With that Chris told his story to the doctor. He'd been hiding his truth for a very long time, faking his way through a life he hadn't chosen and he'd had enough. All he wanted was to get well, get out and get on with whatever was left of his old life. He was back in his own reality with his wife and son. That's all that mattered now. Nothing else.

"And there you have it, Doctor. Life according to Chris Parish, versions one and two; oh, and three if you count the other Chris Parish," he paused and then asked, "Thoughts?"

Judy smiled at Chris's humour.

"Um...ah...I..."

"The way I figure it Doctor, you can run off and tell everyone my story and they'll think you're crazy. They might think I'm nuts too, but the words will be coming out of your mouth, and I can simply deny it, so I have your complete confidence now, right?"

"Of course you do, you always did. I just can't imagine what you've been through. All those years, life relived. So strange."

"Yeah well, it wasn't a picnic. I mean having to convince my wife that I wasn't a loser three times isn't an easy task; you know what I mean?"

"Sure, I get it."

"So, what now doctor? More tests? I mean, this ageing thing sucks, but I have a feeling the Universe is catching me up, so I doubt there's anything you can do."

"We'll have to monitor you, see if it progresses and try to deal with any complications."

"That's it?"

"Pretty much. Rapid aging like this is undocumented. We really have no idea. Right now, it's just the three of us in the room that know about it."

"I expect you'll be studying this and writing a paper, get your name in the New England Journal of Medicine?"

"I haven't thought that far ahead, but it makes sense."

"And what about all my colleagues, are you planning to blow the whistle on them?"

"I don't need to; the authorities are all too aware of them. I'm sure they're being searched for as we speak."

"Hunted down you mean?"

"Probably."

Chris looked at Judy, "Well, looks like you're going to get the old me back, literally although, in this timeline, you never saw me at 52, did you?"

"No, I didn't, I saw you as you were yesterday. I'm scared Chris. I came here to tell you I wanted to give us a try, but now, well, maybe we should see what happens?"

"Meaning?"

"I just think you need to get better, then come home and we can figure it out from there. Is that ok?"

"Sounds perfect," and Chris smiled as a tear rolled down his face.

"One more thing," suggested the doctor, "How do you know you're going to keep aging?"

"Believe me, I know. I can feel it in every fibre and bone. It's happening now and it ain't stopping. I expect in a day or so, I'll be my old self, and that's no joke."

"I see, well I need to talk to my colleagues, see how we can make you comfortable and hope it's not something serious."

"Do whatever you have to doctor. I'll be here."

The doctor left, leaving Judy alone in the room with Chris.

"Where's Caleb?"

"At work."

"Oh, what does he do. I never thought to ask yesterday."

"He's an accountant and a very good one. Runs his own firm now."

"Wow, that's impressive. He got your maths gene I think."

"Yeah, he did."

"And his wife, his son? When can I see them?"

"Amanda and Clem. I brought photos," and Judy pulled out her mobile phone, opened the app and started swiping through hundreds of family photos.

Chris was speechless. He could see the family likeness in Clem and Caleb's wife looked like an amazing woman too. Chris wept with joy and thought that maybe everything he'd been through was worth it. His family was strong and successful and seemed happy. Hopefully happier with him back in the picture, "And what about you Judy, where are you working?"

"Stuck with banking. Got promoted to branch manager a few months ago. I'm a boss!"

"Holy cow! Good for you. I'm so proud of all of you," and he pondered a moment, "I wonder if I'll fit into this life now?"

"Of course you will. You're the reason it all happened, whether you were here or not. Caleb wants to know you and I have certainly missed you. We'll figure it out. I promise."

"Why the change of heart?"

"Well, I had time overnight to think, and I never stopped loving you, Chris. I was angry after you vanished and found out what you did, but I didn't hate you for it and after a while it didn't matter. I just wanted you to come home."

"I'm glad, and I'm sorry. I was hopeless back then but that part of me doesn't exist anymore. I'm a good guy now."

"You never weren't Chris; you just had a gambling problem."

"I know, and I'll always regret it. If I hadn't been a gambler, I would never have been spiked and none of this would have happened."

"But you would still have been a gambler and, from what you've told me, right now we'd be on the cusp of a divorce, so…"

"Good point. Doesn't matter now, I guess. Here we are."

Chris and Judy spent the better part of the day talking, catching up on 26 years. He loved hearing about her life and even her failed lovers. He told her about some of the day-to-day events in his missing years and felt their relationship strengthen with every revelation. It was just good.

Later Caleb arrived with Amanda and Clem. Chris was stunned at the sight of his grandson and swept him up and hugged him. He was about three years old and certainly not shy. He looked just like Caleb, who looked just like Chris and so on. It was uncanny but so very thrilling.

He got to know Amanda too, an equally confident young woman, an accountant who Caleb met when he started out as a trainee.

For the first time in a very long time, Chris felt truly happy and hopeful. Things were going to be fine.

Another day went by and another array of tests. It appeared his doctor kept his secrets, for now, which Chris appreciated but he knew it wasn't going to last. A nurse snuck him a newspaper and he read about the Parallax Incident, as people were now calling it, and he saw references to the survivor in hospital and photos of the paparazzi camped outside waiting for him. He wasn't going to be able to hide forever.

Not unexpectedly the ageing process rapidly caught up to his current day, and he soon looked every bit his 52-year-old self again, albeit much thinner, which wasn't a bad thing at all. According to the doctors the process stopped suddenly as did most of the pain, except for the regular aches that go with being middle aged.

It would have been nice to stay young, but he was glad things were normal again. This was his natural state, and he didn't want it any other way. He'd already cheated the world by living too long, so it was only fair that he accepted this slight adjustment.

As these and other thoughts swirled in his brain, the keystone cops returned for another round. They were utterly shocked at his appearance, "Jesus Christ Parish, did you eat something you shouldn't have," Summers stammered.

Chris thought of making a 'bad pork' remark but decided that diplomacy was probably a better approach, "No, just did a bit of catching up."

"Well yeah, at least twenty years' worth. What gives?" asked Williamson.

Chris looked at the men intently, "Before I say anything I need to know what my situation is. Am I still being accused of murder?"

The officers looked at each other then turned back to Chris, "No. We came here to tell you that a witness came forward, said a woman did it, probably a jilted lover or his wife. Doesn't matter. You're off the hook."

Chris felt a pang of regret about Jason's possible murderer but mostly he felt relief, "Thank God."

"Yeah, well sorry for your troubles," said Summers.

"That's ok. Thanks for, well just thanks."

"No problem, but there's still the issue of the accident. Anything shake loose in your head," Summers enquired.

"I know there's a lot of talk and I know about the media scrum out there and the eyewitnesses, so there's really no point trying to pretend I don't know anything. I was in that crash; I was part of the whole event."

"What do you mean event?"

Here we go again.

For the third time since his re-emergence, Chris told his long and complicated life story. He spelled it out to the Police in vivid detail, naming everyone he could recall by name and why it had all happened. The police scribbled and nodded and more than once gasped or looked shocked, but not once did they call bullshit on his story. When he finished, he looked at their faces, "That's it."

"Well Mr Parish, that pretty much corroborates what we know. Thank you."

"Corroborates?"

"Yeah, we caught up with a couple of your colleagues, and they gave us the same story. Well not all your personal stuff but the overall Parallax side of it. Don't know how we're going to process this one, no precedent and no laws to deal with it. It's all a bit cuckoo," suggested Summers.

"So, what happens to me?"

"Well," said Williamson, "I expect there'll be an enquiry of some kind. You and the others will have to give evidence, and anyone else we find. Maybe there'll be prosecutions but that's for someone else to decide."

"So, I can just go?"

"Pretty much Mr Parish, but don't leave town," Summers said with a smile.

"Thank you for your time, Mr Parish and your honesty," Williamson added.

Chris grinned, "Thank you gents. It's been a pleasure."

"I'm sure it wasn't," suggested Summers and the officers began to walk out, "Oh and I wouldn't say anything to the press just yet. They can get their stories from the enquiry, whenever that is, but good luck keeping them out of your hair after that. Might be a good time for a long holiday," and Summers winked.

"Understood."

Chris was thrilled. It seemed that everything was getting better for him in every way. He was back, cleared of any wrongdoing, had a wife, a son, a daughter in law and a grandson. He could live out the rest of his life and be happy.

The doctors continued to monitor Chris and were relieved to see his ageing hadn't progressed after a few more days and after another week he was given the all clear and allowed to go home.

Judy arranged for him to make a stealthy getaway after scouting the area. At this stage the press didn't know his name or what he looked like, but Chris nor Judy wanted to take any chances and got out without incident through an unguarded exit.

Driving across the city, Chris noticed that everything was 'normal' again. The city was the way it should have been, the way he remembered it, "Can we swing past the Para...um, bank building," he asked.

"Well, we can't get close but if I slow down just up at that intersection you should be able to see something of it," Judy suggested.

"Good enough."

When they got to the lights, they turned red, which put them right on the line giving Chris a perfect view up the street to his right. The road was blocked to stop traffic getting into that section of the city and was guarded by police and all the surrounding building were deserted. Chris looked about a hundred yards down the street, noticing firstly the myriads of emergency and salvage vehicles including heavy lift cranes and bulldozers but then his eyes took in the reason for all that activity. Dwarfing them was a massive tangle of concrete, metal, glass and an array of other materials. Papers littered the streets still, as well as pieces of furniture and cabinetry, most of which had been badly damaged but overall, it was just obliteration. The mass of contorted debris was at least five stories high, and it reminded him of the 9/11 Twin Towers after they collapsed but on a much smaller scale thankfully. Clearly, they were still looking for anybody who might have been inside but so far, they hadn't found anyone, either dead or alive, aside from the body of Jason Milne and of course himself.

"It's amazing that no-one died in that mess," he said out loud to no-one.

The lights took forever to change which he was grateful for. He could take a long hard look at the disaster area. He could see the remnants of the Parallax machine's major parts, remnants of the photon spheres and quantum computers, but he doubted anyone would understand what they were looking at. Then he saw that workers were dragging out pods from the debris and packing them onto trucks. The ones being brought out had been opened but were empty while those on the truck has been closed for transport.

Chris assumed that the time dilation had protected everyone from the actual crash effect, and they were able to simply climb out unscathed but even that didn't make sense. Once the time shift ended and they opened their pods, surely, they would have been buried? Something else must have come into play that protected them, but he had no idea what. He also wondered if everyone made it. Maybe some were trapped in time somewhere else. It was a sobering thought. Those that did escape were now on the run and he knew of at least two that had been caught, and they talked, just like he did.

Probably for the best.

As they got a green light and drove off, Chris noticed two other vehicles; not police or rescue, they were Federal Science vehicles, and they were no doubt looking to salvage as much tech from the machine as they could. He hoped they wouldn't salvage enough to make another machine like it and doubted they could anyway. Some of the World's most brilliant minds had created the thing and they couldn't get it to work. The car accelerated and a second later his view was blocked.

About twenty minutes later they were home. It wasn't the home he knew though, it was another place, a better place, a nicer place. He was glad. A fresh start would be most welcome.

Over the coming days and weeks, Chris got his strength and his appetite back. He spent as much time as he could with Judy, Caleb and the family. It was nice to feel settled and content and with nothing to worry about.

Judy worked while Chris played house husband. He enjoyed the simplicity of his life but knew it would eventually get to him, and he'd have to ultimately find a job.

One day, just after Judy went to work the phone rang, "Hello?"

"Mr Parish?"

"Yes."

"My name is Jackson Priest, Parliamentary Secretary for Science. I'm calling about the enquiry into the Parallax Incident."

"Ok."

"Well, you'll be receiving a document inviting you to the enquiry. I just wanted to let you know. It's starts next week. If you're willing, we'll make arrangements for transport and accommodation."

"Really?"

"Yes sir. I know that's a bit unusual, but this whole affair is well, odd, to say the least. We want to make sure you and the others are comfortable, and we hope, willing to speak freely."

"I have no problem with that."

"Good. Also, it's not a criminal investigation. As far as we're concerned you and the others are victims, so we're not going to pursue charges of any kind. This is about science and learning what happened and why," explained Priest.

"That's very good to know."

"Indeed. Well then, I'll see you next week in Canberra. Thank you, sir."

"Thank you," said Chris and the phone clicked in his ear.

About an hour later he received a satchel delivered by courier in which was a summons to appear at the enquiry as well as travel documents. There was even a small allowance for incidentals.

Wow, they must be keen for answers.

A week later he was on his way to Canberra alone. Judy wanted to go with him, to provide support but she was unable to get away from work. He didn't mind and reassured her that it would all be fine.

He was flown to Canberra, Business Class despite the trip being less than an hour and was met at the airport by a Commonwealth car and driver and was soon at Parliament House, where he was met by the Parliamentary Secretary's personal assistant. She took him to the chamber where everyone was getting settled and showed him to his seat.

He looked around and saw two people that, like him, stood out from the crowd. They were clearly Parallax employees, and he recognised one of them as Jennifer, the young scientist that he'd spoken to about Judy's pregnancy when they were finalising the Parallax machine for the jump. She hadn't appeared to have aged, and Chris wondered why but then dismissed it when he realised, he had no idea when she came on board or what age she was when this whole affair started. The other was a man, around forty years old, but he didn't recognise him at all.

There was a hum in the chamber as the delegates, six of them, settled in. He and the other two Parallax representatives were kept apart, probably so they couldn't share notes or ideas. Not that he expected that would be an issue.

Looking around again, he checked the public gallery which was full to overflowing. The media pit was a gluttony of cameras, lights, microphones and reporters, all eager to get their stories and most likely get a piece of Chris and his colleagues. Until now, no-one knew who they were but as of this moment, all eyes were eager to discover the "survivors".

"I call this hearing to order," and a gavel banged down on the bench three times. Chris felt uneasy for some reason. It suddenly felt like a prosecution. He'd seen parliamentary inquests on TV before and somehow, they always got hostile, but this was different surely. This one involved civilians so he hoped it would be more, civil.

"Firstly, ladies and gentlemen, welcome and thank you for taking time out of your busy schedules to help us today. My name is Senator John Bishop. To my left are the Honourable Keith Nicholas, the Honourable Julie Schofield and the Honourable Neil Piermont. To my right, Senators the Honourable Brian Westlake and James Michaels," he took a breath, "We also welcome members of the Federal Science Bureau, members of the various astronomical bodies such as the Australia Observatory and key faculty members of various universities and other scientific bodies. Welcome all."

A small murmur crossed the room for no apparent reason. Chris looked around once more and spotted Dr Fred Wilson and gave him a smile. Fred nodded. Chris wondered if they knew each other in this timeline given everything that had occurred.

"This hearing has been called to determine the cause and effect of the so called 'Parallax Incident' which occurred on the morning of May 13, 2014. We will hear from witnesses, scientific experts and, of particular interest, the three known survivors of the event."

This time the murmur in the room was much more raucous. Chris could feel the energy in the room intensify and his stomach pulsed nervously. He could almost feel the eyes of the media scanning for him and the others.

"ORDER!"

The room quickly fell silent.

"This will go much more smoothly if we refrain from further outbursts," said Senator Bishop, "I call the first witness, Miss Amanda Skinner."

A young woman stood and walked to a vacant chair next to the bench and was sworn in.

"Please, in your own words, tell us what you saw on the morning of May 13 this year."

"Well, I was out for an early morning jog, I do that most mornings and was turning down Castlereagh Street when I was stopped."

"What stopped you, Miss Skinner?"

"Well, there was a bright light, very bright and too intense to be just office lighting and there was a strange sound, like a whirring; very high pitched, followed by a flash and then the whole building in front of me seemed to expand, like something stretched out from inside, some kind of brilliant halo. Nothing broke; it was like they melded together. The halo was touching the ground and then, suddenly hundreds of people appeared, like out of the halo. They looked shocked. Some ran away; others just stood for a moment looking up at the light then they just walked off like it was nothing. The whole building was vibrating by then, like when you bump a mirror and coming out of it was this weird looking machine. A few seconds later the entire building and the thing, the machine just collapsed and crashed down into the street. I was terrified so I ran. I didn't see much after that."

The members of the panel asked Miss Skinner several questions, most of which she couldn't answer, and she was soon dismissed. Chris realised the witnesses were simply putting their stories on record for the benefit of this enquiry. Most of the information had been documented already but it set the standard in this case.

With that several other witnesses took turns giving their versions of the event, a street cleaner, a garbage collector and some residents of nearby apartment blocks. Their stories were similar, and all were equally nonplussed about what had happened.

Senator John Bishop then asked for Miss Jennifer Wells to take the stand. Chris watched as the young scientist took her seat. He thought she looked very uncomfortable.

"Good morning, Miss Wells, thank you for being here today," said the Senator.

"Good morning," she tweeted back.

"Miss Wells, you're a survivor of the incident are you not?"

"Yes sir."

The gallery gasped and cameras clicked furiously but the Senator ignored the flurry, "Can you begin by explaining your association with Parallax?"

"I am or was employed as a science officer with the company."

"I see, and what did that entail?"

"My job was to work with other engineers and scientists on the Parallax Machine."

The Senator seemed frustrated, "Miss Wells, I'm going to ask you to be more detailed in your answers. I'm sure you've sought legal advice, and they told you to keep your answers as brief as possible and not to elaborate, am I right?"

She nodded in the affirmative.

"Can I just say then, that this is not a trial, it's an inquiry and you are here as a witness, not a defendant. You are not being prosecuted, do you understand?"

Jennifer nodded again.

"So, you can answer openly and honestly and there will be no retribution, so please, what was your job?"

"I worked under the lead scientist, and we were responsible for the building and programming of the time dilation device, the part that created a photon field around the machine and enabled it to slip through, what was essentially a wormhole and leave one time and arrive at the same place in a different time."

The gallery was again animated at the revelation, however Senator Bishop seemed unmoved, "And how did it work?"

"Well, if I were to explain it in technical terms, it would take the entire day to go through the data and to be honest I'm not entirely sure myself. I had a specific job within a fragment of the project."

"Simplify it then, but we may need you to give a fuller explanation at a later date."

"Essentially, we developed a photon accelerator which punched a hole in the space time continuum. You see, a photon is the fastest thing in the Universe and travels at the speed of light. We know that at the speed of light, time essentially stops. We developed a technique to push a photon beyond the speed of light, which creates a wormhole. Basically, if you control the speed of a photon, you can in theory, choose a time and date to travel to or from."

"How did you achieve that? Controlling photons," asked Neil Piermont.

"No doubt you're aware of the Large Hadron Collider? Well, we simply miniaturised it and vastly improved it and, well, we accelerated the particles beyond the speed of light and slowed them as well. I don't know how that was achieved. Those developments were need-to-know. We then had to disperse the photons via large prisms which created a halo around the machine and the whole thing simply slipped into the resulting vortex, like dropping a ball bearing through a soggy piece of paper I suppose."

Chris was curious about the questioning, mainly the fact that they were asking about procedure and not the elephant in the room; why was the machine built?

"Who did you answer to Miss Wells," asked Brian Westlake.

"Um, my immediate manager was Jill Mcintosh, but she only looked after our department."

"Ok, so who did she answer to?"

"I don't know."

"What do you mean, you don't know?"

"It was all very secretive, we talked to who we needed to but above that, the chain of command was shrouded. Probably for security purposes."

"I see," said Westlake, "but surely the staff at your level talked to each other?"

"Yes, we did, and we compared notes and discussed our various roles, but you asked about the chain of command and, as far as my knowledge goes, it stopped at Jill."

"So, is there anyone who might know how high up the chain of command went and who was responsible?"

"Yes," answered Jen.

"And who might that be?"

"Christopher Parish."

"And who is Christopher Parish?"

"He was one of the flashbacks. He had access and privileges that the other workers didn't have."

Oh crap!

Keith Nicholas piped up, "What is a flashback may I ask?"

"Well, I'm not clear on the details myself, but basically flashbacks are the people who started this whole venture. They are people who were sent back in time, that's all I can really tell you. We weren't allowed to really discuss it with them, and they tended to keep to themselves, except for Chris, he seemed normal."

There was an aura of astonishment in the room, excited whispers, a few genuine gasps of shock and others who were clearly not convinced.

"ORDER"

Keith Nicholas continued, "So you're saying they are time travellers?"

"Yes"

"Why are they called flashbacks?"

"It's the name they were given. It's what happened to them when they were struck by Sun Spikes. They were flashed back to their original birth and started life again."

"Preposterous! Lies! Came some shouts from the gallery.

"ORDER" and the gavel crashed down quieting the audience, "Continue Miss Wells," asked Senator Bishop.

"That's all I know really."

"Why aren't you a flashback Miss Wells," asked Nicholas.

"I wasn't struck by a Sun Spike, but I was affected by the time dilation when we first used the machine."

"Are you telling us you have travelled through time?"

"Yes, I have."

Loud murmuring and chatter across the room, this time ignored by Senator Bishop.

"You said Sun Spikes. I've heard nothing of this phenomenon Miss Wells, when did this happen," asked Keith Nicholas.

"It hasn't happened and won't for about three months, according to them. I'm only telling you what I was told. I haven't witnessed anything like it either."

More gasps and shrieks from the gallery.
"ORDER. There'll be no more outbursts, or this hearing will be closed!"

Senator Bishop was getting agitated but not so much by the audience behaviour.

"You expect me, all of us, to believe that the people who build that machine were time travellers, thrust from the future to their own births and started life over again and that you, as an employee of Parallax were exposed to the effects of the machine they build and you too travelled through time," asked James Michaels.

"Yes sir. That's true."

"And this Christopher Parish, he's one of these travellers?"

"Yes Sir, a flashback," replied Miss Wells.

"And is he here," asked Michaels, knowing full well who was on the witness list.

"Yes sir, that's him," and Jen pointed across to Chris.

Suddenly hundreds of pairs of eyes and dozens of cameras were focussed on Chris, and he felt an instant flash of heat under his collar as his face reddened. He put his head down instinctively.

"Thank you, Miss Wells. One more question if I may," asked Senator Bishop, "What was their reason for building this machine?

There it is

Miss Wells continued, "I was told they wanted to make things right, save the planet from itself and, well that's it. I'm unaware of the details to be frank. I was simply paid to do a job. Mostly, I only heard about these things. I wasn't part of the inner circle."

Soft murmuring in the gallery died off quickly.

"Is there anything more you'd like to add Miss Wells?"

"Nothing comes to mind Sir."

"Thank you then Miss Wells. You are dismissed."

Jennifer Wells returned to her seat in the gallery, catching Chris's eye as she moved across the floor. He thought he detected empathy or maybe an apologetic expression, but who could tell?

Chris anticipated that he would be next to face the music.

"The bench calls Joseph Gill!"

It was the other survivor, and he sat, took the oath and clasped his hands together on his knees which were closed. He hunched forward slightly and appeared a bit 'Egor' like.

"Mr Gill," began Senator Bishop, "What was your function on the Parallax project?"

"Um, well, I was part of the catering staff," he said, clearing inhibited by the exposure he felt.

Some laughter in the gallery this time.

"Catering? Whatever for? Why would they need catering?"
"Well sir, there were hundreds of workers on the site, and we worked for years on the project. The facility was fully self-sufficient and, well, people had to eat."

Laughter again from the gallery

"Order."

"I'm sorry Mr Gill, where was this facility," asked Julie Schofield.

"In the desert, very remote, very hot. Not much fun really." answered Joseph with an awkward squirm.

"Was the facility approved? Was it legal." asked Brian Westlake.

"Well, I don't know, I worked in the kitchen."

Stifled laughter again.

"And were you too a time traveller Mr Gill or a, what was it? A flashback?"

"Oh, an employee, yes but I also travelled through time. Nice to be back too."

"Back from where Mr Gill?"

"Oh, um, 1988. We were in 1988 until the machine brought us here."

Loud gasps and shouts of dismay and disbelief again, ignored now by all the delegates.

"1988? Impossible," screamed Neil Piermont.

"Oh, but it's true. I was affected like Miss Wells; we had to go with the machine to get back to our proper time. It was the only way."

"I'm sorry," blurted Brian Westlake sarcastically, "but this, this a circus act, isn't it? All this talk of time machines and time travel. It's got to be a ruse, hasn't it Mr Gill?"

"Um? No," Gill squirmed again and tightened up noticeably looking even more like a hunchback.

"How do you explain it? What the Hell are you telling us Mr Gill?"

Joseph looked confused and overwhelmed. The aggressive questioning appeared to fluster him, "Um, I cooked, so…" He didn't finish his sentence.

The gallery murmured as the delegates looked at each other.

"Do you have any more to add Mr Gill," asked Senator Bishop.

"Um, no?"

"Fine, stand down Mr Gill. Thank you for your time."

The gavel smashed down on the bench, "We will take a ten-minute recess," ordered Senator Bishop.

With that the delegates stood and exited the room, but not before taking a long hard look at Chris. Most of the other audience members and witnesses left too, probably to have a cigarette or to chat about the proceedings thus far. Chris decided he would stay put, hoping it would insulate him from the media for a while. He knew that he had become the centre of attention and realised he'd made a huge error in not having any legal support for this trip. Things hadn't gone as he anticipated. This now felt every bit like a witch hunt. He also noticed that most of the media representatives had stayed put too and ALL the cameras were on him.

Oh shit!

When the hearing resumed, Chris again expected his name to be called but there followed a string of so-called experts, adding their theory and spin to the events of May 13. Chris listened to each speaker, occasionally rolling his eyes and once shaking his head at the ludicrous ideas being touted by so called academics. He didn't really understand what all this theory had to do with the enquiry.

The hearing finally broke for lunch, and he knew this time he wouldn't be able to stay in his seat. He was hungry and in urgent need of a bathroom. He chose the door furthest from the media exit so he could get ahead of the pack that he knew would be upon him at the first opportunity.

To his relief there was a bathroom a short way down the corridor, and he quickly slipped inside and occupied the stall at the very end.

As he sat, he heard the door open and footsteps approaching. They stopped outside his stall, "Mr Parish?"

Chris hesitated, "Yes?"

"I did tell you not to trust anyone didn't I?"

"What?"

"Well, I did try to warn you all those years ago, but you didn't listen."

"I have no idea what you're talking about."

"At your school, with the Minister and your academic achievements, all that media attention. You should have listened. You should have said nothing to anyone. You would have been left alone, like me."

Chris had a glimmer of a memory and as he focussed on it, he remembered, "You! The man who spoke to my parents. We thought you were just a weirdo."

"Yes Mr Parish. That was me, not a weirdo, but that depends on who you ask I suppose but I told you didn't I? Don't trust anyone!"

"Wait a minute, you must be what? 70 or 80 by now?"

"Well, yes but then again, no."

"What does that mean?"

"I'm a flashback too but I also found out that there are ways to stay younger."

"Impossible."

"And yet, here I am. It's not all cut and dried Mr Parish and, I knew who to pay off to get what I needed. Clearly you didn't know about some of the work behind the scenes at Parallax."

Chris was deeply confused and felt somewhat jilted at the news, "Why didn't you get caught? Why don't people know about you?"

"Oh, I kept to myself, stayed away from people I didn't need to know or didn't want to know; didn't get noticed, but I saw your name pop up often enough to keep tabs."

"How?"

"I worked in the patents office. You had quite an impact on the world Mr Parish, quite an impact."

Chris shook his head, "What's that got to do with the hearing?"

"Nothing at all, but I know you need help."

"Why would you do that?"

"Because, you have something I want."

"What?"

"Well, all your patents, I want them, and for that I'll give you the best barrister in the business, how does that sound?"

"Why would I need a barrister?"

"Because you're about to be roasted Mr Parish. So, take my deal and get the best representation available or take your chances."

Chris felt panic rise in his gut, "How do I know you're not swindling me?"

The man laughed, "You don't. It's a leap of faith Mr Parish, a leap of faith."

With that a paper and pen slid into view, "A legal agreement to sign over all your patents."

"Do they still exist?"

"Yes and no. Sign now and you'll have representation, I guarantee it."

"I don't understand."

"Mr Parish. This is a business transaction. I can walk away, but by the end of the day, I doubt very much that you will be able to do the same but it's your call."

Chris looked over the paper, and recognised the long list of accomplishments, "Wait a minute, these don't exist because I wasn't here for the last 26 years, so this couldn't have happened in the current timeline, so how can you have them?"

"Tut tut Mr Parish, does it matter how I got them?"

"Yes, it does! Were you a survivor too?"

"Let's just say I was always in the periphery and had friends in the right places, now sign the paper!"

Chris was confused and overwhelmed but more than that, he felt desperate. He signed.

"What now," Chris asked but he only heard footsteps, then the bathroom door slammed and after that only silence.

That's just great.

Chapter 21

Just before the inquiry resumed, Chris was met by a man in the corridor, "Mr Parish?"

"Yes, who are you?"

"I'm your barrister, Jonathon Quigley. I was referred to you by a mutual friend."

"Interesting you call him a friend. He fleeced me for everything I'm worth so you would represent me. Interesting how I haven't seen him. Slip away, did he?"

"He's a very private man but believe me, you made the right decision. I'm going to advise you to decline to speak today," suggested Quigley.

"Why, what have I got to be afraid of?"

"You didn't think this was just a Q and A and that nothing would come of it did you? They're looking for a scapegoat, and you are the highest-level Parallax employee available to them, so you are in their crosshairs."

"Me? Whatever for?"

"Well let's see, willingly assisting with the construction of a machine that destroyed the better part of a city block. That's terrorism Mr Parish. That's what's happening here. You're looking at prosecution and perhaps twenty years in maximum security."

Chris went white, "What? They never said anything about that. They made it sound like I was doing them a favour."

"Yes, I imagine they did. That's called politics; making it sound like you're a good guy while they sharpen their knives. You've been had Mr Parish, big time!"

"Oh my God! He was so nice on the phone last week. It all seemed so routine. Why would they lie?"

"Aside from that being a political norm in this country, they're embarrassed. A very public event happened with a lot of witnesses and people are asking how and why it happened. They need to look like they're on top of this. It's really that simple I'm sorry to say. The only saving grace is that, somehow, no-one died, or you'd be in a much worse position."

"So, what do I do?"

"I'm going to ask for a recess and see if we can get the afternoon off so you and I can sit down and talk. I doubt we'll get more than that."

"How will you do that?"

"You just leave that to me sir."

Chris liked Quigley's confidence, "OK, I'm in your hands I guess."

"Yes, you are. Oh, have you got a dollar on you?"

"Sure. What for?"

"You need to retain me, so that I'm officially your legal counsel, or they might not let me in."

Chris handed Quigley a dollar and the barrister wrote him a receipt on his letterhead and signed it, "There you go, all official"

Chris felt awkward but he wasn't going to argue about a legal technicality and besides, he felt he had no choice in the matter now. He and his new legal representative entered the chamber, and Quigley showed the receipt to the security guard who inspected it, looked at Chris then let them both through. Chatter filled the air; expectations were high. The delegates took their seats and the gavel came down, "I call this inquiry to order," announced Senator Bishop once more.

The gallery members and press quickly settled, as did the witnesses.

"The bench calls Mr Christopher Parish."

"Chris began to stand but his barrister put a calming hand on Chris's arm, "Wait."

Jonathon Quigley stood and announced himself, "If it pleases the Honourable Senator and members of the panel, I am Jonathon Quigley and I have been appointed to represent Mr Parish."

The Senator and the other panel members looked up in astonishment, "We were not made aware of this," said Bishop as he looked at Chris with a frown.

"Um. Sir I defer to my barrister at this point," Chris said.

The gallery murmured.

"This isn't necessary Mr Parish," suggested Bishop.

"Oh, but I do believe it is sir," said Quigley, "And I will be asking that this inquiry, or whatever you want to call it be recessed for the rest of the day so I may confer with my client."

The panellists looked at each other, a few muttering and shaking their heads then Bishop said, "You'll need more than that to convince us sir, what is your reasoning?"

"Very well Senator, may I ask your esteemed self and the panel members what the purpose of this inquiry actually is?"

"Well," grunted Bishop, "to find out the truth about what happened with the Parallax machine of course."

"Senator, in my experience these inquiries are not generally used to 'find facts' alone. They also tend to find someone to blame, and I think you intend to blame Mr Parish here and charge him under the Terrorist Act, am I right?" asked Quigley. He knew the media would latch onto that.

Loud gasps of astonishment from the gallery now but Bishop wasn't hearing it, "This inquiry is about the truth."

"Yes, sir I agree, but with truth comes blame and with blame comes indictment. My client deserves more than to be shanghaied by this esteemed panel and I strongly request that you allow him his right to counsel."

More mutterings from the gallery as the media filmed and photographed the entire exchange, which very much pleased Quigley. The atmosphere was palpable. Senator Bishop and the other panellists covered their microphones and whispered amongst themselves, hiding their mouths with their free hands so that the media couldn't use lip readers to reveal their discussion later. The exchange lasted a few minutes before Senator Bishop cleared his throat and resumed, "Very well, this hearing is adjourned until 9am tomorrow. You have you recess Mr Quigley."

"Thank you, sir."

With that the gavel crashed down extra hard, and the panellists left the room in a huff. The gallery and the other witnesses also left in less of a hurry. Chris caught the eye of the other Parallax employees who seemed very sheepish, particularly Jennifer Wells. They didn't wait around.

"Wait here a while Mr Parish, the media isn't going anywhere, and I want them to focus on you talking to me."

"What about?"

"Football? The weather? Just keep your back to them, we'll give them some b-roll and something to think about then we'll leave when they get bored, Understand?"

"Yes sir, I do." Chris was finally getting with the program.

As Quigley suggested, the cameras rolled and clicked for a while. Some journalists even called out to Chris for comment, but his barrister told him to ignore them. After a while they packed up and left one by one. Still, the pair waited in the chamber a while longer, just in case a few of the journalists camped at the door in the hope of bailing Chris up for a remark.

After nearly an hour of small talk it was time to leave. They exited through an alternative side door, then weaved their way through a series of corridors that led away from the main entrances. By the time they got outside they were hundreds of meters away from the front of the building. A car was waiting, and the driver opened a door for Chris and then let Quigley in the other side. They were on the road seconds later.

"Right. Now that's done let's get down to business."

"Sure thing."

"You will need to tell me your entire story, from the very beginning up to now. Don't leave anything out. I must know what you know so there are no surprises. I know you've probably done this before, but this is critical, ok," said Quigley sternly.

"I'll do my best."

"I need more than that. Twenty years behind bars could hinge on a minor detail. They must prove intent. They won't if you follow my lead but I'm hoping it won't come to that at all."

"How so? What are you thinking?"

"They need someone to hang, so you have to give them that someone. In turn, you get immunity."

"Oh."

"What's 'oh' mean Mr Parish?"

"The brain behind this entire operation is dead. She was the driving force and head of the company, and I don't even know her name."

"Well, that's…Shit," blurted Quigley, "Was there anyone else?"
"Well, her son John I suppose."

"Then he'll do, he's, their man."

Chris felt uneasy, "He's never done anything to hurt me Mr Quigley. I don't feel comfortable serving him up as a sacrifice."

"I understand that, but this isn't like picking players for backyard cricket Mr Parish, it's your life and if you don't give him to them, they'll take you!"

Chris pondered for a moment, "I don't even know his last name?"

"Doesn't matter, they'll have it on record somewhere in that rubble or at the Securities Commission, we'll find it, rest assured."

"OK, I don't feel good about it, but I'll do it."

"Good. Of course, if they shut that door and still want you, we need a plan B."

"And what's that?"

"We demonstrate beyond any doubt that you were just a victim. You were coerced to help them, or you were under duress. We have to make them believe you had no choice or your life was threatened, or that of your wife and son. Do you understand?"

"Yes."

"Also, they don't want too much more to go public so I have an idea that might get them squirming as soon as you start speaking tomorrow. I'm sure they felt exposed by the existence of that machine and want to save face. We can use that."

"How?"

"I'll explain once we're settled at the hotel."

A short time later the car arrived at a five-star establishment which Chris guessed was at least five hundred dollars a night for a standard room and Mr Quigley wasn't a standard kind of person. They got out of the car, bypassed the front desk and entered a private elevator which took them to the top floor.

"Here we are. The Senator's Suite. Ironical really," laughed Quigley.

They went inside where Quigley made them drinks and then they settled down.

"What now," Chris asked sheepishly.

"You talk Mr Parish, tell me everything."

Chris took a deep breath and a sip on his drink, a nice scotch indeed and then he started telling his story all over again. Quigley listened intently but didn't write anything down, which Chris thought strange. When Chris finished, he slumped back and sighed.

Quigley finally spoke, "That's quite a story. Astonishing really. I don't know how you haven't lost your mind or suffered post-traumatic stress to be honest Mr Parish."

"Maybe that's yet to come," Chris added.

"Perhaps," agreed Quigley, "Ok, now I need for you to talk to me about everyone you can remember of significance in this whole adventure. Who are the players?"

"That's easy, The Boss, her son John, the scientists and engineers that led the project, maybe a few others but I didn't know a lot of them by name, only reputation."

"That's ok, let's start with The Boss and go from there."

Once again Chris found himself explaining his relationship with The Boss. What happened to her and how she unravelled and, in Chris's opinion, lost her way, became corrupted by the idea of controlling time and solving World problems accordingly. He went on to say how her son, John, after her death was driven to reset time to bring her back.

"I see. Between the two of them, there was no choice for you. With or without you this would have happened, right," asked Quigley.

"Definitely. I wasn't a key factor in the plan. I just went along because I saw it as the only way to keep my family together. If I hadn't got on board and I mean literally, the time shift would have impacted me some other way and that might have been worse than going with them. No way of knowing."

"Yes, as you said before, you were once slung into an alternative Universe without being in the machine. Fascinating indeed!"

"My only other option was to destroy the machine, which I simply couldn't do. I didn't have the resources, and they would have killed me, I'm convinced of that."

"Very good, that's what we need to make clear to the panel, if we need to."

Chris and his barrister talked for several hours, taking a small break for dinner then continued talking strategy into the evening. By 11pm they were both quite exhausted.

"I think we're ready Mr Parish. You've done well. I think we can beat this."

"I hope so."

"You need to rest. I have a room here for you, I'll be next door if you need anything." and Quigley got up to leave. As he headed for the door he stopped, "Oh and you'll find a fresh suit in your bedroom. You need to look the part tomorrow," and with that Quigley smiled and left.

Chris's mind was racing. So much to remember, so much to do. He thought of calling Judy and scolded himself for not doing so earlier. It was so late, but he called anyway. She was still awake.

"My God Chris, you're all over the news. They think this is all your fault."

"I know. I was caught off guard but they're only fishing. I have legal counsel now and we have a plan."

"Who is it, how did you find him?"

"It's a long story really but nothing for you to worry about. I'll be fine."

"Oh Chris, I hope so. I just got you back and now this. They're talking jail time," said Judy with a level of alarm in her voice that Chris had only heard once before under very different circumstances, when he lost his job and this whole adventure started twenty-six years earlier.

"It won't come to that," he said trying to sound confident.

He was apprehensive yes, but he believed Mr Quigley would come through for him.

They talked a while longer and when Chris was confident, he had given Judy some reassurance, they said goodbye to each other.

He took a long, hot shower then slipped into bed and fell asleep in a few minutes.

Next morning Chris was up early. He felt good, like a weight had lifted but he didn't know why, given the issues that faced him. He met Jonathon Quigley for breakfast, and they arrived at Parliament House by 8.30. Not much was exchanged about the inquiry, they'd covered all that the night before. It was just a matter of hoping their plan paid off.

They walked straight to the chamber where people were already seated, and others were crowding the gallery. The evening News had certainly given this inquiry a much bigger profile.

They were seated by 8.45 and waited for the delegates to arrive, which they did at 9am sharp. Senator John Bishop didn't waste any time, "I call this inquiry to order," and he hammered the desk quieting the crowd, "The bench calls Christopher Parish to the stand."

Chris looked at Quigley who gave him a nod, so Chris stood and walked to the vacant seat next to the bench and made himself comfortable. This was the first time he'd literally faced the audience and the media, and he was taken aback by the number of people. It was standing room only. Everyone was eager to hear from the time travelling man who was about to be hanged.

Bishop cleared his throat, "Good morning, Mr Parish," he didn't wait for Chris's response and rolled on, "Would you begin by telling us about the events that transpired on May 13 this year?"

Chris kept a close eye on Quigley knowing that he would interject at a moment's notice if he thought the delegates were thrusting for a morsel of guilt.

"I was the victim of a phenomenon known as a Sun Spike. It's thought they were caused by small black holes colliding with our Sun, releasing spikes of energy that hit the Earth and occasionally hit a person. These Sun spikes were thought to be faster than light and therefore disrupted space and time, hence my situation. I was struck and woke up as a newborn child in 1962, but I retained all my former life's knowledge."

Animated astonishment from the public gallery.

"ORDER, ORDER!!! Mr Parish, how do you expect this panel to believe such a story?"

"I would say that the evidence is all over Castlereagh Street in Sydney."

Surprisingly Senator Bishop didn't challenge, "Indeed. So, you lived your new life, what then?"

Chris explained how he came to work for Parallax, their use of knowledge to create technology and enrich the organisation and how their mission was to stop the world from heading down the path of destruction, be it war, global warming or whatever the danger might be.

"And yet, here we are in 2014, no better off as far as I can tell. What did you do wrong?"

"Objection Senator," called Jonathon Quigley.

"Mr Quigley, this is not a prosecution, so an objection cannot be called."

"Senator Bishop, if I may, Mr Parish is my client and has instructed me to interject if I feel he is being led towards incriminating himself. I believe that's what's starting to happen."

"Mr Quigley, there is no intent here. We simply want to learn of the reasons behind the Parallax incident on May 13. That's all."

"And to find someone to blame, is that right? I very much doubt that the Government would go to all this trouble just to hear an interesting story, shake it off and go home. Something else is at play and someone wants their pound of flesh, and I object!"

"Your client has volunteered to speak, and seems more than willing to do so," Bishop turned his attention to Chris, "Mr Parish, will you continue?"

Chris looked at Quigley who subtly shook his head, "No sir."

Shrieks from the gallery this time.

"Mr Parish! You are not under arrest; you are not under any suspicion and are not being prosecuted. You may answer freely, I assure you."

"If I may approach the bench Senator," asked Quigley.

Bishop grunted disapprovingly, "Approach!"

Jonathon Quigley was in his element and strode forward as all the delegates crowded in to listen, "Senator, my client and I are under no illusions here. This inquiry is only the beginning. You know as well as I that everything said here is on the record and that could expose Mr Parish to future prosecution under the Terrorist Act. You know it, I know it, so can we stop playing games?"

Bishop didn't bother to deflect this time, "What is it you want?"

"Immunity for his full testimony. He'll tell you everything but not without an assurance that he is a free man once this is all over, in writing!"

"I can't give such an assurance," answered Bishop.

"Fine, then we leave," and Quigley walked away, "Mr Parish?"

Chris was about to stand.

"Wait," called Bishop, "We need to discuss this. If you will oblige us Mr Parish, Mr Quigley?"

Chris looked at Quigley who smiled widely, "Of course Senator. We'll be right here."

With that Senator Bishop called a recess and the delegates moved to an antechamber to talk. No-one else in the chamber moved, not even the smokers.

"What are they doing," asked Chris.

"Speaking with the Attorney General I suspect. He'll tell them whether to give you immunity for what you know, no not. They'll be idiots to say no," answered Quigley.

"Why is that?"

"Because, if they say no, you walk and then they'll have to pursue criminal charges to get to you. That'll just make it worse for them, publicly. I'll make sure of that."

"I don't like this at all."

"It's not as bad as it sounds. What would you rather, someone gave you a fish for dinner or you must get a boat and go out to catch your own?"

"I see. You've offered them a fish?"

"Indeed, but if they decide to do this the hard way, we'll have plenty of time to build a defence. For starters, you don't have any technical ability to speak of, so how could you have knowingly been a part of the conception and construction of the machine?"

"And the machine existed before I had anything to do with that side of Parallax."

"Precisely. They don't have a case unless they manufacture it, which I will most certainly not allow."

"Thank you, "said Chris feeling slightly relieved.

"Think nothing of it. These are the cases I live for."

"I can tell."

The two men chuckled just as the delegates came back into the chamber. They were quickly seated, and Senator Bishop again gave his gavel a work over, just because he could, Chris suspected.

"Order. Mr Parish, will you stand please."

"Uh oh," said Quigley.

Chris felt a jolt of panic as he rose from his seat with Quigley on his feet also.

Senator Bishop continued, "Under the direction of the Attorney General, these proceedings are terminated. Mr Parish, you will be handed to the Federal Police to face charges of espionage under the Terrorist Act," and he hammered the gavel one more time, "Would the bailiff take Mr Parish into custody."

"Objection," screamed Quigley.

"This inquiry is closed," announced Senator Bishop and he and the delegates left immediately.

The media and members of the gallery were so awestruck there was silence in the room but that soon gave way to shouts and jeers while journalists screamed for comments from Chris.

"What now," Chris asked Quigley as the bailiff cuffed him.

"Sit tight and say nothing and I mean not a word. Silence is your best defence right now. I'll be over to see you very soon," Quigley could see Chris was terrified, "Don't worry, it's all part of the game."

Chris didn't much like this game. He came to them in good faith and now he was being hung out to dry. The bailiff led him away and as they left the building, cameras whirred and clicked while journalists screamed. Quigley was right behind and drew their attention, "My client will make a full statement once we've dealt with this preposterous situation. He is innocent of any wrongdoing. In fact, if anything, he is the victim here and the Attorney General will do well to let this go or face significant embarrassment."

The bailiff didn't know what to do at first and stopped as the media crowded around Chris, blocking their way to the police car.

"Chris, are you a terrorist," screamed one reporter, "Who are your accomplices," came another, "What was that machine supposed to do?"

The questions kept on coming but Chris did as Quigley instructed and remained mute.

"My client will not be answering your questions today, but I do suggest you call the Attorney General's office and ask him why this man is being arrested. Thank you." said Quigley.

With that the bailiff charged through the scrum of people, getting Chris to the car and shoving him in the back seat rather roughly before another officer climbed in with him. Chris looked out at Quigley who mouthed, don't worry! But Chris couldn't help it. He was living one nightmare after another and now his wife and son would see all this on the news with who knows what kind of spin put on the story. The word terrorist wasn't easily deflected in this day and age and Chris knew it.

The car drove off quickly and was clear of the street circus in no time, speeding toward Federal Police headquarters. Chris had no idea what would happen next. They arrived in less than ten minutes, and Chris was escorted inside where several uniformed and well-dressed men and women were waiting. He was taken to an interview room, seated and cuffed to a heavy table and left alone. It was a classic movie scene, one-way glass and all.

Jesus!

He knew that there were people watching through the glass and after a few minutes he realised they were testing his resolve, hoping he would break down. He was determined not to and after half an hour, the only door to the room opened and a very well dressed professional thirty something female walked in. She took one look and called out, "Who the Hell cuffed him like this, take them off!"

Good cop?

A guard flashed in, released Chris and disappeared just as fast. The woman looked at Chris, "I'm sorry about that Mr Parish."

Chris didn't answer.

"Can I get you a glass of water?"

Chris hesitated but then thought it wouldn't be an issue to have a drink, "Yes please."

She didn't relay the message and Chris realised that people were listening as well as watching, "My name is Madeline Hill, I'm with the Attorney General's office."

Chris remained silent.

"I'm going to ask you some questions. How you answer is up to you but if you don't cooperate, there will undoubtedly be consequences. Do you understand?"

"What consequences," Chris asked without thinking.

"Mr Parish, you are facing a dire situation. Your actions brought down a building, endangered civilian lives and caused millions of dollars' worth of damage. This isn't a game."

"I want my legal counsel present."

"You are here under the Terrorist Act. We can hold you for two weeks without charge, did you know that? I'm sure Mr Quigley did. Can you remain silent for two weeks Mr Parish?"

"Ask my wife!"

"Oh, we plan to do that. She's being picked up as we speak, as is your son!"

"They had nothing to do with this!"

"With what Mr Parish. What were you involved in that they were not a party to?"

Chris realised that she was twisting his words, "That's not what I meant."

"Well, it doesn't matter what you meant, a jury of your peers will interpret the meaning for themselves, and it sounds to me like you were definitely involved in something."

Bad cop!

Chris could feel his gut churning, and he fought off the desire to break into tears. He felt he had to remain strong at this point, "Look if you want answers, I need to know what this is all about. I went to that inquiry willingly. I wanted to tell you everything, now this. Doesn't give me much faith in the Attorney General or the system."

Madeline Hill put her hand over the small stick microphone in the middle of the table and said quietly, "The people are scared. An act of terror in the middle of Sydney and one suspect. They want blood."

"But I didn't do anything? I didn't program the machine, I didn't design it, I didn't even conceive the idea. It wasn't even supposed to appear in this era! It was just an accident, a mistake in the programming perhaps, I don't know."

"Why don't you start from the beginning. Tell me everything," suggested Hill.

Chris paused. He realised he may have said too much already and, remembering Quigley's advice he folded his arms in defiance, "I've said enough. Where's my lawyer?"

"Fine Mr Parish, have it your way, but it's going to be a long two weeks."

Madeline Hill stood and walked out, leaving Chris alone to ponder his fate. After two more hours he was thirsty, having never received that glass of water and he was hungry, "Hey," he yelled, "are you going to let me starve to death? So much for civil rights!"

A voice soon beamed out from a small intercom speaker on the wall, 'You don't have any rights Mr Parish." It was a cultured male voice, "You're facing terrorism charges. When are you going to realise that?"

"Who is this?"

"My name is Alexander, Robert Alexander. I'm the Attorney General!"

"Wow, you must be desperate to have come all this way personally. Do you normally visit the unjustly accused?"

"I don't like being embarrassed Mr Parish and what you pulled at the inquiry embarrassed me and my department. I had no choice."

Chris had two hours to consider his position and drew on his days as a card player. He could bluff better than ever, and he was about to bet his life on it, "Of course you had a choice, but I imagine you chose the low road because you didn't want me going public about what happened. All too messy I suspect. How would it look for a government to have time travel machines appearing on their watch and not know a thing about it? Yes, that would be hard to explain."

There was a brief pause, "You're an astute man Mr Parish. Obviously brighter than most people give you credit for. So, let's not play any more games. Yes, we need to get our pound of flesh; to restore the confidence of the people and you need to give it to us."

"I was willing to do that at the inquiry."

"I know, but you're right about the public. I don't want this to get any crazier than it is. The papers are already talking about you giving us next week's lotto numbers. It's becoming a farce. So, you help us, and we'll let you go, all on the quiet of course."

It was now Chris's turn to play, "Where are my wife and son?"

"They're on their way here."

"Send them home. They don't need to be interrogated. If you've done your homework, you will know that I have been AWOL for twenty-six years, they couldn't possibly know anything. You're just using them as leverage, so call off your bluff!"

"Fine Mr Parish. That I can do."

"And let me talk to Judy. She'll be worried sick!"

"Ok."

"And give me my barrister. I'll talk but only with him present. You want answers, I want my lawyer."

"Done."

"And I really could use something to eat."

"It will be arranged Mr Parish."

"And finally, do I need to be in here? I'm not a terrorist. I'm a citizen and should be treated as such!"

"I agree. We'll make you more comfortable."

It seemed too easy, but Chris wasn't pulling any punches, and he just had a feeling that the Attorney General was getting desperate and wanted to put this whole affair to bed.

Moments later the door opened, and he was led to more comfortable accommodations, with leather lounges, a bathroom and food. He was soon met by Jonathon Quigley, "I don't know what you said but it got me in the door. Tell me everything that happened."

Chris quickly filled the barrister in on the last few hours.

"Ok, that's good. You have the upper hand. Let me control the conversation. I think we can get this sorted and you can walk. The media has been going nuts and started siding with you. You have the power now."

"Really?"

"Yes."

Chris was allowed to freshen up and returned to the room where he found Miss Hill and an older gentleman seated on the lounge, "Good afternoon, Mr Alexander," Chris said.

"Hello Mr Parish. Shall we begin?"

"My wife?"

"Home safe, you can call her when we're done."

"Fine."

With that Chris told his story. Save for a few interjections from Jonathon Quigley and follow up questions from the Attorney General. He gave them a complete overview of Parallax and the machine and the people who created it as best as he could remember. Miss Hill took notes and when it was all over the Attorney General had only one more thing to add, "Thank you Mr Parish. I apologise for the turmoil you have endured here today and through your life. You are free to go on one proviso."

"What's that?"

"Retract your time travel and time machine statements in the media. We need to kill that story. You may have to discredit the other witnesses too. I don't really care how you do it, but it must come from you. Understood?"

That really was the bottom line. The government needed to look like they were in control. Chris looked at Quigley who nodded, "Agreed."

"In that case, we're done. Goodbye Mr Parish, Mr Quigley."

The Attorney General left with Miss Hill.

"OK," said Quigley, "ready to make a statement?

"What do I say?"

"Leave that to me," answered Quigley.

"How did I know you were going to say that?"

Later that day an assembled media was champing at the front of Parliament House, waiting on Chris but it was Jonathon Quigley who would speak first.

The Attorney General had already made a statement announcing that Chris was no longer under any suspicion as a terrorist or had any direct involvement with the May 13 incident. He even went as far as apologising, which was very unusual and certainly underlined their deep desire to sweep the whole affair into the discard pile. Now it was Chris's turn to quell the media fire.

Quigley stepped to the crowd of microphones and smart phones, "Good afternoon. I'm Jonathon Quigley, Christopher Parish's legal Counsel. He has asked me to make a statement before he speaks. On the morning of May 13, Mr Parish was found unconscious in the rubble of the Castlereagh Bank Building. His memory of that event is hazy to say the least. My client was simply a victim of that event and was in no way a party to it. The authorities, understandably, looked upon him as a suspect due to his prior association with the company known as Parallax but that's all it was. There was and is no evidence to suggest my client had anything to do with the collapse of the Castlereagh Bank Building. Now you may ask why it happened but that is not within the scope of this media conference. My client will now make a short statement. Thank you."

The gathered crowd of journalists murmured but held back on their questions while Chris approached…

"Good afternoon. Firstly, I would like to thank the Attorney General for listening to my side of the story and seeing it for what it was, a case of someone who was in the wrong place at the wrong time. I am very pleased to have been cleared of any involvement in the collapse of the bank Building and am very much looking forward to getting home and being with my wife and family. Thank you."

As planned, he kept it short with no elaboration but that wasn't enough for the media.

"Mr Parish," called an ABC journalist, "you said at the inquiry that you were struck by Sun Spikes, are you now denying that event and further, denying that you went back in time?"

Quigley had briefed Chris on the likely questions, and he was prepared, "My recollections are limited due to the trauma I suffered in the Parallax incident, as you're calling it, so much of what I think happened and may have believed could be inaccurate. Doctors have suggested that the trauma caused hallucinations, and I haven't been able to distinguish fact from fiction."

"But you said you went back to your birth, and lived out your life again, worked for Parallax, tried to change the World. Are you now saying that's false," asked another reporter.

"Yes, that's exactly what I'm saying."

"How do you explain the eyewitness account of the machine emerging from the bank building," came another question.

Quigley stepped up to repel the question, but Chris held up a hand to indicate he had the question covered, "I'm not denying I was there or that something happened, but as you well know, I was found unconscious and have no memory of the event. I simply cannot give you an answer to that question."

"What about the fact that you've been missing for twenty-six years? Off the grid I believe was the term my source used," asked a slimy looking reporter from one of those magazines that thrived on spin, innuendo or plain lies.

"Your source, like your publication, is misinforming people."

Chris's answer prompted some laughter from the more credible members of the media, but the journalist followed up, "So where have you been for twenty-six years?"

"I've been travelling, working, trying to make a living. There's nothing to it really."

The more questions that were asked, the more Chris deflected or use vagaries to answer, giving the media nothing. Quigley had done a great job, and Chris was cruising through the press conference with ease. He was very convincing to say the lease.

Things were about to wrap up when someone piped up from the back of the media crush, "So Mr Parish, how do you explain your casino win and the prostitute you engaged just before the Sun Spike took you back in time?"

What?

Chris was visibly shocked, and it didn't go unnoticed. He was lost for words, and Quigley was slow to react. The voice came again, "Do you know how many lives you've ruined, how much disruption you created, how much turmoil people like me have suffered because of the decisions you made?"

Again, Chris was gobsmacked and couldn't answer. He looked through the throng of reporters to see who it was but couldn't home in on the voice, "And while these people have no idea of what was done in the past that impacted on the now, I certainly am. Do you have anything to say about that?"

"I don't know. Who are you?"

There was no answer, and Chris was left to face the journalists, "Is she right? What did you change, how are things different now?"

"I don't know, nothing's changed, I don't know…." Chris was losing his train of thought, and the facade was collapsing.

Quigley moved in, "That's all folks," he said comically, "No more questions."

The media wasn't satisfied, "Are you a terrorist Mr Parish," and "Should the public fear you?"

Other pointed questions were flung about as Chris moved off, headed for the sanctuary of a vehicle. His innocence had evaporated as quickly as he'd got it back. Chris and Quigley got into the car and drove off at speed,

"What just happened," asked Chris.

"Our goose just got cooked," said Quigley, "Who was that?"

"I have no idea."

Chapter 22

For several weeks, Chris was holed up in his home. It wasn't the kind of family reunion he wanted or could afford. The mystery woman wasn't heard of again and it seemed like the media wasn't able to track her down either. She wasn't talking now, which seemed like a good thing.

Under the agreement with the Attorney General, Chris couldn't set the record straight and had to stick to the lies he was forced to tell to stay out of jail. It was indeed a tangled web.

Unfortunately, as a web of lies tends to do, this one was unravelling, and the Government was getting a major share of hate from the media as well. Political controversy was News fodder, and the media was bleeding this story for all it was worth.

As the pressure mounted and eyewitness accounts were reviewed and analysed, Chris found himself torn between the truth, which would no doubt make him feel better and the lie which was keeping him out of jail.

Then, the announcement came that the Attorney General had resigned. Chris didn't know whether to feel relieved or horrified. What would this mean for him now?

News crews were camped on his street day and night and if he set foot outside to check the mail or to buy groceries, he was mobbed. He remained silent all the while, but it was starting to fracture his family, and he knew it couldn't go on.

"I can't live like this Chris. I'm freaking out," said Judy.

"I know and if you want me to talk, I will, if it stops this whole affair."

"And see you in jail? No!"

"Well, we can't go on like this. We can't leave the house. We can't do anything, so I'll have to do something."

"Do what?"

"I have no idea."

The stress was having a dreadful effect. Sleeplessness and loss of appetite as well as physical reactions like stomach spasms and occasionally straight out vomiting. It had to end.

The News soon revealed that a new Attorney General had been appointed, Simon Wakefield, and he promised to set the record straight, whatever that meant. It was hard to tell from his first news conference whether he was a good man or another lying bastard!

Then, another survivor of the Parallax Incident came forward, a scientist, Douglas Hershel, who told how he had worked for the organisation on the time machine as an engineer, building some of the photon generators and photon accelerators under the directions of the company scientists. His story was compelling and poured fuel on the whole issues, but worse still, it made Chris out to be a complete liar and the media crowd outside simply grew larger.

The statements were also extremely embarrassing for the government, and they were being hounded about this technology coming into play under their watch and without the slightest clue of its existence. The new Attorney General made another statement in the wake of Hershel's revelations, "It's clear to me now that this affair has not been handled at all well. And while we've tried hard to get to the truth of the matter, the fact is we simply don't know who is responsible or why the Parallax Incident occurred."

Chris knew he was lying of course. He'd told them everything and they decided it was better the public didn't know. He had no doubt that Wakefield was aware.

"I have," continued Wakefield, "reopened the inquiry into the Parallax Incident. I would invite anyone who knows anything about the events of May 13 to come forward. I say on record right now that this is NOT, I repeat NOT about prosecution or blame. This is all about learning what we can about the incident and the implications, if any." He looked directly into the cameras, "I understand that the people directly involved in the incident, the victims, are being harassed severely by the media. I want you to know Mr Parish, Miss Wells, Mr Gill and most recently Mr Hershel that I do not condone the way you have all been treated and, again, hope you will accept the apology of this office. I invite you all to attend the inquiry with my guarantee of immunity and the right to speak freely on the matter. You have been wronged and you particularly Mr Parish have been forced to lie under threat of jail. That's something I cannot allow to remain. Please accept my apology, which I would like to give in person if you are so willing. That is all."

The Attorney General left without another word. Judy looked at Chris and began to cry, the pressure was off for now. Chris didn't hesitate and stormed outside facing the media. As soon as they saw him, they screamed and yelled for his remarks. He stood at the front of his house with his arms folded and waited for them to settle before uttering a single word.

At last things were quiet, "I want to thank the Attorney General for the wisdom he has shown today. All I've ever wanted to do is tell the truth and now, I will have an opportunity to do so. I intend to give a full and complete account of my experiences, including my employ with

Parallax, the Parallax Machine and yes, reliving my life because of the Sun Spikes and time travel."

There were so many questions flying now that Chris couldn't discern one from another and he raised his arms to shush the group of journalists, "I have no more to say. I suggest you wait until the new inquiry. I'll be more than happy to talk after that."

Chris turned and walked inside, ignoring pleas for more comment and ignoring questions.

The next morning all the cars and vans were gone. For now, things were relatively normal.

A few weeks later Chris was back in Canberra, this time, not only with Jonathon Quigley to keep an eye on things but with Judy for moral support. He wasn't going to be blindsided again.

The inquiry was, somewhat unusually, chaired by the Attorney General himself. Quigley suggested that this was a good thing because as chair, he could not recommend to himself to launch proceedings against anyone giving evidence. True to his word, this hearing was simply designed to find the facts and learn whatever could be learned from the people involved.

Chris recognised a great many Parallax employees who, under the guarantee of immunity, decided to come out of hiding; not all, but a good proportion of them. It gave Chris more reason to feel confident.

The inquiry opened with an overview of the previous proceedings and then, one by one the witnesses gave their accounts of Parallax, their roles with the organisation and some of the projects they worked on. Most of the stories were very similar. It was only when they got down to individual tasks and expertise where things varied. Most of the technical talk went over Chris's head and even seemed to bore the media, who were once again there in droves.

Finally, Chris was called to the stand. The Attorney General, Simon Wakefield made a point of again publicly apologising for how Chris was treated and assured him once more that his testimony was never going to be used against him by this or any future Government or Police force, State or Federal, "And thank you Mr Parish for coming here today. I would have understood if you felt compelled to do otherwise."

"Thank you, sir," said Chris, "I simply want to tell my story. The truth as I saw it and experienced it, nothing more. I never wanted anything else." Chris added.

"So noted and that's exactly why we're here. From where I sit Mr Parish, yours is one of the most extraordinary experiences. I don't wish to suggest that the people we've heard from to date haven't seen and done some amazing things but, if I'm on the money here, they were employed by Parallax and therefore experienced their respective time shifts quite differently to yourself. You were one of the people that lay claim to being struck by a Sun Spike which, and correct me if I'm wrong, started this whole process, is that right?"

"Yes sir. The series of events I experienced were indeed caused by the Sun Spike phenomena that occurred in 2014. Technically this year which I'm sure is hard for everyone to comprehend. I was struck by one such spike and sent back to my birth in 1962…"

Chris continued to give details about his incredible life, revealing his true age, his re-lived life, the murder of his parents, time slips, alternative universes, his double identity and so on. Not a sound was heard as he talked; all were mesmerised. By the time he was done the day was almost complete.

Naturally the Attorney General had questions as did the other members of the panel. He answered them as best he could, but some were simply too far beyond his technical knowledge.

"Mr Parish," asked Senator James Michaels, "What happened to all those achievements? The inventions, the leaps in technology? Why don't we see evidence of it now?"

"I think that last attempt to reset time did exactly that. Instead of going back we jumped forward so we couldn't do anything we had done in the first flashback. I can only surmise that by not going back that everything was cancelled out. We have, after all this time and turmoil, done nothing at all. 2014 as I knew it before the Sun Spikes is the 2014 you are experiencing now."

Some gasps of astonishment from the gallery.

"Just one more question if I may Mr Parish. We're fast approaching that time again, when the Sun Spikes are supposed to have happened. Will they happen again," asked Wakefield.

"That's difficult to say. On one hand it's the same time but for me it's history so it's a past event. It would require an understanding of how time and the Universe both work to adequately answer such a question. Has time only been manipulated on Earth or within our Solar System or was it Universal? I really don't know. All I can say is we'll have to wait and see. As far as I'm concerned, I hope not."

That spawned a few laughs from the audience.

Just then a gallery member called out, "Do you know about the effects of a near miss?"

"ORDER!" called Wakefield.

Chris looked into the audience and saw a woman around seventy years of age standing in one of the upper sections of the public gallery, looking at him. He had no idea who she was.

"Please. I must speak," the woman said.

"Who are you," asked Wakefield.

"I'm a Sun Spike victim too."

The audience gasped in surprise.

"Why haven't you registered to give evidence?"

"I wanted to hear what Mr Parish had to say first."

"I see, may we know your name and your connection with Parallax?"

"My name isn't important, but I would like to ask Mr Parish some questions if I may?"

The panel members conferred quickly then Wakefield said, "As this inquiry is voluntary and open, I cannot compel you to identify yourself. And given how unusual this whole affair is, we have no objection." He looked at Chris, "As long as you have no reservations Mr Parish?"

"No sir."

"Very well, please ask your questions."

The woman hadn't taken her eyes off Chris, and it suddenly made him feel uneasy. At the same time, there was something vaguely familiar about her, but he couldn't find the connection.

"Mr Parish, are you aware of the effect of a Sun Spike near miss?"

"I'm sorry, a what?"

"A near miss. Someone who doesn't suffer a direct hit but is within the effect radius of a Sun Spike?"

"I'm afraid I don't know what you mean."

"You were struck by a Sun Spike, a direct hit, correct?"

"Yes."

"Was there anyone nearby at the time?"

"Um, I don't know what you're getting at."

"It's a simple question Mr Parish. Were you completely alone when the Spike hit you," asked the woman.

"Well, no, now that you mention it."

The audience was spellbound.

"Care to explain?"

"I was in a Casino Penthouse, after my win. I explained this earlier."

"You left out the part about the young woman who accompanied you to that Penthouse, isn't that right Mr Parish?"

"I didn't think it had any relevance to the inquiry. I was a different person then and that was, private," the audience murmured, "And nothing happened, she was in the next room! I never saw her again."

"That's right Mr Parish but she was well within the event horizon of the Sun Spike," suggested the woman.

"What are you saying," asked Chris. He was struggling to comprehend exactly what was happening.

"Mr Parish. The effect of a Sun Spike, a direct hit is to send that person back to their birth, to start life again with a head full of knowledge, am I right?"

"I think that's been established, yes."

"The effect of a near miss is to send that person back to the same time as the person who was hit, regardless of their own origin. Your companion went back to 1962 as well and was forced to continue her life from thirty-three years before she was born."

Gasps of shock and surprise now.

"What? I don't understand."

"I was 19 years old Mr Parish, just trying to get by. Being a casino call girl wasn't my life's plan, but it was sure better than what happened next. Because of you I went back to 1962 as a teenage girl. It might have been ok for you. You were home and you were loved. I went back to a Hell you couldn't possibly understand."

The gallery members all cried out, completely shocked by the revelations.

"ORDER," cried Wakefield.

It took some time for the gallery to settle down, "Miss, er…" Wakefield didn't quite know what to say to the woman while Chris tried to make sense of what he'd just heard.

He looked at her once more and strained his memory of that day.

Holly?

"You were reborn Mr Parish, and I was dumped on an industrial site, where the casino would be built decades later. I had no identification, no family, no way to explain myself. I was found by waterside workers and handed over to authorities. Do you remember what I was wearing? In 1962 that was certainly considered indecent. They didn't believe my story and I couldn't prove anything. In the end I was diagnosed as suffering some kind of mental condition and put in an asylum. I spend a long time there, until the World caught up with itself and I was finally found to be perfectly sane and released BUT the damage was done Mr Parish."

"I'm sorry," said Chris, "But I didn't know. How could I have known?"

She ignored his comments and kept talking, "I had a great many years to figure out what to do. I found you thanks to a newspaper article about some child prodigy. You didn't have a clue of course Chris, but I knew who you were and what I needed to do."

Using his first name somehow disturbed Chris even more.

"You know, I even found myself years later. Another strange effect of the flashback is that I was in two places at once, but years apart in age. Sadly, I couldn't get close to warn myself of the coming disaster because of some invisible barrier which pulsated whenever I tried. Call it a time paradox if you like," explained Holly.

"Anyway, I thought of writing to my younger self, but knowing myself as well as I did, it would have been pointless. The young Holly wasn't much of a reader, and she certainly would have thought it all a bit cuckoo, so I gave up and focussed on you instead."

Chris shifted uncomfortably in his chair as Holly continued to tell her story while the panel members and the entire gallery fixated on her, totally mesmerised.

"I made sure, after my release, that I was very much a part of the creation of the Parallax Machine, and I jumped around with those idiots as they tried to fix the World all the while waiting for my moment. You see Chris, it turns out I had a gift for calculus, mathematics, writing code and computer programming. I was able to use my former skills from the casino to gain a lot of knowledge," she smiled, "Men are so weak!"

No-one knew what to do, so compelling was her story.

"So, when everything was set for that last jump I did a bit of a jailbreak on the system, changed a few coordinates and hit the fast forward button and well, The Parallax Incident happened."

"What," screamed Chris as the gallery shrieked.

"Oh yes, it was me. It was the least I could do for all those years of drug therapy and shock treatment! Oh, and I killed your parents too. Remember that little car chase fiasco? So sad."

Chris shook his head, "That was you?"

"I did hope to get you too but those morons I had doing the deed couldn't even get that right. First, they tossed your house which was supremely stupid, then they failed to kill you! Idiots!

Of course I was in the asylum at the time, so no-one ever figured out what happened. Oh, I dealt with those cretins too. It looked like they tried to rape me as employees of the institution, and I defended myself. No one ever thought I could have murdered them; they were too big and too strong. Like I said, men are so weak when their dicks are in someone's mouth. Really, it's so pathetic." Holly paused and made sure she had Chris's face fixed on hers, "As it turned out, having you survive has been a blessing. You've suffered in ways even I couldn't have imagined and I'm glad I could witness it, but it's not enough."

With that she pulled something from her purse. It wasn't a gun and didn't look to be made of metal of any kind but for some reason Chris knew it was a weapon. Unfortunately, no-one else was any the wiser.

"Not all the future tech that was created disappeared in that last jump Chris. Some of us knew how to secure a few things for when we needed them. Too complicated to explain that right now, but this is a photon accelerator, a miniaturized version of one anyway. Very handy for speeding up photons for time travel. You need a cluster of them to do that kind of thing, but, as a single unit modified like this, they make a fabulous weapon and are completely undetectable in 21st Century scanners. This one I made to look like a lipstick case. Neat huh?"

Without hesitation she held it up and fired. A bolt of light burst through a line of audience members and witnesses who fell upon the floor like someone had knocked over a row of toy soldiers with a puff of breath.

Holly remained terrifyingly calm and paused, focussing again on Chris, "Oh remember Dr Chamberlain? Turned out he had a conscience, so I had him suffer an unfortunate heart attack. He put things together because of your friend Jason. And I killed him too, the old-fashioned way. I really hated that casino!"

Panic consumed the room, and people ran in all directions. Security was slow to respond as another shriek of light blistered to life withering another line of souls.

A security guard unholstered his pistol, but he barely had it half out when he rolled to a crumpled heap, dead on the floor along with anyone directly behind him.

The exits were jammed and people screamed as the weapon now relentlessly and unwaveringly flashed the life out of anyone regardless of where they were struck.

Chris searched for Judy but in the panic, he simply couldn't see her. He looked at Holly who was targeting anyone who could stop her before resuming her blitz on everyone else.

Finally, an alarm sounded, and Federal Police streamed in from a secure entry door. Holly noticed them and sent half a dozen to meet their maker as they filed in but a few managed to spread out and raise their weapons.

Realising she couldn't hold them off, Holly turned the accelerator onto a lone target, "This is for you Chris!" and she fired one last bolt just as a volley of pistol shots rang out. Chris could only watch as a bolt of light careened towards him. It only took milliseconds, but his mind had slowed everything down and he had plenty of time to absorb what was about to happen but was powerless to react. In that instant he felt a wisp of breeze and heard a crackle in his right ear, then nothing. He saw Holly smile a second before the police fired.

Several bullets found their marks and Holly's body shuddered at the impact of the lead tips before rolling down the stairs and hitting the banister: the momentum tossing her over the railing. She fell headfirst to the auditorium floor; her skull cracked on impact and bright red blood quickly seeped onto the glazed white tile floor.

Chris looked at Holly in dazed horror as the photon gun fell out of her unclenched hand and rolled harmlessly into a grout filled groove between two tiles. He felt utter relief that the very last vengeful shot she'd levelled at him had missed his right ear by a few millimetres. His next instinct was to search for Judy. He looked around, starting at the seat where she was a few moments earlier, no sign of her. He scanned the auditorium and the exits where the last few survivors were headed but couldn't see her.

Then a voice broke through the fog of his panic, "Chris. CHRIS! Over here."

Chris turned to the source of the call and saw Jonathon Quigley. He was holding the body of a woman. Holly hadn't aimed for Chris at all; she fired just past him aiming at Judy and it was a direct hit.

Chris was so mortified he couldn't even cry out. He rushed to Judy's side and gathered her up in his arms, holding her clumsily as he tried to say her name, but he only managed a few squeaks and grunts before it all gave way to the realisation that Judy, his wife, was dead!

He collapsed into uncontrollable fits of hysterical wailing, and no-one could do anything to help.

It seemed to take forever for the ambulances to arrive but there was little they could have done. Scores of bodies lay all over the auditorium, some in macabre piles and other just slumped where they'd been seated. It was a scene of utter horror but eerily, no blood, no wounds, nothing but dead human beings littering a still clean floor except for the red pool surrounding Holly's body. The photon weapon, it seemed, simply had to graze a victim and their light was extinguished, leaving a stone-dead body.

When the paramedics got to Chris, he was cradling Judy and rocking back and forth sobbing uncontrollably. They hesitated before one of them said, "Sir, I'm so sorry but we need to take you with us, you need to be checked over."

Initially Chris didn't react but then Jonathon leant down, "Chris, she's gone. You have to say goodbye and let these men check you out."

Chris looked at Quigley's face. The sadness it reflected only added to his hopelessness but after a few moments he kissed Judy on the forehead and released her, lying her gently on the floor, "What happens to Judy" he asked a paramedic.

"It's a crime scene now sir, so it'll be up to the Feds and the Coroner. I'm sorry sir. For now, she'll stay here."

Chris stood, feeling incredibly shaky as the shock took hold. The paramedics rolled up a gurney and helped him get on and wheeled him towards a ground floor exit. He watched Judy until he could see her no more, sobbing all the way.

Jonathon Quigley remained, no doubt to give his version of events to the investigators who were just arriving on scene.

Chris was hoisted into the back of an ambulance and seconds later was racing once again to hospital, a place he seemed to have spent a significant part of his various lives.

His brain was frazzled, he couldn't think clearly and swam in a mishmash of hate, love, light and dark. He suddenly felt sick and vomited then collapsed, overwhelmed entirely by the emotional jolt of his wife's murder.

It was hours later that Chris awoke, sedatives enabling him to sleep and get over the initial shock. As he regained consciousness he was confused, but only for a few seconds as the memories broke through and his eyes welled up again.

A nurse noticed and came to his side, "Hello Mr Parish. I'll call a doctor immediately."

With that she simply pushed a button and within seconds a doctor appeared, "Hello Mr Parish. I'm sorry for your loss," said the doctor.

"Thank you," Chris said, slightly offended by the drama television response to his losing his wife.

"Look, I won't beat around the bush. You're suffering from severe shock, which should dissipate soon. We just want to watch you for the night and then you'll be right to go home. If there's anything you need, just hit the buzzer. Is there anything you need right now?"

"Yes. I have to call my son."

"Of course. I'll bring you your phone."

With that the doctor left, and the phone was handed over. Chris dialled Caleb's number. It barely rang once when Caleb answered, "Dad?"

"It's me."

"Are you ok? We're watching the TV; they said there's been a shooting and people were dead. Where's Mum?"

"I'm ok Caleb, mostly. Just a little shaken up."

"And Mum?"

Chris hesitated. He simply didn't have any idea how to tell their son that his mother had been killed, "She's…she's gone son. I couldn't save her."

"No! Oh No! Why?!"

Chris knew better than to try and explain anything at that moment. Caleb was now in his own form of shock and screaming nonsensically at the news. He dropped the phone, and all Chris could do was stay on the line until someone picked it up again. He could hear the commotion and Caleb's wife trying in vain to calm him down. It took all of ten minutes to bring him back down to a communicative level and back to the phone, "Hello Dad, are you still there?"

"Yes Caleb, I'm here."

"What happened Dad?"

"It's a very long story and I'll tell you everything but not right now. Just don't believe all that they're saying on the TV. It wasn't a gunman. It was an employee of Parallax and someone who had a personal grievance with me. It's all my fault Caleb."

"What? No. That can't be true."

"That's all there is to it. I'm so sorry. She was just an unhinged woman with an axe to grind and I was her target. She wanted me to suffer."

"It was a woman?"

"I'm afraid so."

"Who was she?"

"Someone from my deep dark past. She was nearby when I was spiked and it seems she was caught up in the vortex and sucked back to my time and, well, suffered some injustices for it. The system was simply terrible, and she lost her mind and focussed on someone to blame for her lot in life and that someone was me."

"Oh my God," exclaimed Caleb.

"I know son, I'm so very sorry."

Caleb was breathing heavily, and Chris could feel the tension again building in his son, "None of this would have happened if you hadn't come back. Why did you come back? We were fine without you!!?? You did this!"

"I know."

"I hardly knew you Dad and now all I can feel is hate. You might as well have killed her yourself! Never call me again," and Caleb hung up.

"Caleb? CALEB," Chris yelled but he was gone.

Just then Federal Police arrived.

Oh great!

They didn't seem at all perturbed by Chris's dilemma and were by his bed in an instant. They looked at Chris who had tears draining down his cheeks, but they didn't seem to care, "I'm John Mesmer and this is Hamish Woollcott, we're detectives Mr Parish. We need to ask you some questions, while things are still fresh in your mind."

"Sure, why not," he answered sarcastically, "what do you want to know?"

"Who was the woman at Parliament House?"

As exasperated as Chris felt and as fed up as he was to be telling the same story repeatedly, he realised he had little choice in the matter. He explained how he knew Holly and that it had been almost 26 years since he'd met her, if only fleetingly. He told them how he had no idea that she'd been taken back in time with him or that she'd been institutionalised.

He went on to tell them about the people she claimed to have killed or arranged to have killed and that she'd fired her weapon and killed his wife. The detective's recorded the entire conversation. They asked a few questions, but Chris didn't leave anything out and when he finished Mesmer simply said thanks and both men turned to leave.

"How many?"

"I'm sorry sir," asked Woollcott.

"How many dead?"

Mesmer looked Chris in the eye, "Forty-seven."
"Jesus!"

With that the pair left. Chris didn't think he could have felt any worse, but he suddenly did. He'd lost his wife, probably his son and now felt solely responsible for the deaths of all those people as well as those that Holly had disposed of along the way. He felt his very soul breaking as he lay there. There was no coming back from this.

The next day Chris was allowed to leave. The media was waiting for him at the entrance, but he simply put his head down and shoved his way through to a waiting taxi without saying a word. When he got home, he was welcomed to a tidy house. Judy always liked to make sure it was perfect when they went away so that there was nothing much to do when they got back. Little did she or Chris realise that she wouldn't be returning ever again.

Chris broke down as familiar smells filled his nostrils.

Over the next few days Chris fielded a lot of phone calls, most from the media who wanted interviews and comments, which he ignored. Most times he'd just hang up on them. He wanted to turn the phone off, but he was hoping Caleb would call and he had to deal with the morgue and the funeral director, so there was no avoiding the pestering journalists who insisted on calling at the crack of dawn.

The day of Judy's funeral was a deeply sad and sombre affair. Chris was in a fog of despair for most of the service, hardly breathing a word. Most people tended to avoid him, and his side of the church was devoid of anyone except for Caleb and his family who stayed well away from Chris. He was truly alone.

At the wake he tried to approach Caleb but was intercepted by a man who identified himself as Caleb's father-in-law and had clearly been given instructions to keep them apart.

It would indeed take time for these wounds to heal, if they ever could.

Chris went home.

In the weeks that followed the media hounding tapered off as other Parallax stories angles took over the news cycle. Chris had heard it all before of course. It was like a waking nightmare, reliving the life of before. He'd heard more than enough for two lifetimes and decided to stop watching the TV, listening to the radio and reading the Internet and became a media recluse, cut off from the electronic world, as much as was possible anyway. On the positive side though, the media ultimately stopped calling. Chris was glad.

In time he tried to get a job and eventually found work in a small firm doing administration. It paid nothing but it kept him anonymous. He didn't want for much and didn't care about much more except for Caleb and hoped against hope that he would hear from his son again one day.

Every night Chris would go home, heat a frozen meal, eat and then go to bed. He had nothing to live for, and he contemplated ending it all more than once, but they were only ever fleeting moments and, besides, he had no intention of becoming Holly's forty eighth victim.

After a few more months he started to feel slightly better, but the memory of that day kept dragging him into a darkness that simply wouldn't go away.

At the end of another uneventful day, he got home from work, started heating another tasteless meal and was about to sit silently at the table when his mobile phone rang. It was the only thing he hadn't cut off and he grabbed it, it was Caleb.

"Caleb, hi, how are you?"

"Hi Dad."

"Is everyone OK?"

"Yes, we're fine Dad."

"I'm so glad you called and I'm so sorry about everything."

"It's OK Dad, listen, have you seen the News?"

"No, I don't watch anymore. Haven't done for ages. Why?"

"Your Sun Spikes!"

"What about them," Chris asked dismissively.

"They're back!"

Chapter 23

It was an unseasonably hot October day when the two men approached the main entrance of the casino, one somewhat older than the other. They walked in unnoticed and headed for the gaming area.

The younger of the two scanned the room for anything that might interrupt their plan while his senior partner found a table where a group of players were involved in a poker game. He took the only spare seat and tossed a wad of cash on the table which was exchanged for a few thousand dollars in chips. He acknowledged the other players and the game began.

He thought he would have been used to Deja' vu by now, but he was once again surprised by the familiarity of his surroundings and even the people at the table, though he'd never known their names.

The player won his firsthand and increased his pool of cash. As the game unfolded, he carefully increased his bets. Just to keep suspicion at bay, he lost a few hands early on, but he also knew when to make the right moves and his piles of chips steadily grew.

The game soon gained a lot of attention from patrons and casino officials, as winning runs tended to do, and a small crowd watched over proceedings. The man didn't have much to say to anyone. He was a picture of concentration, and it was paying off, he stared winning big.

He checked his watch regularly and after a few hours he looked to his younger partner who nodded. The player suddenly called it quits, walking away with a significant amount of money. He thanked the players and tossed the dealer a one-thousand-dollar tip.

He took his chips to a cashier and was handed an amount of cash and the greater share in the form of a cheque which he signed over to his younger partner. The pair then hugged briefly and exchanged a few words before the younger man left.

The Casino Manager, oblivious to the currency exchange, congratulated the player on his win and offered him the services of the club for the rest of the day and accommodation in a penthouse for the evening.

The stranger agreed without hesitation.

The manager then suggested he take with him a companion, courtesy of the casino, to make his stay more enjoyable and a girl was beckoned over. He looked at her. 19 years old, pretty and scantily dressed. Her face was very familiar to him. He smiled at her then politely declined the offer but did turn back to the girl briefly suggesting she try a different line of work, perhaps go back to school and study mathematics and computer science. She immediately scowled at the thought, as did the casino manager. Oh well. He tried.

The man walked to the elevator with the manager, stepped inside and was taken to an upper floor. On stepping out of the lift he was directed to the penthouse, where he checked his watch again.

After handing the manager a generous tip he entered the room. It was as he remembered. Ornate decorations, a crystal chandelier, spectacular views and a super king-sized bed.

He wasted no time and headed for the ensuite bathroom where a huge gold bath waited for him. Drawing a deep pool of hot water, he stripped down naked and threw his clothes, watch, wallet and phone onto the bed. He then slipped into the water and was enveloped in its warmth and waited.

Thoughts swirled in his mind as he hovered just above the bottom of the bath, his face the only thing breaking the surface tension. He was thinking of the life he had lived and the love he had lost. The emotional pain he felt was still strong but somehow, he relaxed knowing what was about to happen.

A few minutes later there was an incredible flash which illuminated the room, practically blinding him. He felt an incredible pain in his head, like a hammer blow as the brightness intensified and what appeared to be stars circled the room but almost as quickly, they started to fade. He was submerged into the bath water and felt like he was being held under by an invisible force. The world around him then began to spin and become a blur and he felt like he was drowning. Suddenly, he was sucked into a void with a nothingness surrounding him briefly as the last flecks of light dissipated. Then came a feeling of falling and he was soon shrouded in darkness.

He once again felt he was in a liquid environment, but it tasted salty and metallic. Immediately he felt an incredible pressure bearing down on his head. Not a hammer blow this time but a crushing, vice like grip surrounding his entire head and face. He couldn't breathe and noticed weirdness in his body suddenly, like everything was out of proportion, but he knew why.

He could hear muffled voices but couldn't understand what was being said at first, then a bright light appeared, and he was being pushed towards it as if being squeezed out of a toothpaste tube. More voices barked out instructions, "Push, push!"

Through the inky wetness he heard the screams of a woman in pain, "I can see the head," someone shouted.

Then, without warning the pressure released and he was ripped from his claustrophobic cocoon.

Someone picked him up as if he were weightless and he felt like he was being enveloped in an enormous pair of hands before being placed on something soft and warm.

Then he heard a voice. It was clear, calm and controlled, "Congratulations Mrs Parish. It's a boy."

He smiled to himself.

Hi Mum.

The End

###

Thank you for reading my book, Parallax. I really enjoyed creating the story and I hope you enjoyed it too. If you got this far, I assume you did.

It was an idea that formulated in my mind many years before I put pen to paper, or virtual letters to the virtual page as the case may be. When I finally started writing, it just flowed out of me, except for the ending.

I always like to add a small twist or two and this proved a challenge. In the end, I had a dream about the ending and woke up thinking, that's perfect. Funny how the mind works.

If you enjoyed Parallax, please do a review, it helps to get the book up the distribution lists and if you want to check out more of my titles, see below.

Thanks again.

Andrew Dunkley

About the author

Andrew Dunkley was a radio broadcaster/journalist for 40 years in Australia, working in public, commercial and community radio, mostly on air.

While radio was his first love, his passion for golf came a close second and he's enjoyed the game for over 50 years.

Andrew has been married to Judy since 1987, has three children, all boys and 4 grandchildren.

He is now enjoying retirement from radio but still produces a popular astronomy podcast called Space Nuts, available through multiple podcasting platforms.

Other titles from this author…

www.ingramcontent.com/pod-product-compliance
Lightning Source LLC
Chambersburg PA
CBHW071203100726
47908CB00002B/497